The Turtle Run

by
Marie Evelyn

Published by Accent Press Ltd 2016

ISBN 9781783753277

For Medusa

Acknowledgements

Many thanks to Catriona Robb for doing a superb job in editing the book. We now appreciate that, in terms of attention to detail and tenaciously pursuing a favourable outcome, an editor is like a brain surgeon on a good day.

We would like to thank Ursula Martin (Somerset Genealogy) for her research into the Monmouth rebels who were sent to Barbados – and for pointing out that one woman was among them.

Chapter One

'You're not going to break in, are you?' asked the taxi driver, keeping his eyes fixed on the road glimpsed rhythmically through the windscreen wipers.

Becky Thomson laughed. 'I'm obviously going to be one of your more boring passengers. No, I'm not going to break in.'

'Just thought you might be undercover.'

'I wish but nothing that exciting, I'm afraid. Why? Do you get hired by many burglars?'

'No. Shame really; they'd probably tip well.' He cleared his throat. 'Usually when I take people where you're going, they're not – let's just say they aren't so well dressed for the English weather.'

The rear-view mirror framed his eyes as he flicked a curious look at her. Becky wondered what he meant. She was wearing a presentable suit and her long copper-coloured hair was pulled back in a business-like ponytail. Then she realised what was bothering the cabbie: the old coat which enveloped her, dripping water over his back seat. Glamorous it wasn't but she loved it; it had survived journeys across the seas and oceans and a sojourn in the rubbish bin before she had rescued it under her mother's glare of disapproval.

'Ah, you don't think I'm dressed appropriately to be interviewing Mr Darnley.'

'Well, I suppose it depends what you've got on under there.' The taxi driver cleared his throat again, and she sensed he was embarrassed his last comment had sounded more lascivious than he had intended. 'So he's the lord of the manor, is he? Mr Darnley?'

'I guess he is,' said Becky.

'I take all sorts of people there – always dressed up to the nines – but I never knew who actually lived there. So what are you interviewing him about?'

'Architecture,' Becky answered, which was at least half the truth.

'Architecture? For the *Essex Gleaner*?' The cabbie sounded incredulous and no wonder. The local paper maintained a relentlessly pedestrian tone, favouring fêtes above politics, arts and industry. Her own gentle article on a Brown Owl's lament that Brownies no longer had the sewing skills to fix their badges to their sashes had been afforded a generous quarter page last week.

'I'm sorry. I've made a real mess of your cab.'

'That's all right,' he said. 'But next time don't wait outside. Huh? When I pick someone up from your offices I just normally buzz that Patsy woman and she calls them.'

'OK.' But Patsy hadn't been at her desk this morning. The *Essex Gleaner* office had been deserted. No McBride, no Patsy, no Ian (thankfully). No anyone. Only ten minutes late – as her bus to Chelmsford had got snarled in rain-sluggish traffic – Becky would have normally worried she was meant to be somewhere with the others but had dismissed this concern when she found the brusquely worded memo on her desk: get a taxi to Noak Hall and interview Matthew Darnley, Esquire. About a very sensitive topic, but one that he was (apparently) keen to discuss. Familial guilt, maybe? If she'd known about the assignment in advance of course she wouldn't have worn this old coat.

The windows were too misted-up for Becky to see the Essex fields roll by but she felt the change as the taxi slid from smooth A-roads to pot-holed B-roads and the way grew ever more winding. The taxi driver grunted each time he had to change down a gear as though every bend in the road was a personal insult.

'You wouldn't believe some of the people I've taken to this place. They're always late and having a go at me for not going faster round these bloody bends. I ask them if they would rather I just drive straight into a ditch but they don't like to hear that, do they?'

'Well, it's OK. I'm not late,' said Becky, hoping this would mollify the driver's sudden bad humour.

They stopped to turn right and Becky noticed that a vein in his temple was throbbing in time with the clicking of the indicator. He was waiting for a huge agricultural vehicle with metal jaws to lurch past. She rubbed a porthole in the steamed-up side window and saw the sign for Noak Hall.

'Of course you know why the roads round here are so bendy and twisty?' he said.

'It's just the lay of the land, I suppose.'

'Lay of the land?' he repeated. 'Look around. It's as flat as a pancake. The lord of the manor didn't want common roads with common people mucking up his fields so the roads had to skirt round his manor.'

'But that was a long time ago,' said Becky and got a grunt in reply.

They turned down a long drive, along which plane trees formed a guard of honour. In the distance, strobed by the windscreen wipers, a white stately pile was growing larger. Through her porthole, Becky glimpsed a rain-pocked lake sitting in grey meditation among rolling green fields. So much land. Green, boastful land.

'It was the Normans, wasn't it?' said the cabbie.

'Sorry?'

'Nicking our land. All those bloody French names. And the enclosures and all that.' His socialist indignation swelled as Noak Hall grew larger in the windscreen. 'It's the sense of entitlement I really object to. You know? Inherited wealth. Most of the people I bring here can't even be bothered to exchange a few words with me.' He turned round to look at Becky. 'Not you, of course.'

'Oh, good,' said Becky, relieved when he turned back to look where he was going.

'We should have another Peasants' Revolt. Finish what we started.'

'We?'

'My lot's always been in Essex. I reckon some of them would have been involved. Probably all ended up swinging or with their heads on pikes.'

Becky laughed. 'You have a strong sense of history.'

'Don't you?'

'Not really. I'm afraid that I found history pretty boring at school.'

'Yeah, but you've got to know where you came from, haven't you?'

'I've never really thought about it. I don't even know where my grandparents came from,' said Becky, apologetically.

'Ask them!'

'I'd need a Ouija board.'

'Ah.' He toned down his truculence. 'Well, you've got to admit you could feed a county off these grounds – and look at it now – just bloody lawn.'

'Actually, I agree with you,' said Becky. There was something faintly obscene about the cropless green acres that surrounded them.

'He must be a rich bastard, excuse my French. And that bloody mansion. What do you call it? Neo-something.'

'Neo-classical, I think.'

As they approached the Hall itself, Becky could see the main drive ended in a lollipop shape at the head of which lay a small flight of steps up to a grand portico and beyond that an uncovered courtyard. Beyond that stood the huge house. She wondered if all the cabbie's other fares to Noak

Hall felt as daunted as she did right now. Probably not judging from his description of them.

He stopped the cab before the steps and turned to Becky. 'Is Darnley an old bloke, or what?'

'I don't know.' Becky hated arriving for an interview this unprepared. She paid the fare and asked for a receipt but hesitated before opening the car door. A pang of unease hit her as though she wasn't supposed to be here.

The cabbie must have noticed. 'Are you going to be more than an hour?' he asked.

'Probably less.'

'Right, I'm going to wait for you. There's a little area for parking over there by the side of the house. I'll just stay up there, out the way. No extra charge. I've got sandwiches and a paper – that should last me.'

'Thank you,' said Becky. 'Actually, I would appreciate that.'

She got out of the car and ran up the steps, pausing as she spied smoke rising from the chimneys. Once again Becky wondered if she should really be here. Maybe she should be looking for the tradesman's entrance. No, Matthew Darnley himself had suggested this assignment and she was bloody lucky to get a story of substance so early on in her career. She would go to the front door like a proper guest.

The skies were still pouring water as she sprinted over the courtyard so that, by the time she had reached the door and swung the heavy knocker, her coat had more than managed to rehydrate itself. At her third knock the door was opened by a middle-aged woman with flour-patinaed hands and a horrified face. She looked at Becky's coat, then at Becky and then past her to the empty courtyard.

'Has Fielding just dropped you off like this? In the rain?'

'Pardon?'

'Has Fielding – oh never mind. I'm sorry but we weren't expecting you for another hour.'

Becky had assumed it would just be her and Mr Darnley. 'We?' she said.

'Oh, er, *nous ne expectons pas vou*s – I don't suppose you speak English?'

'Yes. Actually it's all I speak.' Becky felt a wave of panic. 'Mr Darnley does know the interview will be in English, doesn't he?'

The woman looked at her and again at her coat, obviously baffled. Becky could hear a digital bleeping from somewhere inside the house, faint but insistent. The woman obviously heard it too for she ushered Becky in with sudden urgency.

'Look, just follow me – we'll sort this out in a second.'

The digital pulsing grew louder as Becky followed the woman along a green entrance hall with ornate plasterwork, past a portrait of an elderly man (Darnley?) and into a huge kitchen, where Becky realised she had interrupted preparations for a big do. As well as the delicious roast lamb smells which were wafting from an oven that looked large enough to be in a forge, the aroma of freshly baked pastry arose from trays of golden-clad nibbles on the kitchen counters. The woman took another tray of nibbles out of the oven and then reset the digital kitchen clock – which looked as incongruous as a microwave would in the kitchen of Downton Abbey.

'Right,' said the woman. 'I'm Mrs Collie, by the way. 'Would you like a drink?'

'I'm Becky Thomson. Please don't worry about me. Can I just sit here, out of the way, until Mr Darnley is ready?'

'Of course,' said Mrs Collie, opening the door of the substantial oven, and testing the meat. Succulent wraiths of steam streamed out as if in happy escape. Evidently satisfied, she shut the door and turned a dial on the oven. 'So you're not from Paris?'

'No, from the *Essex Gleaner.* And I'm from Essex.' Becky pulled a barstool from beneath the central counter and winced as her coat shed water on the kitchen flagstones.

'The *Essex Gleaner*? And Matthew – Mr Darnley's expecting you?'

'I haven't met him before, but yes. He wants to talk about this house. And I can see why. I can't imagine living in a place this enormous.'

'He doesn't live here. He's abroad most of the time.'

'Oh. Now I am confused,' said Becky. 'I assumed if he wanted us to do an article on the house it was his main residence – an old family home. You mean he has other places too?'

Mrs Collie didn't reply but she looked perplexed. 'He's going to be pushed for time,' she said. 'And I didn't think he did interviews. I must admit I'm a bit surprised.'

'To be honest I was,' said Becky. 'Considering the topic he's suggested but good for him for being so open about it.'

'What topic?'

'Architecture and slavery. He suggested the *Essex Gleaner* do an article on the grand homes of Essex and how much of the original money to build them came from the colonies, plantations. Well, the slave trade.'

'The slave trade?' echoed Mrs Collie.

Now Becky was certain she shouldn't be here. She fumbled in her bag and unfolded two typed sheets. One was the memo about the invitation from Mr Darnley, the other a sheet of notes – presumably from Mr McBride – with a list of potential questions to put to him. The questions were surprisingly accusing for an editor who preferred articles on Brown Owl to reports of crime and 'unpleasantness' as he put it. Becky had already thought of some more anodyne substitutes. Even if Mr Darnley's inherited wealth owed its origin to highly unsavoury activities, there was no point barging in with questions like: 'Do you feel personally culpable for your ancestors' involvement in the African slave trade?' Not when Mr Darnley himself had raised the topic as something the paper should do an article on.

Mrs Collie held out her hand for the papers and Becky passed over the memo, hoping Mrs Collie wouldn't also demand to see Mr McBride's list of aggressive questions. Judging by the prolonged silence Mrs Collie was not so much reading the memo as studying it. She looked up and gave Becky a long appraising stare before shaking her head and handing back the piece of paper. Something was definitely not right.

'And you look too young to have made any enemies.'

'What do you mean?' said Becky.

Before Mrs Collie could answer, the kitchen door swung open and a six foot three man in his early thirties walked in, doing a comic double take when he saw Becky sitting on the barstool. He was dressed formally in a dinner jacket, white shirt and well-pressed black trousers.

'Good grief, Mrs Collie,' he laughed. 'Is it Waifs' and Strays' week? You must tell me about these charity exploits.' He grinned at Becky. 'I can claim back tax on them.'

His dark hair and eyes suggested he might be French but his voice seemed a hotchpotch of accents: a jumble of Irish, maybe Welsh, maybe American.

'Just you stop being so unkind,' Mrs Collie scolded. 'This is Becky, a friend of my daughter. The poor girl got caught in that downpour and dropped in here to shelter.' She gave Becky a glance loaded with warning.

He held out his hand. 'I'm Matthew Darnley.'

What? Becky had anticipated an elderly man – someone who was nearing the end of his life and seeking redemption – not a tanned, strapping man who looked like he had no regrets about anything he'd done.

'Hello, Mr Darnley.' She shook his hand and winced as a small shower of rain was shaken from her right coat sleeve onto the flagstones.

'What on earth were you doing out in this?' he asked.

'It's an embarrassing story,' she said. 'And too long to tell.' She hoped he wouldn't pursue the subject as it was now obvious that he hadn't been expecting a reporter and knew nothing of an interview. It occurred to her that the brusque memo hadn't come from Mr McBride at all. There was only one joker on the newspaper payroll who would have the temerity to set her up like this. As soon as she got back to the office, she would show the memo to Mr McBride. Even though his pet favourite had written it, surely he would be furious to see the missive that had been sent in his name.

Matthew was watching her with curiosity and she realised she was frowning.

'Well, then,' he said. 'Can I get you a towel?'

'Oh, no thanks,' said Becky; she just wanted to be as inconspicuous as possible until she found an opportunity to leave.

'At least take your coat off; it looks soaked through. You're not on an illegal hunt, are you?'

Becky shook her head. 'It's not a hunting jacket – it's just my father's old coat.' Having it around was usually a sign he was back on shore leave – except the last time the coat had come home her father was no longer in it.

Matthew grinned. 'Shame. You'd fit in round here. When I started coming to this country it took me a while to work out that the richest people wear their oldest gear when they're fishing or hunting.' And, the grin still on his face, he moved over to a selection of wines standing on the kitchen's granite worktop.

Becky tried not to stare as he examined some of the bottles. If he thought she was of the *Horse and Hound* set he was way off track. She wondered which country he was from. Fortunately he'd lost interest in her now. He turned towards Mrs Collie, who was busy transferring the pastry nibbles to a trolley.

'Did Fielding go to pick up Miss Carette?'

'Left on the dot, Mr Darnley.'

Sitting on the stool, quiet as a mouse, Becky eavesdropped shamelessly. She watched as Matthew Darnley made light work of uncorking the vintage wines and left them to breathe. And she listened to the last-minute reminders of what he wanted served and when, which Mrs Collie was to pass on to 'the girls' – whoever they were. 'And I must remind them the *petillant* is the one Miss Carette prefers.'

'But I thought you said she only drank pink champagne!'

'No, Mrs Collie. You're thinking of the wife of that obnoxious man from Luxembourg.'

'It's the ladies and their fancies that complicate things,' Mrs Collie grumbled. 'You should just give them Babycham and be done with it.'

'You think so?' He grinned and turned to Becky. Apparently he hadn't forgotten her after all. 'Do you drink Babycham?'

'I'm afraid not,' she said. 'Even though I come from Essex.'

'You see, Mrs Collie, your theory is quite flawed.'

'Yes,' said Mrs Collie. 'But I dare say this young lady is more sensible than some of your guests.'

Becky wasn't sure how to respond to what could have been faint praise or a subtle way of saying she wasn't 'guest material'.

'Oh you can see how sensible I am,' she said. 'Choosing a day like this to be out.'

'If I had more time I would love to hear your embarrassing long story,' said Matthew, locking eyes with her. It was a relief when the sound of merry voices approaching the kitchen broke the spell and he finally looked away. A door on the far side of the room opened and three young women, chattering like starlings, appeared. They were dressed in waitresses' uniforms and stood bunched in the doorway for a second, their uninhibited banter dying on their lips when they discovered Mrs Collie wasn't alone. Then they came in, murmuring diffident 'good evenings' to Mr Darnley.

He grinned to acknowledge them and listened as Mrs Collie passed on his instructions. Satisfied everything was in hand he turned to Becky once more. 'Maybe you'll come back and tell me that story when the weather is better,' he told her.

'Maybe, I will,' she responded politely, knowing as well as he surely did that they were unlikely to meet again.

He nodded and walked out; moments later mellow background music floated through to the kitchen. She could hear a tenor sax embroidering the melody with laid-back ease. He was obviously in a room nearby, creating ambience for his lucky guests, having erased Becky from his mind the instant he left the kitchen.

Mrs Collie, a bit pink in the face, pushed the trolley towards the door the girls had come through, summoning one of them to hold it open for her. Before the door shut again, Becky caught a glimpse of a room with a dark gleaming table set with sparkling silver, crystal glasses and a central display of what looked like white orchids. All very elegant, very inviting.

Mrs Collie bustled back into the kitchen. 'Aren't those napkins ready?'

The young woman whose deft fingers had been pleating the napkins so that they fanned out into a perfect crescent assured her that they were.

'Well take them in, love, take them in!'

There was an edge to Mrs Collie's voice now – a sure sign that zero hour was fast approaching.

Becky slid off the stool and thanked Mrs Collie for her intervention. 'I think I was set up.'

'Sounds like it. A nasty trick. Do you know who it was?'

'Yes, a colleague from work. It was someone I turned down. I'm guessing this was his little joke.'

'Just as well you turned him down, then.'

Becky looked around the kitchen, wondering which of the doors was the best to use; presumably as an uninvited guest she should go out the tradesmen's entrance. Mrs Collie noticed her confusion and quickly gestured for Becky to follow her. They retraced their steps to the front door and Mrs Collie opened it. Outside it was still damp and grey.

'Have you got a car?'

'Yes, thanks,' said Becky, stepping into the courtyard. 'A taxi is waiting for me.' Thank God for her socialist cabbie and his insistence on hanging around. 'Sorry to have been a bother.'

'Not your fault.' Mrs Collie shut the door and Becky hurried across the courtyard and down the steps. The first guest was already arriving: a Bentley had stopped at the head of the lollipop. Becky hesitated on the bottom step, wondering whether to run like a panicked Cinderella or adopt a sedate pace. But the young woman in the back of the Bentley was clearly oblivious to Becky's presence: she held a compact mirror in her hand and was making a rapid last-minute appraisal of her face and hair. She needn't have bothered: she looked exquisite.

Becky headed towards the side of the house in the direction her taxi driver had indicated. Halfway there she turned back to see Matthew Darnley running swiftly down the front steps. Although the rain had reduced to barely a bitter drizzle, he unfurled an umbrella before opening the car door and helping the James Bond beauty out. She was almost as tall as he was and her only concession to the weather was a long feather boa worn with a model's casual panache about her shoulders. Becky heard Matthew greet the lady (Miss Carette, presumably) and her reply and realised they were speaking in French. Neither noticed her as Miss Carette, in her shimmering beaded shift, flung her white arms about Matthew Darnley's neck and he, in turn, encircled her slender waist. There was no way that lady was going to be served with Babycham tonight. Becky turned her back on Matthew Darnley and his companion, pulled up her coat collar and walked on to the side of the house, where her carriage awaited – and within it – a very curious driver.

Half an hour later the taxi driver, outraged on Becky's behalf, dropped her outside the *Essex Gleaner*'s offices. She headed straight for Mr McBride's room, with 'his' memo in her hand, and knocked on his transparent door. But the plump editor was on the phone and he gestured with an impatient swipe that he was not to be disturbed.

Returning to her desk Becky was relieved the few other people in the office paid her no attention; presumably they thought her earlier absence was due to a genuine assignment. She checked her emails and ate her meagre salad from a Tupperware box, feeling a twinge of deprivation as she imagined the multi-course luncheon being served at Noak Hall. She googled Matthew Darnley and the first few items on the results list concerned his ownership of the Monmouth Hotel (five star) in north Essex; there was no mention of Noak Hall.

Patsy came in with a shop-purchased sandwich and made a beeline for Becky the moment she saw her. 'Where were you?' she asked. 'McBride called a meeting first thing. Fortunately he didn't notice you weren't there.'

‘That’s good,’ said Becky, though Patsy’s unintended slight cruelly confirmed her earlier lack of judgement. How had she believed that Mr McBride would send a junior reporter to interview someone on a topic as challenging as slavery? She had let her enthusiasm trample over good sense.

‘Don’t look so down,’ said Patsy. ‘You didn’t really miss anything. He gave us a talk on ethics. He’s got it into his head that we’re all hacking phones and going through people’s rubbish bins. Something I can’t imagine you –’

‘Becky’s always going through people’s rubbish bins,’ a voice said behind them. Ian. For an obese bloke he moved with a surprising stealthiness; usually the first indication of his presence was a shadow across the computer screen closely followed by his hand on her shoulder and a cheery ‘I know a much better way of doing that’. Patsy mouthed ‘prat’ and went to her desk.

Becky wondered briefly if she could just ignore Ian. She had refused his ‘help the new girl’ overtures on many occasions, knowing any favour would be called in with an insistence she join him for a drink or a meal and there were more competent colleagues who would help her without starting a tab. Also his unsolicited advice usually involved him balancing one buttock on her desk and cupping a hand over hers to guide the mouse but Patsy had warned her not to upset him until her twelve-month probation was up. After that – with more legal protection behind her – she could tell him where to stick his buttock.

For now though he wasn’t going to take the hint to leave her alone and anyway she wanted to confront him about the trick he’d played on her. Becky turned around.

‘So how was your morning?’ he asked, evidently expecting a temper tantrum because he grinned and dodged an imaginary punch. ‘I suppose you met the lord of the manor.’

‘I did,’ said Becky.

'And?'

'And what? He seemed nice enough.'

Ian's face lost some of its anticipated glee. 'But what about the questions? What did Darnley say when you asked him about the slave trade?'

'I didn't bother asking him,' said Becky. 'It was obvious someone had tried to set me up. By the way, was this to get at me or do you have something against him?'

'He's an arrogant git. Swanning round his manor and not letting people fish in his lake.'

'Ah, so that's what it was about,' said Becky. 'Unbelievable. How did you know he would be at Noak Hall today? I'm told he's hardly ever there.'

Ian tapped his nose. 'Inside information. So go on, tell me what he said.'

Becky ignored the question, reached into her bag and laid the two taxi receipts on her desk. 'How am I going to claim for these?'

Ian casually pulled loose notes from a pocket and threw them on to her desk. He put the taxi receipts in his pocket.

'I bet you didn't even meet him,' he said, scowling.

'Would you like to bet where I'm going now?' said Becky. 'I have to discuss an ethical matter with Mr McBride.'

'Discuss away,' snapped Ian and slimed off. Becky looked round for the memo and Mr McBride's 'instructions'. They were no longer on her desk. At the far end of the office Ian was feeding something into the shredder. Evidence gone.

Chapter Two

Only three weeks to go before her twelve-month probation was up and Becky had managed to avoid any assignments that involved Ian. Until now. She'd barely got into the office before Patsy hurried over.

'Ian says I'm to tell you he's just gone to fill up and then he'll be waiting for you in the car park.'

Oh God; she could look forward to half a day of Ian ogling her breasts while pretending to photograph something. 'I didn't know he was covering the rally?'

'Rally?' said Patsy, frowning. 'That's not what he said.'

'I'm supposed to be covering the vintage car rally at Marsden Common in an hour,' Becky fumed. 'They're expecting me. Right, I'm going to speak to Mr McBride. I know Ian's his nephew and all that, but –'

Patsy sighed. 'Don't bother. McBride hardly ever goes against Ian. Our boss has no children of his own. He thinks the sun shines out of Ian's – camera.'

'What? Just let him get away with it? If nothing else, it's unprofessional.'

'And when your probation is over you can say so,' said Patsy. 'I'm sure Ian's delegated someone else to cover the car rally.'

'Did he say what this is all about and where we're going?'

'Somewhere in the country, I gather. You'd better hurry.'

The telephone on her desk shrilled. Becky picked up the receiver but before she could say a word Ian's voice demanded, 'Are you coming down or *what*?' He rang off before Becky could even reply.

Furious about the sudden change to her day and even more furious she couldn't do anything about it, Becky headed downstairs. In the car park Ian was behind the wheel of his Citroen, revving its powerful engine impatiently.

'What the hell do you think you're doing?' she said.

'That's a fine way to show your gratitude. You should be on your knees, thanking me.'

'Thanking you for what?'

'For arranging the most exciting day you've had since you've been in this sad little office. But if you want to go and tell our esteemed editor that you refuse to go –'

'Your uncle knows about this – assignment?'

'Oh yes,' said Ian. 'You know how it is: I suggest things; he agrees. Now, chop, chop.'

Fuming Becky got in and belted up. She remembered the word 'nepotism' came from favouring nephews – never a more apt use.

'And don't look so sour,' snapped Ian. 'I'm doing you a favour here.'

The F-word again – always ominous. 'A favour?'

He plonked a folder in her lap. 'Feast your eyes on that,' he told her. 'And while you're at it, try to be a bit more appreciative of what I've set up for us, will you?'

She didn't respond but, as he tore out of the car park, she opened the folder and examined the brochure inside. It showed photos of a gloriously mellow stone building cloaked in Virginia creeper and surrounded by manicured lawns that set it off to perfection. 'The Monmouth Country Club UK,' she read aloud, 'Matthew Darnley's newly renovated oasis of calm in today's hectic world.'

She shut the brochure and gave Ian an unfriendly stare. 'We're going to a hotel owned by Matthew Darnley?'

'Yup.'

'Why? Has it been burgled or something?'

'Not yet. Unless I take a fancy to the cutlery.' He giggled as though he had said something amusing. 'Anyway, all you need to know is that I've fixed for you to do an interview.'

'Hang on a moment. I can do a write-up on the place but an interview? Please tell me you haven't arranged for me to talk to Matthew Darnley.'

'Maybe I have. Maybe I haven't,' Ian chanted.

Becky wished now she had found out more about Matthew. Having googled him after their first meeting she had suppressed her curiosity; with no professional excuse to research him she had felt the same unease as when her younger brother tried to 'stalk' potential girlfriends online: it was a bit creepy.

'I know all you have to do is point a camera and click but I can't talk to someone without doing some research first.'

'Got you going!' Ian laughed. ''Course you won't have to talk to Matthew Darnley. Even if he was at the Monmouth today, I don't think he would bother with a junior reporter from a piddling little local rag. No, you'll be speaking to the manager.'

'About what? I'm not prepared.'

'Oh, wing it,' Ian snapped. 'His name is Chris Harris and he happens to be a friend of mine. While you interview him, I'll mosey around' – he was putting on a very tiresome mock-aristocratic accent – 'take in the stately rooms, the lounges. Maybe even take a wander upstairs; see if the bedrooms rate my personal approval. Who knows, I might want to stay there some time soon? I mean look at the brochure. Would you say "no" to a stay in their honeymoon suite?'

'Depends who with,' said Becky.

'You wouldn't say "No" to Darnley.'

Even if this merited an answer, Becky wouldn't have known what to say. Did she want to bump into Matthew

Darnley again? He just might ask about that long embarrassing story. The car jarred over a pothole and she checked to see if Ian was paying attention to the road: nope – he'd been casting a not-furtive-enough look at her breasts. Ian quickly tried to camouflage his inability to stare straight ahead by rabbiting on about the assignment.

'You could say I got him the job.'

'Who?'

'Chris Harris. He was umming and ahhing about accepting the position. I told him to go for it. So now he's manager of the Monmouth Hotel. He'd never have taken the job if it wasn't for me.'

'And how do you know him?'

'He and his wife moved into my street. They didn't know anyone – bit lost really. So I introduced him to a few people, you know, took him down the pub.'

'You're calling in a favour?'

He giggled in that annoying way again. 'What else can you do with them?'

An unwelcome thought flashed through Becky's mind. 'Does this Chris know we're turning up today?'

'Oh yeah. I've told him you're going to write a lovely piece about the hotel – so long as he treats us right. I expect a free lunch out of this at least.'

'I didn't think Mr McBride was into giving free advertisements.'

'My uncle likes us to support local businesses.'

Not that local. They had left the A12 before Colchester, and seemed to be slaloming along the sort of B-roads so despised by her socialist taxi driver a few weeks earlier.

'Got any plans for tonight?' said Ian.

He'd caught her on the hop so she didn't have a chance to invent a night out. 'Er…'

'Obviously not,' he said, smugly. 'Friday night as well. We need to get you out a bit more from whatever dreary bedsit you inhabit.'

Becky sighed inwardly. She was embarrassed that, at twenty-three, she still lived at home with her mother and brother but this was an economic necessity; she was only going to look for somewhere to rent when she knew she had a firm job. She could now look forward to an argument with Ian later about why she wouldn't join him for a drink or meal or whatever evening out he was planning.

But she forgot about excuses to foil Ian's evening plans as they turned into the entrance to Matthew's hotel. The approach to the Monmouth was stunning, a long curving drive revealing a mature, stately building – perfect in its setting of manicured lawns and with an established Virginia creeper hugging the façade. Becky really did feel like she was entering a sequestered place of peaceful loveliness.

'Why don't you take a picture for our piece? The light's perfect right now,' she suggested as they got out of the car.

'All in good time,' said Ian. 'Let's go and winkle out old Chris.'

They didn't have to. A tall figure stood by the main entrance, they saw him right away and she – if not Ian – could tell immediately he wasn't a bit pleased to see them. Apologetically the first thing he did was cry off the interview 'with Miss Thomson' due to the pressure of other commitments. His accent was similar to Matthew Darnley's, which Becky still couldn't place, so he certainly wasn't local despite living in Ian's street. And, unlike Mr Darnley, Chris Harris seemed unaccustomed to the constraints of formal dress; one hand was constantly tugging at his shirt collar and tie. He was obviously still new to the job, treading warily, his face pale with anxiety to make good. Becky felt really sorry for him.

Not wanting to add to the harassed man's problems, she took herself off to explore; Chris Harris was going to have Ian dogging his footsteps as it was, selfishly determined to get whatever favour he was after, and since she was here she might as well get a feel for the place. Having looked over the beautifully landscaped grounds, and watched as a team of workmen created a fiendish bunker on the spanking new golf course, she went indoors.

Becky introduced herself to the pleasant girl at reception and explained she was doing a write-up for a local paper. The young woman agreed with her that the hotel suggested a more mellow, less hectic age than our own. 'It's what the owner wanted to achieve; the atmosphere of a comfortable Edwardian country-seat but with modern amenities and French cuisine.'

'So it's a sort of fusion hotel?'

'That's right. He's very big on the French stuff. Microwaves are banned from the kitchens. It's only been open for three months but it's really taking off. Quite a few famous people have started coming too.'

Becky laughed. 'Really?' She couldn't imagine any A-listers wanting to spend time in Essex.

'Really,' the girl said. 'This bit's off the record, right? Look who we've got staying.'

She twisted her screen and pointed at a name that meant nothing to Becky; presumably someone who featured in the celebrity magazines she didn't read or in the reality TV programmes she didn't watch. Maybe she should gen up on this sort of trivia for the sake of her career. And then the receptionist panicked. 'Promise you won't put that in your article?' she said quickly. 'I'd be out on my ear if the boss knew I'd let you see this. He's really strict about client confidentiality.'

Becky assured her she wouldn't breathe a word then froze, staring at the screen in disbelief. 'Just a moment – that's my name at the bottom. What's that doing there?'

The girl winced. 'Hell. Was it supposed to be a surprise for you? I didn't realise. Your boyfriend just had Chris type the booking in himself. Mr Ian Watt and Ms Becky Thomson – the bridal suite for tonight.'

'The *what?'*

'The bridal suite. That's what it says here.'

Becky's felt her stomach lurch as she read the linked names on the screen again, furious that Ian would take such a liberty. Furious, too, at his conceit in thinking his 'charm' was such that he could actually talk her into spending a night with him here – well – anywhere. And then she remembered Ian's earlier set-up.

She forced a smile at the receptionist. 'I take it you were in on this joke? A very good wind-up, by the way.'

The receptionist looked confused. 'Sorry?'

'Presumably my colleague put Chris up to this and told you to show it to me.'

'No, it's a real booking.' The receptionist looked horrified. 'You mean Mr Watt isn't your boyfriend?'

'No, he is not. Cancel it.'

The girl hesitated.

'You can do that, surely?'

'Well, no,' stuttered the girl. 'It's a special code for free stays. Chris typed it in; I can't undo it.' The telephone next to her rang. 'Look, we'll get Chris to sort it out in a minute. Let me just get this call.'

Seething with indignation, Becky left her to it and sat in one of the classic English antique chairs in the reception area. So this was the extra favour Ian had intended extracting from the manager. And pathetic Chris Harris had gone along with it.

She wondered whether to have it out with Ian as soon as she saw him. Or maybe it would be more satisfying to see how he intended to break the news to her and then deal with it – preferably in front of Chris, who clearly needed to 'man-up' where users like Ian were concerned.

And here they were: Ian coming along the corridor with a jaunty swagger, followed by Chris Harris, looking deathly, his forehead beaded with sweat.

‘Becky,’ exclaimed Ian. ‘Isn’t this a lovely hotel? Are you getting enough for your write-up?’

Chris was looking at her with an anxious intensity. God, he really believed she had the power to influence would-be local customers.

‘It’s a lovely setting,’ she told him. ‘And I’m sure your hotel doesn’t need the publicity.’

‘Everyone could do with good publicity,’ said Ian, quickly. ‘And isn’t it nice of old Chris to insist that we have lunch here?’

‘It’s nice that Mr McBride has agreed to cover our expenses,’ said Becky. ‘Or shall I just ring him now to confirm it’s OK?’

Ian glared at her, while ‘old Chris’ looked resentfully at him.

‘Lunch is on the house,’ Chris murmured, standing aside. ‘Would you like to come this way, Miss Thomson?’

He led them to a table in the walnut-panelled dining room and handed them each one of the Monmouth’s ornate, gold-tasselled menus. He then disappeared into the kitchen, emerging seconds later with a waiter who he brought to the table just as Ian was holding up a knife to the light.

‘Is there something wrong with it?’ asked Chris.

‘Relax, old boy,’ said Ian. ‘I was admiring the hallmark.’

‘You may need to frisk him when we leave,’ said Becky and noticed Chris cast a bewildered look at Ian, who was now perusing the menu.

From where she was sitting Becky could see part of the reception desk through the open dining-room door and made a mental note to ask the receptionist for a screen print of the bridal suite booking. Once she got back to the office she would show it to Mr McBride; surely even his favoured nephew wouldn’t survive this. But then the receptionist moved back into her line of view and it wasn’t the young woman from before; an older man had taken her place. Becky cursed inwardly.

Ian completed his protracted perusal of the menu and settled for moules marinière. 'And, I suppose, let's have a look at the wine list.'

'You're driving,' snapped Becky and then, more gently to the waiter, 'a salad, please. And a glass of tap water.'

'You haven't even opened your menu,' said Ian. 'How can you do a write-up of the food based on a salad?'

'I'm not a food connoisseur,' said Becky.

'How about a perigourdine salad?' asked Chris, 'it has duck and walnuts and –'

'Does it need a lot of preparation?' said Becky. 'We have to be back in the office this afternoon.'

'No more than for a plain salad.' Chris cast a surprised look at a frowning Ian.

'Hang on,' Ian said. 'We're not in a rush.'

'I am. I have work to do.' Becky snatched the menu from him and handed it, together with her own to the waiter. 'I'd like the salad Mr Harris mentioned, please.' The waiter made off with their order before Ian had a chance to protest.

He glared at Becky. Chris, who had been hovering with uncertainty, hurriedly pulled up a chair. 'I'm sorry I was so tied up earlier on, Miss Thomson. Is there anything about the hotel you'd like to ask me?'

Becky felt she had enough information for her write-up but realised Chris was misinterpreting her aggression towards Ian as dissatisfaction with the hotel. She took a notepad out of her bag and tried to think of a tame question. 'What clientele are you trying to target?' she asked.

Chris embarked on a rather rambling explanation about the hotel being within easy reach of both Stansted airport and London and listed the European countries they planned to target, especially France. Becky felt guilty that she was only pretending to take notes. Ian looked bored until their food arrived. Chris moved on to a long account of the struggle to find British staff who could speak French fluently. Becky's attention wandered. How was she going to convince the receptionist now on duty to give her a screen print of the bridal suite room booking? She turned to look at him to see if that provided inspiration but found her view blocked by a man standing in the doorway: Matthew Darnley was scanning the dining room as if to check all was well.

No dinner jacket and formal wear today, of course, just a smart business suit. But other than that, Matthew Darnley was as dark, tall and good-looking as she remembered. His gaze landed on Chris and Becky saw him frown, presumably wondering what his manager was up to. Unfortunately, as she was scrutinising him, he caught her at it. He did a similar double take to the one in his kitchen. 'Hello,' he mouthed silently then smiled at her. Embarrassed, she gave him a small smile back and refocused on her meal.

She made a half-hearted attempt to eat her salad, which was delicious but she could not enjoy knowing they were not paying for it. Ian, who had no such qualms, was eating a mouthful of mussels and dribbling as he talked about the difficulty in getting access to private fishing lakes while Chris tried to look interested. Becky turned back to see if Matthew was still in the doorway. He wasn't. He had walked to the reception desk and must have asked the receptionist to twist round the monitor so he could examine the screen. Panic struck Becky – Matthew would see that booking. She could strangle Ian. The urge to race over to reception and plead with Matthew Darnley not to be misled by what he was certainly going to read was almost overwhelming. Becky twisted her napkin in her lap, agonised – prayed – that he'd miss the damning entry. But of course he didn't and seconds later she heard his raised voice. The other diners stopped eating and looked towards reception too.

Chris Harris went white and pushed back his chair. 'God, it's Matthew. I wasn't expecting him until tomorrow. Excuse me.' He hurried out to the reception area.

'Pathetic, isn't he?' Ian sneered. 'You'd think he was in the army. Jumps to it at the mere sight of his employer.'

'Maybe you would too, if your job was on the line.'

Matthew Darnley stormed into the dining room with Chris in tow.

'Which table?' he said. Chris pointed out where Ian and Becky were sitting and Matthew marched over.

Becky darted a look at Ian, intending to ask him how he was going to deal with the situation he'd provoked. She got a fierce and urgent whisper that amazed her, 'Just remember whatever I did was for both of us, we're in this together – right?'

'No we're not,' Becky hissed back as Matthew reached them, his discomfited manager fingering the knot of his tie and trailing in his wake.

Ian, first, was the focus of Matthew's attention. 'And you are?'

Ian gave his name and occupation on the *Essex Gleaner* then stupidly tried to curry favour. 'You've never met me, Mr Darnley, but I've often admired the grounds of your Noak Hall.'

'Then you must have been trespassing,' snapped Matthew. He picked up Ian's camera. 'I really don't need your newspaper's publicity but, just to satisfy my curiosity, how many photos of the Monmouth did you take this morning for your readers?'

Ian muttered something about the unsatisfactory light. Matthew gestured for Chris to pull back the dining-room curtains fully. Sunlight streamed into the room, motes dancing in the beam.

And then Matthew was standing before her – no inclination now to smile. He didn't say anything for what seemed to Becky an eternity, 'So you're a reporter?'

Becky nodded.

'And I suppose it was just a co-incidence that you were at Noak Hall the other day?'

No, that was another stunt of Ian's, Becky wanted to say, but with her boss's nephew sitting opposite she didn't dare. When she hesitated, Matthew snapped 'Never mind' and rested his hand on the spiral-ringed notebook beside her plate. 'So who did you interview today, Miss Thomson?'

Becky could hardly say she had had an informal chat with the young receptionist who had been on duty earlier.

Impatient for an answer, Matthew Darnley peeled back the cover on her notebook to reveal a page with nothing on it but the name of the celebrity guest who Becky hadn't recognised. She had idly scribbled it down meaning to google the man later and see if it was someone she should have heard of.

He tore out the page and scrunched it in his pocket. 'You're every bit as bad as your boyfriend, aren't you?'

Becky found her voice. 'He is not my boyfriend.'

'No? Well you'll forgive me, Miss Thomson, for assuming that he was. I just saw your names on the monitor booked into the nuptial suite here for tonight. Sorry to be a killjoy but I've cancelled that booking. We don't accommodate freeloaders.'

He turned to Chris Harris. 'Normally it would be your job to escort undesirables off the premises but this time I'll see to it myself.'

Matthew stood there glaring until Ian and Becky put their knives and forks together on their unfinished meals and rose to follow him out of the restaurant. Ian strode ahead nonchalantly, hands in his pockets, but Becky had never felt so humiliated in her life. When she attempted to lag behind Ian, and be less conspicuous, Matthew Darnley firmly cupped her elbow. He didn't make her go faster than she wanted but he didn't release her either. And she'd never forget the pair of snooty women in the lobby who, fully aware of what was going on, gave her the once over before shrinking away as if she were contaminated. At that moment she didn't know who she hated more – wheeling-and-dealing Ian who'd got her into this nightmare situation or Matthew Darnley who was convinced she had schemed to get something for nothing. He saw them all the way to Ian's car and for a moment Becky thought Matthew was going to push her head down – policeman-style – as she got in but he stood back and said nothing. She could feel his eyes on her until Ian pulled away.

'Got to admit,' Ian said, as they pulled out of the driveway. 'It was a bit of a laugh.'

Becky didn't reply and spent the rest of the journey back to Chelmsford planning what she'd say when she marched into the editor's office and denounced his nephew for sexual harassment.

But when they arrived at the *Essex Gleaner*'s premises Mr McBride was already pacing the car park, furious.

'I've had a call from the proprietor of The Monmouth. He tells me how disappointed he is that a pair from our newspaper tried to blackmail the staff there into giving them a free room for the night. So, whose idea was it?'

Becky looked at Ian to see if he was going to own up but he said nothing. Mr McBride angrily waved his nephew away and signalled for Becky to follow him. He showed her into his office, sat down and stared at her, unsmilingly.

'When I call a meeting for all staff I expect all staff to attend.'

'Sorry?' said Becky.

'My ethics meeting – two weeks ago. I assumed you weren't there because you were ill. Now I'm told you spent that morning nosing around Mr Darnley's place. So I want to know who authorised you to look for a story concerning him?'

'No one authorised me, as such,' said Becky. 'But Ian –'

'Did you discuss it with anyone first?'

'No, I couldn't. Because Ian –'

'Your employment is terminated with immediate effect.'

'You can't do that,' Becky blurted out.

'You're on probation. So I can.'

Becky stared at him. She was sure Mr McBride knew who was really to blame.

He blinked under her gaze. 'You don't adhere to the core values of the company and your performance is unsatisfactory.'

No one had suggested that before but Becky could see there was no point arguing. Mr McBride marched her to her desk, and, humiliatingly, called Patsy over to relieve Becky of her smartphone, laptop, and security pass. Everyone in the vicinity kept their heads down. Becky looked around. There was no sign of Ian, which was probably just as well as she had no idea what shape her fury would take if she saw him.

For the second time that day Becky was escorted from a site with no opportunity to explain.

Chapter Three

'Fired?' said her mother, frowning. Having never really got her head around Becky's job at the *Essex Gleaner*, she was now having problems understanding Becky's sudden loss of it. 'But why?'

'I've told you why,' said Becky, wearily. She'd actually toned down the account of her day to say she had refused to go out with the nephew of the editor and they had decided her face didn't fit. Her mother thought that any non-secretarial office job was straying into dangerous territory and tales of illicitly booked bridal suites and being thrown out of hotels would just consolidate this view.

Her brother, Joe, was full of impotent indignation on Becky's behalf. 'You should take them to court for sexual harassment. You have rights.'

'Yes, probably. But taking them to a tribunal is not a great start to my career.'

'Maybe it's for the best,' said their mother.

'How is it for the best?'

'Well, you know, maybe it was a bit too much for you. You need to find a job that's a bit more – steady. Forget this writing business.'

'It's journalism,' snapped Becky. 'And I will get another job.'

'But you said the job market was even worse than last year.'

'You don't have to be so negative, Mum.'

'I'm just saying.'

Becky stormed up to her room. What was wrong with their mother? But she recalled her maternal grandparents had been mired in a sort of old-world working-class passivity too. 'That's not for the likes of us,' was a common catchphrase; one that was brought out when the young Becky had expressed an interest in university or even when Joe, in his early teens, had said (hopefully) that he needed satellite TV to watch the football.

'It's ridiculous,' their grandmother had snapped. 'Working-class people having satellite TV.' She seemed oblivious to the satellite dishes that had erupted like shelf fungus on the other houses in their estate.

Becky needed someone she could confide in – someone who was the antithesis of her mother – and she had just remembered a half-forgotten invitation from someone exactly like that. A quick phone call confirmed her friend would be delighted to see her tonight.

Becky walked out of the house, down the scrubbed front path which crouched in fear between her mother's sparse and regimented flower beds, and to the nearest bus stop where she caught a bus to the much more upmarket area of Hutton. From there it was only another short walk to a property whose front garden was so lush and exotic she could imagine animals breaking out of a zoo just to lose themselves in its thickets of pampas grass and bamboo. She rang the bell and the lady who had created this carefully crafted wilderness opened the door with a delighted smile.

'Becky,' the lady cried. 'Long time no see. Come in.'

Clara Babonneau was one of several people Becky had interviewed while covering an 'Open Gardens' event and by far the most interesting. A very lively lady in her mid-sixties, she was like an exotic migrant who had apparently 'flown in to England to see what English gardens were about', having been informed – or misinformed – that the English were obsessive gardeners.

Exasperated by the sanitised English front garden, Clara had self-published a book on designing 'wild gardens for suburbia' and had been so endearingly appreciative when

Becky plugged her book in the Open Gardens piece, that she insisted Becky came round for dinner one night. Despite the age difference and the fact the two could not have been more different – Becky had seldom left the UK whereas Clara was well travelled – it had been a fun evening and a friendship had been formed. Neither had talked much about their own families: Clara revealed she had been widowed when she was relatively young and, perhaps sensing Becky's ambivalence about her own home, had insisted Becky drop round whenever she needed a break. But aware from their conversation that Clara seemed to have a vibrant social life, with bridge nights and visits from old friends who were passing through England, Becky had been reluctant to take her up on her offer – until today.

Becky followed Clara into the living room and sank into a sofa.

'I was going to offer you tea,' said Clara, 'but you look like you need something stronger.'

'To be honest, I think I do.'

'Then let me have a look in the medicine cabinet.'

Clara rootled through the drinks cupboard, eventually holding up an unopened bottle wrapped in yellow cellophane. 'I picked this up in Paris last month. I've been dying to try it out with someone.'

A few minutes later they were sitting side by side on the sofa and wincing over something that tasted like peppered sherry.

'It's, um, warming,' said Becky.

'It's revolting,' said Clara, cheerfully, 'but I think the English believe that medicine has to taste horrible to be effective.'

Becky laughed as Clara topped up both glasses. She was elegantly dressed but with a hint of 'something other'. Her eyes were very dark, her skin dusky and, though her hair had turned silver, Becky thought that today it was tinged with a rebellious lilac rinse.

'So,' said Clara. 'What's wrong?'

'I've been sacked,' said Becky.

Clara had the foresight to put down her glass before reacting with a dramatic hands-to-face action accompanied by some French words which Becky assumed were expletives; she sensed that Clara thought it unladylike to swear in English.

Becky started to explain about Ian but then stopped. 'Actually, it's a really tiresome story. I won't bore you with the details.'

'Idiots; their loss. But let me think – we're in June now.' Clara frowned and pushed her sherry glass round the table, as though she were at a séance. She beamed. 'But this is amazing timing. Serendipity. I'm going back home.'

'Oh,' said Becky, crestfallen. 'You're leaving Essex?'

'I only meant to stay a year and it's been almost eighteen months.' Clara patted Becky's hand. 'I need someone to help me with a new project. How about working for me?'

'Working for you?' said Becky.

'I have a little – venture, let's call it. Something that's been bugging me for years. There's a book I must write before I lose the energy. I need help with research and editing, and –'

'A gardening book?'

'No, dear. A *history* book. On a subject very close to my heart. Now have you ever heard of the Battle of Sedgemoor?'

Becky smiled apologetically. 'I'm afraid not. Where did it take place?'

Clara rolled her eyes. 'England, of course! The Battle of Sedgemoor was the last pitched battle to be fought on English soil. 1685. Now who was King?'

'Er – a Charles. Um – or a James.' Becky hoped this wasn't a job interview; her knowledge of history was pretty gappy.

'Well done. Charles II and James II were both king in 1685.' Clara's eyes gleamed with something akin to passion. 'King Charles II died without having a legitimate son so his heir was his younger brother. James was a staunch Catholic and not a popular man whereas the Duke of Monmouth – that's Charles' illegitimate son – was by many accounts a charismatic man. And a Protestant.'

Becky tried not to wince at the mention of Monmouth; after this morning's ejection from the hotel it wasn't a name she particularly wanted to hear again but, as Clara went on, it seemed she would have to adjust to hearing it quite a lot.

'The Duke of Monmouth had much support from the people in the West Country, particularly the poorer farming folk. They fought the royal army armed with farm tools, scythes, billhooks – whatever they could get their hands on.' Clara paused, lost in reverie, and Becky wondered if she was picturing herself there on the battlefield, whacking a royal soldier with a pitchfork.

'So what happened?' Becky asked.

Clara returned to the present. 'Well, they lost, of course. Those who weren't executed were exiled. It was tragic.' She sighed. 'I often wonder how many people in Somerset could trace their ancestry back to those poor men who were dragged from their families.'

'Can I ask why you're so interested in the subject?' said Becky. She couldn't recall Clara mentioning any English ancestors.

Clara seemed momentarily lost for an answer then shrugged and said, 'let's just say I feel sorry for the underdog. And that the Duke of Monmouth was a fine man.'

Becky felt Clara was holding something back but was reluctant to probe more; perhaps the reason for Clara's interest in the subject would become apparent later. 'It sounds interesting,' she said, carefully. 'So how would I be helping?'

'Research: collating the hundreds of scrappy notes I've made over the years, typing it all up, and – well everything really. My son has bought me a laptop and done everything possible to entice me to use the thing but I can't be doing with it.'

'This sounds almost too good to be true,' said Becky. 'You promise you're just not feeling sorry for me?'

Clara blinked. 'I promise there's a real job.'

'OK,' said Becky. 'So this would be a book about the Duke of Monmouth?'

'No,' said Clara. 'This will be a book about the poor people who fought to get him on the throne. Effectively, they became white slaves.'

How ironic that on the day of her second encounter with Matthew Darnley the S-word should come up again. But here was a lady of colour wanting to write about white slaves. Becky was intrigued. 'I'm up for it.'

'As I say, I'm packing up here,' said Clara. 'So how about you come away with me. Let's say – I don't know – for three months?'

'Away?' said Becky.

'We need to be where the primary sources are. I want to rely on the original documents. You do have a passport, don't you dear?'

'For Somerset?'

'No, dear. We're not going where they came from; we're going to where they went to.'

'Where is that exactly?' said Becky tentatively.

'My home. Barbados.'

Barbados. Of all the places in the world Clara would choose the one tiny scrap of land that had claimed Becky's father's affections – and from which he never returned. Heaven knows what her mother would say.

'Are you all right, Becky?' Clara looked concerned. 'I thought you'd be pleased but you look like you've seen a duppy.'

'Duppy?'

'A spirit, a ghost.'

Becky tried to calm herself with a deep breath. 'Sorry, I don't know why but I assumed you were from France. It never occurred to me you live in the West Indies.'

'I do love France, it's true, but Barbados is home. Or at least it's where I've made my home.' Clara gave Becky a stern look. 'And I hope you're not worrying about the airfare. All included.'

Becky could hardly believe it but judging by how much Clara must have spent to create a mature garden in a matter of months, money was not an issue. 'It sounds very exciting,' she said. 'Actually it's an amazing opportunity. Thank you for offering it to me.'

'It wasn't really difficult, dear. I'd been remembering how well we got on and how uncomfortable I'd be if I left the choice to Mr R.'

'Who on earth is Mr R?'

'My son. It's what I call him, which he hates.' Clara giggled. 'Anyway, when I did my gardening book, I just wanted a girl to type the thing into a computer, stick in the photographs and sort out the self-publishing. Not much to ask, surely.'

Becky laughed. 'Actually Clara, that sounds like a lot of work.'

'Well, maybe. Anyway, he got me some high-powered young woman with superior airs who thought she knew more about gardening than me; we didn't gel at all. I think at one point I threw a handful of mimulus seeds at her. That's why my monkey flowers are all over the place in the west corner of my garden. You probably noticed?'

‘Er, I’m afraid I didn’t.’ If there were patterns to the flowers in Clara’s front or back gardens, they were not apparent to Becky’s untrained eye.

‘Anyway, back to the matter in hand,’ said Clara. ‘It’s a lot to take in so how about coming over on Friday and we’ll talk in more detail? By then I’ll have a better idea of possible dates.’

The rest of the week passed slowly. Apart from receiving a sweet card signed by Patsy and the other women from work, Becky had little to show for her year with the *Essex Gleaner*. It was almost as though she had never worked there. Occasionally she would find herself brooding over her unfair dismissal, or her humiliating ejection from Mr Darnley’s hotel, but these miserable thoughts were rather overtaken by worry about how to broach the subject of ‘Barbados’ with her mother. She kept deferring that conversation in favour of lying on her bed and reading up about the Duke of Monmouth.

Why had she never liked history at school? She had thought it was irrelevant – useless, over and done with. But she recalled how passionate her socialist cabbie had been about it and she had seen something similar when Clara spoke about the Battle of Sedgemoor. If Clara felt a battle which had happened in 1685 was relevant to *her* then Becky wanted to know more. Maybe it was something to do with religion. Clara had mentioned the Duke of Monmouth was a Protestant and the library book told her people had feared James II would drag the country back to the days of Bloody Mary, a hundred and thirty years earlier. Hardly something within their living memory but then Becky remembered walking by ‘Martyr’s Elm’ on the other side of Brentwood. The tree had been planted to commemorate the burning to death during Mary’s reign of a young man – still a teenager – for preferring to read the

Bible rather than attend Catholic masses. Who would want a return to those days?

Whatever Clara's rcason Becky also found herself on the side of the Duke of Monmouth; compared to the vindictive James II he was certainly the better man.

The book was yanked roughly to one side so Joe could look at the cover.

'*The Stuarts*? Why are you reading that?'

'It's interesting.' Becky quietly despaired of her younger brother. He was bright but had worn his refusal to study at school as a badge of honour. Now he worked in a garage by day and seemed to spend most of his wages trying to service his motorbike so he could get to the garage the next day.

'I must read it sometime,' said Joe.

'You could try reading something.'

Drawn to Becky's room by the exchange of voices, their mother appeared in the doorway. 'You've always got your head in a book nowadays.'

'Why is everyone suddenly in my bedroom?' said Becky.

'Since you were fired you just seem to lie around reading,' complained her mother. 'Shouldn't you be looking for another job?'

Becky sat up; she'd been putting off this conversation but now was the time. Her mother wasn't cooking, which meant she couldn't drop anything hot, and she wasn't gardening, which meant she couldn't say her back had 'gone' – as it was liable to do at times of unexpected news.

'I've got a job.'

'Hey,' cried Joe, launching himself onto the bed. 'Well done. What, how, where?'

'It's a little unconventional,' said Becky. She could see her mother was already mentally fumbling with a large casserole dish. 'And it's only for a few months. I'm going to be working for a female author helping her write a history book.'

'But you don't know anything about history,' her mother said.

Becky waved *The Stuarts* in the air. 'That's why I'm reading.'

'It's good news.' Joe looked defiantly at their mother. 'Isn't it, Mum?'

'So where does this author live?' she asked.

'Her name is Clara Babonneau and –'

'She's French?'

Becky realised she still didn't know where Clara originally came from. 'She certainly speaks French but she seems to move between houses and, er, countries.'

Becky visualised a casserole dish slipping from her mother's grip.

'So where will you be working?'

'Barbados.'

Smash. If this conversation had happened in the kitchen Becky would now be sweeping up shards of glass and lumps of beef.

'Barbados?' Joe and their mother cried in unison.

'Yes. It's relevant to the book Clara's writing.' Becky searched for some familiar words with which to soften the surprise. 'Look, I'll just be like a secretary. And it's only for three months.'

Her mother did not move or speak for what felt like several minutes. 'You can say hello to your father,' she said at last and walked out.

'Bit of a weird reaction but actually she took that quite well,' said Joe.

Nothing more was said on the subject but it was still a relief to get out of the house on Friday. Becky received the warmest of welcomes from Clara, who led her into her bright living room and settled herself on the sofa, patting the seat beside her. 'So, you've told your mother you'll be going away?'

'Yes,' said Becky, sitting down. 'It's fine. Well, she's OK. She asked me if you were French. I guess your name sounds French.'

Clara laughed. 'No, Becky. I'm from Martinique. Anyway, Babonneau is my maiden name. My son prefers me to use that.'

Becky frowned. 'Why?'

'Shall we have another go at that peculiar sherry?' said Clara. 'It wasn't so bad after the first mouthful.' Becky nodded and Clara poured them a glass each, then sat back down with a sigh.

'I want you to know that Barbados is not dangerous but –' Clara took a sip of peppered sherry and made a comical eye-screwing expression, 'the truth is my son has made a bit of money – which he works very hard for – and the police in Barbados discovered a plan by some despicable people to kidnap me and get my son to pay a ransom. This was a few years back.'

'Oh,' said Becky. This was casserole-dropping information.

'Fortunately it was all very amateur so nothing bad happened. It was my son who then encouraged me to use a different name in public. Pointless in Barbados, of course, where everyone knows me, but I suppose it might confuse people when I'm abroad. I think he got a little paranoid but there we are.'

'I can imagine he was paranoid – with good reason.'

'But, trust me, the house in Barbados is as secure as a prison.'

An unfortunate simile, thought Becky. No doubt Clara was trying to put her mind at rest but she wasn't sure she wanted to stay in a jail.

'Who else is in this house?' she asked.

'It will be us, Mr R of course, our lovely old cook and people drop by all the time. It's very relaxed.'

That sounded better.

'My son is due sometime today, back from – oh I can't keep track of him – France, was it? Anyway, it would be good if you can meet him before we all end up in the Bajan house together.'

'That sounds like a good idea. And Bajan is short for Barbadian?'

'Yes indeed. You'll hear it all the time when you're there.'

The doorbell rang, closely followed by the sound of a key turning.

Clara beamed and got up. 'I wasn't expecting him back this early. I'll be able to tell him right away I've found the co-author of my book.' She laughed at the grandness of the title and went out to the hall.

Becky could picture her giving her son an effusive hug as she greeted him. 'When did you get back from – wherever it was? I wasn't expecting to see you so soon.'

'Shall I go away, then?' a jocular voice enquired. Becky sat forward on the sofa: that accent was familiar.

'Certainly not. I see little enough of you as it is. Now come on in.'

There was a clunk and Becky assumed Mr R's head had collided with the potted fern suspended from the ceiling in the hall; Clara and Becky had passed it under safely but evidently he was that bit taller.

'Ouch. I should wear a hard hat in here,' he said, dolefully.

'Oh, that reminds me,' said Clara. 'Can you water that later? Saves me getting out the stepladder. Now come and meet my lovely new co-author.'

'Co-author?'

'For the book I keep talking about.'

'Book?'

There was no mistaking that voice now and Becky looked round hurriedly but the only way out of the room was the door Clara was walking back through, followed by Matthew Darnley. He was wearing an expectant smile but the grin vanished as soon as he saw Becky and his outstretched hand was withdrawn.

'This is Becky Thomson,' said Clara.

'What a co-incidence,' Matthew said quietly, in a tone that revealed he thought it was anything but.

Clara chose that fraught moment to begin singing Becky's praises, telling Matthew just 'what a find she was'.

'How long have you known Miss Thomson?' he said grimly.

'Oh, months,' Clara said vaguely. 'Becky's the clever young woman who wrote that charming piece about me in the local paper. I showed it to you,' she added. 'Anyway now she's agreed to come out and work with me on my book in Barbados.'

He fixed his eyes Becky. 'Has she now?'

Clara looked at him, clearly confused by his unfriendly tone.

'Actually, you know, it's getting late,' said Becky, with no idea what the time was. She picked up her handbag. 'I must go.'

Matthew stepped aside so she could pass but an agitated Clara gave him a look of annoyance. 'Oh, don't leave, Becky. We still have lots to discuss.'

'I'll call you tomorrow,' Becky promised as Clara, no doubt trying to make up for her son's abrasiveness, gave her a particularly effusive and affectionate hug goodbye. Becky just wanted to escape but she didn't want to hurt Clara's feelings so she returned the hug, conscious that Matthew was standing ready to shepherd her to the front door.

‘I’ll show Miss Thomson out,’ he told his mother, leading Becky by the elbow as if once again escorting her from the premises.

As soon as they were in the hall Becky angrily shook him off. ‘We’re not in one of your hotels now,’ she snapped.

He lowered his head so his voice wouldn’t carry back into the living room. ‘How did you trace her?’

‘Trace her?’

Matthew looked like he was barely keeping a lid on his fury. ‘This is not a game; I need to know. Did someone at the hotel talk?’

‘I didn’t *trace her*,’ Becky hissed. ‘She had a gardening open day. I came around to interview her.’

She could see Matthew mentally processing this information, testing the truth of it, looking for loopholes. ‘And when did you find out she was my mother?’

‘I had no interest in knowing who *your* mother was. I found out you were her *son* when you walked in just now. If your mother used her real surname, and referred to you by your real forename, I just might have been in with a chance of working out the relationship.’

His sceptical expression was replaced with a grimacing smile as Clara came into the hall to see why it was taking so long for Becky to reach the front door.

‘Everything OK?’ she asked, an edge of concern to her voice.

‘All fine,’ Matthew assured her. ‘I was just warning Miss Thomson about the mosquitoes in Barbados.’

‘Oh, Matthew,’ cried his mother with annoyance. ‘They aren’t that bad.’

He opened the door and looked at Becky, unsmilingly. ‘Drive safely.’

Becky nodded another goodbye to Clara, walked out and around the corner to wait for her bus. A job in Barbados: of course it had been too good to be true.

Becky spent the rest of the day wondering how much of the Monmouth 'freeloading' saga Matthew would share with Clara to dissuade her from taking Becky to Barbados. She was not sure she wanted to spend three months under the same roof as him anyway but she didn't relish the prospect of telling her mother she might not be going to Barbados after all. Besides, she needed a job and she was sure Clara knew her better than Matthew did and would not be persuaded by his opinion. Still, when the telephone rang mid-evening she half-thought it would be Clara calling to say she no longer wanted Becky to work for her. Joe took the call and handed over the receiver carelessly. 'It's some man.'

Had Clara been so appalled by what her son had told her she'd asked him to deliver the news? It *was* Matthew but he didn't tell Becky her services were no longer required. Instead he sounded sardonic. 'I'm a bit baffled, Miss Thomson. I wondered if you could help me out.'

'Can you just call me Becky?' she said, taking the phone into the hall so her mother and Joe could not overhear the conversation.

'No. I think we'll stay formal.'

Becky sighed. 'OK, Mr Darnley. How can I help you out?'

'I'm trying to understand in what capacity you see yourself working with my mother. Will you be a reporter, snooping around, or do you see yourself on a freebie trip to Barbados?'

'Neither,' said Becky, wearily. 'I'll be working on your mother's book. Doing whatever she wants me to do.'

'I see.' There was a pause while he presumably considered this. 'I'm not sure what I think about this book.'

'Surely you should be asking your mother about that, not me.'

'Sounds rather nice to have an all-expenses-paid job in Barbados.'

'That wasn't my idea.' Becky felt herself getting annoyed at his implication she was freeloading again. 'I didn't even know your mother lived in Barbados. I would be more than happy to work on the book here.'

He grunted in disbelief. 'I can tell you now you won't like it.'

'I won't like what?'

'Barbados. Has my mother mentioned our house is in the most remote part of the island? It'll be very dull.'

Becky had toyed with the idea of telling Clara she no longer wanted the position but Matthew's attempts to warn her off were stirring a rebellious reaction.

'Remote and dull sounds perfect,' she said, sweetly. 'It means I'll get a chance to work on the book without distractions.'

'Really? So you'll drop your job, just like that, and swan off to Barbados?'

'If you hadn't got me sacked I wouldn't have had to accept your mother's offer.'

Matthew did not answer. Maybe he hadn't known that she'd been fired – and because of him. He tried a different tack.

'I hope your boyfriend isn't planning on appearing for a free holiday.'

'As I told you before he isn't a boyfriend. Just a work colleague who was trying it on.'

There was another grunt of disbelief followed by a long pause. 'I want you to tell my mother you've changed your mind.'

'Goodbye, Mr Darnley,' said Becky and hung up.

Chapter Four

The morning after the unpleasant phone call from Matthew Darnley, Clara herself rang: 'I hope you don't mind that I gave Mr R your number yesterday. He seems concerned that you won't like Barbados but I told him I knew you would. Anyway, dear, apologies if his behaviour was a little unfriendly. Sometimes he lets his worries about his business affect his disposition.'

'So you still want me to come to Barbados?' Becky asked.

There was an explosion of assent down the line. 'Of *course*, I want you to come! Our original arrangement still stands.'

'Actually Clara, exactly what is the arrangement?'

Clara sighed in exasperation. 'That's what I asked him to tell you. Six thousand pounds for the three months. He was supposed to be asking you for your bank details. And we leave on June the thirtieth. I hope that's OK?'

'Sounds fine.'

'I'll get Mr R to ring you with the details.'

Becky did not relish the thought of another conversation with Matthew but it turned out he had delegated someone called Alex Wilson to deal with the rest of the arrangements. Alex was pleasant on the phone, with a more pronounced Bajan accent than Matthew's. Despite sounding in a rush, he certainly seemed more kindly disposed towards her than his boss.

'Slight change of plan,' he said apologetically when he rang later that day. 'Matthew's suggested we pay you two thousand a month rather than six thousand up front. I hope that's OK?'

Becky grimaced. Clearly Matthew Darnley was not expecting her to last the course. 'That's fine,' she said.

'I've arranged for you to receive some paperwork to fill in. Sorry for the bureaucracy but I'll need you to send a copy of your passport and a couple of other forms of ID. And I also need your mobile number if you want to give me that now.'

'OK,' said Becky. 'Although I need to buy a new mobile. I haven't got one at the moment.'

'Oh.' He sounded surprised. 'Well, just write the number on the paperwork and send it back as soon as you can.'

The paperwork arrived early on Monday morning by courier. It consisted of a single, official-looking form containing a non-disclosure agreement about Matthew's business (which Becky was comfortable signing as she had no interest in learning about his work, let alone disclosing it) and also a clause requesting her consent to submit to a background check. She put her head in her hands.

'What's up with you?'

Becky raised her head to see Joe, already dressed in his oil-stained jeans. She looked beyond him.

'Don't worry. Mum's got her head in the oven.'

'What?'

'I mean she's cleaning it or something. She can't hear.'

All the same Becky lowered her voice. 'This job I'm going for. They want to do a background check on me.'

Joe uttered a four-letter expletive. 'Just to work for a woman in Barbados?'

'It's complicated. Her son doesn't seem to think I'm serious about the book.'

'Christ. He sounds like a complete pillock.'

Becky listened out for their mother, whose auditory range often had a special extension for blasphemies. Still no sign of her. It would be a very clean oven.

'So what are you going to do?' asked Joe.

'I've got to agree to it, haven't I?'

Joe nodded. 'Looks less suspicious. Then maybe he won't bother.'

'Maybe.'

'What's this book going to be about? The one you're helping Madame Bonbon, or whatever her name is, write?'

'The Monmouth rebels.' Becky expected a sarcastic comment but Joe just nodded and walked out. Shortly afterwards she heard his motorbike pull away.

Becky read through and signed the agreement and went out to the post office to photocopy her passport, birth certificate, and a bank statement. The balance of her current account was alarmingly low and she was embarrassed to think of Matthew Darnley catching sight of it. She also bought a cheap phone on a pay-as-you-go basis.

As instructed on the form, she marked the envelope for the attention of 'Matthew Darnley' at the Monmouth Hotel and posted it.

Alex called again the next day, this time on her new mobile.

'Thanks for filling in the form. Assuming there are no problems, I'll give you a ring to sort out where we should meet at Heathrow in two weeks' time.'

'Thanks Alex.'

Two weeks. Becky had already decided she would not buy anything new for the trip – she couldn't really afford it and anyway she didn't want to tempt fate – so she would spend the time doing as much research as possible. Or at least she would once she had worked out what was going on with Joe. Her brother's habits had changed over the last couple of nights and instead of spending his evenings tinkering with his bike or watching a football match at the pub, he was now to be found on the old PC in the study. Becky was alarmed. Last year she had fought a constant battle trying to remove temptation by blocking one online gambling site after another until in the end she had had to tearfully beg Joe to either break his habit or say goodbye to the computer. It was her tears rather than threats that seemed to do the trick and, until a few evenings ago, he had almost ceased using it.

Now no sooner was he home from the garage and changed out of his oil-stained clothes than he was sitting in front of the monitor. While their mother was busy preparing dinner, Becky sneaked into the study to see what he was up to. She was surprised to find him studying a YouTube clip of a battle re-enactment.

'Battle of Sedgemoor,' he said casually, as she peered over his shoulder. 'You know, you should go to Somerset and check out the battleground.'

Becky smiled – an automatic response to her brother's suggestions – but later when they were eating realised this was probably good advice.

As soon as the meal was over she rang Clara, who sounded harassed.

'I didn't think I'd bought that much since I've been in England but there's so many *things* lying round the house that I realise weren't here before. God knows how I've acquired them all. Furniture, plants. I swear my *objets d'art* have been breeding.'

Becky laughed. 'Can't you just leave them for the next tenants?'

'The agent came round today to inspect the premises; you know, to check for any damage. The stupid man bashed his head on that hanging basket in the hall and I fear it put him in a bad mood. He said that all the *clutter* had to go. He was really quite rude.'

Becky gasped. 'What about the garden, Clara? Did they mind you making, um, a few changes?'

Clara gave a mischievous giggle. 'Making some improvements, you mean, Becky. And no, unless I had dumped a mattress in the garden, the silly agent wouldn't have noticed what was *outside* the house. Now tell me, is it normal in England to leave a few things on the pavement with a sign saying 'help yourself'?'

'It would be normal in some areas but not Hutton, I'm afraid.' Becky could imagine the middle-class neighbours' horrified expressions at the sight of bric-a-brac – however expensive – on their illustrious pavement. 'Can't Matthew find space for things in Noak Hall?'

'What's Noak Hall?'

Having just signed a non-disclosure agreement, Becky knew Matthew was highly secretive about his business practices but was the neo-classical manor even a secret from his own mother? Hardly a family mansion, then. 'I've probably got it wrong,' she said quickly. 'I thought he had a place in Essex.'

'You must mean the Monmouth Hotel,' said Clara. 'Good idea. I'll ask him.'

'On the subject of Monmouth,' said Becky. 'I wondered if it was worth me spending a couple of days in Somerset. There's a Heritage Centre which would have records of the people who were sent to Barbados.'

'Records?'

'Yes, I thought if I started off with a list of names of the people transported, and who they were indentured to, then when we get to Barbados, I could try and trace what happened to them.'

'Oh, don't worry, Becky. You must have enough on your plate.'

'No, not really.'

'You must have: I don't know – packing to do, things to cancel.'

Becky felt quite deflated. Why was Clara so reluctant for her to find out this information? 'I don't really have anything to arrange,' she said. 'And no clutter to dispose of – unless my mother feels the need to rent out my room for the three months I'm away, which I can guarantee she won't.'

There was a moment's silence, which seemed unusual for a woman as bubbly and voluble as Clara.

'It's good you're so enthusiastic,' she said though Becky thought she heard a quiet sigh. 'It shows I made the right choice. And, yes, maybe it would be good to know who was sent from this end.'

'But I quite understand if you say no. I would need some money to travel there and back and maybe one night in a B&B. I think the Heritage Centre is free but I couldn't do the trip in a day.'

'No, of course, you must stay over. And in a proper hotel. I don't know – would £500 be enough?'

Becky laughed. 'Far too much. Halve that and hopefully I'll have change to give you.'

'I'll get some money out. Come round tomorrow. Anything else you need?'

'Names,' said Becky. 'I don't know how many people were sent out there but I thought there might be some particular surnames you'd want me to look out for.'

'Let me think about that.'

Two days later, Becky was sitting on a train, watching through the window as it limped out of Paddington before gaining speed and charging through green fields like a wild animal released into its natural element. She should be happy. It was a summer's day, she had a job in Barbados to look forward to, working for a woman she liked, and right now she was on a mission – a paid mission no less. But every time Becky told herself she deserved a break, and this was it, she was aware of something mocking her from the shadows.

Maybe she was picking up on her mother's discontent that she was going to Barbados, although, unusually, her mum had not said anything discouraging about it. She wasn't worried about the trip herself. She was sure she and Clara would get on. The older lady certainly trusted her – when Becky had turned up to collect the funds for her trip, Clara had just handed over her purse with a careless 'take what you need' and seemed bemused when Becky insisted on counting out £250 in front of her.

No, her doubts were more to do with the project itself, following her employer's apparent ambivalence when she had proposed researching in Somerset. Maybe Clara was just stressed about moving house? Or maybe Matthew was putting pressure on her as he was not sure about the book and did not want Becky to go to Barbados?

Becky tried to banish her forebodings by studying a chapter on the fate of the Monmouth rebels. James II had appointed Judge Jeffreys to dispense swift justice and it sounded like he had savoured the barbaric sentences he handed out, pronouncing death sentences with relish and taking pleasure in outlining the appalling fates that awaited the convicted.

By the time the train terminated at Taunton Becky's dark mood had intensified. Clara had told her to 'take taxis whenever she could' but Becky's natural distrust of extravagance, combined with a determination to counter Matthew's impression of her as a gold-digging opportunist, made her ignore the cabs waiting hopefully outside the station. She caught a bus and walked the remaining fifteen minutes to the Heritage Centre, where she checked in and stowed her rucksack in a locker.

'What are you interested in?' asked the woman on reception.

‘Monmouth rebels,’ said Becky. ‘In particular the names of anyone transported to Barbados.’

She was directed to the Search Room and, within there, a series of volumes, which included lists of the men transported, their occupations and their new ‘masters’, who were presumably plantation owners or overseers. She discovered rebels had been sent to Jamaica, St Kitts and Nevis as well as Barbados but all were sentenced to four years’ indentured labour. Becky concentrated on the men shipped to Barbados. Surnames that were still familiar today (Parker, Dodds, Foot) were listed along with names rendered more exotic with the passage of time, such as the wonderfully titled Randolph Randerwick. Clara had only given her one surname to look out for – Pitcher – and Becky soon found a Daniel Pitcher listed as being dispatched in December 1685 on the ship *Betty* from Weymouth. She soon realised why Clara, or more likely Matthew, had been reluctant for her to carry out this research: Daniel Pitcher’s new ‘Master’ on the island was a William Darnley.

So Ian’s tiresome ‘slave’ prank hadn’t been so far off the mark after all. Becky sat back in her chair and tried to think how the Barbados venture would work. If the plan was to follow the fates of certain rebels on the island, it would be ridiculous to omit the names of the plantations they were assigned to and the men they were indentured to. But would Clara feel compromised by what they discovered? Surely she couldn’t expect an account of the rebels’ new lives to sweep over such details?

Becky ran her finger down the rest of the list of the men transported with Pitcher on the *Betty*. One unusual surname leapt out: Thomas Gehalgod. At the bottom of the list was a paragraph:

The Bille of mortallity of the said Rebells that dyed since they were reced on Board and were thrown overboard out of the said Ship were …

There followed three names, one of which was Thomas Gehalgod. Becky shivered. Would it have been better to be hanged than left in a ship's hold with untreated wounds and then thrown overboard with, presumably, little ceremony?

At least Thomas Gehalgod hadn't had to work for William Darnley, whom Becky instinctively felt would have been as mercenary as his descendent. Maybe that was the only positive aspect to dying at sea.

She had paid five pounds for a photograph licence but found the camera on her new phone wasn't really up to capturing the information. She sorely missed the smartphone she had had at the *Essex Gleaner*. She took the book to the helpdesk to find out if they could photograph the pages for her.

'We could,' said the woman on the desk. 'But you know this book is online, don't you? You could access it anywhere.'

Becky groaned. She could have done the research at home after all. It had been a wasted trip and a waste of Clara's money. God knows what Matthew would have to say if he found out.

'Since you're here you should visit the key places,' said the woman, 'the battlefield itself and the church at Westonzoyland.'

'The church?'

'St Mary's. It's where King James's men locked up the injured rebels – left them there with festering wounds overnight. The church had to be fumigated with frankincense afterwards.'

'Oh,' said Becky, unsure how to react to this generously dispensed information. 'Thank you. I might do that.'

But she knew she wouldn't. It would mean finding a taxi and spending even more of Clara's money being driven round the sights. If only she could drive; if only she had a car.

She went back to where she had been sitting to pick up her things and realised her phone was vibrating. It was Joe's number.

'Just a second,' she said. She retrieved her rucksack, nodded thanks to the woman on the helpdesk, and walked out .

'Is everything all right?' she asked once outside the centre. Joe never rang her when he was at work.

'Fine. Just wondered how you were getting on.'

'So-so,' said Becky, touched he would bother to ring but unsure how much of her disappointment to share.

'That doesn't sound good. What's wrong?'

'You remember I said Clara's son doesn't want me to write the book?'

'No, you said he didn't think you were serious about it.'

'OK, I think it's more than that. I'll explain tomorrow when I'm back.'

'Explain now,' he said and hung up.

Becky stared at her phone, baffled, then turned as she heard the roar of a motorbike pulling up alongside her. Joe raised his visor and gave a big grin.

She didn't know whether to laugh or express astonishment his bike had got him this far. Now she thought about it, he had left much earlier than usual this morning; she had assumed he had a busy day at work planned. 'You haven't thrown a sickie, have you?'

Joe made a face. 'No, I haven't. I do get days off, you know, and I thought you'd like to see the actual locations as well as just visit the Centre.'

'I'm rather touched, to be honest,' she said. 'Actually, it's really nice to see you.'

He shrugged off her affection. 'Come on. Let's go to the battlefield and then you can tell me why pillock son doesn't want you to write the book.'

‘You know where it is?’

‘Yup, I went by on my way here. I’ve even borrowed a fine hat for you to wear.’ He opened the bike’s top box and took out a helmet. Becky hesitated. She was nervous of bikes and could never have made the journey here as a pillion passenger, but she didn’t want to be churlish. She put on the helmet, secured her rucksack on her back and held on to her little brother.

The journey took about half an hour during which Becky only occasionally opened her eyes. She kept them open when she realised Joe had slowed down and they were passing a church. A bit further on he pulled up in a space on a quiet main road and they got off.

‘It’s a fairly short walk,’ said Joe and Becky followed him, impressed (and surprised) that he was so organised.

‘I’ve read up on it a bit,’ he said, casually, once they were some way along the path. ‘Monmouth didn’t want to fight in the end, as he knew he would lose, but one of his commanders persuaded him he had no choice. So he decided to launch a surprise night attack on the Royalist troops camped at Westonzoyland. He led five thousand men – most hadn’t even had any training – and horseback cavalry for miles in the rain – in pitch black and in silence. I mean: respect.’

Becky laughed. ‘Sounds impossible. Surely with horses you’d hear them.’

‘Monmouth had the horses’ hooves bound with cloth to muffle their steps,’ said Joe. ‘Can you imagine that? Seeing thousands of men and horses marching through the fields with no noise?’

‘No,’ said Becky. ‘Spooky.’

‘Apparently some people still see them today, especially on the anniversary of the battle. This is it.’

The battleground looked like a peaceful meadow to Becky. She gazed at the sunlit field but couldn’t conjure up the image of a pitched battle here in the dark.

Joe was looking at a map and turning round at various angles, as if trying to orient himself. 'Right. Got it,' he said. 'You've heard of the rhines?'

Becky shook her head. Her book on *The Stuarts* did not contain many details about the battle itself.

'The drainage ditches. An ancient means of trying to control flooding that were key to the outcome.'

For the next twenty minutes Joe pointed out where the respective armies would have probably stood, where the rhine Monmouth failed to cross would have lain three hundred years before and where Monmouth's commander, Lord Grey, had 'ballsed up' so that instead of crossing the rhine and attacking the Royalist army, he had led his cavalry straight back into his own side.

Becky listened to Joe with amazement and pride. He seemed to have suddenly discovered history, albeit a rather morbid brand. He had certainly devoured facts about artillery, describing the different fire power of the trained soldiers and the badly equipped Monmouth rebels, who bravely yelled at the Royal Army to cross the rhine and fight like men instead of firing over the water at them. He was rather over-fascinated by the idea of men being turned into corpses by musket shot and cannon ball and the injured trying to crawl away.

'In an age without antibiotics,' said Becky.

'Nice.'

Her phone vibrated again and she answered it, while Joe continued studying his map and comparing it with the land around them.

It was Alex Wilson. 'Becky? Bad news I'm afraid. Matthew insisted on a background check. You can't really blame him. If you're going to be living in the house and his office is there too. It was just meant to be a formality …'

Becky knew what was coming next.

'I didn't expect to find anything. Especially not drugs.'

'It was a caution.'

'I know. But Matthew's not taken it too well.'

'OK,' said Becky, walking away from Joe so he wouldn't be able to overhear her. 'I've got a younger brother who's not bad but who got into a bit of trouble. He was caught with dope in his pocket and I said it was mine. I've never tried it and I don't even smoke.'

There was a sigh down the phone. 'Why did you take the rap for him?'

Because he'd only started selling soft drugs to fund his online gambling habit. Because, after a slightly wild youth, he had expressed an interest in joining the police and Becky was so hopeful this could be the answer to his problems she would have done anything to get him sorted out. If she'd known the 'police' idea was no more serious than his other vaguely expressed desires to join the army or the French Foreign Legion she would never have put herself at risk.

'Because he's my younger brother,' she said.

There was another sigh. 'I'll have a word with Matthew.'

'Thanks.' She could hear a conversation in the background and recognised other Bajan accents. 'Where are you?'

'I'm at the Monmouth.'

'The hotel? So you're in Essex?'

'No, I'm not flying over until next week. I'm in the Monmouth in Barbados. Matthew's got two hotels, didn't you know?'

'No, I didn't.'

'Look, I'll ring you tomorrow after I've spoken to Matthew.'

Becky said goodbye and realised Joe had wandered over and was looking quizzical.

'OK?' he said.

'Everything's fine,' she assured him.

Alex had seemed to accept her explanation of the drugs caution but Becky thought Matthew was bound to use it as an excuse to prevent her going to Barbados. Still no need to bother Joe, who was making such an effort to help her out.

He looked over the battlefield one more time. 'I think that's probably as much as I can tell you.'

'You found out loads of stuff I didn't know,' said Becky. 'I hadn't thought about the battle at all to be honest. I was just reading about what happened afterwards.'

'Shall we go pick up the bike, then?'

They headed back to the main road.

'So why doesn't pillock man want you to write the book?' Joe asked when they were part-way there.

'I'll have to tell you a bit about what happened after the battle to explain why,' said Becky. 'As you know, the rebels lost. Many of them were hanged but King James II had others transported to work as indentured labourers in the colonies. Really he was just donating them to his friends who owned the plantations but he did it under the guise of being the merciful Christian.'

'So that's where Barbados comes in?'

'Exactly. Clara wants to write a book about the fate of the rebels who were sent there as exiles.'

'That sounds good. What's the problem?'

'The problem is that, although in theory they were only sentenced to four years, none of them came back. They became, well, white slaves pretty much and the plantation owners wouldn't release them.'

'Bastards. But what's that got to do with pillock man?'

'I learnt today at the Heritage Centre that it was Clara's family – or I think her husband's family – who owned one of the plantations on Barbados that were given many of the men.'

‘Ah. Maybe she feels guilty and wants to – what’s the word when you want to put something right?’

‘Atone,’ said Becky. ‘But she wouldn’t have anything to be guilty about. She’s black, or certainly of colour.’

Joe frowned. ‘So a black woman wants to write about white slaves. Her husband must be white. What does he think of it?’

‘She’s a widow.’

‘Ah right,’ said Joe. ‘So she felt bad that she married into one of the old plantation families but she had to wait for her husband to peg it before she could write the book. But, of course, her son wouldn’t want the book written because basically it exposes his ancestors as slave owners.’

‘Er, I think something like that,’ said Becky, though Joe’s thought processes had jumped much further ahead than hers.

‘But you’re working for her not her son so you can tell him to sling his hook, can’t you?’

‘I’m not sure I can. We’ll all be sharing a house for a start.’

Joe made a face. They had almost reached his bike but Becky realised the church back along the road was the one the Heritage Centre receptionist had mentioned.

‘I want a quick look in there,’ she said. Joe looked pained and she laughed. ‘You don’t have to come in. Just loiter round the graveyard.’

They had both endured weekly church visits to a service their mother must have chosen for its complete lack of joy and vitality. On his fourteenth birthday Joe had said he would never set foot in a church again and had stuck firm, despite their mother’s tantrums, punishing silences and dropped dishes. Becky – either out of loyalty to her mother or maybe because she couldn’t face the emotional consequences – endured the services until, at eighteen, she decided facing her mother’s disappointment was more palatable than hearing about God’s wrath.

Joe followed her reluctantly into the churchyard. Some of the older gravestones looked as weathered as sucked grey lozenges.

‘Do you think we might find rebels buried here?’ he said, becoming interested again.

‘Doubt it,’ said Becky. ‘Anyway the executed men would have been left hanging on gibbets rather than given a decent burial. But their descendants might be here.’

And it was possible some of the men imprisoned in the church had died of their wounds overnight and been buried in the churchyard. She shivered at the thought and was quite relieved to see a sign saying the information centre inside the church was now closed for the day. ‘If a gravestone’s that old you probably wouldn’t be able to read the inscription anyway.’

But Joe was pointing at some grey chunks of stone off the main path, which could only be reached by walking over other graves. ‘What about over there?’

The sun was dipping towards the horizon and, while the church tower basked in the remnants of the evening sun, shadows stalked the gravestones. The area Joe was heading for looked quite gloomy.

She followed him gingerly over the tussocked grass, surprised to find herself inwardly apologising to the inhabitants over whom they trod.

‘These look ancient,’ said Joe, squatting in front of one of the old slabs.

Becky bent down and examined another, which was stubbled with moss and lichens. She rubbed her finger over it but couldn’t tell if the indentations were memories of letters carved or simply natural indentations in the rock.

‘I can see a date on this one,’ said Joe, ‘1721 or ’31.’ He sighed. ‘Too late to be a Monmouth rebel.’

‘He may have been, said Becky. ‘A few managed to escape.’

Joe peered at the stone again. 'T – H – may be an O?' he read. 'And something about "god".'

Becky joined him. 'Thomas.' She scratched off some moss, stared and then scratched some more. 'That is strange.'

'What?'

'I think it says "Thomas Gehalgod".'

'Weird name,' said Joe.

'Exactly,' said Becky. 'It was the name of one of the men who was transported to Barbados. Or at least he was meant to be. He died on the ship and was thrown overboard.'

'His son?' said Joe. He sounded disappointed.

'Maybe. I wish I could read the rest of it.'

To her surprise, Joe kneeled on the grass and produced a key to cut the lichen away. After a few minutes he stopped. 'I feel like I'm rubbing away actual stone.'

'The first word is "my", I think,' said Becky. 'The second word begins with "f". That could be an "e" and an "r" at the end. And the last word looks like "keeper".

'There could be a "t" in there,' said Joe, pointing, 'but the second letter – after "f" – nope, that's gone.'

'My father is my keeper'?'

Joe ran his fingers over the stone. 'Not "is". I think that's "was".'

'My father was my keeper?'

'Could be.' Joe stood up. 'It's not very religious, is it?'

'No,' said Becky. 'It's a small "f", which seems a bit disrespectful if it meant God the Father. Plus it sounds a bit limited, doesn't it? God was my keeper, instead of God is my keeper through eternity.'

He sniggered. 'Maybe Thomas got disillusioned.'

'Maybe,' said Becky. 'Or it could be a simple statement about his real father. Perhaps this is Thomas Gehalgod Junior referring to Thomas Gehalgod Senior who was thrown overboard.'

Joe gave a grin. ‘Or it could be that Thomas Ge – whatever his name was –’

‘Gehalgod.’

‘… wasn’t injured but had a deal with someone on the ship to say he died before the ship got too far and he swam back and lived out his natural life.’

Becky laughed. ‘OK, let’s assume that happened. Thomas Gehalgod survived.’

Thanks to Joe she felt far more positive than she had at the start of the day. They headed back into Taunton for something to eat and then found Becky’s hotel. When she realised Joe was going to get back on his bike and return to Essex she tried to persuade him to stay overnight. But Joe was adamant he needed to go back so he could get to work on time the next day.

As she saw him off Becky wondered at how much he seemed to have grown up in the past few days.

Chapter Five

Two days had passed and Becky had had no contact from Alex. She rang Clara to give her an update following her visit to the Heritage Centre and to point out she still had some money left over but Clara seemed in no hurry for her change.

'Did you find out anything interesting?' asked Clara.

'You mentioned someone called "Pitcher". I found a Daniel Pitcher was sent to Barbados.'

Clara did show some interest in that. 'Ah, that could be the ancestor of our Pitcher.'

'Our Pitcher?'

'You'll meet him soon enough. That is when Alex sorts out the tickets. He and Mr R have gone very quiet on me.'

That meant so as far as Clara was concerned Becky was still going to Barbados but Becky thought Alex and Matthew's lack of communication didn't bode well.

She mentioned her worry to Joe when he came in that night, feeling a little guilty at offloading her concern.

'Why didn't you tell me that was what the phone call was about?' he said, following her into the living room.

'I didn't want to spoil the day.'

'You've got to go to Barbados. One of us has to go. It's closure on Dad.'

Becky smiled. The word 'closure' sounded as incongruous coming from Joe's mouth as would 'embroidery'.

'Why are you laughing at me?'

'I'm not,' said Becky. 'Do we need closure?'

‘I still have dreams – even now – that he comes back. He walks through the house but he doesn’t look at us; he just walks right through and disappears into the garden.’

Joe said this without any trace of self-pity, which gave Becky an even more acute stab of sympathy. ‘Look, I’m probably worrying for nothing,’ she said. ‘I expect I’ll get a phone call later.’

‘If what’s-his-face says you can’t go to Barbados, tell him you know the real reason is he doesn’t want you to write the book.’

The landline rang and brother and sister looked at each other.

‘Quick,’ said Joe. ‘Before Mum gets it.’

Becky reached the phone just before their grim-faced mother but did not pick it up until her mother returned to the kitchen.

‘Miss Thomson?’ It was Matthew.

‘Mr Darnley.’

‘I’m sure you know why I’m ringing. Alex told you about the results of the background check?’

Becky’s heart raced. The gravity of his voice and the fact he was ringing instead of Alex meant he had made up his mind.

‘Yes, Alex rang when I was in Somerset.’

‘Then you know –’ Matthew faltered slightly. ‘Somerset? Was that anything to do with my mother?’

‘Yes. I was at the Heritage Centre doing research for her book.’

‘Ah. I’m afraid that makes what I’m about to say more difficult.’ He paused. ‘Just out of curiosity, did you find out anything interesting?’

Becky decided she had nothing to lose now and might as well take Joe’s advice. ‘Quite interesting, yes. I found out why you don’t want me to do this book.’

‘What?’

'You don't want me to come to Barbados because you don't want your family history exposed.'

There was a hint of a splutter down the phone. 'What gave you that idea? I've nothing to be ashamed of.'

'I didn't say you have. All I'm saying is that I understand the problem now.'

'I'm not sure what you're talking about.'

She didn't really want to spell it out for him. 'I think I know why your mother wants to write this book and I understand why you don't want it to see the light of day. It isn't going to make for a good working environment.'

'I'm rather intrigued now,' Matthew said. 'So you don't want to come to Barbados?'

'I would love to come to Barbados and I would love to do the research Clara wants me to do. But clearly you want it to be a closed subject. And I don't see how we can work like that.'

'I don't know where you've got that idea from,' said Matthew, sounding genuinely puzzled. 'My mother can write a book on any subject she likes.'

'Really?'

'Really.' He went quiet for a moment. 'OK. You'll come to Barbados and let's see what you come up with. Alex will be in touch.'

Becky put the phone down and realised both her mother and Joe were hovering in separate doorways, eavesdropping. She looked at Joe and simply said 'yes' and their mother glared disapprovingly at his triumphant 'just scored a goal' dance.

Alex rang a few days later and sounded his usual harassed but kindly self. 'Congratulations. I don't know how you swung it with Matthew but you obviously changed his mind. You must tell me the secret.'

'I just told him I didn't want to go to Barbados.'

Alex chuckled. 'So maybe if I told him I really wanted to travel to England at every opportunity he would stop sending me over. I must try that sometime.'

'You're in England now?'

'Yes, at the Monmouth. I've got your ticket here for Tuesday. I'll meet you at Heathrow by the British Airways check-in desks. I've arranged for a car to pick you up at eight. That's eight in the morning.'

'Oh, OK,' said Becky. 'I just assumed I would be travelling to the airport with Clara. She's not that far away from me.'

'She'll probably get there with Matthew. She – how shall I put it?' Alex chuckled again. 'Clara doesn't travel lightly. There'll barely be room for Matthew in the car plus all her suitcases. Speaking of which, you'll end up gardening, so do pack accordingly.'

'Gardening?'

'Trust me on this one.'

The morning of thirtieth June came round almost too quickly. Becky tried to relax in the grand car Alex had sent to take her to the airport but trepidation about the weeks ahead kept rising up in cycles. By the time they reached Heathrow she was sure she'd made the wrong decision. The chauffeur must have noticed her nervousness because he said, 'You'll be fine; it's safer than the M4' as he hefted her suitcase on to a trolley.

Her first concern – that she would have trouble identifying Alex at the airport – was immediately allayed as he somehow clocked her as soon as she pushed her trolley into the check-in area. He rushed over, a sandy-haired, brown-eyed white Bajan with a pallid, blotchy, complexion. He was fiddling with an airline envelope and looked very tired.

'There's a problem with your ticket,' he murmured, uneasily.

Half relieved that maybe she wouldn't be able to travel and could go back home, Becky took the ticket from his hands, which she noticed had a slight tremor. The ticket looked fine to her: her name was spelt right, it was the right date, the destination said 'GAIA, Barbados'.

'I can't see anything wrong,' she said, following him further into the check-in area where she soon saw Matthew and Clara having an urgent and angry discussion. Becky heard the words 'upgrade', 'economy' and 'good enough for her'. Alex cleared his throat and Matthew and Clara – like mirror images – turned towards them then immediately back to face each other. They continued their quarrel in French and Becky couldn't recognise any of the words, though Clara's furious hand-waving gestures spoke volumes.

'Look, I'm really happy with economy,' she said, 'if that's the problem.'

Clara gave Matthew a last blast in French and the argument terminated abruptly, with Matthew taking the ticket from Becky's hands and thrusting it at Alex with a terse 'sort it, please.' Alex walked off, without a word, evidently accustomed to Matthew's orders.

Clara turned to Becky and gave her a hug. 'No problem, Becky. It's just our tickets were booked ages ago and booking your ticket at the last minute led to a little misunderstanding.' Becky doubted that was remotely true but appreciated Clara's attempt to smooth things over.

'You'd better go with Alex,' said Matthew.

Becky hurried after Alex's retreating back, weaving her trolley through clumps of irritatingly in-the-way travellers. By the time she caught up with him he had already upgraded her ticket. They checked her suitcase in and he led her to the priority queue through Departures.

'Matthew and Clara will be in the Business Class lounge,' he informed her.

‘Do I go there too?’ Becky asked, realising immediately how naive she must sound.

‘We both do,’ Alex confirmed. ‘Then we can all relax.’ Although he didn’t appear very relaxed himself.

‘You don’t look like you’ve slept for a week,’ Becky said.

‘Tell me about it.’ He sighed. ‘I only flew here four days ago. And now back to Barbados. Again.’

‘That’s ridiculous,’ said Becky. ‘I thought this was the age of electronic communications.’

Alex rolled his eyes. ‘I had to bring some papers. Matthew doesn’t trust the post service.’ He must have felt disloyal because he added quickly, ‘And fair enough. It’s often quicker to jump on a plane with a briefcase.’

Becky didn’t think it sounded fair at all.

‘Do you want to browse the shops or shall we join the others?’

‘I’ve got all I need,’ Becky said and followed him to the elegant lounge where Clara greeted her effusively as if it was the first time they’d met that day and Matthew ignored her.

For the next hour he continued to study the *Financial Times* while Alex constantly checked his phone and Clara dared Becky to try this drink and that snack. For a rich woman accustomed to the good life, Clara was cheerfully ingénue-ish about helping herself to the freebies though Becky couldn’t decide if this behaviour was genuine or just intended to make her feel at ease.

At last they were ushered on to the plane and Becky found there was no need to worry about getting stuck next to Matthew: the seats were more like pods, arranged side-on to the direction of flight.

She put her small rucksack in the overhead locker and arranged herself in her pod. With the cheerful strains of Handel‘s *Water Music* flooding the cabin, Becky put her head back and closed her eyes. After his surprising decision to let her go to Barbados she had thought Matthew might be more friendly but if his behaviour this morning was anything to go by that wasn't the case. All she could hope was that the demands of his business would mean he was often away travelling to Europe or America or preferably Mongolia.

As soon as they reached cruising altitude the stewardesses came round with more drinks and snacks. Becky wasn't really hungry but she took some to keep Clara happy. Her friend had settled back with a book and Becky decided to do the same.

After about an hour Clara got up to go to the toilet and Becky rose to stretch her legs too. As she walked up the aisle, she noticed a little pantomime taking place, a few pods away. Presumably Matthew's looks had not gone unnoticed by one of the stewardesses; a stunning young woman with laser-blue eyes, she had been charming to Becky and to Clara but she hadn't served their drinks by leaning into their pods and delivering an eyeful of breasts, nor had she spent a few minutes fiddling inconsequentially with the items in their overhead lockers so they could admire her chest. Becky wondered what Matthew made of this behaviour but she couldn't see his expression to know what he thought.

He couldn't have been that enamoured because no sooner had Becky returned to her pod than Matthew appeared beside her. She hastily picked up an in-flight magazine and leafed through.

'Where's the lady who reckons you're sugar and spice and all things nice?' he enquired.

'Your mother's gone to the ladies' room,' she murmured, trying to find a page in the magazine that didn't scream 'Retail'.

'I hope they're looking after you?'

She looked up. It wasn't obvious whether he was being sincere or sarcastic. 'Oh they are, thank you. Of course it isn't such a breast-fest over here.' Immediately she wished she hadn't said that – now it sounded like she was bitchy, or, worse, jealous when she was really neither.

He looked surprised and then chuckled. 'In that case I should try and claim a discount on your ticket. We're paying a premium for breasts.' He bent down to look out of the window. 'I wish I could get excited about crossing the Atlantic. Really it's amazing to think that only a thin sheet of metal is between us and all that water.'

Becky turned back to an article about jewellery and responsibly sourced coral. 'I've memorised the location of the emergency exits should we crash mid-ocean.' It would need a little more than that to scare her.

Matthew frowned. 'Better not say that to Alex. He hates flying.'

'Then why do you make him do so much of it?' said Becky, giving him a hard look.

Matthew glared back then straightened up as his mother approached. Becky could see Clara was pleased to find them apparently enjoying some mild banter. Matthew wished Becky 'a pleasant trip' – with a hint of menace, Becky thought – and returned to his seat.

Becky returned to her book – a second-hand one she'd ordered online called *The Monmouth Rebels* – and read until she and Clara were interrupted with a gourmet lunch. But despite all the comforts of Business Class travel the flight still seemed interminable. She soon fell into a fitful sleep.

When she awoke for the final time they were approaching Barbados. There was a palpable air of excitement in the cabin. Flagging stewardesses seemed to summon hidden reserves of energy and hurried along the aisles with brisk step and cheerful chatter – both among themselves and with passengers wanting to know how many hours they should set their watches back or what temperature they could expect on arrival at Grantley Adams airport.

'It's 80.4 degrees,' the breast-fest stewardess announced and faces lifted and smiles broadened in response. Clara leant over Becky's pod, looking as excited as a child on Christmas morning. 'It's just so good to be back,' she gushed. 'It will cheer up Mr R to come home.'

'Has he been in England long?'

'Months. Too long. It took him ages to get the manager of the Monmouth up to speed.'

Becky wondered if Chris Harris really was 'up to speed'.

'Right,' said Clara. 'I'd better belt up. You must look out of the window. The approach to Barbados is always worth seeing.'

Becky twisted in her pod to look down on a sea whose colours ran the full gamut of blues on an artist's palette. Cobalt gave way to turquoise until nearer the shore, and abruptly, turquoise became aquamarine. The sand looked as white as every holiday brochure maintained it was. Her eyes were caught by a candy-striped lighthouse withstanding a ceaseless barrage from the sea, then by a white crenellated castle standing like a chess piece on a board of green.

The plane touched down as smoothly as if it had stepped on to the runway. They walked out into brilliant sunlight and headed towards the airport.

'One of the better flights,' said Alex, walking beside her. 'I hate turbulence, don't you?'

'I haven't flown that much, to be honest.'

Alex looked at her with incredulity.

At immigration control, he offered to stay with Becky in the 'aliens' queue, which was creeping forward with the speed of a snail leaning on a zimmer frame, but she insisted he go ahead with Clara and Matthew and then regretted it when she realised she did not have a work visa.

Fortunately Barbados Immigration had no problem with the length of her proposed stay and the time waiting meant there was no delay in baggage reclaim. Becky collected her luggage, went through Customs and emerged from the main hall to find another quarrel in progress – this time between Matthew and a man who seemed to be in charge of transport. Becky couldn't work out if Mr St John, (if she'd heard the name correctly), worked for Matthew or was hired by him. Either way he was an unfortunate man because it was quickly obvious that the four of them, their combined luggage, plus Mr St John himself, were not going to fit in the car he'd brought for the transfer to the house. And it would have been better, Becky thought, had he not made his blunder worse by offering the excuse that he would have come to pick them up in the company's roomier Suzuki Carry but it was 'in for service'.

'In for service?' Matthew repeated heavily. 'On the day we were coming back?'

'I was expecting to collect three of you,' Mr St John protested.

'Ah,' said Alex, grimacing. 'Sorry, that was my fault. I forgot to tell you that we were one extra.'

Matthew glared at him.

Becky hoped she could travel with Clara in the estate car but by the time Clara had been installed in the front passenger seat, and the suitcases loaded, there was just an uncomfortable-looking little space left.

'Can you fit in there, Alex?' asked Matthew.

Alex's face was expressionless as he wedged himself next to the suitcases on the back seat.

Clara sitting in splendour in the front seat gave Becky and her son a teasing, regal, little wave and the weighted car departed.

Matthew turned to Becky. 'I'm afraid you're stuck with me. I had to let Alex go with my mother to unload at the house.'

They returned to the terminal building. She left him at the counter displaying a 'drive yourself' notice while she kept out of the way by looking at a carousel of postcards.

The rack she was twirling stopped abruptly. Becky looked up quickly. Who could be so rude, so impatient?

The white man grinning at her had sea-blue eyes and was about Matthew's age, maybe a few years over thirty. He was almost as tall as Matthew, too, but fair. Quite good-looking, she supposed but, wearing the scruffiest shorts and shirt, he looked like he should be on the beach selling bad jewellery made from shells.

'You'll get a far better selection in town,' he told her. 'You've got hardly any choice with these.'

It sounded like a bad chat-up line. Becky started twirling the rack again. 'Thanks for the advice,' she said, coldly polite, 'but I'm just looking.'

'Oh, so am I,' Blue-Eyes said feelingly, 'and very nice too. Just off the London flight, are we?'

'Yes.'

'Staying here long?'

Becky didn't answer.

'Would you stop bothering my mother's secretary, Richard?' snapped Matthew, who had materialised silently beside her and the scruffy man.

'Matthew. You're back; what bad luck. I thought I had the field clear, both businesswise and – well, introduce me to this gorgeous creature, for heaven's sake,' Blue-Eyes said in a voice of injured reproach.

'Becky Thomson. Richard Carrington.' Matthew sounded so unenthusiastic he could have been reading the football results.

Richard made a comically sad face at Becky. 'Poor you. So you're staying with the Darnleys?'

Becky nodded. She realised that the two, if not exactly friends, certainly knew each other from a long way back. She turned to look at the rack of postcards again, doubting either even noticed now they were so busy measuring up to each other.

She heard her cheeky accoster ask Matthew if there was any particular reason for this visit to Barbados and saw the latter's sardonic smile.

'I do live here.'

'Do you?' drawled Richard. 'I heard you'd set up home in England.'

'I'm afraid that you were misinformed.'

'Pity. But I'm not surprised. Someone told me you're interested in that little chunk of land near Shermans.'

Matthew said nothing.

Richard laughed. 'I'll take that as a "Yes". I hear it's going to be obscenely overpriced. Actually, I was thinking I just might surprise you and snap it up myself.'

Becky was amazed: Richard looked like he had all the purchasing power of a beach bum.

'I wouldn't be surprised if you tried,' said Matthew, sounding bored.

Becky pretended to study a picture of a beach, which looked similar to every other postcard featuring a beach. It would have been intriguing to know why a bit of land was such a sought-after prize. What trophy could have the pair circling each other like a couple of wary prizefighters? But she was hardly on terms friendly enough with either to ask.

The girl from the car-rental agency waved at Matthew and, as soon as he went over to see her, Richard Carrington sidled next to Becky. 'Well, Miss Thomson, if you find the company too dull, I'll be happy to take you out and show you the sights.'

She smiled a non-committal smile.

'And don't let that slave driver take advantage of you. Bajan laws are strict about employers giving time off to their employees.' He giggled. 'Well, nowadays, anyway. If he gives you a hard time, tell me – and I'll come round and trash his office or something.' He looked round quickly but

Matthew was still confirming details with the car agency woman.

Richard gave Becky a cheerful smile. 'Don't worry. I'm sure you'll have a great time and we will bump into each other soon.'

'Will we?' said Becky, amused at his conviction.

'It's a small island.' He laughed and breezed off in his shorts and flip-flops.

His hair, Becky noticed, was almost as long as hers and someone ought to tell him to shave and tidy himself up a bit. But he seemed nice enough – harmless, at any rate.

'Well,' said Matthew, appearing behind her. 'I suppose I ought to congratulate you.'

She stared at him, mystified. 'Congratulate me – what for?'

'For attracting the scion of one of the richest families in the West Indies – not just in Barbados; they own real estate in many islands. And you did it within an hour of your arrival. That's got to be a record. How did you manage it?'

Becky heard the sarcasm in his voice, the unpleasant insinuation that she, barely off the plane, and with this talent he was convinced she possessed for self-advancement, had assessed that the guy who looked like a tramp wasn't really a tramp at all.

'How did I manage it?' she repeated. 'Easily. I thought because he was dressed like a beach bum, and sounded like a beach bum, he must be heir to the largest chunk of real estate in the whole West Indies so I gave him the come-on, as you could hear.' She looked at him, defiantly. 'Can we go now?'

He held up his hands. 'Sorry, you're right; he does look like the beach bum he is. And, yes we can go.'

He relieved her of her rucksack and when they reached the car held the door open for her. She got in, put on her seatbelt and looked stonily ahead.

He put her rucksack in the boot, got in the driver's side and spent a minute studying the dashboard.

'How far away is the house?' said Becky, really meaning how long did they have to share the car journey.

'Quite a way, I'm afraid. The parishes are almost at opposite ends of the island.'

'Parishes?' Her father hadn't mentioned those.

'The island is divided into parishes. We're in Christ Church at the moment, right on the south coast, whereas we have to drive up north to the parish of St Lucy. That's where the house is.'

'OK,' said Becky. 'Let's get going.'

They left the airport in silence. As they picked up speed a pleasant breeze was drawn into the car and she relaxed a little. She was finally getting to see her father's favourite island.

The lanes – shortcuts she supposed – they were bowling along were hedged by emerald fields of a tall crop.

'Is that sugarcane?' she asked.

'Yes, that's right.'

'Wow, I've never seen it before.'

'And you won't see much of it now, I'm afraid. The industry has been on its knees ever since Europe started growing sugar beet to get sugar. Even though the molasses from sugar beet is rubbish; the molasses from our sugarcane is much nicer.'

'So it's still grown for molasses?'

'Not really.' He sighed. 'The sugarcane fields are being turned into golf courses. When the tourist industry moves in say goodbye to agriculture. Actually say goodbye to anything real.'

Becky smiled inwardly. Considering that he owned two hotels, Matthew didn't seem to recognise the irony of his words. Anyway it was all new to her. She felt on a high, as rounding each bend revealed another treasure with its roots in bygone years: a tiny church on a hill, a derelict sugar-mill, or a spreading flame-coloured flamboyant tree. The sky was probably the same blue as at home and yet she admired its cloudless purity as though she had never properly looked at it before. She also sensed Matthew was less tense now he was on home territory.

'This seems like paradise for everyone,' she said.

He didn't respond; indeed he seemed to be giving her cheerful remark more consideration than it merited.

He slowed down to drive through a village that straddled the road. 'I don't think it's a paradise for them,' he said, sounding almost impatient with her.

She thought at first he meant the drab village itself, which not even the glittering day could make cheerful. Then she noticed he was looking at two painfully thin children: a boy and girl, aged about seven and eight respectively. They were obviously brother and sister – both were flaxen-haired and bore the same expression of pinched anxiety that wasn't wholly accounted for by their present dilemma. Barefooted, they were struggling to lift a container of water that was clearly taxing their strength while a harassed-looking blonde woman shrilled at them from her anything but picturesque cottage to look sharp and turn off the standpipe.

'Don't they have piped water to the house?' Becky frowned. 'I thought Barbados was a relatively prosperous island.'

'It is a prosperous island. But a few people have still slipped through the net.'

The children put down their burden and stared at the passing car with listless faces. 'Who are they?' Becky said uncomfortably. 'They look – I don't know – beaten. As if they don't quite know what they're doing here.'

'I don't think all the Redlegs have ever got over the fact they *are* here.'

'Redlegs?'

'They're descendants of – well, if you're going to help my mother with her book, presumably you know all about this. Somerset? The Battle of Sedgemoor?'

'Yes, of course I'm familiar with it,' she said. In fact she now felt she could go on *Mastermind* specialising in the Monmouth rebels. 'But nothing I've read so far mentions Redlegs.'

'In this area, here, are the descendants of the losers. If you're interested, there's a book at the house on Barbados's history. If you're interested.' He gave her a quick sideways glance.

Becky frowned with exasperation. 'Of course I'm interested,' she said. 'That's why I'm here.'

'OK, I'll show you the book. Most of it recounts the familiar link between sugar and slavery. All horrible and all true. The Redlegs get a mention – just about. They're a mere footnote in history.'

'Why are they called Redlegs?'

'You'd better not mention Redlegs to anyone else. It's a bit insensitive. Or politically incorrect if you prefer that phrase. If you think about where these people came from and where they ended up – they couldn't cope with the sun but they were out working in the fields. You can imagine where the term came from. Actually there's a whole bunch of names for them.' He turned his attention back to the twists in the road, which danced its own route with little respect for straight lines.

'So why didn't the Redlegs just get absorbed with the other people on the island?'

'Some did. But others: the blacks looked down on them, the other whites looked down on them, so –' He stopped.

'Limited gene pool?'

'Quite. It used to be a bit of a joke. I mean it's changed now but it's still a joke to a pathetic minority.'

'So would Alex be a Redleg?'

‘No, no,’ said Matthew, quickly. ‘Really, there aren’t many. Don’t go thinking that every white Bajan is a Redleg. What you’ve just seen back there is a very rare sight.’

He lapsed into silence. Becky couldn’t make him out at all. He must be pretty well off and yet the sight had clearly disturbed him. She wondered if he did have a conscience after all. But he obviously didn’t intend to share his thoughts with her so she returned her attention to the scenery and wondered if the journey would take much longer.

‘Were you really sacked?’ he asked suddenly.

Becky had to mentally drag her mind back to what had happened in England. ‘Yes, your phone call to the editor did it.’

‘And what about that – man?’

‘Ian is the editor’s nephew and has worked for the paper for years. I was on probation so it was easier to get rid of me.’

‘Oh. What about reparation?’

Strange word to choose. It was also used to refer to atonement for slavery in former colonies.

‘I didn’t get a pay-off, if that’s what you mean.’

He didn’t respond but Becky glanced at him sideways and saw he was frowning.

His expression only lightened when they finally turned off the road and on to a long lane flanked by some splendid but unfamiliar trees. She ducked her head the better to see their crowns through the windscreen. Unlike the stately but aloof plane trees that lined the driveway to Noak Hall, these trees bent towards each other, as if the branches at the top were trying to embrace their neighbours on the other side.

‘Mahogany trees,’ Matthew said. ‘Are you interested in trees, plants?’

‘I wouldn’t say I’m knowledgeable but, yes, I’m interested in them.’

‘We lost two mahoganies at the end of the avenue nearest the house in a hurricane two years ago,’ he lamented. ‘I was abroad at the time so I was gutted when my mother told me they’d gone. Originally my grandfather planted sixteen pairs.’ He scanned the tree-lined avenue as if counting to see that none had succumbed to other disasters in his more recent absence.

So this had been his grandfather’s house. She wondered if his grandfather had bought it or if the house had been in the family in earlier generations, stretching back to – well, William Darnley in the seventeenth century. Whatever one thought about the rights or wrongs of inheritance based on slavery, it was an amazing line of continuity.

They seemed to be about to drive into a scrubby, tree-studded field but, just before the lane ended, Matthew swung the car left into a large gravel yard and parked.

‘Welcome to Copper Mill,’ he said.

‘Interesting name.’

‘It would be something to do with sugar production,’ said Matthew. ‘They used huge copper vats.’

She got out of the car and surveyed what would be her new home for the next few months. It was a white stone building with a massive veranda at the front overlooking the gravel yard, which lay between the house and a large garden that had no obvious boundary. Beyond the patch of cultivated plants it seemed to transition into an area of verdant wilderness. Thick green foliage lay to either side of the house like a large green tunnel.

‘Wow,’ she said, appreciatively. ‘This place looks like it’s been here for ever.’

‘It’s just an old plantation house,’ said Matthew but his careless tone could not disguise his love of his home.

He fetched her rucksack from the boot and led her up the steps to the front door.

Clara, already changed into a comfortable and cool-looking caftan, was sitting on the veranda with a glass in one hand. She hailed them exuberantly, 'Come and have a drink. Isn't this wonderful, Mr R?'

Matthew set down Becky's rucksack out of the way beside one of a line of white jalousie doors that opened out on to the veranda. Becky, peering through a window beyond the jut of his shoulder, glimpsed an imposing high-ceilinged living room that wouldn't have disgraced a palazzo.

'Isn't what wonderful?' he asked Clara.

'See for yourself inside. Maureen's kept the furniture polished and she's put flowers absolutely everywhere. Isn't it nice to see her again?'

A young woman, dark and pretty, came out on the veranda. Becky guessed from the grin Clara's statement elicited this must be Maureen – presumably someone who helped round the house.

'You're working late,' said Matthew.

'I haven't seen Clara for a long, long time,' said Maureen.

'This is Becky Thomson. She's here to help my mother with a book.'

Maureen shook Becky's hand. 'I think maybe rum punch?' she suggested.

'Definitely,' said Clara.

It was clear Becky wasn't going to be asked for her preference but she was happy to avoid making decisions about anything just then.

Matthew disappeared into the house after Maureen and Clara questioned Becky about the drive, obviously anxious to know how she and Matthew had got on. Becky exclaimed enthusiastically about the nicer sights she'd seen but omitted any mention of the Redleg village.

'Oh thank you,' she said appreciatively when Maureen reappeared and handed her a drink with a tower of ice in it.

Maureen nodded and leaned towards Clara. 'I didn't tell you. That Francesca woman –'

Clara instantly sat up.

'She's got divorced.'

Becky knew this was bad news because Clara swore in French and put a hand to her face.

'She turned up last week looking for Matthew but I told her I didn't know when he was coming back. Should I let him know?' asked Maureen.

Clara thought for a bit. 'No. She'll be round here again soon enough. Let's give Matthew a bit of a break.'

At some point during this conversation night fell with the speed of a theatre curtain. What had been a sunny evening minutes before turned dark and cool and a chorus of unseen nocturnal creatures started whistling and clicking from the bushes. Clara seemed to have forgotten Becky's presence as she stared out at the garden with an unmistakeably heavy heart.

Chapter Six

With her body clock still on London time, Becky woke at 5 a.m. – her initial confusion about where she was quickly displaced by waves of different emotions. Firstly excitement as she listened to the tantalising sound of unfamiliar birdsong through the open window and then anxiety as she contemplated sharing a house with Matthew's less-than-friendly presence.

She tried to get back to sleep, but eventually gave up. She kicked off her covering sheet, showered in the en-suite bathroom and, dithering a bit between dress and shorts, reasoned she could do her job for Clara as well in shorts and a T-shirt as in a dress. It took a bit of fishing around in her still-not-fully-unpacked suitcase but sandals were eventually located and she ventured on to the landing outside her bedroom. All was quiet. Clara hadn't actually said what time she wanted their working day to start but it obviously wasn't this early.

Becky tiptoed downstairs and through the hall to the front door, realising worriedly that she had just walked past an alarm sensor. Nothing sounded so hopefully it was either switched off or on some sort of timer. The main door itself was securely fastened. What a business it was getting out of an old sugar plantation house. But eventually the door yielded its bolts and the latches obediently slid away. She stepped on to the veranda, saw a sky of never-ending blue and hurried down the stone steps.

Having crossed the gravel yard to the garden beyond, she took off her sandals. The grass felt wonderful under her bare feet. She sniffed at the flowers. Hibiscus, she discovered, disappointingly had no smell at all but made up for that deficiency by the gorgeous array of colours they came in – lemon, pink, a stunning salmon, and mauve. And as for the bougainvillea that tumbled like waterfalls over the walls, it was as though she were seeing colours she had never seen before: pinks and purples which were searing new memories rather than tickling old ones. Becky stood on the grass and spun round like a child with her arms outstretched. She felt high.

She heard a rich chuckle from the veranda and looked up sharply to see Matthew Darnley, still in his pyjamas, studying her antics with undisguised amusement. 'You'll get dizzy,' he called out to her.

Becky froze and let her arms fall by her sides, regretting her childish action.

He nodded at her bare feet. 'A word of advice – if this is how you like starting your day, I'd resist the temptation to go native just yet. You might be unlucky enough to get jiggers.'

Becky sighed. The man was certainly determined she wasn't going to enjoy paradise. 'So go ahead, tell me,' she said resignedly. 'Jiggers are obviously bad news.'

'They *are* bad news – and a real pain to get rid of once they take up residence. Jiggers are a disgusting kind of flea that burrows under the skin, especially under the soft-soled skin of new arrivals.'

If he was expecting a reaction he would be disappointed. Becky wordlessly put on her sandals, crossed the gravel yard and came up the steps. She could see that at any sign of enjoyment he would appear behind her with another dark warning.

'We'll have to take you to the beach,' said Matthew. 'Walking on the sand will toughen your feet up then you won't have to bother.'

'No doubt the beach is also fraught with danger,' Becky said and went inside.

Feeling a sudden bout of homesickness she took out her mobile to text Joe. But her phone simply said *No service.* She cursed her stupidity. It had not occurred to her to check which regions her provider covered. There would be no easy communication with her brother.

A couple of hours later Clara appeared and to Becky's amazement announced that the book was going to have to wait.

'I've just been looking down at the garden from my bedroom window. *Quelle horreur!* It needs a bit of attention.' Clara looked at Becky with a hopeful glint in her eyes. So Alex had been spot on.

Becky took the hint. 'Clara, if you'd prefer to work on your garden first that's fine by me. But you'll have to tell me what to do. I'm no gardener.'

Clara beamed. 'Thank you, dear. I know I never mentioned gardening to you back in England but now that I've seen the state it's in I'd really like to get it straight before we do justice to our poor Monmouth exiles.'

'The Redlegs?' Becky immediately regretted saying the word because she could see Clara was taken aback. Matthew had warned her it was politically incorrect. But then again she wanted to know exactly whom they were writing about.

'Yes,' said Clara, frowning. 'Though that's not a word I use to be honest.'

They had breakfast in the dining room and then, armed with shears and protected by a shady hat, Clara led the way to the garden.

'Hi Alex,' said Becky, as they passed Matthew and Alex on the veranda. The two men were obviously having a business meeting though in rather unconventional dress: Matthew wore nothing but a pair of dark shorts; Alex, also in shorts and a ruffled, creased shirt, was spreading papers over a cane table. He seemed genuinely happy to see

Becky though the fleeting happiness on his face could not hide his bloodshot eyes. Presumably whatever shut-eye he'd had on his first night back in Barbados wasn't enough to repay his sleep deficit.

Becky waved a pair of secateurs at him and he grinned.

'Told you.'

'You did,' said Becky.

'Anyway,' said Matthew impatiently and Alex's attention was pulled back towards the papers.

'We're going to have to be totally ruthless,' Clara said, when they reached the garden. 'The trouble is neither Matthew nor I have the heart to get a new gardener but really all Pitcher can manage these days is the watering and taking out the more obvious weeds.'

'Pitcher?' said Becky. 'As in the man you thought might be a descendant of Daniel Pitcher?'

'Yes,' said Clara, apparently too distracted by the garden's shortcomings to take the bait. 'I'm not sure he's that steady on his feet. He probably shouldn't climb up ladders.'

'I can,' Becky assured her. 'What would you like done?'

'Well, for a start, just look at that poor bougainvillea.'

The 'poor' bougainvillea looked glorious to Becky but she bowed to Clara's superior knowledge that the growth around the inner stems needed 'lightening up' if it was to continue flourishing. 'And all those long shoots thrashing about wildly need to be cut right back.'

For the next few days, under Clara's direction, Becky weeded, pruned and fastened, revelling in the outdoor work. She would love to meet Pitcher – presumably a genuine descendant of a Monmouth rebel – but she was starting to wonder if he really existed. She had seen no sign of him and the weeds seemed to be luxuriating in his absence.

Matthew's work schedule did seem relentless but, as his main office appeared to be the veranda, they were bumping into each other every morning. Though Becky hadn't previously thought of herself as a prude she wondered, rather glumly, if she had inherited a little of her mother's sense of propriety. She was finding it increasingly difficult to walk past Matthew in his natural state: studying papers over the cane table he was always unshaven, bare-chested and barefooted (the jiggers were obviously no match for his calloused feet). A pair of black shorts were his only condescension to decency. He seemed to be oblivious to the same morning sun that had Alex constantly shifting his own chair into the ever-drifting shady patch.

Late each morning Matthew and Alex would drive off in their respective cars, presumably to the hotel, and then Matthew might come back in the afternoon to shower and change into a light suit before heading out again. He always returned after Clara and Becky had gone to bed. Becky got used to hearing the hum of his Nissan Sedan's engine pulling into the drive above the plaintive sounds of the nocturnal wildlife. It was closely followed by the sound of drawing bolts and turning keys, as he shut the house up for the night, and the musical beeping of the code he typed into the keypad to set the house alarm.

On her second day Matthew had warned everyone he was about to test this, which involved some readjustment of timings on a console, followed by a request – to a poker-faced Maureen – to 'break in' by walking through the front door. She then had to repeat the exercise via the back door. Matthew hovered over the console controls ready to silence the alarm the instant it went off as the sound was so piercing it virtually disabled mind and body. Apparently Matthew insisted on this drill once a week. Apart from this, the house routine was peaceful. The alarm, Becky learnt, automatically switched itself off at

5 a.m.; even Matthew and Alex's working day didn't start that early.

The only other live-in resident was the seemingly ancient Cook – which really was her second name and seemed to serve as her first as well. Despite her advanced years she produced wonderful meals three times a day. Maureen drove over on weekdays to keep the house tidy and take care of the shopping. Becky suspected Clara or Matthew had employed her to ensure Cook's tasks were kept to a minimum.

Becky loved the mornings most, working in the garden with Clara. They would share a leisurely lunch after which Clara – often tired from the morning's exertions – would disappear for a rest. It was in the afternoons that Becky most felt a pang of loneliness. With Clara asleep, and Maureen and Cook largely sequestered in the kitchen, she used the time to sit on the veranda and study the *History of Barbados* which Matthew had mentioned. However sometimes she longed for some human interaction.

At about three o'clock on weekdays Cook's little granddaughter Zena would be brought over by her childminder for Cook to look after until her daughter-in-law finished work. The childminder never had time to say more than 'Hello' and deliver Zena safely to the door before she drove off again. Little Zena was a sparkling and engaging little girl but Becky, assuming this was special 'Grandmother' quality time, would immediately take her to Cook and then return to the veranda.

One morning, late joining Clara, Becky rushed on to the veranda just as Matthew was coming indoors to fetch something. She almost bounced off his wall of a chest.

'Sorry,' he said. 'You OK?'

'Don't you ever wear proper clothes when you're working?' she snapped and hurried off to the garden, embarrassed.

The next morning, as Becky passed him, she did a double take. As usual Matthew was wearing shorts – but today there was also a tie knotted around his otherwise bare brown neck. He and Alex dissolved into guffaws.

Becky had to laugh. 'Actually that looks much better.'

'Good,' said Matthew. 'I can take the damn thing off now.' He hoisted it over his head and used it to lasso a mug of coffee and pull it towards him, then looked at Becky. 'I take it you don't mind that your first week has been spent gardening?'

How had a whole week gone by already? Apart from Clara's cheerful explanations about why this or that had to be done to a particular plant, Becky had enjoyed an almost Zen-like immersion in her simple manual tasks.

'I don't mind,' she said.

Matthew nodded at the garden. 'It is looking a little better, though I would prefer it if you could persuade my mother to get on with the history book or whatever it is you're supposed to be doing.' He turned back to his papers.

Becky was annoyed at his peremptory dismissal but couldn't be bothered to think of a suitably cutting riposte. She really couldn't make him out; was he comfortable with book project after all?

It was partway through her second week and Becky was wondering why she was in Barbados. She couldn't see there was much more to be done in the garden but Clara still showed no inclination to discuss the book or track down the original sources she had mentioned. Becky had searched through the *History of Barbados* but found only a brief half page on the Monmouth rebels and just a one-liner about the Redlegs, saying the term was derogatory.

One afternoon she took a little wander down the mahogany-lined driveway to stretch her legs. Ahead of her she saw a figure in a Fedora hat and torn clothes weaving an unstable path beside the trees. There was something tragicomic about the way he moved; his footing was very irregular, as if he were following a huge invisible hopscotch grid. The only clue that he was the gardener Pitcher was a hoe in one hand. Though he was surely harmless there was something about his chaotic ambulatory style that dissuaded Becky from continuing, as that would have meant overtaking him and having some sort of exchange. She returned to the house. No one had said she couldn't take a walk but the long driveway was slightly forbidding, as though it were a passageway to an unsafe world. Becky almost wished that Richard Carrington would turn up with some cheeky excuse to see her.

She hadn't been back long and was reading alone in the living room when the phone rang. Everyone else seemed deaf to its insistent tone so she thought she'd better answer it. The woman at the other end of the line was plainly disconcerted by the sound of an unfamiliar female voice. 'And who are you?' she enquired bluntly.

Unsure of how to describe her role Becky explained that she was doing some research for Clara. There was a heartfelt sigh of relief – and an immediate demotion of her role in the Darnley household. 'Oh, Clara's secretary, are you?' the woman said. 'Well, would you get Matthew? You can tell him it's Francesca.'

Becky said that Matthew was out and Francesca insisted Becky tell him 'the moment he got back' that Francesca had rung. Then she rang off abruptly, without thanks and without a conventional goodbye.

Matthew was not likely to return to the house until midnight so Becky made a mental note to tell him the next day.

Maybe it was something to do with Francesca's rudeness but Becky felt particularly blue that afternoon and when Zena arrived with her childminder she decided that, instead of delivering the little girl to the kitchen and then scuttling off, she would stay. Becky was attuned to any sign that she was not welcome but Maureen and Cook seemed to accept her presence and appeared grateful to have another person to help keep the three year old entertained.

'Don't leave it too late to have children,' Cook warned Becky. 'My son's wife leave it too late.'

As Zena looked perfect Becky could only guess Cook meant she would rather be a younger grandmother.

After that Becky joined the two women in the kitchen most afternoons. When Cook dozed off at the table, as she frequently did, it was Maureen who had to prevent Zena from opening the cutlery drawer or trying to sample the leftovers from the semi-feral cat's food dish. Her relief was evident when Becky took Zena out to examine the garden or simply sat her in a corner and sang songs to her. Sometimes Zena would fall asleep against Becky and if Cook was feeling more 'present' she would share a little gossip with Maureen. Without overtly prying, Becky learnt that Cook had lived in the same room in the house when she was a teenager. Widowed later in life, she had ended up back at Copper Mill and seemed to regard this as her final home. Though often clearly exhausted, the elderly lady enjoyed the female company and her habitual brief utterances would turn into a stream of gossip, descending into a Bajan accent so strong that Becky struggled to keep up.

'Pitcher tek too much rum and now he see tings in de garden daint f'real but instead he cut down de drinking he go to Matthew and mek a request dat he deal wit dese perps and Matthew got bigger tings dealing with his hotel dan dese tings dat don't exist.'

Becky looked at Maureen, helplessly.

'Pitcher keeps telling Matthew that he sees people hiding in the garden,' Maureen explained.

'Could they be real?'

Maureen shook her head. 'Pitcher drinks a bit. I've never seen anyone.'

No doubt it all fed Matthew's paranoia, thought Becky.

She also answered their questions about England – about her own house and situation – though she was a little vague about her former employment status. Cook and Maureen seemed curious why she had, apparently, left a career in journalism to come to Barbados.

'Wouldn't most people?' Becky said. 'Given the chance?' But their joint frowns signalled quiet dissent. She could hardly tell them Matthew had got her sacked from her job. Neither Maureen nor Cook ever said a word against him or Clara though the name Francesca often merited shaken heads and sucked air. Cook asked if the latter had come round again to see Matthew.

'Not *yet*,' said Maureen.

'She rang,' said Becky, making a rare contribution to the gossip.

'When?' asked Maureen.

'A few days ago.' Becky recounted the conversation.

'That woman is trouble,' said Maureen.

'And what did Matthew say?' asked Cook.

Becky had given Francesca's message to Alex as Matthew was busy on his mobile when she walked past them to start work in the garden. Presumably the name Francesca meant something to Alex for he had just raised his eyes and agreed, with noticeable reluctance, to convey the message to Matthew when he got off the phone.

'He was in a meeting,' she said, having no idea whether Alex had remembered to pass on the message nor what reaction the news had elicited.

Now she wondered if Matthew's late returns to the house were connected to Francesca. Not that she cared what he got up to but she felt envious that he had somewhere to go after the sun went down. She was starting to feel trapped in the old plantation house – never more so than at night when the building was ensnared in darkness and she was trammelled by lack of transport.

She sorely missed access to the internet, which would have allowed her to swap daily emails with Joe. It wouldn't have been so bad if she and Clara had been making progress with the book but her employer seemed to have lost her focus.

In the mornings, out in the garden, Clara always sounded enthusiastic whenever Becky suggested they make a start on the book 'that evening' but every day the discussion had to be postponed because Clara wasn't free. Word had got out that she was back in Barbados and her many friends were keen to see her – and even keener to rope her in for their shared passion: bridge. If Clara was not visiting one of their houses, then she was glad-handing coiffured women up to the veranda for drinks before migrating to the dining room to cut the cards.

Becky had joined them on the first bridge night and been introduced to a lady (whose hair was so set and eyebrows so pencilled that she looked entirely artificial) as Clara's 'co-author'. The artificial woman had asked Becky whether Clara was talented: a provocative question to ask when Clara was standing right there – and an impossible question to answer as Becky still hadn't seen anything that Clara had written, apart from the gardening book.

'Well, Clara's certainly a talented *gardener*,' Becky had replied and then said to Clara. 'You are, aren't you?'

Clara had laughed and waved a dismissive hand. 'Oh no, Becky,' she'd said. 'Being a good gardener is like being a lady. If you have to say you are, you aren't.'

That had set the tone for the evening. Becky had felt completely out of place among this grand-seeming set of ladies and sensed her bridge partner's frustration with her slowness to comprehend the rules.

When Clara invited her to join them again she'd politely refused, choosing instead to sit with Cook in the kitchen and encourage her to tell tales of duppies and other colourful malevolent beings that buzzed around at night seeking bodies to possess and torment.

Becky described some of these stories in a letter to Joe along with sharing her frustration that she didn't have internet access. As she signed it she realised it would be the first handwritten letter he received since their father's last note to him with its sketches of the ship.

The letter to her mother was much more difficult. Becky struggled to fill it with meaningful information, as if she were a young girl writing to an aged relative with whom she had little in common. The weather was 'nice', the people were 'nice', the garden was 'nice, and the food was 'very nice'. She went into detail about Cook's dishes though aware her mother wouldn't have a clue what eddoes, yam or plantains were. She was so desperate she even drew a plan of the plantation house as if she were a real estate agent and her mother was interested in knowing that upstairs there were five bedrooms – all en suite – and that downstairs there were three light and airy reception rooms, a bathroom and, further into the bowels of the house, a darker corridor off which lay rooms she hadn't yet been able to explore: Cook's room was somewhere back there and Matthew's office (when he wasn't on the veranda).

She struggled to find some personal anecdote to include and could only come up with the experience of the resident gecko (normally hidden behind a painting in the dining room) once using her head as a brief stepping stone on his peregrinations round the walls in search of insects.

Of her research and secretarial work – the reason she was there – she had nothing to report. And so the letter ended rather abruptly after the lizard story with 'hope you're well, love Becky'.

Most nights she sat alone on the veranda staring into the darkness that lay beyond the reach of the house lights. Despite the nearby laughter and the bidding of rum-warmed female voices, it felt almost as if time had stopped beyond the edge of the light.

Chapter Seven

It was the middle of Becky's third week in Barbados and there was still no indication from Clara that they were going to start on the book. As usual Becky was sitting on the veranda waiting for Clara to appear and list all the things they had to do that morning, which Pitcher either couldn't or wouldn't or shouldn't. She'd nodded to Matthew – on his way to his car today – and would have exchanged pleasantries with Alex had the latter not dozed off in a cane chair the moment Matthew had driven away.

'I'm sorry, Becky,' said Clara, appearing in her dressing gown. 'I'm going to have to give the garden a miss today. Renee's car has broken down and she needs a lift to the care home to see her mother.'

'OK,' said Becky. 'I don't suppose it's near Bridgetown?'

Clara frowned. 'Nowhere near, I'm afraid. Josey Hill's up this end.'

Becky's spirits sank as Clara went back into the house. Gardening in the morning was the only meaningful event in her daily schedule other than helping mind little Zena in the afternoon.

She had to get away from the plantation house. She would just have to walk until she found a bus stop; it must be possible to get a bus to Bridgetown. In her first week Alex had insisted she be given two hundred Barbadian dollars out of her first month's wages as ready cash and it was still sitting up in her bedroom, untouched, so paying the fare wouldn't be a problem as long as the bus driver took notes.

Alex opened his eyes and yawned. 'I've got to go to Bridgetown. Is there anywhere in particular you want to go?' he asked.

'Is there a public records office? I need to start doing something instead of just sitting round here all day.' She could see Alex was surprised at her tone of voice but she couldn't be bothered to disguise her frustration.

'There's the main library,' he said. 'I could drop you off on the way but I've got to warn you I won't be able to pick you up for hours. I've got the bank manager and lawyers to see and a stack of messages to do.'

'Messages?'

'I just mean things. Errands. Boring stuff.'

'That would be great,' said Becky. 'I'll be ready in two minutes.' She ran upstairs to fetch her rucksack, and also asked Maureen to let Clara know she was going out with Alex, then waited by his car until he appeared carrying a briefcase. He put it on the back seat and they both got in.

'You seem a little vexed,' he said as they pulled out of the yard and into the lane.

'I am a bit fed-up,' said Becky. 'Actually, I'm really fed-up. Clara seems to find any excuse not to work on the book and I've yet to see the notes she's apparently been making for years. I'm beginning to wonder ...' She paused, unsure how to explain her concerns to Alex.

They had reached the end of the lane and he turned on to the road. 'What are you beginning to wonder?'

'If she's had second thoughts about writing the book after all. I suspect she felt sorry for me and offered me a job on impulse but now she's embarrassed about the subject matter and wishes she had never mentioned it.'

'And what is the subject matter, exactly?'

'The fate of the Monmouth rebels who were sent here to work on the plantations.' Getting a blank reaction from Alex, Becky added 'the Redlegs.'

Alex whistled. 'That's a difficult one. She could be having second thoughts, as you put it.'

'I already have the names of some of the men sent out from England to work –' Becky was going to say 'on the Darnley plantation' but thought it impolitic to spell out Matthew's family's involvement, 'on one particular plantation.'

'OK,' said Alex. 'And what will you look up at the library?'

'I don't quite know to be honest. I assume there are records of what happened to them when they arrived. Or maybe they just disappear from history. In which case, I might as well fly back home.'

'There are still little communities,' Alex said. 'So they can't have disappeared entirely. In fact there's a tiny settlement on the edge of Matthew's land.'

'Is there? Could you take me there? One day, I mean.' Becky could see Alex instantly regretting what he'd said.

'I've never been there myself to be honest,' he said. 'I think it's just a couple of little houses, shacks really. You'd be disappointed.'

'But I'd love to talk to them.'

'They might not want to talk to you,' said Alex, adding quickly, 'or to anyone. They're Bajan now. I could be wrong but I don't know if they'd be that interested. Or even if they would have much to say. It was hundreds of years ago.'

'I could at least try.'

Getting no response from Alex, Becky looked where they were going and noticed a signpost for Bridgetown. It made her think of her father – who had mentioned it often – and she wished he could see her now, seeing the same sights as he had seen.

'I think the man who does the gardening lives there,' said Alex.

Becky tried to remember where their previous exchange had left off. 'You mean Pitcher?'

'Yes. If you really want to talk to someone you could try him but I don't think you'll have much luck.'

Becky recalled Pitcher walking ahead of her down the lane a few days earlier. She hadn't even wanted to catch up with him, let alone attempt a conversation.

'So you don't think he'll want to talk about it?'

Alex shook his head. 'I don't think he'll understand what you're asking. Most people only have the shakiest idea of where they come from. And from what Matthew tells me Pitcher's grasp of the present is shaky enough.'

Becky sighed. 'How about you, Alex? Do you know where your ancestors came from? If it's not too personal a question.'

'It's not too personal but I don't really know the answer. I've no idea where Wilson came from. My mother's maiden name was Campbell, which I believe is Scottish, but there was nothing Scottish about her. She'd never even been to Scotland.'

'Wouldn't you want to go?'

'Never occurred to me. England's cold enough. No offence but when I'm over there, I can't wait to get back home. Aren't you missing your home?'

'I hadn't really thought about it to be honest.' Becky grimaced. 'I sort of miss my brother.'

'And your mother?'

'I guess.' Apart from wondering what to put in a letter to her Becky had barely thought of her.

She turned her attention to the landscape. The flat green land was furnished with the odd single-storey house or ruined mill or well. Alex occasionally pointed out some landmark but she was pleased Matthew had chosen a more scenic route for her first glimpse of the island. Not that she minded the comparative lack of scenery.

'Thanks, Alex. It's lovely to get away from the house.'

'Has Clara not taken you anywhere?'

'No.' This sounded a bit disloyal so Becky added, 'the gardening seems to tire her out and then, after she's had a rest, it's time to get ready for her bridge friends.'

'Do you play bridge?'

'No.'

Alex gave her a sad smile. 'Poor you.'

'That's part of the problem. Most people would think I'm nuts to complain. I'm getting paid but I'm not doing what I came out for. I'm sure Matthew isn't happy about it.'

'I wish you could take on some of my tasks. You'd probably be better at them than me.'

'I'm sure I wouldn't be.'

She realised they were entering a more built-up area. This must be Bridgetown. She could see palm trees and grand, colonial buildings – all quietly boasting municipal pride. 'Are we here?'

'Sorry, yes – welcome to Bridgetown.' Alex dutifully turned into a tourist guide, albeit one on a tight schedule. 'Look out for Nelson's Column – built years before your one in London. There's the Parliament buildings. Parliament was established in 1639 –'

'They're seventeenth century?'

'No, most of the buildings in this part are nineteenth century. And this is Coleridge Street.' He pulled in to the side of the road. 'That's the library and that building over there is the courthouse so don't get them muddled up. I'm probably going to be busy until five o'clock. Have you got your mobile?'

'I left it at the house. My provider doesn't seem to cover Barbados.'

'OK. No problem. When I'm done I'll come in and find you.'

'Thanks, Alex.'

Becky got out of the car and walked towards the imposing library building. She went to what appeared to be a reception area and asked the young Bajan lady where she could find documents relating to the Monmouth rebels. The young woman looked as blank as Alex had done earlier.

'The what?'

'The records of the political exiles from England who were sent here in 1685.'

'No good coming here then. You'll have to go to the Department of Archives. We don't have much before the nineteenth century.'

Becky was a bit taken aback by her bluntness but realised the woman didn't mean to be rude. 'Is that in Bridgetown?'

'No. Black Rock. In St James.'

Becky's heart sank. She had no idea where that parish was or how she could get there. Even if she could get a bus, there was a chance she wouldn't get back in time to meet Alex. The young woman must have seen her disappointment for she picked up her glasses from the desk and came round.

'There's one book you could try. You go through there and sit down and I'll bring it to you.'

Becky walked into a larger room, sat down at the table the librarian had indicated and shortly afterwards the young lady – now wearing gloves – brought over a musty tome and placed it carefully on the table. The cover was thrillingly old – faded green with a gold letter inscription: *Records of the Trayterous Complices with intent to overthrow the Crown*e.

'Don't touch it,' commanded the lady and walked off, leaving Becky wondering how she could examine the contents without X-ray spectacles. The librarian returned with a pair of disposable gloves and gave them to Becky to put on.

'You're not going to trash this book, now?'

'I promise not to trash it.'

'OK. You just show me first what you're going to do.'

Becky opened the cover and stared at the yellow, mildewed page, on which the title 'Records of the Trayterous Complices with intent to overthrow the Crowne' was repeated in faded ink.

'And the next one.'

Becky dutifully turned the first page, with all the care of a surgeon performing open-heart surgery on a new-born baby. She almost gasped. The pages inside were handwritten. While this was going to be a pain to read, she felt a buzz of awe at the thought these lines had been written three hundred and thirty years earlier.

'So what are you looking for?' asked the librarian, presumably still seeking some reassurance that Becky was a bona fide researcher and not a book-trasher.

'I've got a list of some of the rebels who were sent from England in 1685 and which plantation owners they were assigned to. I just want some information about what happened to them when they reached Barbados.'

That was evidently good enough for the librarian for she said 'good luck' and walked back to her desk.

Becky began to read the introduction but found it tough going and was grateful Alex was going to be a long time. There were many spelling mistakes – if one could describe unstandardised pre-Samuel Johnson English as containing 'spelling mistakes'. It also took her a while to realise the word she was reading as 'Matey' referred to 'Majesty':

A moft Horrid wicked and Execrable Rebellion was raifed and profecuted within his Ma ties Dominions by James Scott late Duke of Monmouth and by his Trayterous Complices with intent to destroy his Majesties moft Sacred person and Royall family, to overthrow his Crowne and Government. The Rebells and Traytors were utterly Defeated, ffor which many of them have Deservedly ſufferred the Paynes of Death, while the reſt were granted clemency by his Ma tie in his Princely and unparrelled Grace.

This was followed by several pages of further sanctimonious twaddle, the author being obsequiously keen to hammer home the message that King James was just and merciful and the rebels barely worth saving from a hangman's noose.

Becky carefully leafed through until she came to what interested her more: the fate of the rebels once in Barbados.

Anyone endaevouring to eſcape before their terme of tenn years was ended should receive 39 lashes on his bare body in publique.

Becky remembered the rebels had been given sentences of four years in England. Apparently some punitive inflation had struck while they were crossing the Atlantic.

There were further proscriptive rules controlling their lives: they were not allowed to marry or have children.

She turned to the list of prisoners arriving and compared the names with the list she had made in Somerset of those dispatched on the *Betty*. The names tallied except there was no mention of Thomas Gehalgod or of the others thrown overboard, which made sense if the records were only of those who walked off the ship. Why would the Barbadian authorities have been interested in the men who were buried at sea and therefore unavailable to work on the plantations? Daniel Pitcher and Randolph Randerwick were listed, along with another thirteen men assigned to William Darnley of what looked like Copper Hall plantation. The writer must have meant Copper Mill or perhaps the name of the house had changed slightly in the past three hundred odd years.

Talk about continuity. Mr Pitcher might now be working the very same land his ancestor had hundreds of years before.

At the very end of the list of prisoners was a name she hadn't expected: Sarah Thomas. In all of her reading Becky had not come across an account of a woman fighting in the Battle of Sedgemoor so it was reasonable to assume Sarah Thomas had been convicted of aiding the rebels. Becky had read previously of the harsh penalties handed out to people for hiding fugitives after the battle, even if they were unaware the men they were helping were rebels. Judge Jeffreys had even sentenced one such woman to be burnt alive.

But in that case why wasn't Sarah Thomas recorded as boarding the *Betty* in Weymouth along with the other prisoners? Unless she was smuggled aboard – willingly or unwillingly – by the crew. Whatever her reason for being on the ship her fate on land was a little more definite: she was described as a 'servant girl' and assigned to William Darnley.

After reading for three hours, Becky was left feeling intrigued but frustrated. There was no more information in the book. Sarah Thomas could have acted as a servant in the Darnley household or she could have ended up working the fields with the men. She might have lived a relatively easy life or she could have been horribly abused.

Still wearing the gloves Becky took the book back to the librarian and thanked her.

'I don't suppose you have a record of deaths and marriages?' Becky asked.

'Not from the seventeenth century. You need the church parish registers.' The young woman tapped into a computer and searched a screen. 'There's quite a bit online. You could try the Anglican church records.' The young woman wrote the website address down. Becky was about to ask if there was a computer she could use when she heard a voice call her name and looked round to see Alex, briefcase in one hand, phone in the other. She had to hide her disappointment at his early appearance.

'I can't believe it,' he said. 'It's gone like a dream today. I've sorted out the bank and done all my messages. You ready to go back?'

'Yes,' Becky lied, sensing Alex wanted to make a quick getaway. Sure enough she had to up her pace as she followed him to the car.

Becky spent the drive back deep in thought. She wondered whether some oral history could have been passed down the generations of Redlegs to the present. Wouldn't it be amazing if she could say something to Pitcher that would trigger a rhyme or a story from over three hundred years ago – carried through time like a spoken gene? It may be a forlorn hope but Alex had already demonstrated the possibility. During the Scottish referendum on independence, the *Essex Gleaner* had attempted to be topical by publishing a tongue-in-cheek glossary of Scottish words. Becky could only remember a couple: *piece* meant a snack, *message* meant groceries. Alex had almost certainly heard his mother or grandmother say she was 'doing the messages' when she was off out to shop and had interpreted this to mean 'doing errands'. Over how many generations had that phrase been relayed?

'You're very quiet,' said Alex.

'I really need access to the internet,' Becky replied. 'I've asked Clara if you have broadband at the house but she just looked blank.'

Alex laughed. 'Of course Matthew has broadband, but, I'm sorry, I don't think it's practical to use the computer in the office. Look, tell him you need a laptop. I'm sure he'd buy one tomorrow if it would help you.'

Becky didn't share Alex's conviction. Knowing Matthew he would assume she was after freebies rather than trying to do any genuine research. Still it wouldn't hurt to ask.

'I guess that means the library wasn't much use. Did you find out anything?'

'Pitcher's ancestor was working for the Darnleys over three hundred years ago. That's pretty amazing, isn't it? I mean the continuity.'

Alex didn't answer and she was surprised to see his face screwed up in puzzlement. She had been about to tell him that a girl had walked off the *Betty* who had never (apparently) boarded the ship in England. But his silence put her off. She felt a little sad. Here she was getting fired up by Bajan history and no one else seemed interested.

That night, as Becky tidied her room, it occurred to her she might be performing the same actions, in the same space, as Sarah Thomas had three hundred and thirty years ago. She looked out of her window at the yard and garden gently illuminated by the lights on the veranda. At least she could assume Sarah had been familiar with this window, though whether as a plantation worker looking up, or a servant girl looking down, Becky had no way of knowing.

Chapter Eight

The veranda was not a peaceful place the next morning as Matthew – in his normal office attire of black shorts – was shouting into his mobile while Alex sat opposite, looking pained. Becky hung around long enough to realise that this wouldn't be a brief conversation and raised her eyebrows quizzically at Alex.

'One of the hotel guests is blaming our swimming pool for giving him Hepatitis A,' said Alex.

'Yuck. Could it be true?'

'Doubt it. He's probably gorged himself on shellfish at one of the Crop Over events but of course there's more money to be made from suing a hotel.'

Becky had heard Maureen and Cook talking about Crop Over, which sounded like a bacchanalian equivalent of the Harvest Thanksgiving celebration in the UK – except that it celebrated the sugarcane harvest and seemed to take up much of July.

'Too much drinking and carousing,' Cook had said disapprovingly.

'That sounds serious,' Becky said to Alex.

'You're not joking. We may have to close the pool until we can get an independent quality check of the water.'

'So now isn't a good time to say that I need a laptop?'

Alex gave a rueful smile. 'Not a good idea. I'll try and remember to ask him later when things have calmed down.'

Resigned to not being able to check the lists of deaths and marriages today, Becky thought she could at least update Clara on her trip to the library yesterday. However that turned out not to be possible either as no sooner had Clara surfaced than she cried off gardening that morning, saying she had to drive Renee to the garage to pick up her now-mended car. Becky didn't bother to conceal her disappointment.

'I promise we'll do something nice tonight,' Clara said, which did nothing to lift Becky's spirits, as Clara's idea of doing 'something nice' usually involved a pack of cards.

Clara did not return for lunch and the day passed slowly until Zena arrived with her childminder. Becky decided that today she and Cook's granddaughter should explore the area behind the house. She was feeling braver after her excursion to Bridgetown and also wondered if she might get a glimpse of the settlement where Pitcher lived.

This area of scrub hadn't received any attention during Clara's garden renovations and looked generally uncared for. The rough grass bumped over the uneven ground until it reached a high wall 'decorated' with broken glass secured in place with concrete – no doubt another example of Matthew's paranoia about break-ins. But a strange little visitor had made it over the wall. Becky approached the flat cream-coloured hexagon lying in the grass and picked it up carefully. It was about eighteen inches long and wide and made of thick paper sewn roughly on to strips of light wood; it felt both rough and delicate.

'What's this?'' she said. It looked like a hat for a person with a flat head.

Zena giggled and took it from her, toddling off at quite a pace and flinging the flimsy object into the air. She screamed with delight as it came down to earth again.

'Careful, Zena,' Becky called. 'We don't know what it is.'

Zena stopped and regarded her with pouty disbelief. 'Kite.'

Becky sighed. What an idiot she'd been. Of course it was a home-made kite: one that had broken free from its tether to land in their little patch of the world. She rather envied it its freedom for, though the wall was low enough in places to see over, Becky couldn't spot anything resembling a settlement in the distance. Even if she were adventurous enough to venture further she had to get Zena back in time for Cook's daughter-in-law to pick her up.

Despite Zena's comedic attempts to get the kite airborne as they headed back to the house, the afternoon had compounded Becky's feeling of isolation. She half-wished Richard Carrington's assertion they would bump into each other would be proven right.

But at least Clara kept her promise.

'Renee's going to drive us to the cinema to see a play,' she said happily when Becky got back.

That sounded odd but any change in routine would be good.

Sure enough Renee arrived in a saloon car a couple of hours later and Becky recognised her as one of the friendlier members of the bridge group, A nice middle-aged Bajan she greeted Becky warmly as they waited for Clara to walk decorously down the veranda steps.

'I just know you'll love it,' said Renee. 'As soon as I heard the film was on I told Clara we have to take Becky. Remind her of home. Shakespeare, Becky!'

'Shakespeare? A film?' asked Becky, bemused, getting into the back seat.

'*Othello*. It's supposed to be really good.'

Clara got in the front and shut the passenger door. 'You've probably seen the play loads of times I know but hopefully the film will be good too.'

'Actually I haven't seen it,' said Becky, amused they should think being English conferred some sort of expertise. She wasn't actually a big fan of Shakespeare but she was pleased to have an opportunity to see the island after dark. Renee was a sedate driver but the slow rushes of the landscape in the headlights were as engaging as any film.

'So where is the cinema?' Becky asked, having lost any sense of whether they were driving south, west or east.

'Holetown,' said Renee, adding, 'on the west coast.'

Becky recognised the name. She'd read that the town had a monument commemorating the first English landing, when the island was claimed for James I. She would have liked to see it but now was not the time.

The layout of the cinema was familiar enough but the rest of the experience was new to Becky. When she went to see a film in Essex she might recognise one or two people and give a little nod of acknowledgement but Clara and Renee seemed to know at least half the people in the audience. There was much hubbub of chatter and exuberant waving.

'Oh there's Richard,' said Clara. 'Richard!'

Three rows in front a fair-haired head turned to wave at Clara and Becky recognised the beach bum from the airport. Tonight he was dressed in a smarter (though still casual) shirt – presumably a concession to his date for the evening, an attractive Bajan, who turned round and smiled at them before resuming her conversation with someone in another row.

'Hey, Becky,' Richard shouted, waving at her with a big grin. 'They're not working you too hard?'

'Of course not,' she said and returned the smile.

'How do you know him?' asked Clara.

'Bumped into him at the airport.'

'And how's Matthew?' Richard called to Clara. 'Any special plans for Crop Over?'

'Oh, he's busy at the hotel,' said Clara. 'Though he'll be at Queens on Sunday for the competition.'

'For the Rotaract Club?' asked Renee. 'It would be great if they could get the competition going again.'

'I know,' said Clara.

'What competition?' asked Becky.

'Judging kites. It used to be a traditional event on Easter Sundays,' said Renee. 'It was great fun and a big proper competition. Nerves stretched to breaking point trying to get some of the larger ones off the ground. There would be competitions for the silliest kite or the biggest kite – quite a few categories.'

'It's a real shame it died away,' said Clara. 'I think the Club are hoping making it part of the Crop Over celebrations will revive the tradition.'

Becky saw Richard was still watching them although he wouldn't have been able to hear the exchange.

'Hey,' he called. 'Has Matthew made his own kite?' He laughed.

Becky sensed some annoyance in Clara though her mouth soon returned to a smile. 'No,' she called back. 'He's handing out the prizes.'

Becky noticed a strange look cross Richard's face – 'crestfallen' would probably describe it best but it was soon replaced by another grin. 'Then I'll see you there,' he shouted. 'You're going, Becky, right?'

As Becky had no idea whether she would be going she just smiled. The film trailers were starting and Richard turned back and slipped an arm around his date's shoulders as the lights dimmed.

'Did you see that look?' asked Clara. 'Or did I imagine it?'

'He's envious,' said Renee. 'Not surprising really.'

Becky wondered what they meant but soon forgot about it as she discovered that watching a film in Barbados was a different experience from England as well. A trip to her local cinema at home was hardly a rarefied event – people constantly checked their mobiles, struggled with supersize cartons of popcorn and chatted to each other – but they didn't interact with the film. In this cinema people were shouting advice to Othello, groaning when the advice was ignored and then got bored when Othello went on and on to Desdemona about a handkerchief. Becky's attention wandered too. She saw Richard's date shrug off the arm round her shoulders; maybe he had done something to irritate her. When Becky's eyes returned to the screen Othello was still going on about a missing handkerchief.

'For God's sake,' shouted a Bajan voice from the back row. 'Use your sleeve, man, so we can get on with the story.'

Becky thought that was the best bit of the evening.

As they drove home she warmly thanked Renee for taking her.

Renee beamed. 'I knew you'd enjoy it. A bit of Shakespeare's good isn't it? I didn't understand half of what they said but never mind.'

'Nor me but I think we got the gist,' said Becky.

Becky's effusive thanks to Renee must have sparked some guilty reaction in Clara. She was quiet for a while before exclaiming 'poor Becky' and turning round to face her in the backseat. 'I haven't really taken you out anywhere, have I?'

'No worries,' said Becky. 'After all I am supposed to be working.'

'Well, you're certainly not working this weekend,' said Clara.

'Clara, I'm not really working at all. I'd much rather get on with the book than –'

'Next week, Becky, I promise,' said Clara. 'But on Sunday you and I are going to go to Queens to see Matthew hand out the prizes.'

'OK,' said Becky, pleased she was going to get to go to the festival.

Although it was Saturday, it was still a working day for Matthew and Alex and Becky found them in their usual places on the veranda when she came down in the morning. Matthew looked a little calmer; presumably his swimming pool was open for business. Alex took one look at her and slapped his head in annoyance.

'Sorry, Becky. I forgot to ask him.'

'Ask me what?' said Matthew.

'Becky needs a laptop for her research.'

'And internet access,' said Becky.

Matthew stared at her. 'Hasn't my mother given you her laptop?'

'No,' said Becky.

Matthew gave a grunt of frustration. 'She's probably left it behind in England.'

'To be fair I think I asked her about internet access rather than about the laptop specifically.'

'Can you check with her first?' He returned his attention to the papers in front of him.

Becky couldn't tell whether he was being deliberately unhelpful or was genuinely distracted by work concerns. She headed back into the house.

'Try Maureen,' Matthew called after her. 'If she can't find it when she's back on Monday let me know and I'll sort out a replacement.'

Becky was so stunned by his answer she could barely get out the words 'Thank you.' Perhaps Alex had told him about their trip to Bridgetown and he now realised she was serious about researching the Monmouth rebels.

Clara came down about an hour later, clearly tired after her day out with Renee, but she insisted on working for a couple of hours in the garden anyway. Becky told her some of what she'd discovered at Bridgetown library but didn't feel the time was right to bring up Sarah Thomas or mention talking to Pitcher. She mentioned the laptop when they were having lunch but Clara went vague.

'I just can't remember. 'I'm sure I'd have brought anything that looked important.' She smiled at Becky. 'I almost forgot. You've got two letters.'

The household custom was for mail to be placed next to the phone on a small table in the hall. Becky had long given up looking – used to seeing nothing but a stack of official-looking envelopes for Matthew – but sure enough today there were two envelopes for her – one from her mother, one from Joe.

She opened the one with her mother's handwriting first. It was somewhat joyless: the gutter was blocked, there were mouse droppings in one of the kitchen cupboards, and someone had fallen in church – literally rather than morally, Becky assumed. The letter made no reference to Becky being in Barbados.

Joe's letter was a welcome contrast, his handwriting a little chaotic but energy leaping from the page. He asked questions about the climate, the wildlife, and did boys really play cricket in the street? (Becky had hardly been out enough to answer that one). Had the pillock tried it on with her? (This was accompanied by a rather rude diagram of where to hit him if he did). Had she learnt anything about their father? (That made Becky feel guilty for she had barely thought about tracing him). There was also evidence Joe had been doing some research of his own though clearly he favoured the *Horrible Histories* approach: he wrote that the Duke of Monmouth's execution was so botched it took multiple axe chops to finish him off and in the end the executioner had to be whisked away before he was torn to shreds by the furious public. Joe finished the letter with a drawing of a tombstone with the words 'Thomas Gehalgod lives' scrawled over it.

Becky smiled. The way things were going she would be better off posting her questions to Joe to have him trawl the internet and post back his findings.

When Clara went up for her afternoon nap, Becky went through the *History of Barbados* again to see if there was any mention of the Darnley plantation but the book didn't go into that level of detail. If she could just get online to check out the Deaths and Marriages websites she had been given at the library she would be in with a chance of finding something about Sarah Thomas. Maybe not marriage – if Sarah counted as a Monmouth rebel she wouldn't have been allowed to marry – but she would have died at some point.

It occurred to Becky that Cook had been in the household a long time and there was the slimmest of chances some folklore had been passed down by the people who worked for the Darnleys. She decided to ask Cook that evening when Clara was hosting her usual bridge session.

Becky noticed that Cook sounded a little breathless when she dished out their stew. After eating Becky helped Clara get the dining room ready for the bridge party then carried the dishes out to the kitchen. Cook's breathing sounded even more laboured than before.

'I'll clear up,' said Becky, putting the plates in the sink and running the water.

Cook nodded gratefully and sat down, leaning heavily on the kitchen table. After a moment or two she said, 'I think I need one of my pills.'

'Tell me where they are,' said Becky. 'I'll get them.'

'Thank you. On the table in my room.'

Becky stopped washing up and hurried to Cook's room. She knew it was at the back of the house but had never been down this corridor behind the main reception rooms before. She passed a downstairs toilet and a locked and bolted door which must lead to Matthew's office and opened the door at the farthest end. Stifling heat hit her and she cursed Matthew for giving Cook a windowless room but, when she switched on the light, she could see there was a large window, tightly shut. She found a small pill bottle on a table by the single bed and brought it back to the kitchen.

'It's too hot in your room,' said Becky. 'Shall I go back and open the window?'

'No thanks,' said Cook.'

'Ah,' said Becky, getting a glass of water for her. 'I forgot that a duppy can get through the smallest crack. So what would it do if it got in?'

Cook shrugged. 'Mess up tings. Trow tings. Mek a fire.'

'Well, your room is duppy-free. It's the neatest room I've ever seen.'

Cook made a face and swallowed a tablet. 'Because I keep the window closed.'

Becky resumed the washing up but did not feel she could raise the subject of Sarah Thomas now. She was pleased to hear Cook's breathing gradually get steadier and before long the old lady heaved herself up and headed to bed.

Becky finished clearing up and headed out on the veranda. Even a few minutes in Cook's room had made her feel in need of air and she could not imagine how Cook got any sleep. Maybe that was why she dozed so much in the kitchen during the day.

Becky sat down and looked out into the night. The laughter of Clara's guests sounded far away, drowned by the whistling laments of the little beasts in the foliage below. A breeze picked up and woke the giant bamboo so that its usual gentle creaking turned into a more ominous sound – like that of an army of men cutting through a forest to approach the house. Another strange instrument joined the timeless orchestra that surrounded her – a whining, buzzing sound that filled the darkness and swelled until the sky seemed filled with malevolent angels. Becky had a sudden vision of transparent floating upper torsos – duppies – following the slave ships from Africa to the West Indies and America. She shook her head to dispel it but knew the sound wasn't just in her mind when the conversation in the dining room died away and the bridge ladies ventured out on to the veranda.

'What on earth is it?' asked the Artificial Woman, who wouldn't have been able to raise her eyebrows any higher without first rubbing off the old ones and drawing a new pair.

'It's horrible,' said another, laying a hand over her heart. To Becky she said, 'How can you bear to be out here alone?'

'I'd like to know what it is,' said Becky who also found the sound deeply unsettling, the more so because she couldn't identify it.

The lady who had put her hand over her heart put her fingers in her ears and hurried back inside.

'It's a singing angel,' said Renee. 'At least I think it's a Singing Angel. Normally there's just one but this sounds like an army of the beasts. I've never heard so many.'

'It's a Mad Bull,' said another. 'I should know. I had to ban my grandson from making them.'

That made Becky feel better. If the noise was caused by something a child could make, it could not be anything dangerous.

'No wonder some people want them banned at night,' said Clara.

'I've never heard it this bad before,' said Renee. 'I hope the wind dies down otherwise you won't get any sleep tonight.'

The noise was such that it brought the curtain down on the act of bridge and soon the ladies were turning out of the yard and pointing their cars towards their own more tranquil neighbourhoods. Clara went to bed, muttering distractedly, and Becky opted to go up too. She lay on top of her sheets, searching for sleep, but it would not come. She tried closing the window but the heat was soon suffocating. Her room had a fan on the table but she tended to avoid using it, as the waves of air interfered with her sleep. She tried one more time with the window open and the buzzing noise increased triumphantly. Matthew came home and she heard the rat-a-tat of the bolts locking out whatever villains lurked outside but the bolts were powerless against this formless intruder. She wondered what Matthew thought about it.

Chapter Nine

Becky tried to sleep with pillows wedged round her ears but at six o'clock she gave up the futile struggle and got up. The buzzing was probably less intense than it had been the previous night but its very unceasing monotony was distressing. She realised she had assumed daybreak would herald a return to normality. No such luck.

She found Matthew on the veranda – like her still in pyjamas – leaning over the balustrade. His face looked worn with sleeplessness.

'When did this start?' he said curtly. There was no point expecting a 'good morning' out of him as this morning clearly wasn't.

'About ten o'clock last night. Where's it coming from?'

'Hopefully on our land. Can you get dressed? Give me a hand?'

'OK,' she said. 'See you back here.'

Ten minutes later they were both back on the veranda, Becky wearing shorts and a T-shirt and Matthew for once wearing a shirt with his black shorts. He was also armed, rather alarmingly, with a machete and a small knife.

'Are we going to need a lawyer for this?' asked Becky.

To her surprise he laughed. 'If they're on someone else's land then we will be trespassing and may have to kill a couple of pit bull terriers before we finish off the owner – then we might need a lawyer.'

'Oh.' She hoped he was joking.

'But as I said hopefully they're on our side of the wall.'

Cook came out on the veranda and regarded Matthew and his weapons impassively. She said, 'I'm going to church later.'

'Are you saying that because you want a lift or telling me because you're going to pray for my soul?' asked Matthew.

A half-smile played on the old lady's face. 'Both,' she said.

'Maybe you could slip in a prayer for an end to this assault on our ears.'

'Maybe I will,' said Cook and went back inside.

Matthew shook his head with something like admiration then turned to Becky. 'You look terrible.'

She certainly felt it. Even Matthew with his darker-toned skin had noticeable circles under his eyes. 'So do you.'

'Cook looks better than both of us. I don't know how she managed to sleep.'

Becky knew it was because Cook kept her window shut but said nothing. She followed him out of the yard towards the area of rough ground at the end of the drive. To the left of the mahogany treeline was the grassy area she had explored with Zena a couple of days before, whereas the land they were heading for was banded by casuarina trees. The noise of the wind playing through their needles was usually a comforting sound but today it was quite usurped by the duppies. Matthew strode ahead, not talking, though he would have had to shout to be heard above the furious buzzing. The occasional swipe of his machete to knock away a recalcitrant clump of tall razor-sharp grass alongside the drive revealed more about his mood than any conversation might.

However one person seemed unaffected by the racket. Beneath the branches of a casuarina tree was a figure, fully stretched out with a floppy fedora over his face.

‘Pitcher,’ said Matthew, with weary resignation. ‘Worn out by gardening as usual.’

As they drew nearer Becky could see Pitcher’s chalk-white arms resting on his stomach. His trousers were so torn they were more like tasselled shorts and his shirt was all but bleached of colour.

‘Looks like he could do with some new clothes,’ she said.

‘I can’t tell him what to spend his money on.’

‘It was an observation,’ said Becky. ‘No need to take it as criticism.’

Matthew grunted. Despite the fact they were standing over him, Pitcher seemed oblivious of their presence.

‘I take it he is just sleeping?’ said Becky, watching Pitcher’s chest to check he was breathing.

‘Let’s hope so.’ Matthew carried on walking.

They came in sight of what Becky assumed was an old plantation wall and – presumably – the boundary of Matthew’s land. He stopped now, seeming to survey the area as if he expected to find something right in front of them. Becky couldn’t see anything obvious. Beyond the low wall was yet more scrub and another wall could be seen ahead, perpendicular to them, roughly threading its way over the land beyond.

Something about that wall seemed out of place here and yet looked familiar to Becky. The buzzing noise seemed to reach a crescendo as she walked nearer to the boundary to look over. For a moment she remembered being with a very young Joe on holiday somewhere in the south west of England, maybe Devon or Dorset. Her father was pointing out a wall to them and explaining that it took real skill to build such a structure without cement; one that could stand for hundreds of years. There was no mistaking it – she was looking at a drystone wall.

Becky would have liked to ask Matthew what use they had in Barbados but he was staring at the sky.

‘Look at that,’ he shouted. ‘There must be at least twenty.’

Becky followed his gaze to see several blobs floating above them, no more distinguishable than skylarks on a summer’s day in Britain.

‘Can you see the strings?’ he asked.

She peered more closely and realised what the objects were. ‘Oh yes. Now I can.’ There were twenty kites tied to stakes in the ground – all screaming with fury at being tethered. She had actually passed between two of them without realising.

‘I’ve never heard kites make this kind of noise,’ she shouted. ‘But at least they’re on your side of the wall.’

‘Yes,’ said Matthew, grumpily. ‘Someone trying to make a point.’ He walked forward and touched the string attached to the nearest stake as if to test the tension. ‘They were lucky with the weather.’

‘They? You think someone did this deliberately?’ It was a stupid question – of course the kites could not have tethered themselves – but she was sleep deprived.

Matthew flung the machete and knife down and started pulling hand over hand to rein in the first kite. As the soaring beast drew nearer, Becky recognised a conventional old-fashioned coffin shape and was surprised to see it was just a shop-bought kite. It lost its nerve fifty or so yards from the ground, its serpentine wanderings abruptly terminating with a slow decline to the grass. Matthew pointed to a flap of plastic, which looked like it had been cut from a normal throwaway plastic bag, stuck fast to the top of the kite.

‘That’s the Mad Bull?’ shouted Becky.

Matthew looked surprised. ‘You’ve heard about them? I made my own when I was young. You had to make them as loud as possible. But that’s the sort of thing that irritating little boys do.’

‘So this was probably just boys messing around?’

'Childish men would be nearer the truth.' He picked up the machete and the knife. 'Now, what to do? I would like to cut the strings; it would certainly save time.' He looked at her. 'What would you do?'

Becky felt like she was being tested but either way her answer would have been the same. 'I think we should pull them down. I don't know what the consequences would be if we just cut them loose.'

He nodded, as if she had confirmed his own thoughts. Matthew put down the knife and machete again and they worked their way along the stakes. Pulling the kites down was surprisingly hard work and Becky appreciated the same breeze that had kept the beasts up in the air overnight; each one had a fold of plastic bag glued to it – which looked quite incongruous with the otherwise professionally made kites.

'It must have taken someone ages to do this,' she said as they worked side by side.

'People will do anything for money.'

When all the kites were captured, and their strings rolled into neat loops, they both stood back, catching their breath. Becky shut her eyes and listened to the day sing through the casuarina trees, the breeze gently rattling the parchment-coloured pods of the shac-shac tree. Only now did she realise how disorientating the sound of the kites had been – almost debilitating.

She opened her eyes to see Matthew looking at her with slight impatience, as if he had somewhere else to be. She picked up the knife and lifted a stack of kites.

'Isn't it nice to talk at a normal volume?' she said.

'Certainly is.'

Matthew took the other stack of kites in one arm and in his other hand he swung the machete. 'Fit?' he asked.

She nodded and they headed homewards. She smiled automatically as the sound of a jubilant hymn wended its way across the land, congregational spirit coursing through the tambourines. 'I read somewhere that Barbados has more churches per square mile than anywhere else in the world.'

'That's probably true.' He tilted an arm to look at his watch and grimaced. 'It's already gone nine o'clock. Poor Cook. I said I'd take her. It's a bit of a walk.'

'Maybe Clara's given her a lift.'

'If she's up this early. The garden's really taking its toll.'

'She loves it.'

'I know. But she reacts quite badly to fungal spores. It's a curse for someone who's obsessed with gardening. After a while she'll overdo it.'

Becky suspected late bridge nights were more likely to be the culprit but thought it best not to mention that. She waggled the stack of kites. 'We did the right thing bringing them down. I don't know how high these things would go on their own but if planes can be brought down by bird strikes, then –'

'Bat strikes,' said Matthew and almost grinned. 'You know the little bats that you see from the veranda?'

'Vesper bats?'

He looked surprised at her knowledge. 'Yes. There have been reports of them hitting plane engines. And I don't think they fly that high. So I suppose a kite strike would be quite possible.' He looked at the bundle in his arm. 'Now I've got to figure out whether to throw these away or –'

'You could hand them out at your hotel.'

'What? Complimentary kites?'

Becky felt a twinge of annoyance. He hadn't paid for them; he could hardly charge his guests for second-hand kites.

'Yes, free. Unless there's an orphanage around.'

'Actually there is a children's home not far away.'

'That would be the perfect solution then, wouldn't it?'

‘We’d have to take off all the bits of plastic first.’ Matthew looked at her. ‘But, yes, children’s home it will be. Good idea.’

He strode off again and Becky was hard pressed to keep up with him.

They approached Pitcher who Becky was pleased to see now sitting up, though he looked dazed, as though the state of slumber had made more sense to him than the waking world. He shook his head several times and then his hands started swatting invisible insects.

‘All right, Pitcher?’ called Matthew.

Pitcher removed his hat and looked round. His bleary eyes were both blue and blotchy red and his skin so pale it looked like it had never seen the sun. He was thin to the point of emaciation and was the unhealthiest-looking man Becky had ever seen. She couldn’t guess his age. He could be anything from late thirties to sixties.

Pitcher stopped swatting imaginary insects and gave a half wave, which Becky sensed was more out of polite acknowledgement than recognition. Most people would have commented on a man and woman walking along with arms full of brightly coloured kites but he showed no interest at all. She could see why Alex thought she wouldn’t have much luck asking him about the Monmouth rebels. Becky couldn’t imagine Pitcher had much idea what had happened yesterday let alone over three hundred years ago.

‘What goes on in his head?’ Matthew sighed as they walked on.

‘Cook says that he sees people in the garden. Or sees things anyway.’

‘He sees both. Though the things aren’t real. I’m not sure about the people.’

‘I’ve never seen anyone,’ said Becky. ‘If that helps?’

‘Good. I don’t mind people walking over the land out here. It’s a short cut to a little …’ he paused, as if looking for the right word, 'village – you could call it. People just step over the old wall, which I don't mind. But if anyone actually comes into the garden then I'm more concerned.'

Becky was surprised considering how security conscious Matthew was but that explained why the outer plantation wall wasn't topped by broken glass and concrete. She supposed people taking a short cut to the Redleg village Alex had mentioned wouldn't pose a threat to anyone at Copper Mill.

'You mean if they're in the garden they might be trying to break in?'

'Yes. No. I mean, don't be worried.' He gave a bitter laugh. 'I suspect that the real thieves would be invited in as guests.'

By the time they reached the yard Becky's arms felt dead with fatigue.

'Shame about later. I have to get enthusiastic about kites and right now I never want to see one again,' Matthew muttered.

Becky remembered it was Sunday and the day of the competition. Right now she didn't feel much like an afternoon out herself but, having heard so much about the festival from Maureen and Cook, she did want to see it. 'Clara said someone is trying to revive an old tradition?'

'Well, hopefully more than one person wants to get it going again. It used to be one of the main events of the year. But – I don't really know what happened. People stopped coming and the sponsors got nervous. Mind you they're quite happy to push every food and drink festival down the tourists' throats.'

This was possibly the longest conversation Becky had ever had with Matthew but she still could not work him out. For someone who owed his wealth to his hotel business he didn't seem that enamoured of the tourist industry. She followed him to an outhouse which held the gardening tools and dumped the kites on an old table. They put away the machete and the knife and headed back to the plantation house. Matthew watched as Becky tried to rub some life back into her arms.

'Thank you,' he said. 'And sorry about your disturbed night.'

'I'm sure it wasn't anything personal. Probably just kids excited about Crop Over.'

He scowled so she changed the subject, 'I'm looking forward to seeing you hand out the prizes later.'

'I'm handing out bribes.' He gave a half-grin and stepped back to let her into the house. 'I think breakfast, a shower and some sleep are called for. Not necessarily in that order.'

Becky agreed and decided to aim for sleep first. She felt worn out.

Chapter Ten

Somewhat to Becky's surprise she did fall asleep soundly and awoke a couple of hours later, feeling much better. She took a quick shower and went downstairs wondering whether it was now time for breakfast or lunch. Clara clearly seemed to think the former as she was still in her dressing gown. She looked quite pale.

'Isn't the silence a relief? Matthew says you helped him with the Mad Bulls. Thank you so much.'

'That's OK.'

Outside on the veranda Becky found Matthew holding his hand out over the balustrade, as if to test the wind. He was looking worried. The earlier breeze had completely died down; the shrubs in the garden were barely shimmering. He withdrew his hand when he noticed Becky join him.

'What exactly is the competition judging – skill at flying?' she asked.

'No, skill at making. Any fool can buy a kite and get it to fly. But making a kite out of paper and sticks and string is quite a craft. It would be really good if we can keep it going. But we need a bit of breeze. Otherwise people won't bother to turn up.'

She wondered why a successful businessman was so bothered about a kite competition. 'You're quite into traditions, aren't you?'

'Aren't you?' he said. Becky did not answer because she could not think of a tradition in England that she really followed but he must have taken her silence as dissent because he snapped, 'Don't expect too much in the way of entertainment today,' and went inside.

Becky was cross. Why had she even bothered? But maybe he had not been able to go to sleep like her and his disturbed night was now catching up with him. She decided she was not going to let a grumpy Matthew Darnley spoil her opportunity to see a real slice of Barbados life. Besides if he was busy handing out the prizes there was a good chance she would not have to spend much time with him anyway.

A couple of hours later they set off. Matthew had changed into a lightweight suit and Becky was wearing a dress for the first time since she had arrived in Barbados. Clara, looking her usual glamorous self, sat in the front, next to Matthew. Becky was pleased to see it was getting noticeably windier as they got nearer the coast. Eventually they pulled into the grounds of what looked like a school and Becky saw a sign saying Queens College. When Renee had mentioned Queens on the night of the cinema Becky had thought she meant a country club or something similar but this was clearly their destination.

Matthew parked in the designated area and helped his mother out of the car. There was a stack of folding chairs nearby. Matthew picked up one for each of them and led Clara and Becky towards a grassed area beyond the main school buildings.

'The competition is held on the school playing fields now,' he said to Becky. 'Probably not what you expected.'

Becky thought there was something accusing about his tone. 'Actually I was expecting a cocktail bar and a string quartet,' she said. 'We always have those at kite competitions in Essex.'

Matthew looked a little surprised. 'I just meant that it's a shadow of what it used to be.'

‘It used to be the highlight of Easter,’ said Clara, seemingly oblivious to the tension between her son and Becky. ‘It was held at the Garrison Savannah.’

‘Where the horse racing happens?’ asked Becky. Her father had mentioned it.

‘Yes,’ said Matthew. ‘It was a major event. You should have seen it before.’

The school playing fields were edged with spectators and although the atmosphere was sober – compared to the Crop Over festivities Maureen and Cook had described – it still had a pleasant and expectant buzz. Matthew opened up the folding chairs for Clara and Becky and, murmuring something about needing to talk to some people, walked off.

Becky was glad to see him go and hoped when he came back he’d be less moody. He headed off towards a clump of men and women clustered around a table bedecked with silver cups of various sizes. Near them stood a reporter with a camera bouncing on his stomach. Becky felt a pang of deprivation: Ian was still happily ensconced in his job at the *Essex Gleaner* but who knew if she was going to have a career in journalism when she returned to England? At the moment she didn’t even know if she had an alternative career as a researcher and co-author – although Clara had promised they would discuss the book once today’s event was out of the way.

‘Good heavens,’ said Clara. ‘Is that Richard Carrington?’

Becky looked at the group of people who were now hailing Matthew. Although they were all dressed smartly, like Matthew, most of the men were wearing short-sleeved shirts with no ties. However, one of them, a fair-haired man standing a little apart from the welcoming committee, was dressed in a full suit with jacket and tie, which must have been stifling under the midday sun.

'It can't be,' said Becky. 'He always looks so scruffy.'

'You know, I think it is. I've never seen him wear a tie before.'

'Why would he come to a kite flying competition?' asked Becky. She didn't know anything about Richard Carrington but from what she'd seen he wouldn't be a natural attendee at an event that involved wearing a suit and drinking no alcohol. Looking around she could see several respectable hawkers selling soft drinks but no stalls for beer or rum.

'All the Carrington brothers are members of the Rotaract Club,' said Clara. 'Though I don't think Richard is very active. Whereas you can see that Matthew does quite a bit for them. I wonder what Richard's up to.'

Becky didn't care what he was up to. She just hoped she might be able to have a cheerful and straightforward conversation with him later as opposed to putting up with Matthew's resentful reminisces and Clara's unwillingness to discuss the Monmouth rebels.

Not that Richard was looking too cheerful at the moment. He was stomping away from the Rotaract Club group.

Becky saw Matthew point her and Clara out to a plump Bajan. The man gave Matthew a slap on the back and then headed their way to greet Clara – obviously an old acquaintance.

'And this is Becky from England,' said Clara. 'She's helping me to write a book.'

If only, thought Becky, wincing inside.

'Wow,' said the middle-aged man, whose face was a study in wrinkled cheerfulness. 'Do you live in London?'

'No, but not too far away.'

'So,' said Clara, with a mischievous face. 'Why is young Richard wearing a tie for the first time in his life?'

The man laughed so much he had to put his hands on his knees to stay upright. 'Oh Lord,' he cried. 'Young

Carrington wanted to hand out the big prize. He pretended he didn't know Matthew had bought all the prizes and was lined up to present them.'

'Oh dear,' said Clara. 'I do hope the Club isn't going to listen to him.'

'Don't you worry. Matthew offered Richard the chance to hand out the prize for the youngest kite-maker.' The plump Bajan held up a hand with his thumb and forefinger a few inches apart. 'It's a little, bitty silver cup.' He laughed some more. 'I think the man is insulted. He go storming off.'

'Oh, Mr R is naughty,' said Clara with indulgent pride.

The man went back to join the committee and, as the competition got under way, various other people came up to Clara to exchange greetings and gossip and find out who Becky was.

A woman from the Rotaract Club announced each category over a PA system and then children in school uniforms took to the field with wonderful home-made kites. Becky could only imagine the children in the youngest category were being taught kite-flying in primary school as they just about managed to totter out holding beautiful home-made creations. The sight of them trying to launch their glued together sticks and coloured paper was both funny and moving. She was surprised to see that Clara was in tears.

'Excuse me,' Clara said, dabbing her eyes. 'They are so sweet.'

'Yes,' said Becky remembering Zena's fierce determination when she was trying to launch the little kite a few days earlier. 'They are gorgeous.'

'Oh heavens,' said Clara. 'And the little boy over there is from the children's home. Let's hope his kite just soars.'

The lad was one of only a couple of boys not in school uniform and was doggedly trying to keep his kite airborne. Every time it fluttered to the ground there was a collective sigh from the crowd. The boy would work out which way the breeze was blowing then lay out the line again and try to lift his kite by running along with his arms raised a few feet in the air. He was the smallest on the field and must have been no more than five or six.

'Remember the kites must be in the air for one whole minute,' said the lady over the loudspeaker.

Other children's kites had been flying for a good ten minutes but this little boy was presumably the only one still in contention in his age category. At last his kite took flight. The crowd cheered and started counting. When the collective voices shouted out 'sixty!' and the little boy's kite was still in the air there were more huge cheers and for the first time his expression changed from worried concentration into a sparkling grin.

He came forward proudly to collect his prize and Matthew bent down to say a few words to him, making the boy giggle, before taking the microphone to announce him as the winner of the youngest kite-flyer category. The boy seemed delighted with his little cup.

Becky looked around for Richard and saw him chatting with a group of men. She wondered if he regretted not taking Matthew up on his offer.

She was enjoying herself. The venue may only be a school playing field but she drank in the colourful kites and bright Bajan outfits and loved the easy-going nature of the crowd. The Sno-Cone man occasionally advertised his wares with the tinkle of a bell and, in the afternoon sun, crowds quickly grew by his handcart. Becky watched him dispense cones of shaved ice saturated with syrups the colours of ruby and topaz and decided she would buy one when the queue had gone down.

Matthew had presented several cups, in ascending order of size, and now there was just one trophy left. It dazzled on the table, drinking in the sun. Already impressed by the home-made kites and the skills of the schoolchildren in their neat uniforms, Becky wondered what the last category would be. The Rotaract lady announced the Large Kites section.

'Let's hope it lives up to tradition,' said Clara, fanning herself with a hand.

There was an expectant hush as everyone stared at the empty playing field. Becky looked over to the presentation table. The Rotaract group was looking slightly jittery and the female announcer held her hand out as Matthew had done earlier that morning, testing the breeze. Matthew just stared ahead, expressionless.

Five teams of schoolchildren, either all male or all female, started trooping on to the field. Resplendent in their uniforms they were carrying kites the size of several dinner tables lashed together.

'Do these things ever get off the ground?' said Becky to Clara.

'We're occasionally lucky.' Clara laughed. 'Let's just say this is usually when the gambling starts.'

The teams laid down their masterpieces and cast sideways looks at their rivals' creations, all of which looked rather vulnerable set on the turf.

The Rotaract lady declared the 'skies open' and immediately the atmosphere changed from sedate charm to naked competitiveness. Knots of malicious youths cranked up the aggro from the sidelines with helpful comments such as 'All you gon need helicopter to get dat one up'. Presumably this was aimed at teams from other schools.

'Some of these will never have been in the air before,' said Clara.

'What? No test run?' said Becky.

'They don't often have enough room where they live.'

There were a few near-disasters, though from the reaction of the spectators this was what they wanted to see; had all five kites flown immediately there would have been little humorous tension.

One group of young boys charged along the grass pulling their kite, accompanied by confused shouts and conflicting instructions, while their stouter companions tugged desperately at the other end of the nylon line. For a moment the great structure seemed to hover on the edge of rising airborne but the brave endeavour ended as a sad jigsaw of balsa and bamboo.

Three of the kites did eventually make it into the air and the winning team, whose kite was almost twenty feet long, drew the largest applause of the day when Matthew presented them with the giant trophy.

It was all huge fun.

Becky wondered what happened now as she watched the photographer attempt the near-impossible task of getting the winning team and their kite all in one picture.

'Can I get you a drink?'

Becky started. She hadn't heard Matthew approach and was surprised he wasn't still needed for official photographs.

'I'd love a coke,' said Clara. 'And I'm sure Becky would like something too.'

'I'll give you a hand,' said Becky. It would be good to stretch her legs even if it did mean a few minutes in Matthew's company. Despite being all smiles when handing out the trophies he was looking serious now.

'Were you bored?' he asked, as they walked towards a drinks stall.

'Not at all. And as far as I could see it was very successful. I can't imagine most children in Britain being this well turned out. I've never seen so many school uniforms.'

'But that's the problem,' said Matthew. 'It's just children. You can always tell when a tradition is declining because all that's left is the children.'

'What do you mean?'

'You have Maypole Dancing in England, right?'

'I suppose so. Our school never went in for it but –'

'Exactly. I mention Maypole Dancing and you immediately think in terms of schools and children.'

'What's wrong with that?'

He looked at her. 'It's a fertility rite, isn't it? So it wouldn't have been children doing it, at least not in the days when it meant something.'

Becky had no idea what to say to that – and felt slightly awkward discussing fertility rites with Matthew – but she was saved from having to reply by a chorus of wolf whistles. They came from the group of men Richard was with, who sprawled on their seats looking good-naturedly tight though no beer was evident.

'Hey Becky, ecky-Becky,' called Richard, cheerfully.

Becky smiled and gave a wave. The men waved back, grinning. 'Ecky-Becky,' they chorused.

'Hey Matthew,' one of them called out. 'I hear you're living the high life. Sitting in the front row now.'

Matthew either didn't hear or chose to ignore the comment.

He carried on walking and the group retreated into angry whispers, their previously cheerful dispositions turning sullen.

Matthew forged ahead and Becky had a job catching up with him. 'That was a bit unfriendly,' she said, as she joined him at the stall.

'Yes, they were.'

'I meant you.'

Matthew ordered three cokes and didn't respond until he had completed the transaction and they were headed back to Clara. 'You don't know what they were saying.'

'They were just playing with my name and I'm not worried about it.'

'No, you don't understand,' snapped Matthew although he obviously had no intention of giving her an explanation.

Becky sipped her drink and mentally counted to ten. It had been such a pleasant afternoon. Why did Matthew have to spoil everything?

Chapter Eleven

Becky slept late on Monday morning and when she came down Matthew and Alex had already left for the day. Clara was not down yet either. The sleepless night on Saturday and the afternoon out yesterday had probably caught up with her too. Becky took her breakfast into the dining room and found Maureen there, polishing the table.

'Hi,' said Maureen. 'I'll have a look for the laptop as soon as I've done my chores.'

'That's fine.' Becky felt a bit guilty about adding to Maureen's workload. 'You know I'm happy to help you search.'

Maureen shook her head. 'Matthew's quite particular about who goes into certain parts of the house.' Becky could believe that.

Maureen stopped polishing. 'Cook told me about the Mad Bulls.'

'Oh, yes it was horrible,' said Becky. 'We got no sleep at all until Matthew and I pulled them down.'

'Who would do such a thing?'

'Kids presumably,' said Becky. 'They probably didn't intend to disturb our sleep. Maybe just some boys having a competition. You know, whose kite could stay up overnight.'

'Uh huh,' said Maureen. 'So these kites were home-made?'

'No, they were shop bought. Though they'd been – customised.'

'Uh huh,' said Maureen, again and resumed her polishing.

'You think it was intentional,' said Becky. That might explain why Matthew had been in such a bad mood yesterday. 'Can I ask you something else?'

'Sure.'

'Is "ecky" a bad word?'

Maureen frowned. 'Ecky? No, I don't think so.'

'It doesn't mean anything, I don't know, sexual?'

'Not that I know of. Why?'

'When we were at the kite competition yesterday some men called out "Ecky-Becky" to me. I thought they were just being friendly but Matthew got quite annoyed. I thought maybe they'd insulted me.'

Maureen looked at her unsmilingly. 'They weren't insulting you.'

'So if someone shouted "Ecky-Becky" at you, you wouldn't be insulted?'

'If someone was so stupid to say that to me I'd ask him why God bothered putting eyes in his head,' said Maureen, picking up the duster and polish and heading for the door. She paused on her way out. 'They weren't insulting you.'

Becky took her coffee on to the cool veranda feeling even more confused than before. It was like she had been given a puzzle to put together by people who had deliberately removed the key pieces. Exasperated she looked out over the yard towards the now-very-well-tended garden.

There was a strange discolouration on the gravel – a little patch of red or brown. And another, and another – each one nearer the house. Becky leaned over the balustrade. There on the bottom step sat Pitcher, minus his floppy Fedora. His feet were bare and he was clutching his right leg. As she headed down the steps to see if he was all right he turned and Becky could see his shin through his torn trousers. She stifled a desire to scream and forced herself to speak quietly.

'That looks a bit nasty, Pitcher. No, no, sit down –' He was starting to lever himself up. 'Stay right there. I'll get some help.'

Becky ran into the house and shouted for Maureen who came running from the kitchen, closely followed by Cook. Clara appeared at the top of the stairs.

'It's Pitcher,' said Becky. 'He's put a hoe or something through his shin. It looks pretty bad.'

'I'll go check,' said Maureen heading out the front door. Becky waited at the foot of the stairs for Clara to come down. 'We need antiseptic,' she said. 'And something we can use as a bandage.'

'I'll fetch the witch hazel, said Cook, heading back to the kitchen.

A minute later Pitcher was surrounded by four clucking and concerned women.

'Why you don't take more care?' grumbled Cook, handing Becky a bottle of witch hazel and a tea towel. Becky gingerly placed the makeshift bandage over the massive gash on Pitcher's leg. She still thought a proper antiseptic would be better but Cook had resolutely held forth the witch hazel.

'Oh Pitcher,' said Clara. 'How did you do that?'

Pitcher made a hacking or chopping gesture with his right hand.

'He needs stitches,' said Maureen.

'And a tetanus injection,' said Clara.

'He needs to go to hospital,' said Becky.

Pitcher started to fidget, craning his head to look at Clara and shaking it.

'It's all right Pitcher,' said Clara. To Becky she said more quietly, 'The hospital is miles from here. He's not happy being away that long.'

'How about the clinic in Speightstown?' said Maureen.

Ten minutes later Clara was driving Becky and Pitcher along the little roads to the clinic, Pitcher half-lying across the backseat and repeatedly having to be reminded to keep the tea towel over the wound.

The clinic was a small, white one-storey building with a negligible car park, the few marked spaces already being occupied.

'I'm going to have to park down the hill,' said Clara. 'Can you take Pitcher in? I don't want to make him walk more than he has to.'

Pitcher needed some persuading to get out of the car and looked bereft when Clara drove away. Still, at Becky's urging, he limped beside her into the building, his bare feet seemingly impervious to the baking ground.

'Your name,' said the Bajan receptionist.

'It's not me that needs attention,' said Becky. 'It's this gentleman whose name is Pitcher.' She looked at him. 'I don't know your first name. What is it?'

'Pitcher.'

'No, that's your second name. What's your first name?'

'Pitcher.'

'Give me *your* name,' said the receptionist.

'Becky Thomson.'

'Another Thomson,' the receptionist said as she wrote it down. 'Quite a few of you around.'

'It's a common enough name,' said Becky, wondering if the process would still be this slow if Pitcher was screaming blue murder instead of standing mute behind her.

'Your address?'

'I'm from England. But I'm staying …' Becky realised with some embarrassment she didn't know the exact address, let alone where Pitcher lived. 'It's a house called Copper Mill in St Lucy.'

This must have been sufficient information because the receptionist nodded and wrote that down.

‘We’re not sure what he’s done to himself,’ said Becky. ‘He’s a gardener and it looks like he’s caught his shin with a hoe or maybe even a machete. He was bleeding quite badly. We’ve managed to stop it.’

‘OK,’ said the receptionist. ‘Why are you here?’

‘I’m just helping him get some attention.’ Becky emphasised the word ‘attention’ as Pitcher seemed to be receiving so little of it.

‘No, but why are you here?’

Becky sensed nothing was going to happen until she was more forthcoming about why she was in Barbados. ‘I’m researching family history. I’m staying with the Darnleys at Copper Mill where this gentleman works as a gardener.’

The receptionist looked confused. ‘I mean why are you here today? Are you a relation of his?’

‘Oh.’ Becky realised what she meant. ‘Let’s just say I’m a friend of the family. Look, his wound is really serious.’

‘Wait there,’ said the receptionist, pointing at some plastic chairs. ‘He’ll be seen next.’ She picked up a phone and Becky overheard her and Pitcher’s names being mentioned; hopefully the urgency of the situation was being conveyed to a doctor or nurse.

Becky helped Pitcher to a seat and looked around the room, relieved that it seemed less crowded than the average A&E at home. A few Bajans regarded her with curiosity and an elderly lady came quite close to have a look at Pitcher’s leg. She winced, sucked air and returned to her seat.

Pitcher looked at his shin but made no fuss about the terrible wound. His slightly agitated gestures of looking around and tugging at his clothes seemed more to do with being in unfamiliar surroundings than the appalling pain he must be feeling. Becky realised she was holding the blood-soaked tea towel. She couldn’t remember when it had fallen off Pitcher's leg and she'd had to pick it up; presumably it was too dirty now to reapply to the gash.

A door off the waiting room opened and an Indian-looking nurse came out. 'Pitcher,' she called, so quietly Becky could barely hear her.

'Come on,' said Becky to Pitcher, wincing as the effort of levering himself up reopened the wound and blood started running down his leg. He limped beside her into a bright room where the forty-something nurse took one look at them and put her hand to her mouth.

'I'm hoping it looks worse than it is,' said Becky, trying not to be put off by the nurse's unfriendly expression. 'He's a gardener and he's probably caught his leg with a rusty hoe or something.' She emphasised the 'rusty hoe' in case the nurse thought she was some wild tourist who had mown him down in a car.

The nurse led Pitcher to a stretcher bed and Becky sat on a chair in the corner and watched her fuss around him. The immediate treatment seemed to consist of scolding Pitcher for being careless. The Indian nurse felt his arm through his flayed sleeve and made an irritated sound. 'You're too thin, man. You drink too much, right?'

Pitcher nodded.

'And you don't eat enough. Am I right?'

Pitcher shook his head then nodded.

The nurse made another irritated sound and walked out.

Becky was a little nonplussed by this behaviour. She wondered where the nurse actually came from; her accent was not Bajan but it had a West Indian sing-song lilt despite her appearance. Her name badge said 'Sairah', which also sounded more Indian than Caribbean.

The nurse came back in carrying a Tupperware box. She opened it, extracted something in pastry – a samosa or a patty – and handed it to Pitcher.

'Eat.'

Pitcher obediently took it and started munching. Becky suddenly felt a ridiculous desire to cry; the nurse had just given Pitcher some of her own lunch. Whether she thought food was urgently required or that it would distract Pitcher from the pain of having his wound cleaned it was a wonderful gesture of compassion.

'I don't suppose you know if you've been fully vaccinated against tetanus?' the nurse asked him.

'Don't know,' said Pitcher, not taking his eyes off her.

'Clara, his employer, said he would need a booster,' said Becky.

'Right, I'll give you an injection in a minute. Don't stop eating.'

The nurse looked at Becky and then quickly away. 'I hear you're over from England.'

'Yes.'

'Researching family history, I'm told.'

Becky nodded.

'Any family in particular?'

'People who originally came from England.' Becky did not want to be more specific, knowing that the Redlegs were a potentially touchy subject, though she was hoping this would be her chance to find out a bit more from Pitcher.

'Any sisters or brothers?'

'I'm afraid I don't know anything about Pitcher's family.'

'I meant you.'

'Oh,' said Becky, surprised. 'I have a younger brother.'

'And he is over here?'

'No, just me.'

The nurse nodded then kneeled down to clean Pitcher's wound, occasionally muttering to herself. A few minutes later she stood up, threw the bloodied wipes and her gloves into a plastic container and looked at Becky.

'I'm going to have to give this man an injection and some stitches. You'd better wait outside.'

Becky wasn't particularly squeamish but she was relieved to have an excuse to leave. Something about the nurse was making her feel uncomfortable.

She was pleased to see Clara sitting in the waiting room.

'Is Pitcher OK?' Clara asked. 'I expected more fuss from him.'

'Actually, he's very brave. I'd have been screaming my head off but he's just sitting there quietly. The nurse has given him some of her lunch.'

'Oh,' said Clara. 'If she's managed to get him to eat something she's done better than me and Cook all these years.'

'They seemed more interested in my details than his when we came in,' said Becky. 'Which was just as well because I realised I didn't know his first name nor his address nor whether he has any family.'

Clara looked at her. 'How could you know? *We* don't even know his first name. He lives about half a mile from our house. I guess he's in his forties.'

'Married?'

'No.'

'So that's the end of the Pitcher line?' Becky realised she sounded disappointed.

Clara looked surprised but smiled. 'I've no idea if he has children. But he has brothers and sisters with family so, no, it's not the end of the Pitcher line.'

Becky was pleased to hear that. 'I'm curious as to where the nurse comes from. Her name badge says S-A-I-R-A-H. Is that Indian? I can't place her accent. Not Bajan.'

'I'll have a listen when they come out.'

Another twenty minutes passed before the door to the treatment room opened again. Pitcher seemed reluctant to leave so in the end the nurse walked out ahead of him and he followed.

'You need to come back in three days to have your bandage changed,' she told him. 'And then you'll come back again next week.'

'She's from Trinidad,' whispered Clara to Becky.

Pitcher was nodding at the nurse's words.

'And you need to rest for a few days. No walking around,' – the nurse banged two fists together to demonstrate – 'causes too much impact.'

Pitcher looked down at his feet and nodded.

'And make sure you don't drink too much and that you eat properly.'

Becky couldn't imagine Pitcher was taking any of this in, though he seemed to be listening intently. The nurse handed him a packet of pills and a note. 'Antibiotics. Take one pill every day. You understand me?'

Pitcher nodded.

'You have to come back. I've written down the dates I need to see you.' With that she gave Becky another unfriendly look and walked back through the treatment room door.

'Oh dear,' murmured Clara to Becky. 'I don't think she understands. I'll try and get that note off him later. Heaven knows if he'll remember to take his antibiotics.'

Becky waited with Pitcher outside while Clara went to retrieve her car. Now his leg had been treated, and he was hopefully in less pain, this was the perfect opportunity to talk to him about his history but Becky was not optimistic.

'Pitcher,' she said. 'Do you know where I come from?'

'England,' he said after a moment.

So far, so good. 'Do you know where your ancestors came from?'

Pitcher swayed.

'I mean your original family. Do you know where they came from?'

Nothing. Becky began to worry that Clara would be back with the car before she had learnt anything.

'England?' tried Pitcher, eventually.

'Yes, your ancestors came from England.'

Pitcher greeted the news without interest but just unfolded and refolded the note the nurse had given him and shook the packet of antibiotics as if to see what sound they'd make. Becky decided not to push it. Poor Pitcher had probably had enough strangeness today.

'I have to come back here,' he said, looking at the clinic. It was the longest sentence Becky had heard him say and she noted his heavy Bajan accent was on a par with Cook's.

'Yes, in a couple of days,' said Becky.

'T'ree days,' corrected Pitcher. 'T'ree days.'

Clara pulled up and Becky got Pitcher settled with his legs extended across the backseat again before getting in herself.

'All right, Pitcher?' asked Clara. 'Soon be back home. You've been away for a while, haven't you?'

'Yes,' he murmured and looked out of the window. As Clara drove away his lips carried on moving and Becky craned her neck to hear what he was saying.

'We backed the wrong King.'

She felt a spike of adrenaline. Pitcher might be able to help her after all.

Chapter Twelve

Clara was tired after their trip to the clinic in Speightstown and went up to her room straight after lunch for a lie-down so Becky joined Cook and Maureen in the kitchen.

'I can't find that laptop,' said Maureen.

'Thanks for looking,' said Becky, disappointed but not surprised. She would have to go back to Matthew.

Maureen and Cook wanted to know how Pitcher had got on at the clinic. Becky tried to give a full description, including the nurse's evident compassion towards Pitcher, while leaving out her less-than-friendly attitude towards herself.

Cook nodded sagely. 'She right. Pitcher don't eat enough.'

Before long Zena arrived with her childminder and must have expended some energy in the morning for the three year old seemed sleepy today and was content to sit on Becky's lap while the adults continued talking. The conversation turned to Francesca.

'Why did her husband leave her?' asked Cook.

'Well –' whispered Maureen and Cook and Becky leaned forward.

At that moment Matthew walked into the kitchen. It was earlier than he usually came home to shower before going out for the evening and he had changed back into his habitual black shorts. He looked surprised to see the three women huddled together like a coven. They straightened up guiltily.

‘I was looking for –’ He noticed Zena asleep in Becky’s arms. ‘Are you a childminder as well as a part-time gardener now?’

Becky half-nodded, trying not to look at him in his half-naked state.

Matthew turned to Cook. ‘Am I allowed to make coffee or is this women-only space? I should add that it’s an emergency as Alex has fallen asleep and I need him awake.’

Becky laughed. ‘Poor Alex. I’ll bring some out.’

‘Thank you,’ said Matthew and left.

Becky handed Zena to Maureen and made the coffee.

She found Matthew and Alex in their usual spot on the veranda.

‘That’s great,’ said Matthew as she set the cafetière and cups down on the table. He shot an impatient look at Alex, who was dozing soundly in his seat, then turned the same impatient glare on Becky.

‘Just when are you and my mother going to start working on her Monmouth rebels project?’ he said.

Becky picked up the accusing tone. She was well aware that money was being paid into her bank account in the UK and at a very good rate considering her daily tasks amounted to a little gardening and some unofficial childminding.

‘What can I do, Matthew?’ she said. ‘I’m happy to start the book whenever Clara wants. It’s not like I’m trying to put her off. Quite the reverse in fact.’

She was confused. It was Clara who had wanted Becky to come over and write the book that Matthew didn’t seem to want written, but now that she was here Matthew wanted her to start the book and Clara didn’t seem interested. Baffling.

‘I wasn’t implying you were trying to get out of it,’ he said. ‘And I know how obsessed she is with gardening. I’m just not sure she should be spending hours in the sun. She's not as robust as she looks.'

If he'd just stay home a few evenings, Becky thought acidly, instead of cavorting with a newly divorced woman, he could speak to Clara about it himself. But his concern was justified. Becky had noticed that Clara's siestas were getting longer.

'On the subject of the project,' she said. 'Maureen can't find the laptop. I really could do with one.'

Matthew nodded. 'I'll take care of it. But I don't understand why you can't start working now. My mother said something about going through notes.'

'I thought maybe we could work on the book in the evenings,' Becky said. 'But –' She wondered how to put this delicately.

'Her friends keep dropping by?' said Matthew.

'Yes.'

'So how do you spend the evenings?' asked Matthew.

He was staring at her. Maybe he was trying to picture her playing bridge and sharing island gossip. 'I have company.' She did not need to tell him she preferred being with Cook in the kitchen.

He looked again at the slumbering Alex and growled, 'I hope it's strong.' He nodded at the cafetière.

'He doesn't get enough sleep,' said Becky.

'Rubbish,' said Matthew pressing the plunger and pouring two cups. He looked at her. 'Do you really think so? Or are you assuming that because he's fallen asleep now? I should add that if you'd just read the new American health and safety guidelines for tourists too stupid to stand *inside* the railings of their hotel balcony unless there's a big notice telling them to, well, you'd be asleep as well.'

'OK,' said Becky. She had probably overstepped the mark in implying that Matthew overworked his right-hand man but she didn't regret saying it.

Alex woke up with a start and murmured some apologies.

'Becky says you don't get enough sleep,' said Matthew, pushing a cup of coffee towards him.

'She's right,' said Alex, wiping his hands over his face. 'I don't mind the day job. It's having to entertain in the evenings that's finishing me off.'

'Oh, well, I hate that too,' said Matthew taking a sip of his own coffee.

Becky was unsure quite what they meant by 'entertaining'. A very odd vision of the two men and a woman called Francesca popped into her mind.

She was heading back inside the house when Matthew spoke again. 'Tonight, you'll come too.'

'That's a great idea,' said Alex, brightening up at the prospect. 'She'll be good.'

'What will I be good at?' asked Becky. She didn't think they were talking about lap dancing but even so.

'It's the time of year when travel companies choose the hotels to put in their brochures for next year,' explained Matthew. 'But of course they can't just come and check our hotel. They have to stay there – free – for a few days and get as much out of us as possible. We have to bribe them with drink and food and witty conversation.'

Of course, thought Becky: Matthew hated freeloaders. But maybe this meant he wasn't spending his evenings with a woman called Francesca.

'You can take care of the witty conversation,' he added.

'Oh no,' said Becky. 'Really, I wouldn't be good at that.'

'Yes, you would,' said Alex.

'And I haven't got anything to wear,' protested Becky.

'We have a great boutique in the hotel,' said Alex. 'Selling dresses for the casinos. There's bound to be –'

'Can I see what you've brought along?' said Matthew, standing abruptly.

Becky nodded and led the way up the stairs to her room, conscious of him padding behind her in his bare feet. Part of her felt she should have told him to keep his nose out of her space but she also knew that he would take one look at what she'd brought and realise she was not the right woman for this mission.

It took more than one look. Matthew examined her clothes with great attention, extricating individual items on hangers and holding them up, sometimes rubbing the material between his fingers. He looked puzzled as if he had been expecting something different. Becky felt a little uncomfortable. It was a bizarrely intimate action. But at least it was affirming what she had said: she really had nothing to wear. Apart from the business suit she'd worn on the flight over all her clothes were inexpensive and practical, chosen for a hot climate. There was not a single thing that could be described as 'sophisticated'.

Matthew put back the last item, closed the cupboard door and frowned. 'We'll have to leave a bit earlier so you have a chance to find a dress.'

Becky backed towards the door. 'Can we have this conversation outside, please?' His barely dressed presence seemed to sucking all the energy out of the room.

'Yes, of course.' Matthew appeared to realise their over-intimate situation too. 'Let's go back downstairs.'

Alex gave them a grin when they reappeared on the veranda. 'Sorted?' he asked.

'Not quite,' said Matthew, looking Becky up and down as if already mentally fitting her out in a dress. 'But if we leave at five we'll have time to choose a dress and get changed.'

'Five o' clock?' said Becky, anxiously. It was four now. 'I want a shower first.'

'Fine,' said Matthew. But don't worry about what you wear. You'll change at the hotel.'

'But –'

'No buts,' said Matthew. 'I'm buying the dress.'

Alex seemed to understand what was worrying Becky. 'It's just drinks with some pompous people, followed by dinner with the same pompous people and then coffee with the same pompous people.'

Becky smiled. 'OK. But I warn you, I'm not –' She looked for the right word.

'Neither are we,' said Alex.

'Anyway,' said Matthew. 'You've been here for weeks. Have you been out anywhere? Apart from the kite competition.'

'We went to the cinema. And there was one trip to Bridgetown with Alex but that was for research. Oh and we took Pitcher to the clinic.'

'I heard about Pitcher,' said Matthew. 'Thanks for helping take care of him.' He frowned. 'So your only real outing has been to the cinema?'

Becky nodded.

'High time you had a night out then.'

'Yes, it is. Thank you,' said Becky. She was baffled by Matthew's seeming change of attitude but assumed this was really about business. However, if he thought she could discuss the effect of quantitative easing on the global travel industry or make similar conversation she was going to fall very short of his expectations.

It was with some trepidation that Becky climbed into the passenger seat of Matthew's Nissan Sedan about an hour later. Matthew, who must have quickly showered and donned a crisp short-sleeved shirt and smart trousers, hung up his jacket and tie on the side bar of the car and got behind the wheel. Alex was driving his own car and Becky half wished she had his easy company for the journey instead of Matthew's.

They drove in silence though Becky suspected this was due to Matthew running through checklists and chores in his mind rather than because he was struggling to find things to say. In fact he'd probably forgotten she was in the passenger seat. It was time to remind him.

'Is tonight particularly important?' she asked.

There was a pause as if he were looking for somewhere to save a thought for retrieval later. 'Very. The biggest travel company in the UK. But of course they aren't sending over their salaried staff to examine the hotel. The chairman himself is coming – a Lord, no less – and bringing his retinue.'

'Ah,' said Becky. 'Freeloaders.'

Matthew looked puzzled. Becky wondered if he remembered using that very word about her and Ian.

'I wouldn't mind if they knew what they were doing. But they won't even bother to check a sample of the guest rooms or find out about the local transport. They just want to stay in the most exclusive suites and be chauffeured to the sights round the island. Anyway, I'm sure they'll like *you*.'

Becky didn't ask any more questions after that. She was wondering if Matthew had brought her along because he thought that being freeloaders they would sense a mutual trait in one another and swap tips on how to scrounge.

After another twenty minutes Becky saw a sign for the 'Monmouth Hotel' and Matthew turned left on to a drive which was in better condition than the roads on which they had just travelled. The hotel was a grand white stone building with crenellated walls and mock towers. Becky had expected it to be located by a calm blue sea and was surprised when they got out of the car that she could hear the water pounding the beach like a wild drummer. She looked over a low wall to the side of the car park to see waves making their own white-knuckle rides on to the beach, breaking furiously over the sand. To breathe was to taste the sea.

‘This is the east side of the island,’ said Matthew, sweeping the horizon with his jacket. ‘The wild side of the Atlantic.’

‘Oh yes,’ said Becky, taking in a deep salty breath and feeling very alive. ‘I’d read that the west coast was tamer.’

‘The west coast is for wimps,’ said Matthew with a slight smile. ‘Though I mustn’t be too disparaging of the sunbathing crowd. I’ll be building a hotel on that side when I get the land.’

Becky remembered what Richard Carrington had said at the airport: the land for Matthew’s new hotel must have been what he was referring to.

Alex pulled up next to Matthew’s Nissan and got out but before he could say anything both his and Matthew’s mobiles went off simultaneously. Becky had to jog behind the two men as they marched towards the white building, each with his head inclined towards his phone.

Matthew ended his call with what Becky took to be a French blasphemy and glared at Alex, who had just finished his own call more quietly.

‘Lord Fotheringham arrived early,’ said Matthew. ‘He’s already complained to one of his directors *in England* who then has to ring me to pass on the complaint.’ He looked accusingly at Alex. ‘Who did you put on reception? Please tell me it wasn’t Caroline.’

Alex groaned. ‘Sorry, I completely forgot to get one of the senior receptionists. I think it is Caroline’s shift.’

‘Go and check what’s happened,’ ordered Matthew. ‘And then take Becky to find a dress. Get a bandage gown – a Léger, not a cheap one. Black or midnight blue.’ He turned on his heel and walked off. He was not happy.

Becky had no idea what a ‘Léger’ bandage gown was and was about to unleash a torrent of annoyance at Matthew’s bossiness but stopped when she saw Alex’s stressed face: dresses were not the first thing on his mind.

'Our receptionists can deal with famous people, rich people, normal people – pretty much anyone,' he said, 'but they aren't used to titles.'

She could see how Alex forgot his tasks. In the short walk to the reception desk he was stopped twice by members of staff telling him of late deliveries of food and problems with the air-conditioning in the dining room and then his mobile rang again. He said 'Hello', switched to French and issued some instructions. 'Tour group arriving from France,' he explained to Becky as he ended the call.

She followed him to the reception desk where a cheerful young woman was dealing with guests. She had a sunny smile and a particularly sing-song Bajan accent.

'The trouble,' Alex said quietly to Becky, 'is that a lot of the old calypso stars are called Lord this or Lord that. You know, they have to have fancy names. If you were in Trinidad at carnival time you'd think you were surrounded by aristocracy.'

Becky nodded. She didn't really know what he meant but didn't want to add to his burdens by asking for an explanation. When the young receptionist had finished telling guests about the floor shows planned for that evening she grinned at Alex.

'Hi Caroline,' he said. 'Now were you on the desk when Lord Fotheringham arrived?'

'Lord Fotheringham. Lord!' Caroline laughed and did a little jig behind the desk. 'Silly man,' she said. 'Couldn't even get his own name right. I had to ask him three times. And he was getting annoyed with *me*.'

'Oh God,' said Alex, weakly. 'Can I have look at the booking?' He walked behind the reception desk, checked the screen and closed his eyes briefly with a 'Beam me up, Scotty' look of desperation.

'Is that wrong?' said Caroline, frowning.

Alex pointed at the screen. 'Lord' should be in the title field not in the forename field. Just leave the forename field blank.'

'Oh,' said Caroline doubtfully, as though she wasn't sure Alex had got that right. She typed in the details then did another little jig.

'Um, did you do that dance in front of him?'

'Yes,' said Caroline, cheerfully. 'I told him I hadn't seen many white calypsonians.'

'Oh God,' said Alex, again. 'We can expect trouble later.'

He nodded to Becky and she followed him to a boutique further down the corridor. The sides of the boutique were glass, enticing hotel guests to gaze within as they walked past. While Alex talked to the very elegant woman in charge, Becky watched as casually dressed or swimsuit-clad guests slowed their pace when they passed – their eyes drawn to the gorgeous suits and dresses hung in tiers within. As for the prices, a few simple dresses had a price tag in triple figure dollars but most of them were over a thousand dollars. Becky felt herself getting annoyed. She could see the forlorn looks of the casually dressed women as they wandered by, glancing greedily at the sort of clothes the femme fatale in a James Bond movie would wear. No doubt some of these holidaymakers had already overextended themselves paying for a Caribbean holiday. Now they were to be made ashamed of their perfectly reasonable holiday attire. No wonder Matthew Darnley had made it in business.

'So it's to be a Léger?' asked the lady. 'Yes, I can see that would suit you.'

'I'm afraid I have no idea what a Léger is,' said Becky.

The woman waved a slender arm dismissively. 'It's just a French fashion house. We have a few of their dresses. So you want dark blue or black.' She took a few dresses off a rack and, after holding them up and darting critical looks at each dress then Becky's body, she handed her a black, sleeveless gown and showed her to a changing room. Becky almost gasped at the thought of getting into something so stylish. The trouble was, if she slithered into that black number, she would need a new bra, new shoes and a new handbag. And probably a new personality.

A few minutes later Becky was staring at herself in the mirror, trying to imagine what she'd look like if white bra straps weren't creeping from under the thin halters and if she wasn't wearing scuffed slingbacks. Thank heavens she'd shaved her legs.

The shop woman stuck her head between the curtains, made an appraising sound in her throat and smiled. 'Bra size?'

'36C'

'Shoe size?'

'Six.'

The curtains closed abruptly and reopened within seconds. A packaged black bra with the thinnest straps was handed to Becky, along with some black shoes, not high-heeled but very elegant.

This time Becky did not recognise herself in the mirror. When she came out the shop assistant looked very satisfied with her choice. 'You're beautiful,' she said.

'What do you think, Alex?' asked Becky.

He looked staggered. 'Um, definitely. Yes, definitely.'

She left him paying for the purchases, presumably with a company credit card, while she changed back into her own clothes. When she reappeared he was clutching several bags and looking a little shell-shocked.

'Right,' he said, hurriedly. 'We haven't much time so I'll show you a room where you can change.'

Becky thanked the assistant and followed Alex out of the main hotel complex to a smaller building set just behind it.

'That dress cost over three thousand dollars,' she said.

‘Prices look worse in Barbadian dollars.’

‘Do you have a wife, Alex?’

‘Three demanding children and a less-demanding wife though I’m ashamed to say I’ve never bought her anything that cost even half the price of this dress.’

He let her into a basic but light-filled apartment. ‘Matthew and I use this to freshen up but hopefully it will be clean. Fresh towels in the cupboards if you need them. I’ll be outside in twenty minutes.’

Twenty minutes later Becky walked out to find Alex popping mints in his mouth and wiping bloodshot eyes. She suspected he’d taken some Dutch courage. He led her into a reception room where a stiff-necked group of suited men were standing with drinks and looking uncomfortable. Matthew – now dressed to kill, or at least dressed as if he were licensed to kill – looked up as Alex and Becky walked in. He nodded at her, though whether this was in greeting or approval of her appearance Becky couldn’t tell. She noticed heads turning and staring at her and saw – with surprise and amusement – that men were starting to stand more upright, fiddling with their ties and checking their collars were patted down. She was not fooled: it was the dress and nothing more. She also noticed – with some discomfort – that she was the only woman in the room.

Only one head didn’t turn, a plump man in his sixties who looked like he was haranguing the hotel owner, so Becky was less than thrilled to see Matthew wave her and Alex over.

‘I don’t call an eight-hour flight “a hop-away from the UK” so I think you’re on a sticky wicket saying –’

‘Lord Fotheringham,’ Matthew interrupted. ‘I’d like you to meet Becky Thomson. Becky is in Barbados for a few months helping my mother write a history book. Becky, I’ll get you a drink.’

Becky was not fooled by the gracious introduction. Matthew was clearly bored of listening to the man’s bellyaching and using the excuse of getting her a drink to dump Lord Fotheringham on her and Alex.

'Good evening, Lord Fotheringham,' said Alex. 'I'm Alex Wilson, the manager of the hotel.'

'Humphhh,' said Fotheringham, clearly miffed that the prime target of his complaints had got away. His eyes wandered between Alex and Becky, as if he was wondering who would be more receptive to his opinions. 'Well, I'm not impressed with a hotel that can't even get the checking-in procedure right. That doesn't bode well for the rest of the holiday.'

'I'm sorry to hear that,' said Alex.

'The girl on reception –' Fotheringham sniffed his wine distastefully and chanced a small sip, as though it might disagree with him later, 'couldn't even get my name right. How many times do I need to say it's Lord Fotheringham. Lord. Lord. She still couldn't get it.' He must have sensed Becky's lack of emotional engagement as he gave her a very hard stare and said, 'Don't you think that's abysmal?'

Becky was starting to feel Matthew was treating her like an escort girl brought along as eye candy to soak up the whinges of pompous old men. She had had enough.

'I suppose being a lord is like being a lady,' she said. 'If you have to say you are, you aren't.'

Lord Fotheringham's jaw dropped. He glared at her and then at the ground. Becky thought he was trying to work out precisely how insulted he was. Alex turned pale and Matthew, who was on his way over holding a triangle of drinks, froze. Oh God. Where on earth had that comment come from?

Matthew quietly put the drinks he was carrying down on a table and walked very quickly through a door behind the little bar area. Seconds later there was a muffled roar from the other side of the door: a strange sound – it could have been despair or anger, Becky didn't know. She was too busy watching Fotheringham's face turn angina red. Then he gave a hoot of laughter.

'Being a lord is like being a lady – damn, I wish my wife was alive. She'd have loved that. Now I've no one to share it with.'

Matthew returned expressionless and led them into the dining room,

Lord Fotheringham pointed at Becky. 'Please put me next to *her*.'

Several hours later, having changed back into her old clothes, Becky relaxed into the passenger seat of Matthew's car. The evening had actually gone quite well. She was less sure how Alex had got on as she had noticed him struggling to make conversation with the men on either side of him. Matthew handled small talk with practised ease, even though she suspected his heart wasn't in it, but ironically she had fared the best. Lord Fotheringham had been a thoughtful dinner companion, interested in the book that Becky was (supposedly) co-authoring and in her views on the island.

She sensed a more relaxed Matthew beside her, handling the car lightly as though he didn't even need the headlamps that were the only light on the dark, twisting little roads.

'Fotheringham rather took to you,' he said. 'He was hanging on to your every word.'

'He wasn't so bad,' said Becky. 'I think he's lonely since his wife died. That's probably why he complains so much.'

'I heard a few of the things you were telling him,' said Matthew, sounding slightly puzzled. 'You seem to know quite a bit about the island.'

'My father spent some time travelling,' said Becky. 'He particularly loved Barbados.'

'He must be pleased that you're over here?'

Becky searched for an answer that was true but unrevealing. 'The last time I saw him was over twelve years ago.'

'I'm sorry. That sounds complicated.'

'It is but never mind. Why did you go out of the room? I mean after I made the lord and lady gaffe?'

'For a start it wasn't a gaffe. As for why I went out –' He chuckled. 'I don't always have the most appropriate sense of humour.'

'You were laughing?'

'Obviously. What did you think I was doing out there?' He chuckled again. 'Arthur – the man behind the bar – overheard your lord and lady putdown so it will be all round the island soon. They'll probably want to stick your face on the currency.'

It did not seem to take so long to get back to Copper Mill as on the outward journey and before Becky knew it Matthew was parking in front of the house.

'Thank you for tonight,' he said. 'If you don't mind we'll do it again.'

'OK,' she said, 'unless of course Clara needs me.'

He opened his door to get out and the plaintive soundtrack of hidden little creatures filled the car. Becky got out too and looked around her.

'It took me a while to work out why those little frogs make that forlorn sound,' she said. 'I suppose they're calling for a companion.'

'There you go again,' said Matthew. 'How do you know that? Most people don't guess that sound comes from frogs.'

'But I don't know what they look like,' said Becky.

'One day I'll find you one and show you. If he sees you maybe his whistling will become more cheerful.'

Becky glanced across at Matthew, no more than a dark silhouette in front of the lights up on the veranda. Had he just paid her a compliment?

He looked up at a fat smudge of white in the sky. 'Soon be a full moon –'

Was he about to say something romantic?

'Which means Casino Nights at the hotel.'

She should have known better. 'What are Casino Nights?' she said, wondering what gambling had to do with a full moon.

'You'll see,' he said. 'Fortunately, you have the perfect dress for it.'

He laughed mysteriously and let her go ahead of him up the steps to the veranda. They swapped goodnights on the doorstep and Becky headed up to her room. She heard the military drill of the bolts being drawn across the front door and the incongruous tune of the alarm being set.

Chapter Thirteen

'Matthew told me that you were quite a hit with a lord last night,' said Clara, before popping one of Cook's amazing plantain fritters into her mouth. They were having lunch on the veranda where they could survey their work on the garden.

It had been a morning of fairly light pruning. There really was not much left to be done, which was just as well as Clara's energy had faded after the first hour, leaving her to direct Becky's activities from the veranda steps.

'Oh, Lord Fotheringham. We just chatted,' said Becky, embarrassed. 'In fact he was asking me about the book. Your book.'

'Was he?'

'Yes he was very interested in the subject. Clara,' Becky hesitated, 'if you don't mind me saying, are you scared of starting this – project?'

Clara put her fork down and looked thoughtfully at her plate. 'Whatever makes you say that?'

'Well, it's just that when you've planned for years to do something, when it becomes a quest –' Becky shrugged. 'People can get scared of actually following it through. Maybe we've become defined by our quest and think we'll lose something of ourselves when we start or maybe we're scared it won't turn out like we hoped.'

'Sounds like you have a quest of your own,' Matthew said behind her.

Becky turned to see him standing right by her chair though at least wearing more clothes than usual: shorts *and* a T-shirt. She hadn't even realised he was in the house but he must have done his infuriating panther-like creeping to appear on the veranda unnoticed.

'Mr R!' snapped Clara. 'I do wish you wouldn't do that. Becky has just said something very insightful and I need to consider it without being startled by you appearing like a ghost.'

'Sorry.' Matthew grinned. 'You know I hate shoes.'

'I shall insist you wear them,' said Clara, imperiously. 'Tap-dancing shoes in fact.' She closed her eyes, presumably to consider Becky's question.

Matthew pulled up a cane chair and sat down next to Becky. He watched his mother intensely with a look of impatience and hope.

Clara opened her eyes. 'Do you know, you're right. I am scared of starting. I've been planning it for so long.'

She leaned forward in her chair. 'The trouble is I don't know where to begin. I have a file with years of notes in, snippets on different characters, many scraps of paper. They'll be all over the place, I'm afraid. I know I've written the first chapter so that'll be in there too, though it will probably need rewriting.'

'I can collate all your material with my notes,' said Becky. 'I've discovered a few interesting characters associated with this estate. In fact do you remember coming across someone called Sarah Thomas?'

Clara shook her head.

'Who was she?' asked Matthew.

'A servant girl who came off the ship with the exiled rebels. I'm intrigued because she's the only woman mentioned.'

'I want to hear more,' said Matthew.

'Why don't we find your notes and then I can type everything up on the computer,' said Becky, looking at Clara. 'That will make it easier to arrange all the information into some order.'

'Computer?'

‘Your laptop, mother,’ said Matthew, with mock weariness. ‘I bought it for you ages ago but I’m guessing you left it in England. Alex is buying another one right now.’

‘Oh, yes, I suppose that would be a good idea.’ Clara looked doubtful. She took a deep breath and winced. ‘Oh dear, I’m suddenly so tired. I don’t think I’m going to be able to do justice to Cook’s fritters.’

Matthew was instantly on his feet. ‘Do you want to go and lie down?’

‘Yes, I think an early siesta. That’s all I need. Thank you, Matthew.’

He stood alongside ready to help her.

‘No I can go by myself.’ Clara scraped back her chair and stood up then placed a hand on her side and grimaced.

Matthew took her arm and this time she did not protest.

‘Becky,’ she said, trying to smile though she was clearly in pain. ‘I’ll have Matthew give you what you need.’

‘Yes, I’ll certainly do that,’ said Matthew ushering his mother indoors.

He did not reappear so Becky finished lunch by herself and took the plates back to the kitchen. She put her empty one and Clara’s barely touched one next to the sink.

‘Was something wrong?’ Cook asked immediately from her seat by the table.

‘Not with the food. It was delicious as always,’ Becky reassured her. ‘But I’m afraid Clara’s not feeling very well. Matthew has taken her up to bed.’

‘I hope it’s nothing serious,’ said Maureen, scraping the leftovers into the bin.

‘I think she’s just tired, that’s all,’ said Becky.

Cook was asleep in her chair in the kitchen and Maureen looked so busy that when Zena arrived with her childminder Becky took her out ‘insect-spotting’ in the garden. High in Becky's arms, Zena reached out to turn over leaves, shouting 'bug' or 'spider' with delight when she struck lucky. They both watched entranced as nearby a hummingbird shimmered on the spot, hoovering up a hibiscus. Then Becky realised that Zena was pulling some leaves towards her mouth.

'No, Zena. Oleander is poisonous.'

'Now how do you know that? Your father again?' said Matthew. He was standing on the grass a few feet behind them. Of course Becky hadn't heard him approach.

'How do you do that?' she said crossly. 'You must have been a ninja in a previous life.'

'Ninja,' repeated Zena. 'Ninja, ninja.'

'Oh Zena, what a word to pick up,' said Becky. 'Can't you say "hummingbird" or "hibiscus" instead?'

Zena considered this. 'Ninja,' she said firmly.

Matthew laughed. 'So your father really was in Barbados a lot of the time?'

'Sort of. I think he was on a ship most of the time.'

'He was in shipping?'

Becky smiled at the thought of her father as a shipping magnate but before she could put Matthew straight a car turned into the drive. Cook's daughter-in-law got out and waved.

'Mummy!' cried Zena.

Becky set her down and watched her run to her mother. 'Mummy, I saw a ninja.'

'Did you darling?'

'I blame you,' Becky said to Matthew as Cook's daughter-in-law put Zena in the car and drove away. 'Anyway, how's Clara?'

'Resting. Let's hope it doesn't turn into pleurisy this time. If she's sensible she might get away with it. But I have come to lead you to your office. Well, my mother calls it the "morning room". No idea why; every time I've checked in the evening it's still there.'

'Have I got a computer?'

'Yes, Alex has delivered a no-expense-spared laptop. He bought a printer as well but the bad news is we can't get it to work. It will be a while before he can get back down to Bridgetown to change it. It's a pain.'

'No worries,' said Becky. 'It will be a while before I have anything ready to print out.' She looked at the yard. 'Where's Alex? I should thank him.'

'He's gone off again. He's showing some architects around a plot I'm buying.'

He led her to a sunny little room overlooking the veranda. It held a fair-sized table, on which lay a laptop and a bulging box file. Neatly stacked next to them were notebooks, pens, a memory stick and a few postcards featuring the Monmouth Hotel. Becky picked these up, confused.

'It occurred to me you might want to send some and I realised you hadn't really had a chance to buy any,' said Matthew.

'That's very thoughtful. Thanks.'

He shrugged then became business-like again. 'Sorry about the printer. If you need hard copies of anything in the next few days, copy them on to the memory stick and we'll stick it onto my PC and print it out. Just come to the office.'

'OK.' Becky assumed he meant the room at the back rather than the veranda.

'I've set you up an account. The password is "monmouth3" – all lower case.'

'Three? As in the number?'

'Yes and as in the number of Monmouth hotels I'll soon have.' He grinned.

'And can I access the internet?'

'All set to go,' he said. 'It's wireless and should connect automatically.'

'Great. Then I have everything I need.'

‘If you do need anything else, come and find me. I have to go out later but until then I’m –’

Becky had a sudden thought. ‘Hasn’t Clara got friends coming tonight?’

Matthew winced. ‘Right. I’ll ask Renee to ring around and cancel. The trouble is they’ll all want to visit her if I say she’s ill. I might have to station you on the veranda with a shotgun. The moment one of her friends arrives waving a pack of cards and a bottle of sherry, you’re to pop them off.’

Becky shook her head as he walked out of the room. She was still getting used to his sense of humour. She logged on to the laptop and heaved a huge sigh of relief at finally being able to get online. She typed in the URL the librarian had given her for looking up church records in the seventeenth century and went through the laborious process of entering the names of the Monmouth rebels she had noted down. There was the option of Deaths or Marriages; she clicked ‘Deaths’ and winced at some of the dates:

1686 *Burial of John Foot*
1686 *Burial of Henry Dodds*

There were further familiar names in the next few years. Many of these men had barely survived the first year or two of their working lives on the plantations, which could suggest they had been severely mistreated. She couldn’t find any mention of Sarah Thomas’s death. Having got off a ship that she’d not (officially) boarded, she seemed to have disappeared.

As the rebels were forbidden to marry Becky did not expect to see any of their names under the Marriages option but she decided to check it anyway. And then Sarah reappeared. Becky discovered that in 1690 Sarah Thomas had married a Randolph Darnley, presumably a son of

William Darnley. She could be a grandmother (prefixed with a stack of 'greats') to Matthew.

Becky felt goosebumps. She had wondered on which side of her bedroom window Sarah would have stood and now she thought she knew: Sarah Thomas, servant girl, had likely become 'lady of the manor'. She had moved through the same rooms as Becky moved through. She would have sat on the same veranda surveying the same patch of land in front. She could have sat in the same space where Becky now sat. Hopefully she had had a happy marriage and Randolph Darnley had treated her well. As Becky was absolutely certain a marriage across such a marked social divide would have brought opprobrium raining down on the couple from 'high society', it appeared the Darnleys were not your average plantation owners. She had been projecting a few negative thoughts on to William Darnley, but maybe he – and his son Randolph – were more reasonable than she'd previously imagined.

She went back to Deaths, looking for Darnleys: William had died in 1701, Randolph had died in 1730 and Sarah in 1731. As Sarah had been described as a 'servant girl' when she got off the *Betty* with the transported rebels Becky assumed she would have been about sixteen years old. That would put her in her early sixties when she died, which was probably a decent lifespan in those days; certainly she would have fared much better than the men working the land.

Maybe there would be some reference to Sarah under her married name of Darnley in Clara's notes. Becky took out a wodge of paper from the box file. There were a few photocopies of official documents but most of the pages were handwritten. She decided to start by transferring these to the computer. Clara's handwriting was a beautiful loopy style – easy to read – when it was in English.

However Becky found some notes written in French. Clara would have to translate these when she was feeling better.

Becky had not discovered any more information about Sarah and Randolph by the time Matthew appeared in the doorway. He was wearing pressed trousers and a short-sleeved shirt, an unknotted tie draped round his neck. At least he had shoes on so Becky had some warning of his arrival.

'How's it going?'

'It's fine,' said Becky. 'Though I'll need to print some pages out for Clara to translate. For some reason she's written quite a bit in French.'

'Because it's her first language. Though she only uses it when she's tired – or cross with me.' He grinned. 'I can translate them but it will have to be tomorrow. I'm late meeting Alex.'

'You're off to the hotel?' said Becky, aware the interchange was getting uncomfortably close to a wife waving her husband off to the office.

'Yes.'

'Have a good time.'

'Lord Fotheringham will miss you. It's his last night.' He paused in the doorway. 'I would ask you to come but if you don't mind –'

'It's better if I'm here in case Clara needs me.'

'Yes. And you shouldn't be bothered by anyone this evening. Renee's told my mother's bridge friends you'll shoot on sight.'

Unfortunately Becky was going to be bothered that evening. No sooner had she watched Matthew's car slide out of the yard than the phone rang. Unsure how busy Maureen was, and wanting to prevent the ringing from disturbing Clara, Becky jogged into the hall. She had barely managed a 'hello' before an imperious and familiar woman's voice charged down the phone.

'Now who's that?'

'This is Becky.'

'Ah yes, Clara's little helper. Can you get Matthew?'

'I'm sorry; he's just gone out. He's not usually back until quite late.'

'He's probably been trying to call me these last couple of weeks. Unfortunately I just *had* to go to Philadelphia.' There was a pause. 'You did tell him I rang, didn't you?'

'Not directly. He was busy at the time. I gave the message to Alex to pass on.' Becky was not sure if Francesca would know who Alex was but evidently she did because a huff of indignation came down the phone.

'*That* idiot. In that case we can guarantee Matthew didn't get the message.'

'I'm sure Alex's not an idiot but he does seem to have a lot on his mind. I don't know if he passed the message on or not but I could leave a note out for Matthew.'

A disbelieving silence followed. Then Francesca said, 'I'd like to speak to Clara.'

'I'm sorry,' said Becky. 'She's in bed. She's not well.'

'In bed with what? Is it infectious?'

'I really don't know,' said Becky. 'I'm sorry. I must get back to work now.'

The phone was put down at the other end without any goodbye and Becky returned to the morning room, feeling unsettled. Something inside her had cheered at the thought Matthew hadn't rung Francesca but the other woman's hunch was probably correct: Alex – with his head full of land purchases and problems with the hotel – had forgotten to pass the message on. It could well be that Matthew would be annoyed when he found out Francesca had rung and no one had bothered to tell him.

Becky continued inputting Clara's notes. It was only when Maureen brought her a cold coke and, mystified to find Becky working in the dark, turned the light on that Becky realised she'd been too engrossed in the lives she was reading about to notice the sun had packed up for the day.

'Must be good,' said Maureen, nodding at the notes.

'It's just tragic,' said Becky. 'Have you heard of the Redlegs?'

'Yes,' said Maureen, quietly and then seemed keen to change the subject. 'Did I hear the phone earlier? I couldn't make it on time.'

'I got it,' said Becky. 'Francesca.'

Maureen sucked her teeth and they both looked up as a car swept into the drive, the automatic lights on the veranda welcoming the unexpected visitor.

'Talk of the devil,' said Maureen and went to the door.

Becky could hear Maureen talking, firmly and deliberately off-putting, but there was no dissuading this guest. Becky recognised the imperious voice as it rose higher, insistent and insincere. 'No, I'm afraid I simply have to see poor Clara.'

Francesca must have pushed past Maureen and headed for the only lighted area visible from the veranda because within seconds she was in the same room as Becky and dropping a bag on the table over Clara's notes. A woman in her late thirties, she was stunning rather than beautiful, attractive rather than pretty, very tall with brass-coloured shoulder-length hair, brown eyes, white but tanned. She looked as if she had arrived for a cocktail party, wafting a mix of perfume and hairspray – and confidence.

'So *you're* Becky!' Francesca looked her up and down.

Becky had no make-up on and was dressed in short trousers and an old shirt whose faded flowery pattern was only bright in the places where Zena had happily rubbed hibiscus petals into the cheap material. She could see that Francesca was pleased with what she saw, as if it confirmed a previous opinion.

'Francesca.' Becky held out a hand, which Francesca squeezed rather than shook. She pulled up a chair.

'Now what are you doing here?' she asked, picking up bits of paper and barely glancing at them before putting them back on the table.

'Just typing up some of Clara's notes.'

Becky could see Maureen standing in the doorway, cursing herself for letting this dragon over the threshold, though Becky thought even a shotgun would have failed to repel Francesca.

'One of Clara's little projects. God, I wish I had a secretary; life would be so much easier. When Clara's finished with you come and work for me, Becky.' Francesca looked round. 'Maureen, I'm sure one of us could do with a drink.'

Maureen came in and picked up Becky's half-drunk coke. 'I imagine you'll be needing some rum in that.'

'I meant for *me*,' snapped Francesca. 'I'd like a G & T.'

'I'll get you a drink,' said Becky. 'I think Maureen should already have gone home.' But Maureen made a 'Don't worry about it'' gesture and went out. Possibly she was curious about Francesca's arrival.

'Are you allowed to drink?' asked Francesca. 'I mean, are you on duty?'

'I'm pretty much finished for the day,' said Becky. She had hoped to type up more notes but that was clearly out of the question now. Not that she could expect anything like a conversation with Francesca, who had already established a pattern of disengagement by asking a question and then looking bored when the answer came.

'You're from England are you? I haven't been there for years. My ex-husband was always keener on America than Europe. In fact I've left him in Florida. Best place for him, really.' She picked up the bag she'd unceremoniously dumped over Clara's notes and looked inside.

'Has Clara eaten yet?'

'I doubt it,' said Becky. 'She's been in bed all afternoon.'

‘Well, she’s probably desperate for some good food and some company. Can you go and get her? Tell her I’m here.’

Becky paused awkwardly. ‘I’m afraid Matthew said –’

‘Never mind what Matthew said. I notice that he isn’t here to look after his mother.’

Becky was spared further argument as Clara walked into the morning room, clutching a dressing gown round herself, just as Maureen brought the drinks.

‘Ah Maureen, bless you. You’re still here,’ said Clara.

‘Just wanted to know if I could get you anything,’ said Maureen.

Clara pulled the dressing gown round herself more tightly. ‘Actually I would love a hot –’

‘Clara! You poor thing.’ Francesca rose and gave a startled Clara a distant hug, air-kissing either side of Clara’s expressionless face.

‘Francesca,’ said Clara, with no enthusiasm. ‘I’m afraid I –’

‘I’ve brought you some lamb chops. You probably need some protein.’

‘Cook is cooking,’ Maureen murmured.

‘That’s sweet of you, Francesca,’ said Clara. ‘But it sounds like we already have a meal on its way.’

‘Yes, but Cook must be over a hundred by now,’ said Francesca. ‘Look, I’ll cook the chops myself. Or maybe Becky or Maureen could do it.’

‘Maureen should already have gone home,’ said Clara. ‘And Becky is not here to cook.’

‘OK,’ said Francesca, dropping the bag on the table again. ‘How about we have a quick drink on the veranda and then I’ll leave you to it?’

‘Maybe I could manage a little sherry.’ Clara sighed. ‘But I warn you I can’t talk too much. I’ll have to just listen. Are you coming to join us, Becky?’

‘I’m afraid it will be very boring for you, small island gossip,’ said Francesca. ‘Though of course you’re welcome to join us and hear me talk about people you probably haven’t heard of.’

‘I’ll do a bit more on the computer,’ said Becky. ‘And then I’ll see how Cook is doing.’

‘I’ll get the sherry,’ said Maureen. ‘But then I’ll be off.’

‘Thanks Maureen,’ said Clara as she and Francesca headed out to the veranda. Becky tried to type a few more notes but felt she may as well have been sitting on the veranda with them, for, with the window open, Francesca’s voice carried through and banished any chance of Becky concentrating on her work.

‘– and after Barbara ran off with the pilot, I’m afraid that Simon was caught making hoax bomb calls to the airline. Such a shame he took it so badly.’ The sound of Maureen’s car departing could barely be heard above Francesca’s gossip.

Becky wanted to shut the window but it would have seemed like a very purposeful statement. There was no way she could carry on working so she typed an email to Joe and wrote a postcard to her mother. She knew her mother would have preferred another letter but there really wasn’t much new to say. Even by the standards of most bland postcards this one would have won the ‘Blandest Postcard posted in Barbados’ competition: the weather was still nice, the flowers were pretty, she had been to a kite festival. Her mother would have been interested to hear that Becky had met a lord but Becky didn’t feel she could put the Lord Fotheringham anecdote on a postcard.

An hour later Barbara was with a chef, Simon was in prison for threatening to torch a restaurant and a host of other people had got married, divorced or were facing tax-evasion charges. The only name she recognised was Richard Carrington and apparently he was being pushed to take a paternity test by a single mother. Becky realised that Clara's responses – initially monosyllabic – now seemed altogether absent, which was surprising as Francesca was now talking about how wonderful Matthew was, a subject normally close to Clara's heart.

'Everyone is talking about how amazing his Casino Nights are. Such a brilliant idea.'

Remembering she'd said she would check on Cook, Becky went to the kitchen where sumptuous smells came from the oven, which had been left on a low heat. She presumed Cook was tired and had retired to her room. Becky turned the oven off and plated up for three, though she left her meal in the kitchen protected by a fly cover.

'How sweet,' said Francesca, when Becky appeared on the veranda with two trays. She took one tray from Becky, looked at the heaped plate and placed it on the cane table. Clara did not say anything. Her eyes were closed. How could Francesca have failed to notice her hostess had apparently dozed off?

'Clara?' said Becky, softly. 'Clara?'

After a few seconds Clara opened her eyes and looked at the plate, confused.

'I think I'll have to have this is my room,' she said, struggling to her feet. 'Francesca, it was lovely to see you but I'm afraid my energy has deserted me.'

'Oh, I'm so sorry,' said Francesca. 'I do hope I haven't tired you out.'

Clara gave no answer and headed slowly upstairs. Becky followed with the tray assuming Francesca would see herself out.

Once in her room even the action of slipping her dressing gown off seemed to tire Clara and she got straight into bed.

Becky hovered uncertainly with the tray. 'Where would you like me to put this?'

Clara just murmured 'Poor Cook' and fell asleep.

Becky returned to the kitchen, hurriedly ate her own meal and threw away Clara's uneaten dinner. She went back out to the veranda and was surprised to find Francesca still there, looking out into the dark garden as if willing Matthew's car to appear.

'Is there anything I can get you?' asked Becky.

'No. No, I'd better be on my way.'

'Oh hang on,' said Becky. She fetched the bag with the lamb chops from the morning room and handed it over to Francesca who took it wordlessly and walked down the steps with not a backward glance; she was certainly not into saying goodbyes. Or thank yous. Becky watched her reverse her car out of the yard and was left with another heaped plate of Cook's lovely beef stew to feed to the rubbish bin.

Chapter Fourteen

The next day, concerned that Clara had still not surfaced by ten o'clock, Matthew asked Maureen to go up to her room to check on her. Maureen reported that Clara had refused breakfast and her breathing was 'raspy'. Matthew immediately called a doctor, who arrived at the house soon afterwards – a Bajan woman of about his age, graceful and sombre, she seemed to know the family well. Matthew and Becky followed her upstairs and waited while she examined Clara.

'I'm afraid it's the usual,' the doctor said, as she came out of Clara's room. Matthew uttered a string of harsh-sounding words in French.

'The usual?' asked Becky, wondering whether she was in any way to blame for not being more assertive with Francesca.

'Pleurisy,' said Matthew.

'Well, it's the most likely cause,' said the doctor. 'I've given her an anti-inflammatory and I'm leaving some antibiotics. I'll come in a couple of days; sooner if you think I'm needed. We could give her an X-ray but I think for now just rest – and make sure she doesn't talk.'

Poor Clara. Becky wanted to see her but if the older lady wasn't meant to talk Becky ought not to look in on her. She headed downstairs after Matthew and the doctor and could hear them discussing how often Clara should take the antibiotics and in what quantities. Matthew showed the doctor out and then gestured for Becky to join him on the veranda.

Alex was in his usual place squinting at some paperwork and they joined him at the table.

'Did anyone come round last night?' said Matthew, quietly.

'Francesca.'

'Francesca?' He looked confused.

'Oh damn,' said Alex, rubbing his eyes. 'Sorry, I forgot to pass the message on. Becky told me, oh, ages ago that she had rung and wanted you to ring back. It completely slipped my mind.'

'So she came out to find me,' said Matthew.

'She said she'd come round to see how Clara was,' said Becky. 'But she did wait for a while after Clara had gone to bed.'

Matthew gazed out at the garden, apparently looking at a crooked-tailed black bird strutting across their lawn. 'Was it just her or was her husband with her?'

'Just her. She said that her ex is in Florida.'

'Ex?' He looked at Alex, who nodded. 'You knew this? So her last marriage failed as well?'

'Marriage?' said Alex. 'It was more like a flash in the pan.'

'I'd better get to work,' said Becky. Alex smiled as she got up but Matthew seemed oblivious to her leaving.

Becky fetched herself a coffee and went into the morning room. She fired up the laptop and took out another wodge of Clara's notes, picking out the ones in French to type up so Matthew could do all the translation in one go. She was distracted by the low voices of him and Alex on the veranda – such a contrast to Francesca's shrill tone the previous evening. Now and again she'd pick up a few words but mainly it was a low rumble.

'You need an escort.' Alex said. 'We don't want a repeat of last night.'

Matthew's reply was indistinct.

'How about Becky?'

Again Matthew's reply was impossible to pick up.

'Becky is better at talking to people,' Alex said and then they must have moved from the veranda for the next thing Becky heard was Alex's car pulling away. She wondered what that exchange had been about.

By early afternoon Becky had typed all the French notes into the computer. It was time to get them printed off. She saved them to the memory stick and went to the office at the back, where Matthew was typing at his computer.

'Matthew?'

He looked round and gave a half-smile. He looked tired.

'Now who's the ninja?' he asked. 'I didn't hear you.'

'Sorry. I was wondering if I could print out what I've typed up?'

'Sure. Sit down.' He got up, took the memory stick from her and plugged it in the back of the base unit. It was a fiddly operation as the computer base was wedged close to the wall with a mass of wires protruding. She found herself fascinated by the way his thick hair whorled from the crown of his head. He didn't go for Richard Carrington's neglected hippy look but he wasn't short, back and sides either. As usual he hadn't bothered to put on a shirt.

Trying not to examine his bare torso as he fumbled on the floor, Becky looked at the screen. Matthew had been typing a document:

With respect to the sealed-bid auction for the land near Shermans: plot 106.85B, I Matthew R Darnley of Copper Mill, Cowcross Lane, St Lucy bid US$2.3 million.

She looked away guiltily as Matthew got to his feet.

'There you go,' he said. He looked at the screen, frowned, quickly closed down his document and opened the memory stick folder. 'So how much have you typed up?'

'It's probably just a few pages actually. It's all the notes that were in French. I thought it would be easier for you to correct the translations if you saw them on paper.'

'OK,' he said. 'I won't manage it today now. Maybe tomorrow.'

'Sure, whenever. It can wait until Clara is better if you're too busy.'

Matthew's mobile went off and he wandered away to answer. Becky located her document and started printing. She tried to imagine what two million and three hundred thousand dollars would look like if it were spread over a table. And this wasn't Barbadian dollars but US dollars. A massive amount considering that he would still have to bear the cost of actually building the hotel. He was clearly certain that his bid would be successful. She wondered if he had any other competitors apart from Richard Carrington.

Matthew came back, strangling his phone with one hand, his face like thunder.

'Problems?' said Becky.

'Chris Harris has been signed off with stress. I can't believe I didn't see that coming.'

Becky wondered how much Ian's little stunt with the freebies had contributed to Chris's angst. She felt a stab of guilt then angrily pushed it away; it had hardly been her doing.

'Will you have to go to London?' she asked.

'Probably. I could do without it right now.'

'I can look after Clara if that's what's worrying you.'

'Thanks, Becky. That is one factor. But there are others too.'

Yes, she thought: the sealed bid and a newly divorced Francesca. She collected the printed pages, closed down the document on the computer and made the memory stick safe to eject. 'Thanks, I'm done. I just need to get the stick.'

But he'd already forgotten she was there. He was staring into space, tapping his mobile with one hand. It was only when Becky knelt down to try and find the memory stick that he snapped out if it and knelt down, extracting it immediately.

They looked at each other for what seemed to Becky to be an uncomfortably long time though in truth it was probably a few seconds. She took the stick from his outstretched hand, stood up and walked away.

As she passed the kitchen she could still smell the wonderful eddo soup they had had for lunch. She inhaled then had a thought and checked the clock in the hall: Zena should have arrived by now. Becky rushed into the kitchen to find Cook's granddaughter standing on tiptoe trying to reach a saucepan on a back ring – still bubbling gently – while her grandmother dozed soundly at the kitchen table. Becky switched off the heat and swept the child away.

Becky hugged Zena to her with rather more intensity than usual and still had hold of her when Maureen walked back in a few moments later.

'Oh Lord, I was checking if Clara needed anything. Cook was awake when I left. Did Zena burn herself?'

'No but she was reaching for the pan.'

Maureen closed her eyes in horror at what might have been.

'I'll take her outside,' said Becky.

The little girl was soon squatting on the yard poking what Becky initially thought was a centipede, which might bite her.

'Oh, it's just a Christmas worm,' she said with relief, watching the poor little striped beast curl around to avoid Zena's rather harsh prods. 'No, don't hurt it, Zena. Just let it lie in your hand.'

Zena spent a few happy minutes watching the worm undulate over her fingers and then have to do a balancing act as Zena turned over her hand.

'Choose one of them.' Becky heard Alex say from the veranda. She hadn't heard his car come back though now noticed it in the yard. 'It'll keep the silly girls away. Becky or Francesca. Either that or don't bother going tonight.'

'You know I have to go.'

Becky realised that Matthew and Alex weren't even aware she was in the yard, below and to the side of them. Matthew leaned over the balustrade, deep in thought. If he turned his head, he would see her but he just stared ahead at Clara's well-pruned garden.

'It will have to be Francesca then,' he said. He sounded weary.

Alex's sigh was so loud Becky heard it.

'Well, I can't leave my mother alone,' said Matthew, a hint of defensiveness in his voice.

Becky had no time to try and fathom this strange conversation, as Zena's mother pulled into the drive. Becky took Zena over and quietly shared her concerns about Cook's ability to look after Zena in the afternoon. Zena's mother was concerned but surprised. 'She's never said she was tired.'

'I don't think she's aware,' said Becky. 'Poor old Cook makes lunch and then falls asleep.'

Zena's mother promised she would make alternative arrangements as soon as possible and then put her daughter in the car with more care than usual.

Becky headed back inside to find Matthew on the phone in the hall.

'Matthew! What a lovely surprise.' Francesca's voice on the other end was so loud Becky wondered whether the phone was needed at all. However by the time she reached the morning room only Matthew's side of the conversation could be heard.

'I was sorry to hear about the divorce.' He paused. 'Oh well, sorry to hear about it, all the same.' Becky smiled. Obviously Francesca was saying that *she* wasn't sorry about it.

'I was wondering if you're free this evening? No, it has to be at the hotel and you'd be doing me a favour.' Francesca must have asked for clarification. 'I need the protection of a strong woman,' Matthew said and laughed. 'I had a really embarrassing experience last night. I got mobbed by single women. It was very odd.'

Becky hovered by the door of the morning room curious as to what exactly had happened last night.

'It's Casino Nights,' continued Matthew. 'I have a brilliant compère who teaches people the games but he needs someone to act as the pupil. I have to play this ridiculous James Bond character who turns up in Casino Royale but doesn't know how to play. Then the guests watch me learn and they have a go themselves. We ham it up quite a bit and usually it goes well. But last night – let's just say that a few women took the James Bond character a bit too seriously.'

Francesca must have said something teasing about his virility because Matthew laughed again and said: 'No, I'm sure it wasn't anything to do with me. Single women see a man on his own and decide he needs a mate. I blame the full moon.' He paused again. 'No, really, all I need is an escort. I think if I have a beautiful woman on my arm it will be enough to put off the desperate and drunken dames. Though obviously you can slap them if you really feel the need. That was a joke by the way. I'd rather you didn't slap the guests.'

Becky closed the door to the morning room. She had no interest in participating in whatever happened on Casino Nights. No wish to encourage a gambling habit in people who had probably bought their holidays on creaking credit cards, from a man who could afford to bid over two million dollars for a plot and ruin another patch of Barbados's tiny land mass with one of the new hotels her father had despised. She had no wish to grasp Matthew's arm in a predatory hold, no wish to slap the faces of teary women who threw themselves at his feet. But nor did she wish to picture Francesca doing all these things.

She spent the rest of the afternoon online, trying – without success – to find a reference to Randolph Darnley and Sarah née Thomas. Rather annoyingly images of the present Mr Darnley – dressed up like James Bond – kept breaking her concentration. A more welcome distraction was an email from Joe. He was delighted she had finally got online and brought her up to date with life in Brentwood: the kitchen cupboards were now a minefield of mousetraps, he had accidentally run over a hedgehog on his bike, and the garage was paying for him to study for the next NVQ level in motorbike maintenance. He finished with a one-liner about how Thomas Gehalgod swam back to a beach in Weymouth, hitched a lift on a manure cart to his village and was now considering a career in accountancy. Becky laughed out loud – it looked like this was going to be a shared surreal saga. She emailed back *Accountancy!!? Ploughing NVQ, surely.*

She heard Matthew and Alex leave and, after working for a bit longer, decided to check how Clara was by taking up her dinner tray. She was shocked to see poor Clara looked years older than her age. Even sitting up in bed seemed to cause discomfort in her chest.

'Is it really uncomfortable?' asked Becky.

'Well, dear, you know that joke: it's only painful when I breathe? It's true.'

Becky kept Clara company while she tried to eat something but she didn't manage very much before she fell back asleep. Becky took the tray back downstairs and ate her own dinner alone in the kitchen. Cook had retired early and the house felt like a morgue.

Becky cleared up and went to sit on the veranda, listening to the frogs sadly whistling for a mate. She rather missed the normal laughter that spilled out of the windows on bridge nights. She decided to turn in early but found it hard not to lie there imagining what Matthew and Francesca might be doing. Eventually she fell asleep.

She was woken by the sound of Matthew's car pulling in – around his normal time a little after midnight – and found it comforting to know he was home and had not gone on anywhere with Francesca. She heard him slide the bolts across the door and set the alarm and tried to picture him moving through the rooms but, as his first action was always to dispense with the hated shoes, there was no further evidence he was there at all.

Chapter Fifteen

The doctor came in to check on Clara and afterwards told Becky that she was doing OK but 'in need of rest, rest, rest.' She gave Becky a comically fierce look. 'If she gets up you hide the gardening tools.'

Becky laughed and waved as the doctor drove off. As she was finishing her coffee on the veranda, Alex drove into the yard. There was no sign of Matthew's car – he must have gone to the Monmouth earlier.

'Has Matthew left you to it?' she asked, as Alex reached the veranda and sat down, sighing – presumably in anticipation of the day's work that lay ahead of him.

'He's flown back to the UK.'

'This morning?' Matthew must have snuck out of the house before dawn. Did the man not need any sleep?

'He should have left you a note. I don't think he trusts me to pass on verbal messages any more.' Alex gave a wan smile.

Becky went in to check the hall table; sure enough there was a folded note. It was roughly scribbled on Matthew's business stationery. He apologised for his sudden departure and left the phone number of the doctor – should his mother need medical attention before the next scheduled visit – and a few instructions to pass on to Maureen. He thanked Becky for looking after Clara. The final paragraph read simply 'I am sorry that I didn't take you to the Casino Night as I said I would but there is always next month. I look forward to seeing you again, Matthew'.

She took it out to the veranda, where Alex was now poring over some paperwork.

‘Is he gone for a whole month?’ The disappointment in her voice surprised her.

‘No,’ said Alex. ‘I wouldn’t have thought he’d be gone more than a week or so. He has an idea of who can act up to the manager’s role in the Essex hotel while Chris is off; hopefully it won’t take too long to sort out.’

‘Oh.’ Becky looked at the note again. ‘Does he only run the Casino Nights monthly then?’

‘Pretty much. If there’s a full moon.’ Alex turned back to his paperwork clearly assuming this was an adequate answer.

Becky was still intrigued to know why there was a connection between gambling and the lunar cycle, though knowing Matthew he’d probably read some research which concluded weak punters would splash out more when the moon was full. She was also curious to know why Alex had driven out to Matthew’s house to work when Matthew wasn’t there. Surely there would be more convenient places for him to work? She had her answer shortly afterwards when she brought them both a coffee and, not finding Alex on the veranda, headed for the office. Alex was just opening it up. The process involved conventional keys but also entering numbers into two keypads.

He saw her with the coffee and smiled gratefully. ‘That for me? Thanks. Just what I need.’ The door clicked and he pushed it open. ‘Like Fort Knox in here.’

‘I haven’t seen the opening ceremony before.’ Becky followed him into the office to put his coffee down and noticed there were industrial-size bars on the windows and several fixed safes on the wall. She was embarrassed to think she had been too preoccupied with looking at Matthew to be aware of them before. ‘This must be one of the most secure places on the island.’

‘It is. Matthew is paranoid about security.’ Alex fired up the computer. ‘And with good reason: you’ve heard of industrial espionage – you know, companies stealing each other's designs? Well there's also hotel espionage.'

'What does that involve?' said Becky, genuinely interested. Or maybe she was interested in knowing what made Matthew so paranoid.

'If you want to find out what a competitor's hotel is like you can send in a mystery shopper – you know, pay for a friend or an employee to stay at the hotel and report back. Or just go yourself. It's an open secret: competitors expect to see each other acting like hotel guests.'

'If it's an open secret what's the problem?'

'People are also desperate to find out what their competitors are planning to do –what land they are looking to buy. What they would pay for it.'

'Like the sealed bid?'

Alex looked surprised. 'Did Matthew tell you about that?'

Becky cringed. She could hardly say she had read a private document. 'Not as such,' she answered, hoping Alex wouldn't probe. Fortunately, he didn't.

'Yes, it's particularly bad at the moment. I don't think anyone would be stupid enough to try and break in here – well, they wouldn't get very far. But Matthew knows that there have been attempts to hack into our email accounts. He's even reluctant to put in the sealed bid until the very last minute in case someone opens it and leaks the bid price to Carrington or someone else.'

Becky thought back to the document she'd seen on the screen; Matthew had been unusually unguarded with her around.

'When does the sealed bid have to be in?'

'Midday August thirty-first. Hopefully Matthew will be back well before then but if he isn't I'll have to deliver it to the realtors in person. Probably with an armed escort.' Alex grinned. 'Joke. Sort of.'

'Is Richard Carrington really so bad? I met him at the airport. He seemed, – I don't know – too laid back to be bothering with all that.'

'I agree. I don't think he'd have the brains or the inclination to be devious. But he has brothers who are a bit more savvy. Also Richard and Matthew – they have history.' Alex did not elaborate and as he was clearly overwhelmed with the tasks his day held Becky didn't push him further.

She went to sit on the veranda and discovered Pitcher standing at the bottom of the steps, his bandage still securely wrapped round his right shin. He waved a note at her.

'One second, Pitcher. I'll be right back.' Becky ran inside and found Maureen and Cook. 'I'd completely forgotten. Pitcher's got to go back to the clinic today. We can't ask Clara to drive him. He's waiting outside.'

Maureen sighed. 'What state's he in?'

'Well, actually, he looks pretty good.'

That was obviously enough for Maureen as she agreed to take them in her car. They settled him on the back seat with his leg up as before and headed for Speightstown.

'Why's he different today?' asked Maureen, when they had driven for a few minutes.

Becky turned round in the passenger seat and regarded Pitcher who was looking out of the window. He had on a pair of cut-off trousers, a very faded shirt and some ancient-looking sandals but he looked clean. His eyes seemed a blotch-less blue and his demeanour suggested concentration rather than confusion. Or maybe it was simply that today he was sober.

'Oh God,' said Becky, turning back to Maureen. 'I think he's in love with the nurse.'

Maureen didn't take her eyes off the road but her eyebrows rose like an impatient soufflé.

Maureen had no more luck than Clara finding a parking space when they reached Speightstown so she dropped them off outside the clinic before going in search of a space on the road.

As Becky walked with Pitcher to the clinic reception she warned him that he might be seeing a different nurse today. Pitcher looked bereft then shook his head, as if rejecting this scenario.

Fortunately the same receptionist was on duty and she remembered 'Becky Thomson from England' so Becky didn't have to go through the same rigmarole as before.

They waited, Pitcher sitting upright with his eyes fixed on the treatment room door. Eventually the same Trinidadian nurse opened it and called out 'Mr Pitcher'. Becky noticed with some amusement that his limp became a little more pronounced as he walked across the room.

She half-rose from her chair wondering whether she should accompany him.

'You don't have to come in,' said the nurse, regarding her without any warmth, then she turned to Pitcher and ushered him into the treatment room with a pleasant smile. Pitcher beamed back at her.

Becky sank back on to the plastic chair. She wasn't offended by the rebuttal but she was puzzled by the nurse's unfriendliness towards her. Maybe Pitcher was going all out for the sympathy vote by telling the nurse Becky regularly beat him with garden implements?

Maureen appeared after fifteen minutes and promptly picked up a health leaflet with which to fan herself.

'Long walk?' said Becky, sympathetically.

Maureen rolled her eyes and nodded.

Less than five minutes later Pitcher re-emerged, a gleaming white bandage on his shin. The nurse didn't come out this time. Poor Maureen had barely had time to sit down and enjoy the relative coolness of the waiting room before she had to go off again and fetch the car.

'I got to come back next week,' Pitcher said as they waited outside. Becky noticed he was still holding the note. Or maybe it was a different piece of paper; either way he was holding it as tightly as a love note. He made a scissors action.

'To have the stitches out?' asked Becky.

'Yes.'

Becky felt the back of her neck burning in the sun and tried to pull up the neckline of her blouse to cover the skin.

'Is England cold?' asked Pitcher.

Becky felt a little surge of energy; had Pitcher been thinking about their previous conversation? 'In winter it can be very cold.'

'That's what I heard. Have you met the Queen?'

Becky laughed. 'Afraid not. Not for the likes of us.' She frowned. She'd just parroted a typical phrase from her grandmother's vocabulary. She could see Maureen's car approaching in the distance. She wouldn't have long but Pitcher seemed more 'present' than usual and it was worth a try.

'Have you ever heard of a Sarah Thomas?' she asked him.

'Sarah Thomas.' He paused then grinned. 'Yes.'

'*Really*? What do you know about her?'

'I came on a boat and I was all alone, then I met a man and we mek a home. Then my poor love died, and …' He stopped, as if he knew he'd once known the words but now couldn't retrieve them.

Was it a song? It certainly sounded like a rhyme. She prompted him. 'Then my poor love died and –?'

Pitcher seemed to go into a trance. 'What does this Becky want from me? Will she leave me in peace?'

Maureen's car pulled up and she got out to help Becky get Pitcher settled in the back. Becky greeted her cheerfully but her heart was thumping as if she'd just walked over the grave of someone who resented it.

Becky found Clara's handwritten 'first chapter' and spent the afternoon typing it up. However her thoughts kept turning back to Sarah Thomas. She realised (with self-mocking amusement) that she was rather projecting her own situation on to Sarah for, although Sarah could have lived in this house from her teens to her sixties, in Becky's mind Sarah was the same age as her – a twenty-three-year-old moving in the same space and not quite fitting into the fabric of the household.

The more Becky thought about it, the more she suspected she had misinterpreted Pitcher's little display of spiritualism. Maybe he had some little rhyme lodged in his head, which he would have recited whatever name she'd mentioned. Next time she saw him she would ask if he'd ever heard of Nicole Kidman and see what he came out with.

But when darkness fell Becky had to admit that Pitcher's words had stirred up some rather odd feelings. When she had first learned that Sarah Thomas had married into the Darnley family, Becky had willed herself to try and sense Sarah's presence as she moved through the house; she'd tried to imagine what Sarah would have seen when she walked into the kitchen or dining room, what she'd have seen when she looked out of a window or stood on the veranda. But since Pitcher's little outburst Becky didn't have to try so hard. She almost felt the presence of a young woman, fleeing from room to room ahead of her as if to escape her. Several times that evening Becky sensed movement in her peripheral vision; she switched the light on in the dining room and thought she saw the leaves on the potted plants tremble, as if someone had just walked by. Becky was a little unsettled: one English teacher at school – while being encouraging – would urge her to 'let go' and try and let her imagination run free. Now she would surely get full marks for imagination. Unless of course she wasn't imagining things at all.

That evening Becky took the laptop up to Clara's room to show her how the notes were progressing and go through the first chapter. It started with the Battle of Sedgemoor in Somerset and descriptions of the Royal and Monmouth armies; the Monmouth armies being the larger but worse equipped.

Becky didn't know where Clara had sourced her information from but her own research confirmed what was in Clara's first chapter: that portion of the Monmouth army who were armed with more than scythes used old-fashioned matchlock muskets, which always had to have a match burning, so revealing the fighter's presence. The Royal army, by contrast, would have used the more efficient flintlock rifles, whose spark came from the striking of flint against steel. It was never going to be an even battle.

Becky wished she could travel back in time to discover what it had really been like. She could find all the technical detail she needed but neither her research nor Clara's notes gave even a hint of what the experience must have been like for a poor young Monmouth rebel on a battlefield. Ironically Joe's morbid interest and gory imagination would probably have helped here.

Maybe Clara would have some ideas about how to bring more vitality and individuality to the descriptions.

Unfortunately Clara's technophobia extended to reading from a screen so Becky had to read the first chapter to her.

When she had finished Clara frowned. 'Can you read it again please?'

Becky began to read aloud once more but Clara stopped her after a few paragraphs. 'It sounds more like some parish council's dull annual report than a battle, don't you think?'

Becky didn't want to upset Clara so she chose her words carefully. 'It's quite technical.'

'Technical? It's leaden. Do you think we should remove all the information about weapons?'

'No,' said Becky. 'I think you need to compare the weapons of the two armies and I thought some of the details were quite interesting. I've always wondered where the expression "flash in the pan" comes from. Now I know it's a reference to flintlock guns.'

'Yes, but something's wrong with the way it's written.'

'I think the problem,' said Becky, 'is that there is no emotional involvement. People need to follow a character on the battlefield, to understand how he came to be there and then to care enough to know what happened to him.'

Ah,' said Clara. 'You mean: one death is a tragedy; one million is a statistic.'

'Exactly,' said Becky. 'But our problem is finding one person to follow. I know the names of some of the men who were sentenced to death or exile for fighting, but the trail runs pretty cold when they reach Barbados. I know when they died. I know they were worked into the ground as they weren't a long-term investment and the plantation owners had no incentive to ensure their survival for longer than ten years.'

'You've found out a lot,' said Clara, with admiration.

'But it's still dry facts.'

Clara thought. 'Yes. Yes, I see. And do none of my notes give a hint of individual lives?'

'Not unless your notes in French reveal something. I still have some of your notes in English to read but so far they seem to be snippets from the nineteenth century. The nearest we have to a continuous line is the Pitchers. The original Pitcher was called Daniel and he was a woolcomber, which makes sense, as south-west England was – and is – sheep-farming country. He was sentenced for transportation and arrived in Barbados in January 1686 to work for this plantation.'

'So he definitely is an ancestor of our Mr Pitcher?' said Clara.

'Seems likely. And here is Pitcher – three hundred and thirty years later – working the same land. Isn't that incredible?'

'Not working it,' said Clara, with an exasperated sigh.

'Whatever. But the point is that I don't know what happened in between.'

'Becky, I'm ashamed to say I have never even asked him what he knows,' said Clara. 'I can't imagine that he knows anything.'

'I have asked him.'

Clara leaned forward. 'And?'

'He does have some notion that his ancestors came from England and why. But I suspect that's it.' Becky chose not to share Pitcher's outburst on Sarah Thomas – at least not until she had tried the 'Nicole Kidman' experiment.

Clara leaned back again, wearily. 'We're asking too much, aren't we? No one records the lives of servants or slaves.'

'Unfortunately not.'

'I really thought I'd collected more,' said Clara. 'My mind playing tricks, obviously.'

'But the person who intrigues me the most is the one I mentioned before: Sarah Thomas, the only woman to get off a ship with the rebels. You know, she was probably Matthew's great-times-nine grandmother.'

Clara looked confused. 'That would be interesting but I'm afraid I'd never heard of her before you mentioned it.'

'But she married a Darnley. She would have lived in this very house. She could have slept in this very room.'

'Oh. I didn't realise the house was that old. But actually I have no idea how old it is.' Clara yawned. 'I think I've had enough Monmouth rebels tonight.'

Becky felt quite deflated. She now seemed to be far more fired up about the fate of the exiles than Clara was. Clara must have seen her face fall because she added quickly. 'Becky, I am interested, really. I'm a bit tired now but maybe you could leave me what you've typed up so far.'

'I'll leave you the French notes but I'm afraid that for the first chapter I'll have to leave you the laptop,' said Becky.

'Oh no,' said Clara. 'Becky, I'm sorry, my dear – you're going to have to print this off.'

Becky didn't manage to catch Alex the next morning before he had to dash off to the hotel. He had religiously locked up the office when he left so she would have to wait until he was back before going in with her memory stick. Alex was unfailingly pleasant and accommodating but she baulked at having to disturb him with a request to print off something when he was clearly so busy. In the meantime she carried on scouring the internet for any clue as to what happened to the rebels who remained in Barbados.

She was looking after Zena when Alex finally returned and had to wait until the three-year-old's mother had collected her before she could speak to him. He had looked shattered when he drove in so she made him some coffee and took it to the office. There were no sounds of activity as she pushed open the door and she felt a flash of irritation with Matthew when she saw Alex literally asleep on the keyboard. There was a faint smell of alcohol. He woke with a start as she put the coffee cup down and rubbed his red eyes.

'Why doesn't Matthew get someone to help you?' she demanded.

'He doesn't trust anyone else.' Alex grinned ruefully. 'We were at school together.'

'That sounds rather sweet.' Becky held out the memory stick. 'Would you mind if I printed off a few pages?'

As they were waiting for the printer to finish, a thought occurred to Becky. 'How did Matthew know Chris Harris?'

'Chris? He was at school with us before he moved to Britain. Poor old Chris, nice guy, but I don't think he was ever really cut out for the hotel business.'

'You mean Matthew just appoints people because he was friends at school with them?' Becky regretted saying it instantly; she hadn't meant to imply that Alex wasn't up to the job. Fortunately he didn't interpret it as a personal slight. In fact he chuckled, though somewhat bitterly. 'Us poor boys have to help each other.'

Becky suspected that he was maudlin with drink.

Becky had not needed to follow the doctor's instructions to hide the gardening tools as Clara barely had enough energy to come downstairs let alone go outside. Her chest did not seem to be as painful though so Becky trusted the antibiotics were working.

On Tuesday morning Pitcher turned up at the bottom of the veranda steps, the floppy Fedora hat on his head and the note from the nurse in his hand. Becky sighed inwardly when she saw him. Maureen was off with family commitments and Alex was at the hotel. Clara had seemed quite tired when Becky took a breakfast tray up so Becky was reluctant to bother her but she was out of ideas regarding getting Pitcher to the clinic.

'Oh, poor Pitcher. I'd forgotten about him,' said Clara.

'He seems to be OK,' said Becky. 'But I think today is when he has his stitches out.'

'It will have to be our transport man, Mr St John, then,' said Clara. 'I hope he's got a car free. He's more used to collecting hotel guests from the airport but, well, he'll just have to do it. I'll give you the number. Just explain that I asked.' She gave a mischievous smile. 'You'll have to say it's hotel business.'

Becky followed Clara's instructions and was relieved when Mr St John said he could provide a car but there would be a delay. She went out to where Pitcher was still waiting and told him Mr St John would take him to the clinic but there would be a wait of several hours. Pitcher nodded stoically and sat calmly on the veranda steps.

Becky returned to her work. Half an hour later she broke off from the computer and went out on the veranda to give her eyes a rest. The sun seemed more relentless than usual and, although Pitcher had positioned himself on a higher step so that his head was in the shade, his sandalled feet were in a sheet of light; he had solved the problem by positioning the Fedora over them.

'Why don't you come and sit on the veranda?' said Becky.

He shook his head.

'It's cooler up here.'

He turned round and looked at the veranda as if considering the offer but resolutely shook his head again. He seemed to think there was a demarcation line that he couldn't cross, though Becky was certain this was not the result of anything Clara or Matthew had said: they treated Cook more like family and their relationship with Pitcher clearly went back years. She wondered if his self-exile 'down the steps' owed more to a race memory.

She fetched him a glass of cold water and he raised his Fedora in acknowledgement. It would be nice to think that gesture had been handed down over the generations but it could just as easily be behaviour learnt from seeing an old Hollywood movie; if indeed, Pitcher ever had. That reminded her of something.

'Have you heard of Nicole Kidman?' she asked him.

Pitcher made a show of thinking about it then shook his head.

'Have you heard of Sarah Thomas?'

He grinned and tapped his head. 'I hear she. I see she too.'

'You *see* her?'

'At night. I see her here' – he tapped his head – 'but really she in that other place.' He looked at Becky though, as usual, avoided meeting her eyes. 'She know you tryna find out about she but her don't like it.'

Becky stared at him. There must be a logical explanation for what he'd said. She just couldn't think of one right now. She went back to the morning room.

It was early afternoon when Mr St John pulled up in a fine saloon, which gleamed in the high sun. He got out and immediately extracted a large white handkerchief from a pocket and dabbed his face.

'Hi,' called Becky.

Mr St John raised a hand in greeting and then looked at Pitcher on the steps.

'Is this the patient?'

'Yes.'

Mr St John put the handkerchief away, removed some plastic sheeting from the saloon's boot and laid it over the back seat.

He turned to Becky. 'Are you coming too?'

She was tempted by the thought of an excursion out of the quiet house but wasn't confident they would get back in time for Zena; with no Maureen to keep an eye on the three-year-old Becky thought it best to stay to look after her in case Cook fell asleep.

'No, sorry,' she said to Mr St John and watched them drive off.

The rest of the day slipped by, uselessly. Even Zena seemed subdued by the blazing afternoon heat and was half-asleep when her mother collected her.

Clara did not venture downstairs at all and when Becky took up her dinner she saw the older lady had found a use for the French notes – she was fanning herself with them.

'I don't suppose you've had a chance to translate them?' Becky asked.

'Sorry, not really,' said Clara sadly. 'As soon as I try to read I get a headache.'

Becky wasn't surprised. The day had started without promise and delivered just that at the close. And still no word from Matthew.

The next day seemed even more hot and airless. Becky sat in the morning room feeling quite depressed. She was feeling trapped on the plantation again, wishing she had gone to the clinic with Pitcher yesterday after all.

But at least she had found something promising on the internet: a link to a collection of old wills; she was delighted to discover one for the William Darnley who had died in 1701. Becky called up the transcribed document and read through it, her mood gradually sinking again. William Darnley had left Copper Hall to his wife with separate bequests to his three daughters. There was no mention of Randolph and Sarah.

So they had been disowned. What other reason could there be for excluding them than their society-defying marriage? Sarah Thomas/Darnley had probably never been in this house, which meant that Becky's recent heightened awareness when moving through the rooms had been a fantasy. The realisation brought her a small pang of loss, as her dual awareness had added some depth to her days. Plus she was really annoyed that she had indulged herself in a childish fairy tale: the servant girl who had become lady of the manor.

Most of all Becky was depressed to imagine the fate of Randolph and Sarah Darnley. There was no entry in the Wills section for either of them – because (she suspected) they had nothing to leave anyone. Sarah Darnley née Thomas had not only been exiled from England; she had also been rejected by society in Barbados.

Desperate for escape from the house, Becky found Maureen in the dining room and told her she was going for a walk.

'A walk? In this heat?'

Becky nodded and smiled when Maureen rolled her eyes and twirled a 'mad woman' gesture with her finger at her head.

Becky headed out through the yard and on to the mahogany-lined lane. The morning was so hot even the wildlife seemed to have been parched into extinction. The casuarina trees were as still as cacti. Becky felt like she was the only living being outside.

Not quite. There was a rustle and Pitcher appeared on the lane in front of her, probably not deliberately blocking her path but certainly in her way. Ironic that in this heat he was moving with a strange urgency. After her recent discovery Becky didn't want to play the 'Sarah game' today but she could not get past him without saying something so she picked what she hoped was a safe topic.

'Your shin's healing really well, Pitcher.'

He looked confused then followed Becky's gaze down his leg, doing a double take as if he'd never seen the bandage before.

'Have you had the stitches out now?' tried Becky, wincing at how patronising she sounded but keen to keep the conversation in the present.

Pitcher seemed to nod and shake his head simultaneously, as though any answer would do. 'She get nothing from the Will, she want nothing from the Will. She asks what does this Becky want from me?'

‘Who said this?’ said Becky, dreading what she thought the answer would be.

‘Sarah.’

Becky’s immediate impulse was to run but she forced herself to stand still as Pitcher went on.

‘She says she take his name, no more, just his name. She marry, she not really marry. She want nothing from the Will, she get nothing from the Will.’

‘She said this to you?’

Pitcher blinked. ‘She take nothing from the Will, she get noth –’

‘Who did she tell this to? She said this to you?’

Becky could see Pitcher’s attention fading in and out. ‘Who did she say this to?’ she repeated.

‘She marry, but she not really marry.’

‘‘Thank you, Pitcher,’ said Becky, deciding she was not going to get anywhere and wanting to cut the conversation short. ‘I’m going for a walk now.’

‘No,’ said Pitcher. ‘Go home.’

‘Thank you Pitcher, but no – I want a walk – alone.’

His head started swinging from side to side. ‘Not now. Rain, rain, rain.’

Becky ignored him and walked on, turning around after a few yards to see if he was staring after or, please no, following her. But he had disappeared. She couldn’t deny she was somewhat freaked by the encounter. What explanation could there be? She had discussed finding William Darnley’s will with no one so how could Pitcher’s imagined Sarah choose that as a theme?

Becky had almost walked to the end of the lane, and was wondering if she should continue on to the road, when a warm breeze started as if warning her to turn back. There were a few drops of rain – just enough to make Becky halt – and then it was as though God had moved a weather-control to ‘violent storm’. The rain started pelting down, the causarina trees writhing like souls possessed, shedding twigs, and the mahogany trees' hard nugget seedcases were peppering her like flak.

Becky broke into a run but could barely keep her eyes open for the stabbing rain. A car drove up and Becky made out Maureen beckoning frantically from within. She stumbled into the passenger seat and effusively thanked Maureen as they drove to the end of the lane and turned round in the T-junction. Maureen sucked her teeth when she saw the streams of water running down the sides of the little road.

'I'll take you back,' she said. 'Then I'm driving home.'

'You think this will last?' asked Becky.

'Yes,' said Maureen. 'This will last.'

Maureen was right. For the next two days, everyone at Copper Mill was stuck in the house. From the windows Becky could see the crowns of trees bowed so deeply that some snapped, while the rain chanted angrily at anyone who dared to set foot on the veranda. Matthew rang once and said he could hear rain in the background but Becky did not want to worry him by saying how severe the storm was. She was unable to persuade Clara to come downstairs and, as Clara's technophobia extended to using mobile phones, Becky had to relay Clara's answers to Matthew's solicitous questions: yes, she was fine, she was not playing bridge or overdoing things and he was to look after himself rather than fussing about her.

It felt a little bizarre being the conduit for this mother-son conversation but it was endearing to hear Matthew's gruff concern. And not just for his mother.

'And how about you?' he asked.

She could have said: I feel like a trapped animal and the situation is being exacerbated by Pitcher passing on messages from an ancestor of yours who's been dead for almost three hundred years. But instead she said, 'I'm fine. Plenty to read.'

‘Are you sure? The rain can get a little claustrophobic.’

‘No problem, really.’

But Becky did feel as if she were in a prison cell with watery walls. In fact everyone seemed trapped in some sense: Clara confined to her room and Cook restricted to the ground floor. Yesterday she had found Cook hovering at the bottom of the stairs and realised with a stab of sympathy that the elderly lady wanted to check on Clara but was daunted by the staircase.

‘I could help you up,’ said Becky gently.

The old lady considered this then shook her head. ‘Thank you. I could get up, but I don’t think I would come down again.’

She wandered back to the kitchen muttering about her ‘old, old legs’.

Nor did Cook have the pleasure of her granddaughter’s company. Cook’s daughter-in-law had decided it was better to take time off work to look after Zena at home rather than to risk the drive to the childminder. Becky was surprised at feeling a pang of deprivation; she hadn’t realised how much pleasure she got from the little girl’s antics.

With Clara ensconced upstairs, neither Alex nor Maureen risking the journey to the house, and no Zena to play with, Becky’s world consisted of the laptop – and the seventeenth century. She had decided to widen her research into the people who made up Barbados’s population.

It seemed there were few Bajans – black, white or mixed – whose ancestors had come willingly to the island. Redlegs was a generic term which covered the Irish people who had been sent to Barbados by Oliver Cromwell, the Scottish – who were the first to be brought over as indentured labourers – and the West Country folk who had ‘backed the wrong king’. Now she knew why she sometimes heard a hint of Irish in the Bajan accent, at other times, a hint of the West Country. And she learnt that there was even an area nearby called 'Little Scotland'.

At least one mystery was solved. Becky read that the drystone walls, which had caught her eye when she was out with Matthew collecting errant kites, were probably built by the Redlegs using techniques remembered from 'home'.

The plantation owners had soon realised the white people they had 'imported' to work the land were as unsuited as could be and turned their attention to the west African coast for slaves, dragging people from their roots and re-planting them in a tiny island thousands of miles away from home. Ironic that now people were desperate to live on the island and willing to pay millions of dollars for a chunk of real estate.

But it was true, no matter how horrendous the facts, they had to be wrapped around a few individuals to have real impact. She went back to Clara's odd scraps of paper. Some were copied from gravestones, others from rich landowner's wills:

'To my son I grant 10 head of cattle, 2 horses, my servant Blue-eyed Boy, 2 copper stills …'

Useless, thought Becky. If the landowner had bothered to name 'Blue-eyed Boy' she might have been able to determine if this was a descendant of a Monmouth rebel but, without a name, he could have been anyone.

Against a soundtrack of near-ceaseless rain she trawled the net for personal stories but caught little. One could get a glimpse of individual tragedies back in Dorset and Somerset: of the widows and wives left behind in poverty (their land and homes often confiscated), of land left untilled because there were insufficient men to work the earth.

But in Barbados, once the prisoners were brought off the ships, little remained. Pitcher was a rarity – very few of the old surnames could be found on the island today.

'You seem very engrossed, dear.' Clara certainly didn't move around the house as quietly as her son but Becky had been so focused on her reading that she had not heard her approach.

'I'm sorry, Clara. I was far away.'

'Oh Becky, I do hope you haven't been working all this time?'

'It's interesting. Anyway, it's not like I could go outside.'

Clara gave her a funny look. 'Well, you can now.'

It was only then that Becky noticed there was sunshine streaming through the slats in the window blinds. She hadn't heard the rain stop.

'Any news of Matthew?' asked Clara.

'Er, no more than that one phone call,' said Becky, surprised. Clara must have known that if Matthew had rung again it would have been to find out how his mother was doing rather than to have a private conversation with Clara's 'secretary' (as Francesca would have it). 'Anyway, Clara, how are you?'

'Much better. I was just finding the rain so oppressive.' Clara sat down. 'Do you drive, Becky?'

'No, I'm afraid not. Why? Is there something you need?'

Clara looked through the window. 'No, not really.'

Her face brightened as the phone rang. Becky rushed to answer it.

'Do you not let anyone else answer the phone?' snapped a familiar voice. 'Or do Matthew and Clara pay you to do it?'

'Hi Francesca.'

'Is Matthew there? Or is he in a meeting?'

'No. Well, he probably is in a meeting. But in the UK.'

A pause, then: 'He's flown off without a word to anyone? Just like that?'

Becky resisted the urge to say Matthew had left *her* a note, even if he hadn't contacted Francesca, but she responded politely. 'There was a crisis with the hotel in England.'

'Silly man. Why doesn't he appoint proper managers instead of sticking these idiots into jobs they aren't up to.'

'I don't know,' said Becky, noting that while Francesca might be superficial, self-centred and bitchy, she was no fool. Clearly *she* would never value friendship and loyalty above aptitude.

'When is he back?'

'Alex thought sometime in the next week. I don't think there's an exact date.'

'So probably back by the twenty-first. Hmmm. Is Clara there or is she in bed?'

Becky realised Clara was standing right behind her. 'She's here,' she said, raising her eyebrows at Clara who nodded and held out a hand for the receiver.

'Francesca,' Becky mouthed, silently.

'I guessed,' Clara mouthed back and then out loud: 'Hello Francesca. Much better, thank you. Just starting to get a bit of cabin fever but I don't fancy driving at the moment.' She paused. 'No, she doesn't drive.'

Becky left them to it and wandered out to the veranda to marvel at the blue skies. The weather of the past few days seemed like a fading bad dream.

It seemed that Clara had barely put down the phone and joined her on the veranda than Francesca pulled up in a different car to last time: this one seemed to be a roofless jeep. She carelessly spun the steering wheel with one hand so that by the time the car stopped, it was pointing the right way to take off. With an elbow draped carelessly over the door, she used her other hand to raise her sunglasses. 'Fancy a spin?'

Becky realised the extent of Clara's boredom when she beamed at Francesca. 'Oh yes, that sounds fun.'

'Tell old Cook to take the afternoon off,' said Francesca, merrily. 'We'll grab a crab salad at Shermans.'

'OK,' said Clara. 'And I'm sure Becky needs to get out of this house too.'

After the briefest of pauses Francesca flashed her teeth at Becky. 'Of course she's welcome.'

'Do we go anywhere near Holetown?' asked Becky.

Francesca wrinkled her face. 'Not really; that's further down the coast.'

'Actually, would you mind if we did, Francesca?' asked Clara. 'I need to go to the bank.'

'OK. Holetown then Shermans it is.'

Sitting in the back, with the wind pouring over her (a lovely sensation), Becky had no chance of hearing what Francesca was telling Clara, though the latter was certainly responding with laughter or nods or headshakes as was appropriate to the tenor of the anecdote. Becky marvelled at how Francesca could keep up a stream of light gossip so effortlessly: surely Barbados simply wasn't big enough to generate so much tittle-tattle?

Anyway right now Becky was feeling almost positive towards Francesca. It was lovely to be an al fresco passenger, watching the greenery and small wooden chattel houses flow by. Then suddenly the sea was on their right – just a few yards away – separated from the road by a thin strip of yellow beach. Becky stared – so this was supposed to be the tame west coast? The sea had obviously crossed the inconsequential barrier of sand during the recent storm, as the road was flooded in parts, but that had no bearing on Francesca's speed. She splashed several people walking along the road – either oblivious to or dismissive of their presence – though, if she had bothered to look in her rear view mirror, she would have seen what Becky saw on turning round: soaked people waving their fists at the retreating car.

Once in Holetown, Francesca parked near the bank and Clara got out and walked off with a steady stride.

'She's looking much better,' said Becky, relieved.

'She just needed to get some fresh air. It's a real shame you don't drive.'

'I'm going to nip out for ten minutes, if you don't mind,' said Becky. 'I think the monument is just over there.'

'What monument?'

'The Holetown Monument. Apparently it's near where people first arrived in Barbados.'

Francesca made a face. 'Is that what you wanted to see?' She laughed and shook her head. 'Well, don't let me stop you.'

Becky jogged across the road and towards the beach, assuming the monument would be near a quay. She had imagined being able to stand in the same place as the prisoners and slaves had. She had pictured old stone wharves, unchanged in hundreds of years, and thought she would be able to visualise the ragged people, dragged up from fetid holds and brought ashore, blinking beneath a sun they hadn't seen during their several months' voyage. Instead the Holetown Monument turned out to be a large white obelisk at the side of the road and the commemorative plaque 'celebrated' British possession of the island rather than paying tribute to the poor unwilling souls who were brought onshore here.

'Was it worth it?' shouted Francesca.

Becky looked up to see that the roofless jeep had pulled up opposite: Clara looking curious, Francesca amused. Becky walked over and got in the back.

'No. I knew it commemorated the first Englishman to land on the island but I suppose I was expecting something more.'

‘What more is there?’ Francesca gave a tinkly laugh.

‘Well, I thought there might be something to mark the spot where prisoners landed.’

‘I’m afraid there’s very little left,’ said Clara.

‘Move on,’ said Francesca. ‘History is history.’ She pulled away with a G-force that flattened Becky against the back seat and had her fumbling to engage the clip of her seatbelt.

Francesca drove them to a beach restaurant and they got out and sat at a table on the sand. Francesca ordered for them (and insisted on paying) but Becky would have preferred to spend some of her still-untouched-cash if it had meant buying some peace while they were eating. Francesca’s gossip only paused when she was chewing a mouthful of crab while making ‘heavenly food’ humming noises. She would often think of some new information just after she’d taken a mouthful and would wave her fork like an excitable conductor might try and control an unruly band. Not that she paid too much attention to Becky, apart from asking her why she didn’t drive.

‘I never got round to having lessons,’ Becky said simply. She chose not to add she had saved up for and even booked them but had had to cancel when Matthew got her sacked from the *Essex Gleaner*.

‘That’s a shame,’ said Clara, who was probably thinking the next time she hired a ‘co-author’ driving would be an essential skill.

Full of crab salad, they sat and watched the sea. Becky could see Clara had really benefited from the outing; her face looked bright and happy. Francesca also seemed contented, assuming silence indicated contentment although Becky sensed she was working up to something.

‘Poor Matthew,’ Francesca said, suddenly. ‘Missing this.’

‘He works too hard,’ said Clara.

'What have you organised for his birthday?' Francesca said this so casually Becky suspected it was the reason for the phone call and the outing.

'That's not until the twenty-eighth of August,' said Clara.

'But that's only two weeks away. He's going to be thirty-five, isn't he? Quite a landmark really.'

Clara's hands flew to her face and even Becky understood her French expletive. 'This blasted illness. Poor Matthew. His own mother not realising it's almost his birthday.'

Francesca inclined a head towards Becky. 'You thought he'd be back by the twenty-first?'

'I can't be sure,' said Becky. 'That's what Alex seemed to think.'

'Let's assume he will be back for his birthday,' said Francesca, 'in which case maybe we should organise something to welcome the poor boy home after all his hard work.'

'What, like a birthday party?' Becky couldn't imagine Matthew liking that.

'A birthday party! Clara, Becky has just come up with a brilliant idea.'

'Oh no, I didn't mean –'

'It's a great idea. What do you think, Clara? Let's fill your house with Matthew's friends. Of course I'll help.'

Becky could see Clara was excited at the prospect but also doubtful about Francesca's suggestion.

'I'm not sure. What do you think, Becky?'

'I don't think Matthew is a party animal,' said Becky.

Francesca snorted with contempt. 'Becky, Matthew *loves* being centre stage. You won't have seen him playacting at the Casino Nights but he has to pretend to be James Bond. He's brilliant; he loves performing.'

'Shall we see what Alex thinks?' asked Becky.

Francesca made a face. 'Becky, I can promise you I know Matthew a lot better than Alex does.'

Clara nodded. 'OK, a birthday party. Maybe just a few guests.'

Chapter Sixteen

Francesca was a frequent visitor over the next few days, arriving with guest lists and menus for Clara to approve though, in truth, it seemed to Becky that Clara had gone a little downhill after their outing and would often agree with Francesca's suggestions without much engagement.

'We can still call it off,' said Becky, gently, when she brought Clara's breakfast tray to the veranda one morning.

'I'm not sure we can, Becky. Francesca's sent the invitations out already. Anyway our main problem is we're holding a party for Matthew when he probably won't even be here.'

That was true. Matthew had phoned his mother the previous night but had been vague about when he would return. He was presumably communicating with Alex, who confided in Becky that Matthew was having problems finding someone who could assume the role of hotel manager when there was a likelihood Chris would be coming back after a break. It would be much easier if Matthew could simply replace Chris but friendship and employment laws complicated the issue. Not to mention Chris's wife, who was so angry at seeing her husband fall apart with stress that she was threatening Matthew with legal action.

Matthew's return on the twenty-first became the twenty-third, and then the twenty-sixth. Becky wondered if the best solution would be if he arrived back a few days after the party – unaware that it had happened. It would be embarrassing for Clara (as Francesca had sent out the invitations in her name) but everyone would surely understand the complexities of Matthew's business. Well, all except Francesca.

She arrived later that day and barged into the office where Alex was working at the computer. She seemed particularly annoyed to find Becky there although Becky had only brought Alex some coffee.

'What's keeping him in England?' Francesca shouted.

'He's busy,' said Alex.

Becky left them to it and went back to the morning room. She tried to concentrate on Clara's notes but the peace of the room was soon broken by Francesca storming in.

'Alex seems very furtive. Have you told him about the party?'

'No, but I think he should know.' Becky was uncomfortable she had been expressly instructed not to tell Alex. It was ridiculous when invitations had already been sent to houses all over the island and someone else was bound to mention it.

'Well, stop thinking,' snapped Francesca. 'It's supposed to be a surprise and that idiot wouldn't be able to keep anything from Matthew.'

Becky wanted to ask if Francesca's real concern was that, if Alex told Matthew, the guest of honour would instantly put off any return to Barbados until well after his birthday. But she kept quiet.

In the end, on Friday the twenty-eighth – the very day of his thirty-fifth birthday – they heard Matthew would be flying back that evening. The moment he received the email early in the morning, Alex delivered the news to Clara and Becky as they sat enjoying breakfast on the veranda. Before they could respond Francesca's car swept into the yard.

'She seems to be visiting very early and often these days,' said Alex, drily. 'I hope it is nothing to do with these rumours of a surprise party for Matthew later today.'

'You've heard?' said Clara.

'From Richard Carrington, no less,' said Alex. 'He turned up at the hotel last night for dinner and asked me about it. I had to say it was such a surprise, even I hadn't heard about it. That certainly amused Carrington.'

'I'm sorry, Alex,' said Clara. 'Francesca's rather taken over. If it's any comfort I think she's mainly invited people she knows. Certainly my bridge friends haven't made the guest list.'

Alex shrugged and went back inside. Becky decided Clara could give Francesca the good news that Matthew would be at his own party and went after Alex. He was already back in the office. 'I wanted to tell you,' she apologised, 'but I was – how shall I put it – *expressly forbidden*.'

'Why? On the grounds I might turn up?'

'No, I think on the grounds that you would tell Matthew.'

'Francesca was right. I would have done. And Matthew would have probably stayed in England managing the bloody hotel himself rather than come home.'

'So you think it's a bad idea?'

Alex momentarily shut his red-rimmed eyes and wrinkled his forehead as if visualising the scene that lay ahead. He reopened his eyes. 'Becky, I cannot tell you what a bad idea it is.'

'Can you warn him?'

Alex checked his screen, looked at his watch and made a quick calculation. 'Five hours ahead. No way. No way at all unless the plane has been delayed and they haven't taken off yet.' He picked up the phone and started dialling but quickly replaced the handset.

'Too late.' He sighed heavily. 'All I can do is collect him from the airport and give him fair warning.'

'Francesca won't like that,' said Becky.

'Tough. She can hardly stop me.'

Becky suspected that she could. Francesca always radiated confidence but today her demeanour verged on despotic. She swept through the house issuing commands to everyone and looking amazed if people didn't immediately follow her instructions. Clara escaped Francesca's attentions by ensconcing herself in her bedroom and ignoring Francesca's occasional entreaties from the bottom of the stairs to come and help with some choices regarding décor. Although Becky had no intention of being a lackey she joined in the preparations for the party simply because she had to abandon any hopes of working and would rather be doing something than nothing.

Ironically the only person to resist Francesca's demands was Pitcher. Neither Becky nor Clara had ventured out to clear the garden of the twigs and branches brought down in the recent storm but the usually absent gardener had appeared that morning and begun to rake them into heaps.

'Pitcher!' yelled Francesca.

Intrigued Becky peered out of the front door to see Francesca leaning over the veranda balustrade. Pitcher was now transferring the garden rubbish to a wheelbarrow.

'Stop that for a second,' Francesca called to him. 'This is more important. I need flowers – lots of flowers.'

Pitcher stopped and looked at her impassively.

'What flowers?' he said.

'Pink ones and those red things over there, and – I don't know – whatever those yellow things are called.' Pitcher continued to look at her dully and she gave a roar of exasperation. 'You are capable of cutting flowers, aren't you?'

Pitcher put his head on one side then the other and then fiddled with the bandage on his leg. 'Yes,' he said eventually and resumed his task of loading up the wheelbarrow, suddenly deaf to shrill repetitions of his name.

'Inbred half-wit,' fumed Francesca. 'What the hell is wrong with him?'

Becky joined her on the veranda. 'You asked him a question and as far as he's concerned he's answered it.'

Francesca turned on her heel and stormed back inside. Becky fetched some secateurs and spent a peaceful few minutes snipping pink ixora and red heliconia before the tranquillity of the garden was shattered by the arrival of a catering van and a series of yelled instructions from Francesca who had returned to the veranda. A small stream of people flowed from and back to the van – carrying covered food, ice and plates.

Becky sighed and went into the kitchen to find some vases.

Alex wanted to collect Matthew from the airport himself but Francesca even managed to prevent that. Or, at least, Becky suspected she was the culprit.

'Maureen, have you seen my keys?' said Alex on his knees searching the floor beneath the hall table. Becky had already searched there when he had first noticed the keys were missing.

'Last time I saw them they were right on that table,' said Maureen, pausing on her way to the dining room.

'Who else could have taken them?'

Maureen sucked her teeth. 'Must have jumped off the table,' she said. 'Or more likely the duppy take them.'

'Quite,' said Alex. 'Where is she?'

'Changing in the guest room,' said Maureen. 'Oh, not any more – speak of the devil.'

They heard the staccato sound of Francesca's high heels ruining the wooden floors as she came down the stairs followed by the scent of perfume. She clip-clopped towards them in a deep blue cocktail dress, her hair piled up like a golden snake poised to strike. She looked at Alex, still kneeling on the floor.

'Whatever are you doing?' she asked with what Becky thought was exaggerated surprise.

'Where are my car keys, Francesca?'

'Oh Alex, you're so absent-minded. I haven't got a clue what you've done with them.'

'How are we going to get Matthew back from the airport?' he snapped.

'I've asked Mr St John to pick him up,' said Francesca. 'I thought you'd have gone home by now.' She glowered at Maureen. 'Have you set up the bar area?'

'I'm doing it now for now,' said Maureen, with no urgency.

Francesca strode off towards the dining room and within seconds an imperious 'Maureen!' was heard.

'I'm going to kill her,' said Alex.

'Get in line,' snapped Maureen.

'Maureen!' Francesca yelled again.

'Coming fast as my legs can carry me,' Maureen called back, setting off for the dining room at the pace of a sedated sloth. Francesca had 'engaged' Maureen for the evening to help serve though Becky suspected Francesca had little concept that overtime must be paid.

Becky went upstairs to see how Clara was doing. She found her, dressed for a cocktail party but sitting at her mirror looking worried.

'Are you all right, Clara?' asked Becky.

'Thank you, Becky. Actually, I'm already tired. I'll just put in a brief appearance tonight. Poor Matthew.'

'I'm sure he'll understand.'

'No, I mean, I'm not sure this party was a good idea. The guests are due now and poor Matthew will arrive to find the house full of people when all he probably wants to do is collapse. If I'd known he'd be arriving after the party started there's no way I'd have agreed to it.'

They heard clip-clop sounds coming up the stairs and across the landing. 'Clara, how are you doing in there?'

'I'll be down shortly, Francesca.'

'It's just that people will be arriving soon.' Francesca pushed the door open and looked surprised to see Becky. 'Heavens, you really are Clara's little helper.'

'I think "confidante" would be a better word,' said Clara.

'I suppose I'd better get changed,' said Becky. She hadn't even thought about what she'd wear. In fact the idea of reading quietly in her room was far more appealing than making small talk with people she didn't know. Or maybe she would have a leisurely wash, throw on some simple clothes and hopefully miss both the arrival of the guests and the look on Matthew's face when he reached the sanctity of his beloved house to find that it had been invaded.

Francesca regarded Becky's simple cotton dress and bare feet with a mischievous smile. 'You look fine. Come as you are. Well, some sandals maybe.'

That did it. Becky went to her room and took out her new black dress.

Chapter Seventeen

Despite what Francesca had said about their arrival being imminent, the guests were clearly sticking to West Indian party time as, when Becky arrived on the veranda, the only figure in sight was Francesca. She was pacing like a tethered horse.

At that moment the first car pulled in and Francesca took up a 'lady of the house' welcoming stance on the steps. Becky decided she had as much right to welcome guests as Francesca and went to join her, enjoying Francesca's baffled then horrified expression as she turned to look at her. Becky hadn't bothered to pin her hair up – she hadn't even bothered with make-up – but she knew the black dress and shoes seemed to have some transformative magic of their own. Francesca's face fell, her jaw fell and then she fell, tumbling down the remaining steps until gravity dumped her unceremoniously on the dusty yard. Becky, in her more practical shoes, ran down to help and the couple who had just arrived got out of their car and came over to assist Francesca to her feet too. Her golden hair had uncoiled and was striking in all directions like a paranoid Medusa.

'Francesca, you poor thing,' said the woman, brushing dust off Francesca's blue satiny backside – something Becky had spotted was necessary but not an action she felt she could accomplish without it seeming like a spiteful spank.

'I'm fine,' Francesca snapped. 'Really, thank you, Margaret. I didn't expect Becky to sneak up on me like that.'

‘I’ve told Matthew his steps can get a bit slippery,’ said the man, eyeing Francesca’s pencil-thin heels with a wrinkled forehead.

‘Anyway do follow Becky up and get a drink. Becky is Clara’s secretary by the way. Go on Becky; up you go.’

The couple obediently followed Becky up the steps to the ‘Drinks’ area on one side of the veranda; they must have heard Maureen mutter, ‘Put a cow on stilts, what do you think’s going to happen?’ as she served them rum and cokes.

Maureen poured Becky a drink too and Becky joined the couple, who looked as though they were in their forties. They introduced themselves as Margaret and Robin Turner.

‘I don’t suppose Francesca will want to see us again after we witnessed her fall from grace,’ said Robin with a wry smile. His wife laughed and shook her head.

‘So how do you fit in?’ she asked Becky. ‘I can’t imagine that Clara needs a secretary.’

‘I’m just in Barbados for a few months,’ said Becky. I’m doing some research for a project of Clara’s.’

‘That sounds interesting. Speaking of whom, where is Clara?’

‘She’ll be down soon,’ said Becky, with more hope than certainty. ‘Unfortunately she’s still a little poorly.’

‘Sorry to hear that,’ said Robin. ‘And where is birthday boy?’

‘He’s on his way back from the airport now. He’s been in the UK.’

Robin frowned. ‘He does know about this party, doesn’t he?’

Becky shook her head. The Turners looked at each other and Becky noticed their next gulps of rum and coke were large ones.

‘Your dress is gorgeous, by the way,’ said Margaret. ‘You really have to be slim to wear one of those. No wonder Francesca looked at you and fell over. Up to now she's been one of the few women on the island who can squeeze into one.'

'But I think it's been more a squeeze recently.' Robin grinned.

The three of them wandered further along the veranda to allow other people to fetch drinks. The yard was now full of cars parking, doors banging as their stylishly dressed occupants disembarked to meet their air-kissing hostess.

'Is Clara still unwell?' asked one person.

'Sorry to hear about your divorce,' said another.

'How lovely,' exclaimed another, 'who'd have thought you two would get back together?'

Up on the veranda Robin spluttered into his rum and coke. 'Oh God, is Matthew going out with her again?'

'I'm afraid I'm the wrong person to ask,' said Becky. 'I didn't even know they had been together at all.'

'Well, it was a long, long time ago,' said Margaret. 'We were all just kids really.'

The veranda was gradually filling with people and there was constant toing and froing as people plenished and replenished drinks, with occasional traffic jams when they got stuck en route as they were waylaid by acquaintances. Occasionally Robin and Margaret would nod and smile at people though they seemed in no rush to actually talk to the nodders and smilers.

'Do you know everyone here?' asked Becky.

They laughed. 'It's a small island,' Robin said.

'Though to be fair,' Margaret added, 'we would only count a couple of people here as close friends. Matthew and Clara among them.'

'If they were here,' Robin added drily.

'Margaret and Robin!' a familiar voice cried and they turned to see Clara, dressed impeccably but with her make-up a little more heavily applied than Becky was used to seeing. Margaret gave her a peck on the cheek then looked at her searchingly.

'Clara, you look a bit tired. I heard you'd not been too well.'

'No, I'm fine. Anyway I'm looking forward to seeing Matthew.'

'I'm sure everyone is,' said Margaret.

Clara surveyed the people around them and frowned. 'I'm not sure everyone here knows him that well.'

'Hmmm,' said Robin knowingly.

'Lots of Francesca's friends,' said Margaret.

Clara looked around again. 'Where's Alex?'

'He wasn't invited,' said Becky.

'Well he should have been,' snapped Clara. 'Look. His car's still here; he's probably in the office.'

'Shall I drag him out?' asked Robin.

'Yes please – immediately,' said Clara. 'It would be ridiculous to have a birthday party for Matthew without his oldest friend.'

As Robin disappeared Clara turned to Becky. 'My dear, you look wonderful. Well, you always look wonderful but in that dress you're just amazing.'

'Don't let Francesca hear you say that,' said Margaret. 'She took one look at Becky earlier on and fell over. Literally.'

Clara smiled impishly. 'I *am* sorry I missed that.'

Robin reappeared with Alex in a mock arm-lock. He released him with a cheerful 'I'll get this a man a drink' and headed for the bar area.

'I'm not dressed,' Alex complained.

'Yes you are,' chorused Margaret and Clara.

'Yes, but look at Becky. I'm not dressed like her.'

'I should think not,' said Becky.

Alex laughed and accepted the beer Robin gave him. 'To be honest, I forgot the time. I was hoping to make a quick getaway before the party kicked off.' He looked at the multitude of cars in the yard and winced. 'How many people has she invited? I can see my car is completely hemmed in.'

'Bad luck, Alex,' said Margaret. 'You're stuck with us. Besides Matthew will need all the familiar faces he can see.' Then she grimaced. 'Sorry, Clara. I just made the assumption that maybe you hadn't chosen all the guests.'

'You assumed right. If I had, Alex's wife would be here for a start.'

'At last!' Francesca's voice somehow carried over the blend of conversation and everyone turned to see a car turn gingerly into the yard and stop abruptly in the entrance. Mr St John seemed to freeze in the driving seat as he looked at what was now a parking lot.

A hush fell over the veranda. In the house muffled conversations quietened as the guests indoors realised something was happening outside. The veranda swelled with people, even filling the steps to the yard.

The front car passenger door opened. Matthew got out slowly and looked at the house. Becky wondered how she would feel if she came back from a difficult business trip and an eight-hour flight to find her house bloated with people.

Francesca turned to her audience and held up a finger. 'One, two, three. Happy Birthday to you …'

They all joined in the singing while the birthday man stood leaning on the passenger door, his face in shadow. When the 'to you-ou' had finished he quietly got his suitcase out of the boot, carried it across the yard and up the veranda steps. The crowd parted like the Red Sea, uncertain what to do.

On the top step Matthew put down his suitcase and looked round.

'Bastards.'

And then he grinned. There was a massed sigh of relief.

'Darling,' cried Francesca. 'You must be exhausted.' She kissed him on the cheek and then made a theatrical wince. 'And wonderfully unshaven.' He ruefully felt his chin and nodded as she draped his other arm over her.

The crowd quickly reformed into little cliques and Becky saw some raised eyebrows and surprised smiles as though the scene they had just witnessed was going to form the main theme of their immediate conversations.

'Let me take care of that,' said Alex and disappeared into the house with Matthew's suitcase.

'Hello darling,' said Clara, kissing her son's cheek, and giving him a one-armed hug on his free side (as Francesca was occupying the other).

Matthew looked at the Turners and at Becky, giving a nod and a thin smile. 'I'm not kissing anyone else until I've had a shower and shave. Mothers are more forgiving.' Then he spoke to Clara in French, usually a bad sign though Becky couldn't glean his mood from the even tone of his speech. His appearance was more revealing: a crumpled suit, lines of exhaustion on his face which was still handsome but haggard. Clara and he exchanged a few more words and then he gently disentangled himself from Francesca and disappeared into the house.

Robin drained his glass. 'That didn't go too badly.'

'You don't speak French,' said Clara.

Francesca, suddenly marooned in a group of less friendly people, homed in on Becky.

'So Matthew told me that your father is in shipping.'

Becky laughed. 'No, I said he was on a ship. He was a merchant seaman.'

'Oh.' Francesca managed to endow the word with several syllables.

'I didn't know that,' said Clara. 'How interesting.'

Francesca obviously didn't think that 'interesting' came into it. 'I fear that you gave Matthew completely the wrong impression.'

'Not deliberately.'

'You said he *was* a merchant seaman. So has he found a better job now?'

Becky held up her empty glass.

'Excuse me. I'm going to get another drink.' She walked away.

Becky didn't get a drink but instead sought sanctuary at the back of the house though Cook was not around to talk to. Becky didn't know whether Cook had been insulted or relieved that her culinary skills had been rendered superfluous by the caterers brought in by Francesca but she'd elected to spend the evening at her son's house. Maureen was tied up making sure that the drinks table didn't run dry. Becky wished it was earlier in the day and she had the distraction of looking after Zena. That would have been a great excuse to get away.

As she walked down the back corridor she saw a plump middle-aged man gingerly open Cook's door and step inside her room. Becky rushed to see what he was up to and almost knocked him over like a skittle as he came out again.

'Can I help you?' she snapped.

She must have looked angry because he actually raised his hands as if to repel an attack. 'Yes, you can, please. Someone told me that there was a washroom down here.'

'You've come too far. You need to go – I'll show you.' She led the way back towards the hall and pointed out the door of the downstairs bathroom.

He frowned. 'Sorry, I don't know you. Can I ask what you were doing back there?'

'I live here. But if you want a character reference we could go and find Matthew.'

The man's face blanched. 'Matthew. Has he arrived?'

Becky wondered how long the man had been 'looking for the washroom'.

She saw him go into the downstairs toilet and headed back down the corridor to check that Cook's door really was shut but, as she walked past the office, she thought she heard a sound inside. She knocked on the door.

Matthew opened it, gestured for her to come in and closed it immediately behind her. 'Whose idea was this?' he snapped.

Becky sighed. 'It wasn't your mother's. I think she got a bit swept along.'

'And Alex?'

'He tried to warn you but he didn't officially find out about the party until you were already on the flight.'

'How could he have not known what was going on?'

Becky didn't know what to say to that. Matthew stared at her impatiently. 'And he left the office open and the computer on.'

'Surely not.' Becky couldn't imagine even Alex being that forgetful.

'As good as. He simply locked the outer door without setting the keypads. Any idiot with a skeleton key could have broken in.'

'I think he was rather coerced into joining the party.'

'For heaven's sake, he's a grown man. He could have locked up properly first.'

Becky's temper flared on behalf of poor Alex. She was tempted to explain how Francesca had taken over but it felt a bit like telling tales. 'If you knew what the situation was like here, you'd have more sympathy for him.'

Matthew looked about to answer this but said instead, 'You're really telling me that half the island was invited here tonight, people who would barely recognise me in the street, and the most expensive caterers called in and Alex–'

'Ah, I've got it now,' said Becky. 'This is about freeloaders, isn't it?'

'Freeloaders?'

'Why can't you just be happy that so many friends turned up to celebrate your birthday?'

'Friends? I've seen at least two people here tonight who would happily search this office for information on my business. What a dream. To be invited to my house and find the office virtually open, the computer on and God knows what paperwork left lying around.'

Becky inwardly groaned at Alex's carelessness. Then again he had probably worked a 12-hour day and wasted valuable time searching for his car keys and trying to reach his fierce boss. Alex had looked almost as tired as Matthew looked now.

'I'd better get back to your party,' she said and walked away before Matthew could respond with something sarcastic.

Chapter Eighteen

Becky wanted to make sure Clara was all right and looked first in the dining room. She had to concede Francesca had chosen her caterers well: the dining table was covered with attractive platters of prawns, cold lobster, king fish, and smoked salmon with olive eyes and cucumber smiles, all swimming among dishes of luxuriant green salads.

People were now attacking the buffet and taking their spoils to the lounge or out to the veranda; the lucky ones finding a seat, the unlucky ones on their feet trying to balance drinks and plates of food. As Becky approached one small group, she heard '… and then she said "being a lord is like being a lady, if you have to say you are, you ain't"'. Everyone in the group laughed. Becky sensed a collective turning of heads as she walked past, but suspected this was owing to the magic black dress, rather than any recognition she was the originator of that anecdote.

She found Clara in the lounge and was pleased to see the older lady had a seat but there was no room for Becky to join her. Anyway Clara looked brighter and was chatting happily to Margaret Turner. Becky went on to the morning room where Francesca was holding court with a small cluster of giggling ladies. One of them reached out to stroke the blue material of Francesca's dress.

'It's *gorgeous*! How did you afford it?'

'Alimony, darling!'

The other women's voices did not carry as clearly but Becky heard one of the coterie mention Florida.

‘Just left him there,’ tinkled Francesca. ‘Anyway, silly man. He hired old Belly Baron as his lawyer. He obviously forgot that Belly was a great friend of mine from years ago.’

Becky carried on walking, looking for a friendly face, but the few people she knew were all busy. Robin Turner was talking with a mixed group and Alex was swigging back a beer while listening to a man who was talking intensely. She could have joined in many conversations – small groups of men looked up admiringly as she passed – but she kept going until she reached the veranda. There was no Maureen to talk to – she must have left earlier – and the drinks table appeared to have descended into a chaotic free-for-all.

Becky ignored the small chatting groups and leant over the balustrade, drinking in the sounds of the lonely whistling frogs. She was wondering if she could slip away unnoticed to her room when a pair of arms seized her from behind.

‘Where the devil have you been all evening?’ Richard Carrington demanded, rubbing a bristly cheek against hers. ‘The only reason I accepted this invitation was to see you. Matthew will probably poison my drink if he knows I’m here.’

He released her and his roguish blue eyes roamed over her appreciatively. ‘You look wonderful,’ he drawled. ‘That dress looks amazing. Or at least it looks amazing on you.’

‘Thank you, Richard. And nice to see you made a bit of an effort too.’

He grinned and gave a mock twirl. His sandy hair was tousled as usual but he was dressed in pressed trousers and shirt and smelt like he’d just walked out of a shower. His only other concession to dressing up was a gold earring.

‘Have you eaten?’ he said. ‘There’s so much sea life next door Francesca must have sent out a private fishing fleet to hoover up the Atlantic.’

Becky laughed. ‘Actually, now you mention it, no I haven’t.’

‘Come on, let’s enjoy Matthew’s hospitality.’

Becky followed him into the dining room where he managed to find them a couple of seats and insisted she sat down while he loaded the plates. She could see he would be gone some time: the food was so good people were coming for seconds and thirds and haphazard queues had built up near certain dishes.

At least it meant he wasn’t in view when Matthew walked into the dining room moments later after what must have been a lightning shower. His hair was still wet but he had changed into fresh clothes and had a beer in his hand. As he moved through the room small groups of people stopped him for a chat and occasionally someone seemed to know him well enough to clap him on the shoulder. Nothing could disguise the weary lines on his face but he seemed to have recovered his social humour.

He was standing only a few feet away but he had his back to Becky and hadn’t yet noticed her. She felt like a spy observing his interactions with people. She assumed it was Francesca’s friends who blew up to him speaking in hurried sentences.

‘Gorgeous buffet, Matthew.’

‘Happy birthday.’

‘Super party.’

And then a couple of women from Francesca’s coterie rushed up to him in tandem.

‘Francesca tells me you’ve been in London,’ said one.

‘I suppose you’ve got your Christmas shopping in early?’ asked the other.

Matthew laughed, seemingly unsure how to answer. He looked round, caught Becky smiling at the ridiculousness of the question and gave her a rueful grin before answering the female duo.

'That's right. Though I did manage to squeeze in some business between shopping trips.'

He turned back to Becky and looked like he was about to join her – since there was a vacant chair beside her – when Francesca cantered over, telling off the duo.

'Don't be silly, you two. Poor Matthew has been on a business trip. Clara has just told me he's only had four hours' sleep in the last three days.'

'Oh, you should try lettuce leaves. Brilliant for insomnia,' said one of the pair, clearly not getting it. Matthew saw Becky laughing at this latest conversational gem but before he could respond his arm was taken by Francesca, who spun him towards the veranda.

'It's not that he can't sleep,' she told the duo, sternly. 'It's that he hasn't had *time* to sleep. Now, poor Matthew, let's see if we can find you somewhere to sit down while you wait for all these horrible people to go.'

Francesca propelled Matthew towards the veranda so that the duo were left like disoriented bees bereft of their queen. Becky felt quite sorry for them.

She was quite hungry now and was pleased to see Richard coming back with their plates, tastefully decorated with a selection of each dish. Evidently he knew his food for after a few bites he could names the spices that had been used and the cooking method. He looked hurt that this surprised Becky.

'I do run hotels as well, you know. My family have several in the islands. I oversee the restaurants. And I'm a fantastic cook.'

He was also a fantastic source of gossip, telling her gentle anecdotes about some of Barbados's more eccentric residents as they ate. They were joined by a few stray women whose husbands were talking with other husbands. Richard chatted easily to all, making them laugh, though his eyes always returned to Becky. After a while the husbands noticed their wives were chatting to Richard Carrington and came to claim them. Only one lady remained with Becky and Richard.

'It's your reputation, Richard,' she laughed. 'Shame it doesn't work on my husband. I can see that Frank's boring some poor blighter with his plans for the land near Shermans. He's convinced that Barbados needs yet another golf course.'

They looked where she was pointing and Becky recognised the man who had been 'searching for the washroom' earlier. He was sketching plans on a napkin and talking animatedly to another man, who was nodding at regular intervals but scanning the room for an escape route whenever Frank lowered his eyes to add more marks to the napkin. Frank and Richard, thought Becky: they must have been who Matthew meant when he said there were two rivals at the party. At the time she had thought he was being paranoid.

'Has he got his bid in yet?' asked Richard.

'Yes, he got it in weeks ago.' Frank's wife's hand flew to her mouth. 'You're the last person I should be telling. Don't you dare ask me how much he bid.'

'Wouldn't dream of it,' said Richard. 'How much did he bid?'

'Oh, you're naughty. Ouch.' She gave a squeak and rubbed her tummy. 'See, even my baby kicks me when he thinks I'm going to be indiscreet.' She leant towards Becky. 'I'm seven months pregnant.'

'Congratulations,' said Becky, aware now of a bump under the lady's loose-fitting dress. 'And you know it's a he?'

'Must be. Every time someone mentions the words "golf course" or "sealed bid" he gets restless. Ouch, there he goes again. Now who knows where the nearest washroom is? That little game of football has just made me realise I'm desperate.' She grinned.

Becky was about to direct her to the downstairs bathroom when Richard cut in. 'Just go across the hall and take a left towards the kitchen. There's a little room on your left that looks like a cupboard.'

'Thanks, Richard. Yes, I forgot you would know.' The woman cast a despairing look at Frank – now on his second napkin – and walked off slowly.

Becky frowned. 'What did she mean, "I forgot you would know"?'

Richard chuckled. 'I used to live here. In fact which room have they put you in? The one straight over our heads now? With the view over the yard?'

Becky thought. 'Yes, in the middle.'

'That was my old bedroom.' Richard grinned. 'What a delicious thought. We've been sleeping in the same space – maybe even in the same *bed* – but separated by time. Hmmm.' He gave a dreamy smile and made his eyebrows dance.

'But why were you staying with Matthew's family?'

'I was staying with my family. It was our house.'

Becky's mind swam with confusion while Richard looked amused and in no hurry to help her out. 'How could it have been your house? Matthew's family have been here for generations.'

'I suppose they've *worked* here for generations. Yes, come to think of it, Matthew's grandfather was here, though I only remember his father to be honest.'

'Matthew's grandfather planted the trees down the drive.'

'He probably did. He was the gardener. Then, when he died, Matthew's father took over. And old Cookie was our cook. Well, one of our cooks.'

'If it was your family's house why aren't you still here?'

‘I grew up; my brothers grew up. We all wanted our own houses. My parents wanted to relocate to America. I think they were delighted when Matthew made them an offer.’

‘But it’s lovely. How could you bear to leave it?’

Richard grinned. ‘Who wants an old house with no air con? I always wanted to design my own place. And I did. You should come and see it. In fact, I seem to remember, Miss Thomson,’ he said, assuming a ponderous voice, ‘that you once promised to have dinner with me.’

‘You’ve got a terrible memory, Richard. I didn’t.’

‘Well, maybe you didn’t actually promise,’ he allowed, ‘but how about I take you out tomorrow at seven-thirty?’

Becky had no idea whether to accept or not. It would be lovely to get out of the house and spend some time with an uncomplicated and good-natured man. But this was clearly a date and she wasn’t sure she fancied Richard.

‘Hello?’ he said, comically.

‘Oh, sorry. I was –’

‘Worrying what the gardener’s boy would think?’

‘Evening, Richard. I do hope you’re not bothering Becky.’

They looked up to see Matthew standing over them. Becky cringed inwardly. Had he heard what Richard had just said?

Richard seemed unfazed, greeting Matthew with a lazy smile. ‘And a happy birthday to you, Matthew. Though you look like you’re working too hard, old boy. It’s a lovely party by the way.’

‘Yes,’ said Matthew. ‘And apparently I have Becky to thank for it.’

‘Me?’

‘Your idea, I’m told.’

‘Clever girl,’ drawled Richard. ‘It’s a great party.’

A familiar tinkle of laughter carried from the veranda to the dining room, followed by Francesca saying something that reduced people to helpless laughter.

Matthew seemed to be waiting for confirmation. Becky was suddenly weary of his oblique accusations – this time that she was to blame for his unwanted party.

'I suppose it must have been my idea, then,' she said, 'if that's what you've been told.' She turned to Richard. 'Seven-thirty would be lovely.'

'That's great. I'll pick you up then.'

Matthew looked like he wanted to say something but he turned round and walked off.

Richard grinned at his departing back. 'He's furious,' he chuckled. 'I think maybe I'll take my leave before he *does* poison my drink. And before this drunken lot all try and drive their cars out of the yard at the same time. Expect to see a lot of people swapping insurance details later.'

Becky laughed. 'I think I'll call it a night, too.'

'See you tomorrow, gorgeous.' He gave her hand a squeeze and left.

So she had a date. Something pleasant to look forward to even if it didn't set her heart racing.

The party showed no sign of winding down so Becky decided to let Clara know she was going to her room and check whether the older lady wanted to go up too. As soon as she walked into the lounge she realised that, in the midst of all the jollity, Clara – sitting by herself on a sofa – was in real distress.

Becky rushed over to her. 'Clara, what's the matter; are you all right?' The level of noise had risen to such a pitch she had to bend over, her curtain of hair brushing Clara's cheek, to repeat the question.

'No dear, I am not all right. I'm just summoning the energy to go up to my room.'

Becky took Clara's arm and helped her to the stairs, wondering if she should run to the veranda and summon Matthew to help. She could see him framed in the main doorway, listening quietly to an anecdote of Francesca's. Then Francesca's arm encircled his waist so that they stood together, an item.

Francesca wasn't about to let Becky take him away now.

She began to help Clara up the stairs, unable to decide if the wave of negativity she felt was due to envy or annoyance that Francesca's elaborate and duplicitous plan had worked. She realised her strongest emotion was disappointment in Matthew. How had a man with such an incisive mind been fooled by someone as shallow as Francesca?

Halfway up Clara had to pause, her hand on the banisters. 'Stupid of me,' she said breathlessly. 'I should have stuck to my original plan to come upstairs earlier.'

Francesca's laugh was so excessive it seemed to be following them up the stairs.

'And will you just listen to Francesca's voice.' Clara sounded edgy and petulant, perhaps because she was overtired.

'Matthew seems fond of her,' Becky murmured at which Clara grunted and continued her ascent.

Once in her room Clara sank on the edge of her bed while Becky found her dressing gown and nightdress.

'To be honest, Becky, I blame myself. I think back to when Francesca took us out for lunch. At the time I thought she was just being sociable but now I wonder if the whole point of the trip was to engineer this party.'

'She obviously likes Matthew.'

'Oh I do hope he doesn't fall for her again. It completely wrecked him the last time. Would you open that window more for me, Becky? It's stifling in here.'

As if on autopilot Becky crossed the room and pushed open the window. She was learning more about Matthew in this one night than she had during the weeks they had been sharing a house.

'So what happened?' she asked. 'Was Francesca not interested?'

'Oh she was interested, all right. They were engaged. At the time I was worried – just because they were so young. Matthew's father was delighted, though. I think it broke his heart as much as Matthew's when the engagement was called off.'

'Francesca changed her mind?'

'No, she didn't. Francesca's parents put a stop to it. They refused to let her marry him.'

'But why? Couldn't they see he was going to be successful?'

'No,' said Clara with disgust. 'They couldn't see anything beyond their own snobbish noses.'

'Because he was the son of a gardener?'

Clara cast a slightly surprised look at Becky. 'Yes. And because he was the son of a –' She sighed. 'A Redleg.'

'What? Matthew?'

'I'm afraid I just assumed you'd realised that. That's the point of the book. I want to write it for Matthew's father – for his memory.'

'But Matthew is so driven; he's so *dark*.'

Clara gave her a look. 'As am I, obviously. My parents came to Barbados from Martinique. They were completely oblivious to the island snobbery. My husband, in his youth, was what my mother called *un bel homme*. Tall, blue-eyed – just wonderful in every way. Far too easy-going, of course.'

'Ah,' said Becky. 'Now I know why Matthew named his hotels "Monmouth".'

'Of course.'

‘But how come Matthew and Francesca didn’t marry when he was getting successful? Surely her parents would have had a job objecting then?’

‘Francesca didn’t wait for him, that’s why. Now two husbands, and two divorces later, it seems she’s decided that her first love is the one after all – whatever her elderly parents now think.’

Clara yawned. ‘It’s not that I don’t want him to get married. Actually, I wish he would hurry up. I would love grandchildren. But he’s shown no serious interest in any woman – apart from Francesca.’ She groaned. ‘I can’t believe it’s starting all over again.’

‘Hang on, Clara. This makes no sense. None of the Monmouth rebels had the surname “Darnley”. In fact, fifteen of them were handed over to work for a William Darnley. Darnley was the name of the plantation owner.’

Clara shook her head. ‘No way, Becky. This is a small island with long memories. When it suits people,’ she added, with bitterness. ‘Matthew’s father was definitely Redleg stock.’

Clara looked so tired that Becky was reluctant to keep her talking and let her get into bed. She went to her own room but found she could not sleep. It could have been because the social chatter and Francesca’s laugh seemed to run through the night with all the longevity of a super-strength battery. Or maybe it was the sound of car doors banging and engines revving up to leave the yard beneath her window. Maybe her lack of sleep was due to trying to solve the puzzle of how Matthew’s ancestor had ended up with the same name as a plantation owner. Or maybe it was simply the thought that Matthew – gardener’s boy and Redleg – had been reclaimed by Francesca.

Chapter Nineteen

Becky woke up to the sound of someone banging on the front door. Still in her PJs, she hurried down the stairs and went through the laborious process of drawing back the bolts. She opened the door to find Cook standing on the veranda.

'Sorry you couldn't get in. I'm afraid everyone has overslept.'

But Cook didn't come straight in. She was looking at the veranda and her expression was very weary. 'Who's going to clean all this up?'

Becky stepped out to see what Cook meant. Glasses (empty, half-empty, on their side, broken) perched under chairs, on windowsills, on the balustrade. Flies landed repeatedly on plates, marching over the leavings of fish and salads.

'Not you,' said Becky.

They went inside and did a post-party tour with Cook looking more miserable as they inspected every room. The lounge and morning room were liberally sprinkled with food-smeared plates and dreg-soiled glasses but they saved the worst until last. The dining room looked like the fish equivalent of a massacre – eviscerated carcasses with knives and forks scattered over the table like discarded weapons. Flies were joyfully using each serving dish as a landing pad. And there were cockroaches. To Becky's horror she could see a couple of the antennaed beasts playing happily with the bits of fish and salad careless diners had let fall on the floor. She even noticed the resident gecko had glued itself to a blank stretch of wall so it could gaze, bog-eyed, at the scene of devastation.

‘Oh Lord,’ said Cook. It was a prayer, not a blasphemy.

‘Oh God,’ said Becky. It was a blasphemy though she found herself praying that Francesca’s caterers were on their way back to clear up.

They still hadn’t appeared when the phone rang a little later. Neither Matthew nor Clara had yet surfaced. Becky answered the call and heard a sigh of disappointment.

‘I suppose Matthew’s not up?’ said Francesca.

‘Haven’t seen him,’ said Becky. ‘Do you know what time the caterers are coming back to pick up the plates?’

There was a pause. Presumably Francesca had forgotten what the scene after a party looked like. ‘I suppose it will be Monday.’

‘*Monday*?’

‘I don’t know what it’s like in England, Becky, but the caterers here aren’t going to be working over the weekend.’

Becky could not believe what she was hearing.

Francesca must have conjured up a post-party scene in her mind. ‘Is it really that bad?’

‘It’s pretty bad.’

‘All that’s needed is to stack up the plates and cutlery in one room; it will be gone on Monday. Can’t Maureen do that?’

‘She doesn’t work weekends.’

‘Cook?’

‘Is over eighty years old.’

‘Well then, can’t you –?’

‘Actually, Francesca,’ said Becky. ‘I’m kind of overstepping the mark here. Probably best if you ring back later and have this conversation with Matthew or Clara.’ Becky put the phone down, quietly triumphant. Francesca wasn’t the only one who could end a conversation without a goodbye. She turned round and saw that Matthew had padded up silently in his infuriating manner, dressed in just his pyjama bottoms. He still looked a little tired but he was pretty much back to his natural, rugged-looking self.

'Did you just put the phone down on Francesca?'

'I'm afraid so.'

'Hmm.' He didn't seem annoyed or even surprised. 'Was she suggesting that you clean up after the party?'

'Yes, she was.'

He shook his head and laughed. 'She's a character, isn't she?'

Becky could think of much better words to describe Francesca but kept her response to a non-committal 'yes' and her expression deadpan.

'I was a bit ungracious last night, wasn't I?' he said.

'I suppose it was a surprise birthday party,' said Becky, 'and you certainly seemed surprised.'

'Still I should apologise for my rather miserable attitude in the office. I'm afraid all I've been thinking of for the last few weeks has been getting back to –' he paused, 'this house. Then to come home to find it full of people and that I was expected to *perform*.' He groaned.

'I was told that you love being centre stage.'

He looked pained. 'Who on earth told you that?'

'Doesn't matter,' said Becky. 'Anyway, the caterers aren't going to be here until Monday and I don't think we can let Clara come down to this mess.'

'Absolutely not, Miss Thomson. But what can this poor gardener's boy do?'

Becky winced. So he *had* heard what Richard had said. But he had also solved the problem. 'Can he hold a garden hose?' she asked.

'Yes, obviously,' said Matthew. 'Do you have a plan?'

Becky looked at his PJ bottoms. 'Change of clothes, maybe?'

Becky would love to have taken a photo of Francesca's appalled face when she drove up a little while later. She had clearly come to the rescue, for – stacked neatly on the jeep's passenger seat – were plastic gloves, aprons and antibiotic wipes, ready to deal with any unclean plates that came her way. But instead she found the job very much in progress – along with a water fight. Becky and Matthew – now in swimsuits – had moved the cane furniture inside and turned the veranda into an outdoor wet room. They had brought out the plates, arranged them over the veranda floor and were in the process of hosing them down and each other. There was plenty of childish squealing and dodging the jet of water.

'Matthew!' cried Francesca, getting out and waving a fistful of plastic gloves at them. 'Don't worry with that. Leave it to me.'

Matthew turned, hose in hand and the spray caught her shoes, which made her do a strange little dance. 'Sorry,' he called, cheerfully. 'Actually, I think we're almost done here. We just need to stack the plates.'

Francesca stood – clutching her redundant plastic gloves – and watched Matthew and Becky do this. When they started to bring the cane furniture back out on to the veranda she seemed to realise she should offer to help. 'I'll just put these down first,' she said, waving the gloves and heading to her car. By the time she got back they had finished the job.

She looked from Matthew to Becky obviously wanting to stay but no longer having an excuse to. 'Some friends of mine are having a soiree this evening. Why don't you join us, Matthew?'

He shook his head. 'I'm giving myself this weekend off.'

Francesca stared at him, baffled. 'This is a social occasion, not business.'

'Sorry, I'm still rather tired.'

'That's a shame,' she said. 'Well, do you fancy a little light lunch later? Mangos have a new Carib-Asian Fusion menu.'

Before Matthew could reply Cook came out with a plate of stacked pancakes. She gave Matthew one of her restrained smiles. 'If you were here yesterday morning I would have given you a birthday breakfast so you have it today.'

Matthew beamed like a little boy. 'Thanks Cook; you remembered my favourite meal of all time.'

The sight of towering pancakes drenched in maple syrup evidently did not tempt Francesca in the same way it tempted Becky as she declined Matthew's invitation to join them and walked back to her car without even a 'goodbye'.

'Come on. I think we've earned breakfast,' said Matthew, sitting down. 'You do like pancakes, don't you?'

'Yes, but I've only had them on Shrove Tuesdays.' Becky joined him and took a bite. These were not Shrove Tuesday pancakes. These were a syrupy homage to pure heathen pleasure. 'Wow. Nothing could beat this.'

'I agree. This is a banquet for a gardener's boy.'

'On that subject,' said Becky. 'If you're happy discussing it, and please say if you're not, I only found out last night that your father was –' she hesitated.

'A Redleg?' said Matthew, scooping up stray maple syrup with a fragment of pancake. 'It's no secret.'

'But here's been me trying to find someone with a Redleg history to talk to and getting little sense out of Pitcher' – Matthew raised an amused eyebrow – 'and all along there's been a genuine rebel descendant under my nose.'

Matthew chuckled. 'I'm afraid you're not going to get much sense out of me, either.'

'No stories? Nothing handed down at all?'

'Knowledge of working the land, I suppose – though as you can see, I don't get much time to garden.'

'No family history then?'

Matthew licked his fingers. 'Sorry, no. I got the sense from my grandfather that there was a sort of shame that hung over the family – which I think was partly imposed by other people and partly carried by the family themselves – but he didn't talk about it.'

'I'm baffled. None of the rebels had the surname "Darnley". Darnley was the name of one of the plantation owners who took on some rebels.'

'Really? You know more than me. I can't see how that squares with us being Redlegs.'

'Unless,' said Becky, 'the Redleg side of your family comes from a woman. All the rebels were men but there was a servant girl who was taken off the boat as well. Someone called Sarah Thomas.'

'What did she do wrong?'

'That's the trouble; I don't know. It's very possible she was convicted for helping a rebel. Even if she had just brought food to someone who was hiding that would be enough to be executed, let alone transported. There's no record of her getting on the ship in England. But she walks off it here and goes to work for William Darnley. And then a few years later she marries someone called Randolph Darnley, William's son, presumably.'

'So she did OK for herself?'

'Well, hopefully,' said Becky. 'But maybe that's where the Redleg element comes into your family.'

'Hmm.' Matthew stopped eating and frowned. 'It's a great theory –'

'But?'

'No offence to the fairer sex, people would have discounted her. If she married into a planter's family I think her children would have been seen as coming from that social level.'

'Ah, but I think they were disowned by the Darnley family. I've looked at William Darnley's will online. He left everything to his wife and daughters. No mention of his son Randolph.'

Matthew contemplated this then shook his head. 'I think the snobbery lay more in bloodlines. Even if this Randolph Darnley was ostracised people still would have known he was of planter stock.'

Becky leaned back, exasperated. 'I give up then. It's a mystery.'

'Sorry,' said Matthew. 'Right. We're down to the last one. Half each.'

Cook stepped forward bearing a plate with another stalagmite of syrup-doused pancakes. Becky realised she must have been standing by the door listening to their conversation. The elderly lady looked thoughtful as she placed the plate on the cane table, nodding slightly at Matthew's effusive thanks and giving Becky a look as if she wanted to say something. She hovered for a second then walked back inside. Becky was intrigued but also distracted by the sight of Matthew happily spearing three pancakes with a fork and trying to deliver them to his plate without spilling buttery syrup everywhere.

Clara came down and waved away Matthew and Becky's questions as to how she was feeling. She looked surprisingly rested, Becky thought, considering that she could barely make it up the stairs the previous night. She sat down with a coffee and regarded them as Becky tried to wipe maple syrup from her chin.

'What a sticky mess,' Clara said, amused. 'Cook remembered, then.'

Matthew made an indistinct sound of agreement.

'Was that Francesca's car that left earlier?'

Matthew nodded.

'I'm afraid I have no idea what the caterers cost in the end. We'll be invoiced at some stage.'

Matthew laughed. 'No surprise there.'

Becky contemplated having a sixth pancake but thought better of it. 'Clara, do you want to work on the book today?'

'I shall finish translating all the French pieces you so nicely printed off for me. But, no, Becky, I want *you* to have the weekend off. I'm feeling very badly that you've had to put up with Francesca's endless visits and my bridge friends and being stuck here without much to do while I wouldn't get on with the book.'

'I'm not working today. I could take you to see some places,' said Matthew. 'I'll show you the land I'm going to buy.'

Clara rolled her eyes. 'Not business, Matthew. Take Becky somewhere nice.'

'Actually, I would like to see it,' said Becky. 'But there's also somewhere else I want to visit.'

'Ah,' said Matthew, leaning forward with interest. 'Something to do with your father, maybe? Francesca told me last night he was a merchant seaman.'

'Yes, it is to do with my father. I've only got the name of the cemetery but I think it's quite far south. Southbury Cemetery, do you know it?'

Matthew frowned and Clara was wide-eyed with shock. 'My dear, I'm sorry. I had no idea your father was dead.'

'I was told he was alive,' said Matthew. 'Or at least, I thought – let's just say that I was given the wrong impression.'

Becky shrugged. 'It was my fault for not being more upfront about it.'

'Southbury,' said Matthew. 'Yes, it's down near Bridgetown but, hell, it's a small island. Let's go.'

'Hmmm. Maybe dress first,' said Clara and Matthew and Becky both looked down at their swimsuits and laughed.

Twenty minutes later Becky was ready, more soberly dressed and clutching a card from Joe and herself. She'd been wondering when would be the right time to do this and it was ironic that her visit to her father's grave was going to happen on what had been her happiest day in Barbados so far. She was also very aware that she was carrying some responsibility for Joe and wondered if this visit would bring the closure he needed.

Either way the last chapter of their father's life should never have been so casually dealt with. Perhaps one day their mother would tell her and Joe what had gone wrong with the marriage but so far there was no sign of her wanting to do so.

As she came downstairs Cook appeared at the kitchen door. She signalled to Becky. 'Come in.'

Becky followed her into the room and waited while the old lady drew back a chair from the kitchen table and sat down.

'Are you all right, Cook?'

The elderly lady nodded. 'Cook,' she said. 'Someone give me the name.'

Becky sat down beside her. 'Because you cook?'

Cook shook her head. 'My father was also called Cook. But it wasn't his real name.'

Becky was lost. 'Then what is your real name?'

'I don't know. You think we came from Africa with names like Cook and St John and Babonneau?'

'No, now that you mention it. It seems strange.'

'Slave names. The slaves get given the names of the plantation owners.'

Becky frowned. Why was Cook telling her this?

'How do you know William Darnley had a son called – what was he called? Ran –?'

'Randolph. Because he was a Darnley.' Becky sighed as realisation hit. 'You mean he wasn't a Darnley. He could have worked for William Darnley and ended up with his name.'

Cook nodded. 'Maybe.'

Becky thought about it. If what Cook said was true it would explain William Darnley's will and why Matthew's family had the Darnley surname but also the Redleg label. She looked at the old lady. 'Genius. Thanks, Cook. I would never, ever have thought of that.'

She headed out to the veranda to find Matthew, now wearing a shirt and trousers, waiting for her with Clara, who was carefully wrapping some flowers in paper.

'I've picked you something to take,' said Clara. 'If you'd like to take flowers, of course.'

'Oh, thank you,' said Becky. 'Yes, of course I would. It will probably be the first time anything has been left at his grave.'

Clara blinked rapidly and Becky realised with surprise her friend was trying not to cry. 'My tube roses and yellow ixora are at their best now. And asparagus fern always shows everything off to advantage so I cut some of that too while I was about it.'

'Thank you, Clara.'

'Least I could do,' Clara said, a wobble in her voice.

She handed the flowers to Matthew and Becky followed him down the veranda steps and watched him put them carefully in the car boot. He held the passenger door open for her while she got in and Becky had a flashback to a rainy day in Essex, when she'd spied a suited Matthew run down the steps of his stately home to assist a beautiful boa'ed woman out of a Bentley.

She smiled, recollecting.

Matthew smiled back. 'What?'

'Nothing, I was just remembering the first time we met. In England. At your house.'

He frowned. 'My house? Oh, you mean Noak Hall. You're blushing so I definitely want to hear about this memory.'

'I'd wondered who the banquet was for. As I was leaving I saw you run down the steps to raise an umbrella over a young woman. I was a little envious of your girlfriend to be honest.'

'Girlfriend? The spoilt daughter of a wealthy family in Paris. They run Anglo-French excursions. I'm trying to push both the hotel here and the one in England as bilingual concerns. It just means that I have to schmooze in French and sound knowledgeable about French cuisine. And I have to dress up like James bloody Bond and look like I know what I'm doing.'

'Oh.'

He looked at her, smiling. 'You do know that it's all fantasy, don't you? The dressing up, the silver cutlery, the stately pile?'

'Yes, of course. But sometimes the fantasy is nice.'

'So, if I wanted to impress you, I wouldn't have to buy you a new car, or employ a masseur, or name a hotel after you?'

'No, just sort out a posh dinner in a stately home. And run down the steps to greet me. That would be my fantasy.'

He laughed. 'Then you'd be easy to please.'

He switched on the air conditioning and Becky relaxed back into her seat, realising her shoulders had been tense. She wasn't sure if this was because she was alone with Matthew and had just shared a fantasy she should have kept to herself or because she felt the weight of her own expectation when this journey ended. How would she react when she saw her father's gravestone? Would she feel anything? Would she fall apart? She just didn't know.

It was a magnificent day and the road they took towards Bridgetown wound its way past the now familiar fields of sugar cane. Edging the fields arching manes of some platinum-coloured grass rippled gloriously in the sunlight. The lanes they were bowling along bore delicious names like Featherbed Lane, Pie Corner or Cow Watering Place. She read them out as they flew past for their mutual amusement.

'My father used to send us drawings – his own maps of Barbados: plants and trees for me, ships and cars for Joe. I think he felt more at home in Barbados than in England.'

He took his eyes off the road to glance at her. 'So did he actually live here?'

'I don't really know. All I know is he was in the merchant navy, made several trips to Barbados and eventually died here.'

He glanced at her again then said in a careful voice. 'I don't want to pry but the way you said that sounds like you didn't care for him very much.'

'I did. It's just there are lots of things my brother and I don't understand. For a start Joe and I weren't that young – I was eleven, he was eight – so we don't know why our mother kept Dad's death from us for a year.'

'But didn't you ask, you know, when's Dad coming home?'

'We did wait surprisingly long to ask that question. I guess because, in the past, there'd been times when we'd thought he was never coming back. Then one day he'd just turn up and it was like celebrating Christmas and birthdays all rolled into one. He always brought us fun presents. But really it was having him there that counted.'

'So how did you eventually find out?'

'I think it was coming up to Christmas. Mum realised Joe and I were convinced he'd finally come home so she told us that he had died. Later we found out that he'd died almost a year before but our mother had chosen not to have his body returned to England. And what was chilling was that she hadn't even flown out here for the funeral. Her excuse was that she couldn't leave us. But at the time of his death her mother was still alive. She could have stayed with us for a few days while Mum went off.'

'Money?'

Becky shook her head. 'The shipping company Dad worked for would have seen to all her expenses. Plane fare, accommodation at a guesthouse here. I found the letter with their offer when I was rummaging around in her desk for Christmas tags not all that long ago. I think she turned down the offer because she simply didn't want to come to Barbados.'

'But why?'

'I guess it wasn't the happiest marriage. When Joe and I were older and tried to get to the bottom of it she just got upset and, worse, resentful that we kept asking her – in the end we gave up.'

'So what memories do you have of your dad?'

'Good ones.' Becky smiled. 'I remember he invented a hilarious game called "navy speak". He was Captain Bligh, sitting in an armchair and shouting orders to his useless, scurvy-ridden crew. "Hoist that lug sail," he'd shout. "Trim the binnacle lamp!" His scurvy crew, Joe and me, would run around the house like mad ants searching for something we thought might look like a binnacle lamp – whatever that was. My mother's stockpot I seem to remember came in handy and we'd dash back to his chair. "Perfect," he'd say and pretend to trim it. We'd laugh ourselves silly.'

'Did he ever tell you what a binnacle lamp was?'

'No. I think he just enjoyed seeing what Joe and I would come up with.'

'He sounds like fun.'

'He was. Mum was more serious. But to be fair she had us day in, day out. We didn't see him that often so of course it was easy for him to seem wonderful and exciting.'

'I take it your dad was comparatively young when he died. How did it happen?'

'I can't blame my mother for keeping *that* from us until we were older. She thought it would upset us and she was right. He was the boatswain and he was carrying out some sort of ship maintenance when he fell. Heights had never bothered him and he had done that particular job dozens of times apparently. But that day he lost his footing.'

Matthew kept his eyes on the road ahead but she saw him grimace. It occurred to Becky that she wasn't the only one who had lost a father.

'If you don't mind me asking how did your father die?'

'Heart trouble,' said Matthew. 'He was only fifty-three and he looked quite fit. He was a lean man, always doing something in the garden. My mother was brilliant for him but I think, even with her support, it was too late. His problems had "set", for want of a better word, when he was much younger.'

'Problems?'

'I mentioned the sense of shame that hung over the family. I think he always had a feeling that he wasn't good enough. That can bite away at some people; really sap their strength.'

'Now I understand why Clara feels so strongly about the Redlegs.' And her ambivalence about writing the book, thought Becky. She had mistaken it for guilt at being complicit in the exploitation of indentured labourers when it was probably more that Clara was finding it emotionally draining examining the circumstances that had contributed to her husband's premature death.

'I was once engaged to a girl who came from an old family on the island,' said Matthew. 'Our equivalent of the upper class, I suppose, which – believe me – used to be more snobby than anything you'd find in England. Her family made her pull out of the engagement because they thought I was – well, not suitable. My father was dead within the month. Heart attack.'

'That's dreadful.' Becky wondered why he didn't admit he was talking about Francesca. 'Were you besotted?'

'I was young,' he said then pointed out an old well in a field on her side of the road. 'Look, an uncovered one. Most of the old wells have been covered up to stop goats and children toppling in. When I was a kid I loved playing round wells. Unfortunately they are magnets for children.'

Becky tried to imagine Matthew as a young boy, running around with Alex and Chris Harris. She pictured them chasing each other barefoot through the fields.

'On a different subject, how's the research going?'

Becky sighed. 'It's gone nowhere to be honest. There isn't really much new material to work on. I know Clara has a lot of faith in the notes she's scribbled over the years but – how shall I put this? It's as though she wrote them ages ago and then left them alone so they have kind of grown in importance in her mind. Not that I'm criticising her.'

'No, I realise that. The funny thing is she hasn't mentioned writing a history book since – I can't remember when – perhaps since I was in my early twenties. It was something that played on her mind for a few years after my father died but the enthusiasm gradually faded.'

'Oh God,' said Becky. 'Maybe it was just because she felt sorry for me she invented it as a job.'

'She could have been thinking about it all those years even though she said nothing. I'm sure she still often thinks of my father.'

They continued in companionable silence until Matthew asked, 'Did you say no one would have tended his grave for years?'

'That's right. Probably not for – I don't know – twelve years.'

Matthew groaned but said nothing further.

The area they were now driving through looked familiar to Becky; she guessed they had reached the outskirts of Bridgetown. Matthew turned into a cemetery and parked next to a chapel that could have been any one of those pretty little churches you come across in the English countryside, except for the row of pink and white frangipani trees ranged along its borders.

They got out, Matthew opened the boot and handed her the flowers. She sensed he was holding back telling her something. It was quite a large cemetery. Maybe he was wondering how they would find where her father was laid?

'I expect it'll be an unkempt grave with rank weeds and knee-high grass,' she said.

Matthew slammed the boot shut. 'It might be worse than that.'

'What do you mean?'

'There's been quite a bit of controversy recently about old bodies being dug up and reburied in communal graves. You know, so the graves can be re-used.'

Becky nodded. 'I think we have that in the UK. After fifty years or so, if no one has visited, some graves can be reassigned.'

'The controversy is that in Barbados, in some cases, it has happened after just five years.'

Becky could not believe she had finally made it here and there was a chance she might not find her father's grave. 'Thanks for warning me. I won't get my hopes up.'

They went through the gate and walked down the first path, stopping to peer at any headstone where the grave wasn't in pristine condition. 'What was your dad's name?'

'Philip. Philip Thomson.'

'Right, let's keep our eyes peeled.'

Before long they came to a tall granite tablet engraved with the names of the luckless midshipmen, drummer boy, captain and officers of a warship that had been stationed in the West Indies in Nelson's time. The memorial recorded how, like some phantom ship in a legend, the warship had drifted into Barbados one day and people had watched its erratic progress, wondering why there was apparently no one in charge. When it was boarded the entire crew was found to be dead or dying of yellow fever. The monument stood where they were all buried in one mass grave – in the same cemetery as Philip Thomson. Matthew and Becky still had not found his grave but the memorial was a useful way of getting their bearings. It was so large it was visible from every point of the cemetery.

When they found themselves back at the grim memorial for the third time Matthew stopped and frowned. 'We could just keep going round like this forever. You sure he's buried in Southbury, Becky?'

'It has to be this cemetery. I made a note of it from my mother's papers. She keeps everything related to his death in one big envelope. Autopsy, death certificate. Funeral details. I don't understand why we can't find his grave.'

'There were a couple of men back there, digging. If anyone knows the layout it will be the gravediggers. I'll go and ask them.'

'OK, thanks.'

Becky wandered over to an area of well-tended graves where the grief was still sharp judging by the fresh flowers and unfaded cards; some had flower arrangements spelling out 'DAD' or 'MUM'. She paused by one grave commemorated with a simple collection of flowers – handpicked by the look of them, which somehow increased their poignancy. She noticed that a solitary card had fallen to the side of the grave and automatically picked it up to lean it against the flower receptacle. It read: *I'll never forget you, my dearest one. Rest in Peace.*

Matthew was wandering over to her. 'Apparently this is the right area,' he called. 'Any deaths to do with ships seem to be round here, they tell me.'

She stayed where she was until he reached her then pointed to the gravestone. 'It's here. We missed it because it isn't overgrown with weeds.'

The gravestone looked faded in contrast to the bright flowers beneath it but (unlike the tombstones back in Somerset) it was easy to read:

Here lie the Remains of

Philip Thomson

Who lost his life aboard *Abigail*

1951–2003

'It's well tended,' said Matthew. 'Flowers too. That's nice.'

'Is it?'

Matthew looked momentarily confused then seemed to understand what was bothering her. 'Look the flowers probably come from the seaman's union. Or, if not, we'll find out who the Good Samaritan is and you can show them your appreciation.'

'Here's the Good Samaritan's card,' Becky handed it to him. 'I guess I know now why my mother didn't want to come out for his funeral.'

Matthew read the backward-sloping handwriting and turned the card over. 'She hasn't put her name.' He handed it back to Becky.

'No, she hasn't.'

She replaced the card among the flowers and as she straightened up he put an arm round her shoulder. 'I'm sorry. You had no idea?'

She shook her head. 'Naively, I didn't. But my mother obviously did.'

'Listen,' he said gently. 'You told me you have good memories of your dad. Whatever went wrong between your parents doesn't change the fact he obviously loved you and your brother. And it shouldn't change your affection for him. Why don't you put your flowers on his grave and think of the good times you spent together when he was at home?'

Matthew was being so eminently reasonable she couldn't argue with what he was saying but she couldn't get over her shock. 'I'll put the flowers there but I'd brought a card from Joe and me. I don't know whether to leave it or not.'

'If you've brought something all this way of course you should leave it.'

He removed his arm from her shoulder and wandered away to look at the yellow fever monument again. Becky sensed he was giving her some privacy. She spent some minutes staring at the gravestone. While seeing where he was buried made it easier to accept her father would never be coming back, it also raised new questions. It seemed his life away from them would always be a mystery.

And now she had a dilemma: should she tell Joe? That thought reminded her she should capture the scene for her brother but she didn't have a camera and she'd consigned her mobile to the bottom of her case when she'd realised her provider didn't cover Barbados.

'Matthew,' she called.

He came straight over.

'I'm so stupid. I need to take pictures for Joe but I haven't got anything to take them with. Do you have a mobile?'

He got out his phone, clicked a few buttons and handed it to her.

Becky took a few shots of the gravestone and some of the wider cemetery to give Joe a flavour of the setting then handed the phone back to Matthew. 'Thanks.'

They made their way back to the car and drove out of Bridgetown in silence. Becky sensed that Matthew was giving her space to think and she was grateful for it.

'The grave looked like it was being tended weekly, didn't it?'

‘At least,’ he replied.

‘And Dad died twelve years ago.’

‘Mmm. That’s quite a long time, really.’

Becky sank back into thought.

After a while she realised that Matthew was taking a different route homewards. She could see the sea on her left and couldn’t help smiling at a sign for Brighton Beach, as she suspected the area would have little in common with its English counterpart. Strange to think that her father might have seen this and had the same thought.

‘Whoever she is, she must have really loved him to do that week in, week out for twelve years.’

Matthew gave her a grin as though he had reached the same conclusion earlier and was glad she’d finally caught up. ‘They probably made each other very happy,’ he said, softly.

‘Yes.’

‘Would you want to find out more about her?’

‘I’m not sure. Whoever she was she would have been left with nothing. I mean Mum got the widow’s pension. It might get too complicated.’

‘You may be right,’ said Matthew.’

‘I think so.’ She turned to him. ‘Thank you for taking me.’

‘But are you pleased you went?’

‘Definitely. I suppose it’s good to know that there was someone here who cared for him.’

Matthew signalled left.

‘Do I sense a detour?’ said Becky.

‘Business,’ said Matthew, happily.

‘I’ll tell your mother on you.’

‘I want you to see what’s occupying my waking thoughts when I’m in Barbados.’ He gave her a look. ‘When I’m thinking about business, that is.’

Becky had no idea what to make of that comment. She decided not to read too much into it for, although she now knew why Matthew was so driven to succeed, she hardly knew him well enough to guess what non-business thoughts occupied his mind.

Matthew turned left up a small track and parked off to the side.

'A short walk,' he said.

Becky got out and was delighted to find that she was already walking on sand. Although she sensed they couldn't be far from the beach, all she could see ahead were casuarinas towering over stubby trees. As they kept going she could see palm trees and the sunlight sparkling on the water. Further to each side were gleaming white hotels, like huge teeth, facing the sea. Except there was a missing tooth where they were walking on a long, thin patch of earth, strewn with casuarina needles. Matthew stopped beside a small chattel house perched on a bed of rocks.

'Ah, the chickens have gone,' he said, sounding a little disappointed.

'Chickens?'

'The old lady who lived here all her life kept chickens and a goat. Every developer in the island beat a path to her door. They promised her anything she wanted: huge houses with swimming pools and heaven knows what. But she saw them all off.'

'She wouldn't sell?'

'No. She liked her house, she liked her land and she said that her goat liked it here.'

'Wonderful. But what changed?'

'She died, sadly. Unfortunately her children don't feel the same way about the land as she did.'

'That's a shame.'

'Yes, it is. She was such a great old character. You could almost hear the gnashing of developers' teeth every time she turned down another proposal. The bloody

Carrington brothers really tried to put the pressure on. She told them to jump in the sea.'

Becky groaned. 'I'd forgotten. Richard's picking me up this evening. Damn.' She wondered if there was any way she could get out of it.

'*I* hadn't forgotten. I was going to wait until he turned up at seven-thirty and then set the dogs on him.'

'Have you got any dogs?'

'Not *yet*.'

Becky laughed. 'What a shame this patch of land can't stay as it is.' Then she wondered if he would be offended since he was planning to build a hotel on it himself.

'I know,' he said to her surprise. 'If I was an absurdly rich man I'd buy it and move a tenant on here with some goats and hens and a huge dog that she could set on the developers.' He sighed. 'Sadly, I'm not *that* rich. But at least if I build a hotel here I will make sure the beach stays public.'

'You mean the hotels have private beaches? Are they allowed to do that?'

'Not really but some will find ways to put off non-guests. Maybe the only way to access the beach is through the hotel, for example, and then you have to negotiate an obstacle course of the hotel's furniture on the beach.'

Becky laughed. 'Matthew, I had no idea you had a conscience.'

He looked hurt. 'Of course I do. Well, a little one.'

Becky looked out to the sea, indeed much calmer than the one she had glimpsed from Matthew's hotel on the east coast. 'When will you find out whether you've got it? It's a sealed bid, isn't it?'

'Yes. The deadline is midday on Monday. I'll submit it about an hour before. And we find out who wins on Tuesday morning. It's all over very quickly.'

'What will you do if you don't get it?'

'I haven't really thought about it. It will be a blow to be honest, if I don't win. It would be really helpful to have a hotel on the west coast. Then I can offer people a week at each: experience the wild Atlantic, experience the tame Caribbean Sea. I'm sure that would be attractive to many people.'

'It would appeal to me.' Though Becky was really fantasising about living in the little chattel house and running out into the blue water first thing every morning.

'Anyway, I should get it,' continued Matthew. 'Loads of people will throw in their bids for a few thousand dollars – nothing to lose really with a sealed bid. There's just a handful of us who will be talking serious amounts.'

'And that chap at the party, Frank, was it? Is he really a contender?'

Matthew sighed. 'He's serious in terms of the money he can bid but I can't imagine his plan would get anywhere. He thinks he can build a golf course though, as you can see, it would mean golfers having to shout "Fore!" every time someone swims past unless they're scoring points for hitting other tourists. On the plus side I suppose it would give some employment to the locals to snorkel round looking for all the lost golf balls.'

'You're quite funny, actually.'

He looked at her. 'Funny good or funny bad?'

'Good, obviously.' She could hear the waves swishing invitingly on to the beach. 'Can I just get my feet wet?' She saw a slight line of concern cross his forehead. 'Or aren't we supposed to be here?'

He laughed. 'Technically we're trespassing but if you can do a quantum leap over the high water mark and onto the beach, then you're legal again.'

'How do I know where the high water mark is?'

'That line of seaweed there. That's as far as the tide gets.'

Becky ran and did a series of jumps until she had cleared the seaweed line. Then she rolled up her trousers and paddled. He soon joined her – barefoot – his own trousers rolled up.

'Something I've been meaning to ask you,' Becky called out above the gentle chanting of the waves. 'Why does your mother sometimes call you Mr R?'

'My second name is Randerwick. As was my father's and my grandfather's. And if I ever have a son apparently the poor little bugger will have to have Randerwick as his second name too. My father made me promise.'

'Wow, that's amazing,' said Becky.

Matthew looked comically pained. 'My mother hates the name. There's nothing amazing about it.'

'Yes there is,' said Becky. 'Randolph Randerwick was one of the rebels who came here in 1686. You must come from a long, long line of Randerwicks.'

'God help me,' said Matthew.

'And you are infuriating.'

'Am I?'

'I asked you this morning if there was anything related to the rebels handed down in your family and you said no, nothing at all.'

Matthew looked surprised. 'Sorry, it never occurred to me that the name was anything but a family joke.'

'So your great, great, lots of greats grandparents were Randolph Randerwick and Sarah Thomas.'

Matthew laughed. 'If you say so. Then where does Darnley come from?'

'Possibly Randolph Randerwick took the name of the plantation owner he was assigned to, which was William Darnley.'

'Really? I'm a Randerwick rather than a Darnley?'

'Afraid so.'

'How on earth did you solve that puzzle?'

'It was Cook's idea, actually.'

‘Cook?’ He shook his head with admiration. ‘Congratulations to you both for finding out more about my family than we ever knew.’

‘And you’ve been associated with Copper Mill for over three hundred years. Isn’t that amazing?’

‘That is amazing. I knew it was old but I assumed it was eighteenth or early nineteenth century.’

‘Your family probably didn’t get to go inside back then. Wonderful irony that you own it now.’

‘Yes.’ He grinned. ‘I suppose you could say that it’s pretty cool.’

Becky marvelled that they were alone, with no tourists wandering by; the beach in front of the chattel house was naturally adorned with seaweed, while the sands in front of the hotels on either side were pristine. In the distance it looked as though a pod of miniature whales had beached themselves on deck chairs. Maybe the plump tourists had eschewed this patch of land because the sand wasn’t a sterile yellow.

‘Do the hotels clean the beaches? I mean of seaweed?’ asked Becky.

‘Yes, by hand or with a special machine. Obviously they left this bit alone.’

‘It’s nicer.’ Becky looked up at the casuarina trees, which were whispering in the sea breeze. ‘I wish I could legally walk down to the beach just here, every day.’

‘Well, come Tuesday I’ll be the new owner and I might let you.’

‘But it’s Saturday, so as soon as I cross that line of seaweed I could be locked up in a Bajan prison?’

‘Yes, you would be a common criminal,’ agreed Matthew, cheerfully. ‘Whereas I could just about get away with it by saying that, as a serious bidder, I was coming down to inspect the site.’

‘That seems so unfair, especially when *you* brought me here.’

Matthew laughed and picked her up, carrying her out of the water and up over the line of seaweed. Becky assumed he would abandon the grand gesture once they were screened by the trees but technically they were still trespassing and she was happy that he seemed in no hurry to set her down. He paused by the chattel house to sigh – though whether this was in homage to its former owner or to his own ambivalence about building a hotel on this unspoilt area Becky couldn't tell; either way it was very endearing. He seemed oblivious to her weight in his arms, the only clue to any exertion being a lock of hair falling over his eyes. Becky automatically reached up and swept it back. Matthew grinned at her and resumed the walk to the car. He gently put her down next to the passenger door and stayed close while she found her balance but, just as Becky was wondering if it was more than a line of seaweed that had been crossed, he got out his keys and went round to his side.

'You need to get a haircut, Mr Darnley,' she said.

'Mr Randerwick – according to you. Yes I probably do need one. Do you have any talents in that direction, Miss Thomson?'

'I'm very good with secateurs.'

'Hmm. I'll book an appointment at the barbers.'

Matthew was quiet on the way back and Becky sensed that his mood was turning more sombre. God knows what was going on in his head: he could be deep in thought about buying the land or thinking about being a Randerwick rather than a 'real' Darnley. Or maybe he was thinking about her and regretting his lack of action back at the beach.

'When is your next Casino Night?' she asked, to break the silence and test his mood. Matthew ducked his head so he could look through the windscreen at a higher part of the sky. Becky did the same. The moon was a dumpy pearl in the sky, almost fully round.

'Monday night,' said Matthew. 'I'll probably start them again on Monday.'

He had said he would take her 'next time' and, while she had zero interest in an evening of cards or throwing dice, it would be nice to know he had meant it. Becky waited but he didn't repeat his previous offer.

'What is it with gambling and the full moon?'

'You'll see.'

If that was an invitation, it certainly wasn't an inviting one.

Becky didn't bother attempting conversation again but sat back in her seat, baffled and a little hurt by his gloomy silence. They were still travelling up the west coast and she recognised the odd house in a field or the occasional signpost. Of course, she'd been this way with Francesca and Clara. They drove through Holetown and, later on, through Speightstown with its mix of brightly painted rum shops and decaying old colonial buildings. It was only after Matthew had turned right, heading north-east into St Lucy, that he spoke.

'Exactly where is Richard taking you?'

'I don't know. For a meal so I guess a restaurant somewhere.' Was he jealous? Or was this about a wider rivalry with Richard?

'You could cancel,' Matthew said, a few minutes later.

'It's a bit late. He may have booked somewhere.' Two hours ago she had been thinking of excuses to cancel her date but Matthew's moody behaviour was starting to make an evening out with Richard seem quite pleasant.

'I don't suppose you've any idea when Richard's bringing you back?'

'No. I'm sure he'll bring me straight back if I say I want to go to bed.'

'If you say you want to go to bed then he won't bring you back at all,' Matthew said darkly.

Becky gave him a look. 'You need to talk to me. Is there a reason you don't want me to go tonight?'

He didn't answer but his grip suddenly tightened on the wheel. 'Hang on. How did you know about the sealed bid? Did Alex tell you?'

Becky sighed. 'No he didn't.'

'Did you speak to Frank at the party?'

'I'm afraid I accidentally saw it on your screen.'

'I see.' There was a long silence. 'And does Richard know this?'

'Of course not,' she snapped. 'Richard hasn't asked me anything about your business. And even if I did know something, I wouldn't tell him.'

'But you do know something,' muttered Matthew.

So it wasn't that he was jealous that Richard liked her; this was really about his concern that he would be wrong-footed by a business rival. Feeling annoyed she remembered what she had learnt over the last twenty-four hours: although it was near impossible to imagine Matthew's relatives working for the Carrington family it must make the situation very difficult. The trouble was she couldn't think of anything to say that would make Matthew feel better about it. They drove the rest of the way in heavy silence.

It occurred to Becky she might be being naïve. Maybe Richard's invitation did have a more sinister intention but she thought it unlikely. Richard was basically shallow and frivolous; she just couldn't imagine him having the guile to plan a dinner date with an underlying business motive. All the same she would make sure she stayed in control – no drinking.

When they reached Copper Mill she got straight out rather than risk more uncomfortable exchanges in the sealed world of Matthew's car. He got out too, looking murderously at the ground.

'Thank you,' she said, politely, 'for helping me find my father's grave.'

'And after that? Did you enjoy the afternoon?'

She nodded. 'I did. It was a lovely fantasy.' She turned away quickly and went up the veranda steps. Fortunately Clara was not around as she would have been naturally interested in the cemetery visit and Becky really couldn't face talking about any aspect of the day.

She went to her room and lay on her bed for twenty minutes, her mind rambling and blundering around like a clumsy trapped animal. Eventually she decided whatever the history between Matthew and Richard it was nothing to do with her. She had done nothing wrong and she would make sure she did nothing wrong tonight.

Chapter Twenty

Becky had just finished getting ready when she heard a car coming at speed up the mahogany-lined lane. She closed her bedroom door (or was it Richard's old bedroom door?) and reached the veranda just as a silver Italian sports car turned into the yard, provoking the security light into announcing the arrival of an intruder. Becky watched while Richard did a similar spinning-wheel manoeuvre to Francesca, turning the car so it was ready to depart promptly.

He got out into the security spotlight and shouted a cheerful 'hello' and Becky was surprised to hear Matthew answer with a terse 'Richard'. She stepped forward and saw Matthew sitting on a chair, staring at Richard in a manner that could not be described as friendly. All that was missing was a shotgun across his knee. Beyond the light that illuminated the two men, the night throbbed with darkness as the frogs whistled warnings.

'So,' called Richard lazily. 'Got your bid in yet?'

'Not yet. You?'

'No, I'm not in a rush.' Richard turned to look at Becky and even from where she was standing she could see he was running his eyes over her appreciatively. 'Well, hello.'

'Hi,' she said, evenly.

Matthew rose and walked over to Becky. 'Before you go, do you have my mobile number?'

Becky shook her head.

'Do you know the number of the landline?'

Becky had only answered the phone; she'd never had to dial the number. 'No.'

Matthew grunted as though exasperated. ‘I wrote both down in case you need them later.’ He handed her a piece of paper, which she put in her handbag.

‘You are a fusspot, Matthew,’ drawled Richard. ‘Why on earth would she need to ring you?’

Matthew didn’t answer but Becky could feel his eyes on her as she went down the steps and got into Richard’s car. She deliberately didn’t look back. The sight of Matthew staring balefully at their departing car would not put her in the right frame of mind for what she still hoped would be a light-hearted evening.

‘Yee hah!’ cried Richard, delightedly, as he pulled out of the yard. ‘I feel like I’ve rescued you from the clutches of the Prince of Darkness. He’s always such a grim man.’

Yet just that morning she and Matthew had been soaking each other with a garden hose and squealing like children. ‘He’s quite protective of me,’ she said.

‘I hope you warned him you’re going to be late coming home.’

‘Am I?’

‘Very.’

‘Richard, I can’t be too late. You have no idea what security locks are on that door.’

‘Matthew’ll have to leave it unlocked then.’

For a dreadful moment Becky wondered if the whole evening had been engineered to compromise the security system at Copper Mill so mysterious men could break into Matthew’s office. Then she chastised herself; she was not going to let Matthew’s paranoia rub off on her.

Richard gave her a roguish grin and switched on some music. Becky couldn’t name the genre other than it sounded Brazilian: full of drums and carnival and sex. Richard seemed to revel in the decibels he was broadcasting to the countryside, obliterating the normally insistent cries and whistles of the nightlife. Becky had always worried that drivers listening to loud music drove erratically and her view was confirmed by the way he was navigating the road as if he were playing pinball.

If they were going to be very late they must be eating at a hotel where, during the tourist season, cabarets were staged after dinner. Alex had confided that the late nights at the Monmouth were 'doing his head in', because either he or Matthew had to be present to ensure that whatever entertainment was scheduled ran smoothly and this could mean the working day only finished at 11 p.m. Maybe that's what Richard had planned for tonight.

Assuming they didn't end up in the middle of a sugarcane field – or worse vertical in a ditch – which seemed a more likely outcome at the moment.

'Which restaurant are we going to?' she shouted. She had to yell her question several times as Richard seemed to favour repetition over turning down the volume.

'*Chez moi,*' he yelled back. Becky hoped that was the name of the restaurant but had an uncomfortable suspicion Richard meant his own home.

He turned down the music a little and looked at her sideways before rapidly adjusting the steering wheel to reclaim the road. 'You don't mind, do you? I really want you to see my house. Plus I love showing off my cooking.'

'OK,' said Becky, aware a more sensitive person would have picked up from her tone that it wasn't really OK. She had been so determined she wouldn't be tricked into divulging details of Matthew's intended bid she had forgotten the other unwelcome possibility. A snippet of conversation between Francesca and Clara came back to her: 'the girl is insisting Richard Carrington is the father – we're all waiting to see if he agrees to take the paternity test.' Even if Francesca's gossip was unreliable, Becky felt a wave of apprehension. Maybe it was just as well Matthew had given her those phone numbers.

‘It’s taken years between me first buying the land, then doing the design, getting it built and actually being able to move in,’ Richard said. ‘I hope you’re going to like it.’

He made it sound as if her approval of his newly built house was of the utmost importance to him and went into detail about where the various materials had come from, including the kitchen marble tops specially imported from Italy. Becky didn’t do very much but smile and nod for the rest of the drive – pointless actions in the dark but she was worried that a conversation would further distract him from following the sinuous road. She was finding it hard to get her bearings but sensed they were heading south-west, back towards the coast road she and Matthew had driven up earlier. And yet the car seemed to be climbing slightly, which wouldn’t fit with driving down to the coast.

After twenty minutes Richard slowed down so she could fully appreciate the first sight of his house. It was certainly striking and lit up in a very un-eco-friendly way. Unlike Matthew’s sedate plantation house, Richard’s home was a modern metal and glass affair with rooms jutting out so that it looked like a series of goldfish tanks piled on top of one another. Whatever you thought of modern architecture there was no denying he’d maximised his own view. Becky knew that Barbados could not boast a surfeit of commanding heights and yet Richard had managed to find himself a definite rise in the landscape – he could overlook his neighbour. Except, Becky noticed, he didn’t have any neighbours to overlook.

He stopped the car on a large gravel area at the foot of the house. Becky got out and looked around, momentarily disorientated by the absence of lights close by; it was as though Richard’s home was using up all the available energy in the surrounding area, plunging the immediate district into darkness. ‘Isolated splendour you’ve got yourself here?’ she said, as he joined her.

‘Yep,’ he said proudly, ‘and that’s the way I like it. No intrusive neighbours popping in at inappropriate moments. No stray tourists wanting directions to Cobblers Cove. Come up and see my view.’

He led her up some steps and unlocked the door to the first goldfish tank, which was a huge open plan area. Becky could not find a conventional name for it: lounge? front room? There wasn’t anything that adequately described the expanse of space with such an all-round view. She could see a far corner of it was a recognisable kitchen and there was also an area of seating grouped around a coffee table.

Richard was standing in an open doorway, watching her with amusement. ‘Come on,’ he said and Becky followed him on to a terrace to find a table already laid with linen napkins, gleaming silver cutlery and tall candles waiting to be lit. Richard beckoned her over to the railings. She looked out and had to admit – this was amazing. The elevated position of the terrace gave them a panoramic view of the western coastline. ‘Please note that I arranged to have that liner steam past right at this moment especially for you.’

‘That’s most kind, Richard.’ Yes, there really was a cruise ship, ablaze with lights, gliding parallel with the shore. ‘I’m impressed.’

‘You’re worth impressing.’ He was standing just that bit too close for comfort and Becky found herself moving away, involuntarily. He automatically came nearer.

‘Richard,’ she said, straining her face away from his. ‘Who else is here?’ There had to be other people in this huge house: brothers, or hired helps, or someone.

She heard his chuckle close to her ear. ‘Just us. Really, I don’t need anyone to help me prepare dinner or set the table.’

‘Looks like you’ve gone to a lot of trouble.’

‘True,’ he said cheerfully.

‘You are just planning on dinner?’

‘Yes, dinner. And dessert.’

She decided to ignore what she assumed was meant to be a double entendre. ‘Can I have a coke?’

‘A coke? You can’t drink coke in my house.’ He took himself off to the kitchen.

Becky peered over the railings to see Richard’s car parked below and remembered she hadn’t seen him lock it; clearly he was a man who had no worries about his own security. She heard the pop of a cork; minutes later he brought out a tray and two flutes of champagne.

‘Like it?’ he asked after he’d insisted they clink glasses and have a sip.

‘Yes, it’s quite nice.’ She didn’t want him to know how nice it was; otherwise he would be refilling her glass and her resolution to stay sober would be weakened.

‘I’m down to my last two bottles of a case the old man gave me at Christmas.’

She looked at her glass then back at him. ‘I’m afraid this is wasted on me. To be honest I can’t tell it from Babycham.’

‘Babycham?’ He frowned. ‘Then we must make you a connoisseur. I’d adore teaching you about fine champagne,’ he enthused. ‘Bring your glass into the kitchen. I just need to do the salad and the finishing touches to the Lobster Carrington.’

‘Lobster what?’

He giggled. ‘To be honest it’s my own take on Lobster Newburg.’

Becky followed him into the kitchen, clocking the open bottles of sherry and cognac that stood near a pot on the hob; evidently his own take on a dish she had never heard of involved plenty of alcohol. She watched – astonished – as he fetched a bottle of Madeira from a corner of the counter, poured a substantial amount into the pot and turned the heat on high.

She made a mental note to go easy on the sauce with the meal.

'I saw you enjoyed the fish dishes that Francesca did' – he laughed – 'or that her caterers did, so I thought you'd be OK with a lobster meal.'

Becky perched on a high stool at the kitchen bar and watched as Richard chopped up an array of different vegetables. She noticed, with some concern, that there were two bottles of champagne in an ice bucket on a kitchen counter – evidently Richard didn't think that one was going to be enough. He kept up a conversation, frequently looking at her, while his knife seemed to effortlessly fly up and down to the chopping board, converting whole carrots and peppers into even slices.

'How are you on the water? Ever been sailing?'

'No. My sole experience on the water was a trip on a ferry to France.'

'Did you get seasick?'

'I don't think so.'

'Then you'll be fine.'

'Fine for what?'

'Every year there's a regatta. A group of us race from Barbados to the Grenadines. Will you come with me? It's always huge fun. And they've built a couple of new casinos on the islands.'

'I hate gambling.'

'OK, forget the casinos,' said Richard smoothly. 'You'll adore the Grenadines. All have dazzling beaches and sea as clear as gin. A bit short on shade, it's true, but that won't be a problem – we can retreat to my yacht at any time. The cabin is very large and very cool.'

She ignored any inference she was supposed to draw. 'I don't even know where the Grenadines are.'

'Just ask Matthew. He'll tell you. And don't forget to tell him *why* you want to know. That'll ruin his weekend.'

'You really do like irritating Matthew, don't you?'

'Only way I can get my own back,' Richard said unrepentantly. 'He's smarter than I am and a good-looking bastard.'

He arranged the salad so the different colours of chopped vegetables were spread over a plate in a mini-rainbow and turned off the heat beneath the pot. 'I think we're done. We're eating outside, of course. Candles first.'

He topped up her glass with 'the bubbly' and led the way back on to the terrace to light the candles. After the synthetic air-conditioned atmosphere inside it was nice to feel the natural evening breeze. As soon as his back was turned, Becky tipped some of the champagne over the railings, put down her glass and followed him back into the kitchen to help bring out the plates.

'I'm looking forward to this meal,' she said. To be honest I've never eaten lobster warm.'

Richard sighed. 'So much to learn. I can't wait to teach you.'

He served up the Lobster Carrington and carried both plates out while Becky brought the salad to the table so they could help themselves. She had to admit the setting could not have been better. Now she noticed the terrace seemed garlanded in magenta bougainvillea; the candles flickered in the light warm breeze and the night seemed to sing through a line of casuarina trees that bordered his yard. They both sat down and began to eat.

The food was a match for the setting. 'Wow,' said Becky, after a mouthful. 'This is good.' She dreaded to think what proof the sauce was.

'Please try not to sound so surprised.' He gave a comically hurt look and topped up her still full-ish glass again. 'So what do you do with yourself all day in my old house?'

'I'm helping Matthew's mother write a history book.'

'History?' He gave a big mock yawn.

'It's a book about the Redlegs.'

'Oh, them. Why do you want to waste your time on their history? They fought a battle. They lost. Move on.'

'You're very unsympathetic, Richard. The Redlegs' story is an appalling one.'

'I know it is. The story of how most people came to be here is an appalling one. But the truth is that their descendants live in paradise. Anyway there's an unwritten law in Barbados, you know.'

'And it is?'

'If you're Bajan you're allowed to whine and whine but no one's allowed to be unhappy.'

'It's good that you love your island so much.'

'Though after Barbados the second most beautiful place to go to,' he added slyly, 'is the Grenadines, which is why you really should go there with me.'

But he didn't push that topic and instead was happy to answer Becky's questions about himself and his connections to Matthew and Alex.

'So did you know each other from school? I mean you all seem the same age.'

'No. Matthew and Alex went to a local school. I was sent to America. Then there was Yale. Which was boring as hell.'

'That explains the accent,' said Becky. 'I can recognise the Bajan accent now but I thought yours seemed to have a touch of American.'

She relaxed a little and chided herself for being suspicious of his motives in dining at the house. He was fun, nice. While he was sitting opposite her all was well. It was easy to enjoy his humour. And he was refreshingly honest in admitting that, unlike Matthew, he'd had things handed to him on a plate.

'Though Matthew was lucky it was only him,' said Richard. 'I've got two older brothers. Not as good-looking as me, I should add. But the girls always go for the older ones. I think they figure the older ones inherit the money.'

'So your parents are still alive?'

'No idea.'

'You've no idea if your parents are still alive?'

'I mean they live in Florida now. I've no idea if that counts as being alive.'

'With Francesca's ex?'

'Probably all play golf together. He was a pompous old man. God knows why she married him. She must have looked at all his houses in Hawaii and Florida and felt sorry for him.' His sense of humour reminded her of Matthew only more sardonic.

Dinner eaten and the plates returned to the kitchen they came back to the table to chat. Becky suspected Richard was impatiently monitoring her champagne intake. He was certainly being excessively attentive to keeping her glass topped up.

'Oh, no more,' she said. 'It's gone to my head.' It hadn't but only because she was drinking it slowly and had tipped some away.

'The great thing about champagne is that you don't get a hangover,' he said, adding yet more to her glass. 'By the way has Matthew taken you to see the little patch of land he's interested in?'

'Yes. It seems perfect as it is. Shame anyone has to build anything on it.'

Richard raised his eyes. 'Wait until you see the monstrosity Matthew has planned. I've been told he's wants to build a Las Vegas style casino.'

'Really?' Becky suspected if she had said she hated shopping Richard would be telling her now Matthew planned to turn the beach into a shopping mall.

'Well, if he's going to pay four million dollars, which is what I've been told, then he'll have to recoup the money somehow. He won't get enough of a return on a straightforward hotel.'

Becky knew he was fishing. He was so transparent. 'Things do sound scary in Caribbean dollars,' she said, which she thought was a neutral comment.

Richard leant forward. 'Actually I was talking four million *US* dollars. Anyone who gets it for a million or so could probably get away with a simple hotel.' Richard stared at her with not very innocent blue eyes. 'But anything over three million US dollars then I'm afraid you're looking at gambling to get a return.'

'Such a shame,' said Becky. 'Surely Barbados has some other industry than tourism.'

Richard ignored her attempt to change the conversation. 'Have you been to Matthew's Casino Nights? At the Monmouth?'

'No, as I say, I really don't like gambling.'

'Ah, then you'd hate those nights. I'm told that some of the guests can barely afford to buy meals for the rest of their stay if the Casino Night happens early enough in their holiday.'

Becky thought that was as likely to be true as the other things he said he'd been told. Becoming irritated with him, she got up and leaned over the terrace railings, staring at lights twinkling from the bay. 'I can't imagine living with such a good view.'

'You're not seeing the best of it,' said Richard. He took a remote control out of his pocket and pointed it carelessly over his shoulder. Instantly the lights in the lower fish tank dimmed into darkness and the world outside glistened in response: the boats on the sea sparkled and it was as if a million stars had been switched on – though the moon was the great scene-stealer, luxuriantly round as if she had just polished off a fabulous meal.

Unfortunately while Becky marvelled at the night he came to stand beside her – one arm sliding across her shoulders, the other presenting her with her full glass as if she had mislaid it. Becky drifted out from under his arm and put the glass back on the table.

'Ah, you're bored with champagne,' said Richard, cheerfully. 'Time for a brandy. I'll pour us each a glass.'

It occurred to Becky he might use a 'too drunk to drive' excuse to keep her there overnight. 'I don't know how much you've had but you will be OK to drive me back, won't you?'

Richard laughed. 'You're in Barbados now, not England. Unlike yours, this is a civilised island.'

'What do you mean?'

'There aren't any drink driving laws in Barbados,' he said, happily. 'So brandy? Or would you prefer whisky?'

'I don't want any more to drink,' she said, 'Where's your bathroom?'

Richard gave a sly giggle. 'The grandest one is up the stairs and on the left. Take a peek at my bedroom while you're there.'

'Could you light the way so I can find it?'

He glanced at his remote control, pressed a button and subdued lights appeared up the staircase. Becky crossed the dim fish tank and climbed the stairs. It was impossible not to 'peek' into Richard's room as it lay directly ahead with the door open. There were black sheets on a large bed under a gentle pink light. The effect had all the seductive appeal of a dentist's chair.

The huge bathroom held the sort of over ornate, semi-opulent bathroom furniture that in the UK would only be chosen by two groups of people: those with artificial tans who require a bathroom in which to admire their orangeness or those who thought such a choice of bathroom furnishings demonstrated they were being 'ironic'.

The only positive thing about the bathroom was it made the tackiness of Richard's bedroom seem less acute. Although the bed had appeared to be a king size at least it was to scale, whereas in here the sink, bath and bidet were so large they looked like they should host koi and water lilies. The only thing Becky did admire was a printed blind that hid the central portion of the bath: no cheap shower curtain for Richard.

She looked at herself in the mirror trying to ignore the surrounding gold-painted curlicues. She looked young. And she looked irritated. The meal had been very pleasant and the conversation had flowed easily but something had changed once Richard thought she was drunk: not only was he probing to find out what she knew of Matthew's intended bid but he was dropping more obvious sexual hints. While he seemed interested enough in her, Becky wondered if Richard's business and sexual objectives were primarily driven by his rivalry with Matthew, in which case any attempt at seduction would be doubly irritating.

She suspected Richard's game plan was to get her drunk, take her to bed on black sheets and under pink lights and have her scream out Matthew's intended bid at the pinnacle of passion.

How on earth was she going to handle this tactfully? Ringing Matthew was overkill – assuming she could find a phone in the near-darkness downstairs. She certainly wanted to try and end the evening with Richard on reasonably pleasant terms but she also suspected that Richard was not sensitive to subtle dissuasions. She could throw champagne over him but he would probably take that as foreplay. She might have to try the 'I'm in love with Matthew and no other man will do' line but the effect of that was unpredictable.

She finished bathing her face, and paused, thinking she heard a noise. Yes! It seemed fate had intervened to end her evening with Richard 'pleasantly'. There was the sound of a car outside, the unmistakable crunch of tyres going over gravel. Curious as to who had unwittingly disturbed Richard's plans for seduction and/or business espionage, she turned off the light and opened the bathroom door quietly; if she sensed that his uninvited guest was someone reasonable she would dash downstairs and cheerfully thank Richard for a pleasant dinner but say that it was sadly time to go home, now. It would be very difficult for Richard to refuse then.

Someone banged on the front door several times. Richard must be taking his time to get there from the terrace. She heard him give a small, frustrated exclamation as he opened it.

'Know who I am, Carrington?'

The hairs on Becky's neck stood up. The voice was male and decidedly unreasonable.

'I've already paid,' Richard said. He sounded more annoyed than perturbed. Then he said 'what do you need that for?' and this time he did sound frightened. The next moment she heard shouted obscenities and the sound of blows but it wasn't clear who or what was being hit. It sounded like there was more than one visitor.

She couldn't hear Richard's voice any longer; he seemed to be neither putting up a fight nor trying to reason with them. What if they came upstairs? She could lock herself in the bathroom but a locked door would almost certainly attract attention and it wouldn't take long for them to smash it down. Presumably this was something personal rather than a random burglary and what they would do to her probably depended on who they thought she was in Richard's life: if they thought she was significant to him then she was really in trouble.

The blind down the middle of the bath was not completely opaque but if she scrunched herself into a ball in the centre of the tub she might just stay undetected. She climbed in and no sooner had she crouched down than the whole house seemed to vibrate as they pounded up the stairs.

She couldn't tell which room they were in now as their footsteps were drowned out by a terrifying whirring noise. It sounded like a power saw. What were they doing? Surely Richard would be screaming if they were using it to hurt him?

The sound seemed to go on forever. But then suddenly it stopped and she heard raucous laughter. Becky had no doubt now they would find her: her heart was beating so hard that she may as well have been hitting a kettledrum.

Someone came in and turned on the light. A cabinet door was opened and a man laughed.

'What?' Another voice.

'Look.'

The second man laughed too and Becky could hear packets or plastic bottles being swept on to the floor or grabbed. Whether they had found Viagra or heaven knows what she was grateful that whatever Richard had in his bathroom cabinet had distracted them from doing a more thorough search. They moved on to another room. More doors were opened, drawers rifled. She heard the sound of the power saw again. And then they clattered down the stairs and left.

Becky heard their car receding down the drive and, pressing her face to the wall's cool tiles, closed her eyes. Never again would she be scathing of Matthew's insistence on security. Never again would she grumble, along with Clara, at the periodic testing of the alarm system which always set their nerves jangling.

'Richard,' she called out in a rusty-sounding voice. There was no answer. She almost stumbled as she stepped out of the bath; she felt like she was walking on wooden legs across the landing.

She checked all of the rooms upstairs and found three bedrooms in the same state: the beds had been sawn into pieces. The bed in Richard's own room had been the prime focus of attention: not only were the legs sawn off and the bed frame in separate chunks but they had run the saw along the foam mattress itself so that it looked disembowelled.

She wondered what she was going to find on the ground floor. The fish tank was still dimly lit, though the effect was now more eerie than subdued. As she came down the stairs she could hear a strange groaning – prolonged and jarring – and there was Richard's body by the front door. He was tucked into the foetal position as though he had tried to protect himself against kicks to his testicles or stomach. The fingers of one hand still curved round the stem of a brandy glass though the glass was horizontal on the floor and its contents had drained away. There was an extensive patch of blood over the front of his head.

'Richard?' said Becky. There was no obvious reaction to her voice. She repeated his name louder, then louder still as she approached him but he just carried on groaning. She leaned closer and touched his shoulder; instantly he seemed to get agitated, twisting and twitching as a sleeping person might try to shake off a heavy blanket in the night.

What had been the motivation for this dreadful attack?

There was something stuck with blood in Richard's hair – a little blue pill. As he twitched some more, Becky could see more blue pills all around and beneath him; they must have been scattered over him before his random motions shook them off.

She removed the brandy glass from his hand and tried to find a flat surface to put it on – finally having to go into the kitchen, as the coffee table in the main space had been knocked over. Individual packets of condoms had been thrown over the remains of the salad and the kitchen floor. It seemed reasonable to assume Richard was either bothering the sister or daughter of someone who objected or maybe this was related to his refusal to take a paternity test for a woman he had already 'bothered'.

She must get help. She looked round the fish tank but couldn't see a phone; no doubt it had been tastefully recessed. She knew there were no nearby houses to run to though she doubted Richard would find his isolation so splendid after this. And then the obvious occurred to her. She went back to where Richard was lying and reached into his shirt pocket. There was his mobile – switched off, but there. She switched it on and prayed he hadn't put a password on it. Of course he hadn't; Richard was too optimistic to bother with precautions like that.

Where had she left her handbag? She found it still on her seat at the terrace table and dialled the landline number for Copper Mill. Matthew answered within seconds; she imagined he'd been sitting on the veranda waiting up for her return. Her words came out in a rush. 'Matthew, something terrible has happened. Some people have attacked Richard. He's unconscious. I can't get him to come round –'

'Where are you?'

'At Richard's house. It's – I don't know where it is.'

'Don't worry, I know it. Have they gone?'

'I heard them drive off.'

'Have you locked the door?'

'No.' Becky grimaced at her lack of clear thinking. That should have been the first thing she did.

'OK, do that now.'

Mobile clasped to her ear, Becky went back into the fish tank and stepped over Richard to turn the key in the door. 'Locked,' she said.

'Are *you* all right?'

'Yes, yes, I am,' she said. 'I hid.'

'That's good. Do you know if Richard is breathing?'

'He must be; he's groaning.'

'OK, I'll be right there. I'll send the police and an ambulance too.' Matthew hung up.

She looked down at Richard to see if there was anything she could do. The twitching of his arms and legs was becoming more pronounced so she fetched towels from the kitchen and bathroom to use as buffers between the wall and his head and limbs. She used a separate hand towel, soaked in cold water, to try and stem the bleeding from his head but the slightest pressure seemed to provoke more urgent twitching.

He was as swaddled as she could make him and, as she seemed to be able to offer no comfort to whatever primeval consciousness was left in his brain, Becky went to stand on the terrace and wait for Matthew and the emergency vehicles to arrive.

Just earlier that day she had stood barefoot on the land that Matthew and Richard so wanted to buy, on the rug of brown needles from the casuarina trees, looking up at them and delighting in the lulling sound of the breeze through their leaves. But now, in the lively evening breeze, the shushing of the branches sounded less like gentle waves breaking on the sand and more like sinister crones, whispering a threat: *He's brain damaged, he's brain damaged.* However irritating Richard could be Becky's visions of him in a coma or a wheelchair filled her with horror. By the time car-lights lit up the drive relief at her own escape from the violence had been swamped by grim thoughts about Richard's future.

She leaned over the railings. It wasn't the police or the ambulance: Matthew had got there first. He barely brought his car to a stop before he got out and ran towards the entrance.

Becky hurried back inside to let him in and the moment the door was open buried her face in his shirt.

He put his arms around her and his lips brushed her forehead. 'It's probably not as bad as you think. Come on, let's go and have a look at him.'

'He's right here.'

Matthew let her go and bent down to examine Richard. Becky stepped back to give him more room. He moved aside some of the towels she had put around Richard and checked his ears and nose.

'I think that's good,' he murmured. 'At least the only blood is on his head though I know that looks pretty awful.'

Becky knew that head wounds could pour blood so it wasn't so much the red mat of Richard's hair that distressed her as the twitching. There was something so alien about those body movements.

Matthew brushed more blue pills off Richard – his only comment a raising of his eyebrows – and called loudly: 'Richard. Richard. Richard.' He left it a few seconds then kept repeating the three words. Eventually some connection must have been made in Richard's brain because his eyes opened and he blinked furiously: presumably trying to make sense of the pain he was in, his body position and Matthew's face so near him. Suddenly he looped an arm towards Matthew. It was a wild and hopeless gesture but an unmistakeable attempt at a punch.

Matthew laughed. 'That's more like it. Maybe he recognises me.'

'Ecky-Becky.' It was indistinct but definitely what Richard was trying to say.

'On second thoughts maybe I'll just punch him myself,' said Matthew, smiling ironically at Becky.

He stood up and gestured for her to swap with him. 'He'll be more reassured by your face than mine.'

She crouched down beside Richard, gently talking him back into a conscious state by repeating over and over where he was. Richard's growly attempts at speech gradually became coherent words.

'There were two men. They were big buggers.'

'The police are on their way,' said Becky.

Sirens could now be heard getting nearer. Matthew edged past Richard and Becky and went outside to meet them.

Richard grimaced. 'It's coming back to me now. Sorry, Becky.'

'That's OK.'

His eyes opened wider. 'What about you? Are you all right?'

'They didn't find me. I hid in your shower.'

He gave the smallest of nods. 'That's good.'

She straightened up and got out of the way to let Matthew and the two policemen come in. A second siren blared then was silenced as it reached the yard. The ambulance had arrived and shortly afterwards it left again with Richard inside.

It must have been nearly midnight when the police finished asking her questions. They wanted to know whether the 'blue medicine' and the 'packets of rubber objects' (as they judiciously described them) had been scattered around before or during the intrusion. Despite the gravity of the night's events Becky had to suppress a smile when they also asked if the beds had been sawn up before or after the men had arrived.

Of the men involved Becky could say little other than that their accents were Bajan and that Richard seemed to have recognised them or certainly that he was aware of the reason for their visit.

When the police finally said they could go Matthew gently led Becky to his car and drove her home. A mile or so into the journey Becky gave a sigh.

'Are you all right?' he asked.

'It's the relief of you driving,' she said. 'Richard seemed to think he was a character in a computer game.'

'He's been through a few cars.'

‘Will the police catch his attackers, do you think? I mean, it’s a small island.’

The moonlight through the windscreen illuminated his face; he seemed to be smiling. ‘If Richard decides to press charges they’ll have no problem catching them. But he won’t. He’s probably made some girl pregnant or chased after someone’s wife. He just never, ever thinks about the consequences.’

Whereas Matthew clearly did and that was why he’d made sure she had a means of contacting him before she left for her date. Thank goodness for his good sense.

Before long he was turning into the mahogany-lined lane that led to Copper Mill. ‘I sounded a bit unsympathetic back there,’ he said, ‘but I can’t forgive him for getting you involved. It could have been disastrous.’

She was pleased his concern for her was personal rather than just to do with the rivalry between him and Richard then remembered Richard coming round and trying to punch him.

‘What does Ecky-Becky mean? I thought it was just a play on my name.’

‘I wish it were,’ said Matthew. ‘But it isn’t. Ecky-Becky, Becky Neck, Baked-neck, Redleg. As I told you once there are lots of names.’

‘So Richard was being –’ She sank back in her seat. ‘I’m sorry. I didn’t know it was aimed at you. How nasty.’

‘He is nasty. And spoilt. And lazy. And stupid.’

‘I had no idea it was possible to be so frightened. It was the sound of the power saw and having no idea what they were doing with it.’

Matthew looked at her. ‘The best way to get rid of a bad sound is to replace it with a good one.’ He stopped near the bottom of the lane, just short of the yard, switched off the engine and opened the windows. Instantly the chorus of whistling frogs flooded in.

Becky laughed. ‘Am I being serenaded?’

‘I can do better than that. Stay here a second, will you?’

He got out and, as far as she could tell, was delving around in the undergrowth. He returned, his hands cupped together. ‘Ready?’

‘Yes,’ she smiled. ‘What is it?’

He opened his hands and there sat a frog little bigger than his thumbnail. ‘A genuine Barbadian whistling frog. He’s an ugly little bastard, isn’t he?’

The frog looked up at Becky with big black eyes.

‘He’s lovely. To think that something that small can make such a racket.’

‘When you’re that ugly, you have to have some skill to attract a mate.’

‘Ahh, no; he’s cute.’

Matthew returned the whistling frog to the foot of a croton shrub. It immediately hopped out of sight, its shrill cry now sounding less like an amorous call for a mate and more one of piercing indignation at being discovered.

Matthew got back in. ‘So, if you think he’s cute then I must be in with a chance?’

Becky looked at him, baffled. Surely he must know how good-looking he was. Although he seemed serious, she wondered whether there wasn’t some old-fashioned gallantry at play; was he trying to replace her bad experience with a light-hearted one?

‘If you learn to whistle like that, then yes, I’d have thought your chances are very good.’

Matthew whistled a few sad notes then stopped. ‘I’ll have to take lessons from the experts.’

He re-started the engine, turned into the yard, parked and they both got out. The old-fashioned house sat under the moonlight looking untroubled and secure. The security light came on as they walked arm in arm up the steps, looking like an urbane couple about to join a sedate gathering. As they stepped on to the veranda and the light switched off, returning them to darkness, Matthew’s self-control seemed to desert him. He turned Becky round to face him and kissed her.

A few lonely frogs whistled at the unfairness of it.

Initially he was tentative, as if testing her reaction, but as soon as Becky put her arms around his neck, his kissing became more urgent and his hands slid under her top. Soon they were playing with her bra strap.

Becky drew back slightly to catch her breath and take the time to look at Matthew's face. She could see he was so full of longing that, at the slightest encouragement, he would be happy to make love on the floor of the veranda. But after their long day there was a good chance they would then fall asleep and the prospect of being discovered by Clara or Cook in the morning …

Becky put her head on Matthew's shoulder and tried to stifle a yawn.

'Is the gardener's boy boring you?' he murmured.

'Absolutely not,' she whispered. 'But I think things have caught up with me. I'm just desperate for sleep suddenly.'

Matthew sighed. 'Probably just as well. I'm not sure you should be stripped naked on the veranda. Which would have been my next move.'

He sighed again, then turned, unlocked the door and quickly punched some numbers into the keypad. 'I know you think I'm a – what did Richard call me? – a fusspot but with my mother and Cook here alone –'

'*I* didn't call you a fusspot,' whispered Becky. 'I just wish Richard cared more about security.'

Matthew chuckled then tried the impossible task of bolting the door quietly, grimacing exaggeratedly as each one creaked and squeaked its way into place. 'Remind me to oil these tomorrow,' he hissed.

They crept up the stairs, hand-in-hand like naughty teenagers. Outside her door he kissed her lightly on the mouth then walked off towards his room.

Chapter Twenty-one

Becky slept well for a couple of hours but then went through stabs of nightmares: the front door of Copper Mill was wide open and men were making their way up the stairs to her room. Then she was falling from a height on to her father's grave, which was smothered with black flowers. No amount of pillow turning could induce sleep of more than a few seconds before some uncomfortable image jolted her awake again.

She wished she could talk to Joe and tell him about the night's events. She could imagine his reaction – furious on her behalf that she'd been put in that position and totally unsympathetic towards Richard who he would, no doubt, proclaim sounded like a 'prize pillock' who got what he deserved for trying it on. But she couldn't share any of this in an email to him. Not only would it burden him with knowledge that he'd have to keep from their mother but she would have to share her relief at Matthew riding to the rescue – and she hadn't quite come to terms with the change in her feelings towards him.

Which was another issue: how would she and Matthew act when they saw each other later today? He had seen her in a very vulnerable state.

Becky finally fell into a dreamless sleep and woke to hear the sound of clapping and happy hymns riding the wind. It was a cheering sound to listen to. The next she knew a car was driving into the yard below her window and she could hear Clara and Cook chatting. Clara must have brought Cook back from church.

Becky got up, showered and dressed, and went downstairs to the veranda. Evidently Matthew had already relayed the news to Clara and Cook for Clara put down her paperback and rose to give Becky a huge hug. Cook must have decided that a special breakfast was the best way of soothing troubled nerves, as – for the second day running – she placed a plate of pancakes in front of Becky.

'Thanks, Cook.'

'The Lord will get them if the police don't and the Lord will get them if the police do.' Cook patted her shoulder and went back inside. Becky wondered if Cook had prayed for her that morning – she probably had; it was a strange feeling. She told herself she had no right to dwell on last night's events any more: she had prayers and pancakes on her side.

'So, you're OK?' said Clara.

'Yes, fine thanks. Matthew turned up so quickly.' Becky looked at the yard and saw his car was not there. 'Has he gone to work?'

'Something to sort out at the hotel. Nothing serious.'

'Not much of a weekend off then?'

Clara laughed. 'I was delighted that he took yesterday off. Though I think Alex is on duty tonight and Matthew wanted to spare him having to come in this morning as well.'

'I guess Alex's wife doesn't see much of him.'

'Nor his children. And what with Francesca's – well – Matthew's birthday party, I can't imagine they've seen much of poor Alex this weekend.'

Becky wondered if Matthew was avoiding her after their dalliance on the veranda. He'd asked if he was in with a chance but he'd probably just said it to boost her spirits after such a dreadful night. They'd both been in a state of heightened emotion. Maybe he was embarrassed now. Or maybe he had really had to dash to the hotel because the air-conditioning had packed up and he was having to hose down overheated guests.

'Are you sure you're all right?' Clara asked.

Becky nodded and started eating her pancakes.

'By the way,' said Clara. 'I had a look at the French notes that you've typed up. I'm afraid there isn't much there. I scribbled them so long ago I'd forgotten they were nothing but a few scraps I'd collected from here and there. I can't see any name come up more than once.'

'To be honest I'm not surprised. I don't think there are any personal records anywhere apart from dates.'

Clara sighed. 'Maybe I need to accept that this is a hopeless mission. As you said we need the stories of individuals – some continuity from England to life in Barbados – but the information just doesn't exist.'

'Clara, I have to disagree with you. We have evidence of continuity right in front of us.'

'Pitcher?'

'Him, as well, of course. But I meant Matthew. Matthew Randerwick.'

'My Mr R?'

'Yes. Randerwick would have been the real family name.'

'So where does Darnley come from?'

'It's possible Matthew's ancestor took the name of the plantation owner he was assigned to. Maybe that helped him to get married to Sarah Thomas since rebels weren't officially allowed to marry. I don't know.'

Clara gazed out at the garden. 'Does Matthew know this?'

'Yes. I told him yesterday. He seemed quite cheerful about it. And interested too.'

'And you can trace both of his ancestors – this Sarah and Randerwick back to England?'

Becky sighed. 'I can trace Randolph Randerwick back to England but not Sarah Thomas – she just magically walks off the boat in Barbados.'

It occurred to Becky now that Randolph and Sarah's first meeting could have been aboard the *Betty* and that, amidst the horrors of that journey – during which they would have witnessed Thomas Gehalgod and others die and be tossed overboard like animal carcasses – love could have blossomed. Amazing.

'How mysterious,' said Clara.

'Give me time,' said Becky. 'I'll figure it out.'

'You can have all the time you want.'

That wasn't quite true, thought Becky, as she was due to return home in a month but she didn't point this out to Clara.

Feeling much better after a plateful of Cook's delicious pancakes, Becky fired up the computer and was delighted to see an email from Joe. There was no news on the home front – but in his continuing saga Thomas Gehalgod had not only swum ashore and made his way back to his village, he had also passed his NVQ in sheep dipping with distinction. Evidently Joe had been doing some research of his own: he said that '*Judge Jeffreys had been pissed throughout the court cases, as he drank brandy to deaden the pain of kidney stones. The gaols had been chaotic, crammed with men, full of cholera and smallpox. The authorities barely knew who was who.*'

Although Joe's interest in horrible history was morbidly entertaining it did make Becky wonder if any coherent record of the sentencing had been kept. If Judge Jeffreys was handing out sentences in an alcoholic haze would Sarah Thomas even get a mention or would her fate have been decided en masse with that of other Monmouth rebels? Had she even had anything to do with the rebellion or was she simply rounded up with them for convenience in a judicial job lot?

She thought for a long time about her response to Joe. In the end she thanked him for the details about Judge Jeffreys but kept her own news short, only mentioning that she had found their father's grave and laid flowers and their card on it.

When she got back she would tell him about the card she had found. She realised now that both of them had silently resented their mother's lack of emotion over their dead father but, with her new awareness of his 'other life', she would help Joe appreciate their mother had just cause to be ambivalent about the marriage.

Despite trying numerous internet searches, she had not found out anything more about Sarah Thomas before the phone rang at lunchtime. Becky answered it as both Clara and Cook were busy and braced herself for Francesca's querulous voice.

'Becky?' said Matthew. 'You sounded a bit – resigned.'

'I thought it would be – never mind.'

'Did you sleep OK?' he asked.

'A little, thanks. A few silly nightmares. How about you? You couldn't have got much sleep.'

He laughed. 'As it happens I didn't sleep at all well. Your fault entirely.'

'Oh dear,' said Becky. 'Sorry about that. Anything I can do to make it up to you?'

'Maybe. Do you fancy dinner tonight? We'll leave about seven?'

'That sounds great,' said Becky, pleased he wasn't avoiding her.

'I want your opinion on some cuisine.'

That was typical of his sense of humour, making a date sound like a business excursion. 'My working life is so tough,' said Becky. 'I might have to join a union.'

Come seven o'clock Becky was in the smart blue dress she'd worn to the kite competition and waiting on the veranda. Matthew came out of the house, showered and dressed casually, and led her down to the car. 'Madam,' he said, opening the passenger door for her with a mock bow. She giggled and got in.

He got in the driving seat and drove them out of the yard. 'I have some gossip for you. Something I forgot to tell you yesterday.'

'You? Gossip?'

'Yes. From the UK. That guy you were with at the hotel – Ian what's-his-name?'

'Ian Watt?'

'Yes him. Chris bumped into him in a pub one night where he was moaning he'd been sacked from his job. He said – and this was his side of the story – he'd been showing a new girl how to use her computer and she'd mentioned it to her boyfriend, who was a complete nutter and was waiting for him after work. There was a bit of scuffle and the police were called and the boyfriend said Ian had tried to molest his girlfriend. Anyway Ian got sacked, which, according to him, was very unfair. It seems he was particularly bitter that the women in the office ganged up on him and told the editor he was always sexually harassing the new girls.'

Becky laughed. 'Justice, finally.'

Matthew looked sideways at her. 'So you really didn't know he'd booked a double room for you both in the hotel?'

'No, of course not.'

'Then you must have thought I was a bit of a jerk.'

'Actually, I thought you were a complete jerk.'

Matthew whistled. 'Hope that opinion's changed.'

Becky giggled again. 'I'm working on it. Anyway, how's Chris?'

'He'll be fine. Effectively he's been demoted to assistant manager – I've got someone else acting as manager – but he seems happy with that. I'll go back and check on things in a few weeks but, for now, emails and Skype are all I need.'

He turned off the air-conditioning and opened the windows so they could let the warm air rush through the car. Becky loved it: it was rare in Britain to feel warm on a grey, overcast day. The closest she felt to this in the UK was just before an autumn storm.

'Does Barbados have seasons?'

'Sure. Fine weather, more fine weather, ditto, ditto, bit of rain, sometimes lots of rain, fine again. We're just about at the end of the rainy season now.'

Becky recognised the turn-off to the Monmouth but to her surprise they drove past it. 'Oh, I assumed we were eating at your hotel.'

'Certainly not. Even if Alex's there, if the staff see me they'll keep interrupting, badgering me with problems they're paid to resolve themselves. Or guests I'd hate to upset will feel affronted if I don't linger to chat.'

'We're not going to a Carrington hotel, are we?'

'No. We're going to one in St Joseph, further down the east coast. Their restaurant has a new chef – he's supposed to be a master at seafood so I'd like to check it out.'

Becky felt mildly deflated. Maybe he really did just want a second opinion on the food. On the other hand, it took the pressure off – they could just chat as friends and not worry about that other 'stuff'. 'So will they know who you are or are we in deep cover?'

'That would have been more exciting but I'm afraid I reserved a table in my own name.' He laughed. 'In the name of Darnley, that is. Anyway, I know it sounds boring but everyone who owns a restaurant expects to see their rivals there occasionally. And not only to check out the food; sometimes we just want to have a nice meal without being involved. I find it impossible to eat at my hotel and not feel responsible for whether other guests are enjoying themselves.'

Becky sensed that Matthew was driving inland but as the only light was from his car lamps and the scenery was cloaked in darkness she had no idea if she had been this way before.

After driving for about half an hour after leaving Copper Mill they pulled up at the St Joseph hotel – a smaller affair than the Monmouth but equally sedate. The restaurant was separate from the main building, with most of the tables inside and a few under the covered decking outside. The maître d' showed them to one of these, lit the candles and removed a small 'Reserved' sign. He stood back while they sat down and Matthew consulted the wine list.

'White OK? Or do you prefer red?'

'White sounds good,' said Becky.

If the restaurant staff were aware Matthew was checking out the restaurant, far from resenting it, they seemed pleased to have his patronage – almost anxiously pleased. After the chilled white wine was brought to the table and he approved it, Matthew pleasantly, but firmly, discouraged any more fussy attention so they could study the menu without feeling rushed. It turned out Matthew was particularly interested in the lobster dishes so Becky elected to have some sort of salad with lobster and mango. He chose a lobster pie. She thought it prudent to avoid mentioning Richard had cooked her lobster last night.

'I suppose Richard won't get his bid in now if he's in hospital.'

'His brothers will. When Richard says he's doing something business-wise it's really his older brothers who are doing the actual work. Richard just sits on their coat-tails for the ride.'

Matthew's mobile rang. 'Sorry, I thought I'd switched it off.'

'Don't worry, go ahead,' said Becky.

He answered the call and listened to the person on the other end, giving Becky a pained look. 'Well, don't poison them then.' He ended the call and pointedly turned off the mobile.

'What did I tell you? That was the headwaiter at the Monmouth in a panic because Derek Carrington – that's Richard's oldest brother – has taken a friend there for a meal. What do they expect me to say? Poison the potatoes? Do him in with a steak knife?'

Becky laughed. 'I assume Richard can't be that poorly if his brother is eating at the Monmouth.'

'I'm sure he'll be fine. His family would pay whatever they had to to get him the best treatment.'

The maître d' arrived with their dishes just as a dam above was breached: rain pouring down with such force that it seemed to bounce off the ground and collide with itself. Becky watched, bemused, as a few other diners pushed back their chairs and started the chaotic procedure of collecting their bags, drinks and, in some cases, their half-finished meals, to take into the restaurant.

'Would you like to move inside?' the maître d' asked. Matthew looked at Becky who grinned and shook her head. They were perfectly dry and the rain crashing down just a few feet away charged the air with energy.

'We're fine here, thanks,' Matthew said and the maître d' told them to enjoy the meal and went back inside.

'Do you mind if we share?' asked Matthew. 'I'd like to taste both dishes.'

'That's fine,' said Becky.

They each helped themselves to some of the other's meal before trying their own and neither could decide which was the nicer dish. 'Yummy,' said Becky. 'However are you going to compete?'

He took the teasing good-humouredly. 'No problem. I can match it – at least my very fine young chef can. But I have to admit this is really excellent.'

'Is everything OK?' The maître d' reappeared, looking anxious.

'The lobster pie is absolutely superb,' said Matthew, 'and my companion has pronounced the salad – what did you call it?'

Becky winced. 'Um, I said "Yummy".'

'So please pass on our compliments to the chef.'

The maître d' looked relieved and promised to pass on the comments verbatim.

The rain continued as they finished their main course making conversation a little difficult but they were both so relaxed in each other's company it didn't matter.

The waiter took away their empty plates and brought them the dessert menus.

'It all looks lovely,' said Becky. 'But I don't think I can manage more than a coffee.'

'Same here.'

Matthew ordered two coffees and the waiter nodded and went inside.

'We must do this more often,' he said.

'That means,' she said wryly, 'that you've got a busy day tomorrow and you want to go home now. I can read your mind.'

His gaze lingered on her mouth. 'I doubt that very much.'

Becky laughed. 'Well now I can definitely read your mind.'

Matthew grinned then looked past her and frowned. 'What are they doing here?'

Becky turned round to see Francesca holding an umbrella over an elderly man, as he hung on to the banister of the short wooden stairs leading to the covered terrace and levered himself up. Francesca saw him safely to the top and he looked around him disapprovingly as she disappeared down the steps again. At least Becky thought he looked unimpressed – his frown may just have been the stock expression of an elderly person trying to adapt to unfamiliar surroundings.

Francesca reappeared with a similarly disapproving-looking elderly woman who also looked around as though she found everything wanting. Their gazes flickered over Matthew and Becky without interest but Francesca, once she had dealt with her soaking umbrella, looked up and first smiled then scowled as she saw Matthew, then Becky.

'Mum, Dad, look. It's Matthew.' She came over and gave Matthew a peck on the cheek while her parents peered at Matthew with apparent lack of recognition or, at any rate, a complete lack of enthusiasm.

'Huh? Matthew? Have we met him?' said her father.

'Yes, you remember Matthew,' said Francesca loudly.

'Oh, Matthew,' said her mother. 'Yes, of course we do.' She obviously had no idea whether to smile, shake hands or turn away. She smiled awkwardly.

'And this is Becky,' said Matthew.

'She's working for Matthew's mother,' said Francesca.

'Hi,' said Becky, brightly.

'Hwuh?' said Francesca's father, which could have been a greeting or an outward expression of his internal confusion, which had been made worse by being introduced to a girl he'd never seen before, who worked for the mother of a man he still couldn't place.

'Shall we join you?' asked Francesca. 'My parents are over from Philadelphia for a few days so I thought I'd bring them here. All my friends are raving about the food.'

'It's certainly an excellent restaurant,' said Matthew with bland politeness.

'Is there a table inside?' asked her mother.

The maître d' shook his head and regretted they were absolutely full up inside so the choice was either to take one of the unoccupied terrace tables or to come back in half an hour.

'It's going to have to be outside then,' said Francesca. Becky could see her eyeing an empty table a few feet away. 'Can you move that table over here and –'

But just then the waiter brought out Matthew and Becky's coffees. Francesca looked disappointed. 'Ah, you've already eaten.'

Whatever Francesca's motives for getting the two parties together, her mother had already sat down at the table which was furthest away – though the terrace was too small for this gesture to be very meaningful. Francesca's father followed her, sat down, and said 'Hwuh?' again.

'It's Matthew. *Matthew*,' hissed his wife.

Francesca's father buried his head in the menu the waiter handed to him and shouted to an unspecified audience, 'Why can't you get turtle soup any more? Can get it in Philadelphia, can get it in Singapore, but Barbados – not even a turtle head.'

Francesca smiled at Matthew, rolled her eyes then joined her parents. 'Because it's illegal, Daddy,' she said loudly.

'Hwuh.'

Matthew and Becky swapped a look and quickly drank their coffees.

'Bill, please,' Matthew said to the waiter. He leaned forward to Becky. 'I really do want an early night tonight. Not just because of the unexpected floor show but because Alex will be round at nine tomorrow morning and I want to make sure I have the bid ready to go.'

'So tomorrow's the big day?'

'And midday's the time.'

He paid quickly and they ran through the rain and got into his car. Matthew had called a brief 'goodnight' as they passed Francesca's table but even if a response had been forthcoming they were moving too quickly to hear it. He drove off promptly.

'So they'd have been your father and mother-in-law?' asked Becky, then remembered Matthew had never admitted to her that his first love had been Francesca.

He just made a 'disgusted' face. 'Hwuh.'

The journey home took slightly longer than the outward one because the roads were awash with water in parts though the rain had stopped by the time they reached St Lucy. There was no goodnight kiss tonight as Clara's three bridge-playing friends came out to see how Becky was after 'her ordeal' at Richard's house. While Becky could see Renee was genuinely appalled Becky had had such an appalling experience, (which she insisted was 'very rare in Barbados'), Becky felt the other ladies were more interested in some gossip.

'And do you know why he was attacked?' asked one of them.

'No idea,' said Becky though Matthew was watching her with rather mischievous eyes. To his credit it seemed he had not divulged details of sawn-up beds and scattered Viagra tablets to Clara.

In front of the bridge-ladies, Becky formally thanked Matthew for the dinner and he formally thanked her for helping with the 'restaurant review'. Then he went off in the direction of his office and Becky went upstairs to bed.

Chapter Twenty-two

Becky woke up later than usual – nine o'clock, which she put down to the sleep deficit from two nights before. There was no sign of Clara – presumably having a post-bridge night lie-in, so Becky had some breakfast and exchanged a few words with Cook before going to the morning room. She looked through the window and marvelled at how the sun bounced off Matthew's Nissan Sedan: what a contrast to the previous grey day. Then she was surprised Matthew's car was still in the yard – and there was no sign of Alex's. Maybe they had already headed off to Bridgetown in Alex's car.

She went out to the veranda and found Matthew sitting quietly, head bowed, holding a sealed envelope in both hands. He was oblivious to her, checking his mobile, staring at the envelope and checking his mobile again. Something was wrong.

Becky went back in to get him a coffee and, when she brought it out for him, he looked at her and smiled a 'thank you' but then immediately turned back to the yard.

'Alex isn't here yet?' she asked.

Matthew shook his head. 'He's late.'

Becky's one experience as a passenger in Alex's car had shown him to be a competent driver but she worried that, when negotiating the sinuous single-lane roads in this area, he was very much at the mercy of boy-racers like Richard coming in the opposite direction.

'Have you tried his home?' she suggested. 'Find out what time he left?'

Matthew got up and Becky followed him into the hall, watching while he dialled a number. It must have been answered immediately. His voice was quiet but there was no mistaking his concerned tone. 'He's not there? No, he's not here either. And he's not answering his mobile.'

He listened to the person on the other end and his voice became graver. 'OK, let's not worry yet. He was at the hotel last night. He probably worked too late and stayed over rather than waking you up. I'll ring them.' Becky thought she could make out a woman's voice coming through the receiver, not shouting but definitely a tone of distress.

'Of course I'll call you straight back, Deborah.' Matthew ended the call and immediately dialled another number.

Becky looked up and saw Clara coming down the stairs. She waited for her to reach the bottom then told her what was happening.

'That's worrying,' said Clara. 'No matter how late Alex works I'm sure he always makes a point of getting home. Poor Deborah must be beside herself.'

'So Matthew's got two hours to get to Bridgetown?'

'Which of course is doable,' said Clara. 'But it leaves no contingency time.' She sighed with exasperation. 'I wish Mr R wasn't so paranoid. I'm sure everyone else simply posted their bids days ago rather than leaving it to the last minute.'

Matthew appeared behind them, obviously furious.

'Would you believe it? Today of all days Alex's crashed out at the hotel. He's OK but they're having a job trying to wake him up.'

'That doesn't sound good,' said Clara.

'They think he's just very tired.' Matthew looked at his watch then at Becky and Clara.

'Would you two like to be my bodyguards instead?' He gave a slight smile. 'Mum, I thought you could be a decoy while Becky holds the envelope and fends off any would-be attackers as she's had the practice recently.'

'Matthew,' admonished Clara. 'Poor Becky.'

'No,' Becky laughed. 'It's better to joke about it.'

'I must change,' said Clara, worriedly.

'No, Mum. What you're wearing is fine. No make-up, no formal dress, no time. It's just if I can't park the car properly at least I can leave you two in it while I deliver the bid.'

'I'll be ready in one minute,' promised Clara. 'Just need my handbag.'

'I'll ring Deborah,' said Matthew. 'Becky, can you tell Cook?'

Maureen walked through the front door at that moment and seemed to pick up on the urgency in the atmosphere. She looked at Becky and raised her eyebrows quizzically.

'We have to dash off to Bridgetown,' explained Becky.

She left Maureen to update Cook, grabbed her own bag from the morning room and shepherded a handbag-clutching Clara into Matthew's car before getting in herself. Matthew ran down the steps after them, jumped into the driver's seat and passed Becky the sealed envelope. She noticed, with relief rather than amusement, that his first action after starting the car was to engage the central locking; her experience at Richard's had left her believing anything could happen. It was unlikely but still possible that someone could open the door when the traffic lights turned red and make a lunge for the envelope.

Once they were well on their way and no landslides caused by yesterday's rain or traffic accidents seemed to be hindering them they chatted more easily. Matthew was driving fast, but not recklessly, and Clara was enjoying the ride.

'You know I think I'm almost back to normal,' she said. 'I shall start driving us around, Becky.'

They pulled into Bridgetown at eleven-fifteen, giving Matthew ample time to park the car legally and disappear with the envelope.

While Clara and Becky were waiting for him they were approached by two sandy-haired men in casual suits. Something about their fairish hair and blue eyes looked familiar.

'Clara?' said one.

'Hello Bobby,' said Clara. 'Have you met Becky?'

'No, but we've certainly heard of Becky,' he said, sticking his hand through the car window for Becky to shake. 'Hi, I'm Bobby Carrington.'

These must be Richard's brothers, looking business-like but cheerful. Becky assumed Richard's condition wasn't too serious.

The other man introduced himself as Derek Carrington.

'How's poor Richard?' said Clara. 'Horrible business.'

'He's going to be fine,' said Bobby. 'We thought his skull was fractured but he seems to have escaped that. They'll probably let him out tomorrow so long as we can promise someone will be around to look after him.'

'Which means he'll stay with me,' said Derek. 'Being waited on hand and foot by my wife, needless to say.'

'We thought we'd see Matthew at the solicitors but figured he must have been earlier,' said Bobby.

'You've just missed him,' said Clara. 'We came a little later than we intended. Did you put in a bid?'

'Yes, we did,' said Bobby.

'Anyway,' said Derek. 'Say hello to Matthew for us. Oh yeah and tell him that his cook or one of his cooks at the Monmouth is brilliant. I ate there last night with a friend. Really impressed.'

'I shall pass it on,' said Clara, whose delighted smile revealed her pleasure in hearing her son's hotel praised.

'See you then.' The brothers waved goodbye and walked off at an unhurried pace.

'The Carrington boys aren't too bad, really,' said Clara. 'Though Richard is perpetually young.'

Becky wondered how difficult meeting like that was considering Matthew's father would have been known as 'the gardener' to the Carringtons but she had detected no awkwardness in the exchange.

'Ah, here he is,' said Clara, excitedly, as Matthew walked towards them looking more cheerful and relaxed than he had earlier. He got into the driver's seat and let out a theatrical sigh of relief.

Clara patted his shoulder. 'Well done, dear. Everything went OK?'

'Ten minutes before the deadline. It would have been earlier but there was a queue of people leaving it until the last minute. Amateurs.'

Clara laughed. 'Yes, dear, of course they are. Oh and we saw Bobby and Derek Carrington. They said they were looking out for you but hadn't seen you.'

'No doubt I just missed them. What a shame.' He grinned.

'Derek said your chef is superb,' said Becky.

'No surprise but always good to hear. Now, you two, I want to drop in on the hotel to make sure Alex is OK. And maybe lunch in the restaurant?'

'That sounds lovely,' said Clara. 'I'd kill for a coffee.'

Matthew took the more scenic route back. A couple of times on the way he shook his head and made some reference to the fact that 'Alex would choose this day of all others to be ill'.

'But you're probably made of stronger stuff than most,' said Becky, trying to lessen the possible flare-up when Matthew came face to face with his right-hand man. 'No doubt you'd have made it to the solicitors even if you were attached to a drip.'

'Too damn right,' said Matthew. 'If I'd had a notifiable disease I'd have rolled along in a huge isolation bubble.'

Before long they had reached the hotel. They found Alex leaning on the reception counter, beside himself with contriteness. Becky thought he appeared to be in a dreadful state; with his bleached face and red-streaked eyes he looked as if he'd been poisoned. She suspected too much alcohol was to blame rather than just tiredness.

'Sorry, Matthew,' Alex said. 'I wasn't feeling that well last night. I meant to lie down for half an hour before driving back home but I was out of it. Did you get the bid in?'

'Yes, just been,' said Matthew, failing to disguise the note of impatience in his voice. 'Have you rung Deborah? She assumed you had come straight to the office after sleeping at the hotel. She was really worried when I said I hadn't seen you.'

'I have.' Alex's grimace suggested it had been a difficult conversation.

'Everything OK here? Anything I need to know?' asked Matthew.

'No. It's fairly quiet now.'

'Great. Well we're off to lunch. Oh, remember, it's Casino Night tonight. I assume the would-be Bond is booked?'

'All sorted.' Alex turned to Becky 'Sorry to hear about Saturday. That must have been terrifying.'

'It was,' said Becky. 'Though of course Richard was much worse off. But his brothers say he'll be out of hospital tomorrow.'

Matthew and Clara headed for the restaurant and Becky was about to follow them when Alex stopped her. 'When did you meet Richard's brothers?'

'They put their bid in just before Matthew got there so Clara and I had a few words with them while we waited outside.'

Alex frowned. 'Today?'

‘Yes, just before we came here.’ She waved a goodbye (which Alex seemed too preoccupied to return) and rushed to catch up with Matthew and Clara.

It was a rare occasion when Matthew, Clara, Cook and Becky shared an evening meal but having checked everything was all right at the hotel earlier Matthew decided he did not need to go in again and suggested a barbecue in the yard. It was a group effort: Matthew and Becky in charge of the marinating and barbecuing, Clara and Cook in charge of frying plantains and fritters. They ate up on the veranda and eschewed cutlery for fingers. Halfway through the meal Clara noticed that a branch of her avocado tree was hanging down, possibly displaced by the previous day’s rain.

‘Oh look at that,’ she said, crossly. ‘If I’d seen that earlier today I would have chopped it.’

‘It’s just one little floppy branch,’ protested Matthew.

‘Your father had to chop off all the top branches,’ said Cook. ‘Mr Carrington told him to because the boys kept falling out of the tree.’

‘What? The Carrington boys?’ asked Becky.

‘Yes, if it wasn’t Bobby or Derek falling out they would climb up and holler for Richard to follow. And then he’d fall out. And the tears –’

‘Wimp,’ said Matthew.

‘It would almost make your father cry too,’ said Clara. ‘He hated hacking away at healthy trees unnecessarily.’

As they looked at the tree it was as though someone had turned a huge celestial dimmer switch to low: within minutes the branches were almost in silhouette and, after a brief period of tuning up, the whistling frogs’ orchestra was in full swing. The moon looked as though it was coming in to land. Maybe to put an end to the melancholy that now tinged their mood Matthew changed the subject.

'Now, Mother, we're not going to have your bridge ladies turn up suddenly, are we?'

'And see me like this?' (She was using both hands to gnaw on a pork chop). 'Certainly not. Though I must admit I'm getting a little bored of bridge.'

'What?' exclaimed Matthew in faux horror. 'I thought that was impossible. I assumed it was like golf. People discover the game, play it obsessively and then drop dead having done nothing else with their lives.'

'So negative, Matthew. Though what you've said is true about people who play golf.'

'Do you play for money?' asked Becky. She couldn't remember any gambling on the one occasion she'd tried her hand at bridge.

'Sometimes we play for tiny stakes. Just a dollar here and there to liven it up,' said Clara. 'Maybe it would be more exciting if we increased the stakes.'

'Oh no,' cried Becky and Cook.

'I fear that both Becky and Cook think any gambling puts you on the slippery slope,' said Matthew, looking amused at their prim reactions.

They finished eating and cleared away the plates. Clara and Cook retired, leaving Matthew and Becky on the veranda.

'So what is it about the full moon?' Becky asked, 'Does it make your poor hotel guests more reckless?'

Matthew looked puzzled. 'How do you mean?'

'Is that why you have Casino Nights around the full moon? So that they gamble away more of their cash?'

'Maybe they do spend more when the moon is full – that hadn't occurred to me. But no, that's not the reason.' He leapt up and grabbed her hand. 'Come on. I said I'd take you to a Casino Night.'

'Oh no,' protested Becky. 'I have no interest in gambling.'

'I know. Nor me.'

'And I'm not dressed properly. Well, neither are you.' They were both wearing light trousers and shirts.

'We're dressed perfectly.' He locked the front door and firmly led Becky down to the sedan.

'Why is it so important that we go?' she asked, as he opened the passenger door for her.

'Because I have a feeling you think I'm a bit of a bastard who wants to make as much money as possible out of innocent punters.'

'I think you're very focused on business,' said Becky. A couple of days ago she would have completely agreed with what he'd just said but she was now much more sympathetic, recognising what it had taken for Matthew to build up enterprises in two countries. Remarkable for a gardener's boy who had probably started with no capital.

'Focused on business?' He grinned. 'You're being diplomatic. Which means you'll never really like me until you understand what these nights are about.'

Becky admitted to herself he probably had a point, got in and let him close the door. She hated gambling as much as she could hate anything but decided to trust Matthew wouldn't make her do something she didn't want to do. He got in the driver's side and they drove in silence to the hotel.

Matthew parked beside the sea wall again and Becky paused to listen to the waves crashing below as she got out of the car. She looked at the floodlit entrance of his hotel, gleaming white in the moonlight. Small groups of people were standing outside smoking by a designated ornate ashtray off to one side. They were dressed up to the nines; one woman was even using a black cigarette holder, though presumably the effect was a little diffused by having to come outside to show it off. Still the people were clearly very light-hearted, enjoying plenty of laughter. A melodious alarm sounded: not the harsh post-interval bell of theatres but a cheerful noise; it sounded to Becky like someone was playing an old James Bond theme tune on a xylophone. The smoking groups giggled, stubbed out their cigarettes and cigars and headed back inside.

'We might be overdoing the James Bond theme,' said Matthew, cheerfully. 'But I think people like it. Also they know it's just fantasy.'

'But they could still lose lots of money?'

'It would be very, very difficult. The stakes are fifty cents, a maximum of a dollar on the games which involve more than spinning a wheel. People can learn the rules of roulette, Baccarat etc but, to be honest, it's more about entertainment. They also get cheap drinks and the buffet is half-price.'

'They'd never want to leave your hotel.'

'Exactly,' said Matthew.

'But you can't be making a profit either.'

Matthew looked at her. 'I barely break even on Casino Nights.'

A doorman wandered over and grinned when he recognised Matthew. 'Evening, Mr Darnley. You coming in to throw a dice?'

'Not tonight, Don. Off duty.'

The doorman smiled and made his way back to the entrance. Matthew indicated a path from the car park, which looped down towards the beach.

'We're not going in?' said Becky.

'No. Now careful – the path leads to some steps; there's a rail on your left and it's a bit steep in parts.'

Despite the moonlight Becky was glad to have something to hang on to as she followed Matthew down the uneven steps and onto the sandy beach. She could see he was watching her but he said nothing, allowing her time to appreciate her surroundings.

The hotel's beach furniture had been neatly stacked far above the seaweed line, indicating the high-water mark and, apart from some very low-level orange lights beside the steps, the moon had full responsibility for illuminating the shore.

'We'd better take off our shoes,' said Matthew, quietly. He slipped his off and stuffed his socks in them. Becky leant on him while she undid her sandals and laid them on the sand, which glowed lightly in the moonlight.

'We just leave them here?' she asked and then mentally kicked herself. 'Yes, of course we do.'

'I promise they won't be stolen,' said Matthew. She couldn't see his face but she knew he was laughing at her.

The feeling of cool sand beneath her bare feet was extraordinary. Becky marvelled at the intensity of the experience: the waves rolling in made a crashing sound far louder than was noticeable during the day – and bizarrely – the sea actually smelt of fish as though shoals had come into the shallows for the night. As for the moonlight reflected on the water – it was as though the sea had turned into a huge kaleidoscope with only silver glitter to play with.

'I've just realised – I've never been on a beach at night,' said Becky.

'Then you've never really lived,' said Matthew.

He took her hand and led her further along the beach, staring at the sand as though he were looking for something. After a few yards he stopped. Almost immediately she felt her naked instep being brushed by scoops of sand. She giggled. 'There's a crab playing games with me.'

'Oh, in that case let's take a few steps back. It isn't a crab.' He was speaking very softly, his eyes fixed on the area in front of them. They moved back a little and released hands so they could sit down. As Becky's eyes tuned into the moonlight she realised the area she had just been standing on was becoming agitated. Little lumps of sand were being pushed up. A few minutes later a solitary grey head emerged, followed by little flippers.

‘Oh my God,’ she cried, delighted. ‘A baby turtle. Isn’t it gorgeous?’

‘There’ll be more,’ said Matthew, happily.

The solitary fellow paused, as if waiting for a round of applause, then used its flippers some more and made it out on to the beach. Behind him the sand gradually caved in to reveal a hole filled with his sand-encrusted, squirming siblings. Clambering over each other, desperately trying to find a way out, each would have bouts of paddling up the sandy sides of the hole before resting, seemingly exhausted by the effort of freeing themselves.

‘These are hawksbill turtles,’ said Matthew, softly. ‘And it is almost impossible not to intervene. I try and resist unless they get really stuck or head the wrong way.’

Becky could see exactly what he meant. She had to stop herself from giving the baby turtles a helping hand, as their escape seemed to take so much out of them. She was surprised how emotional she felt and surreptitiously brushed away a tear, though she suspected Matthew had noticed. Once out the baby turtles scrambled in fits and starts towards the sea, looking like ridiculous wind-up toys that needed their batteries constantly changing. But at least their path to the sea seemed unerring, the moonlit water drawing them onwards as naturally as the moon pulls the tides. They seemed to know that the sooner they got into their true element, the better.

The ones at the bottom of the heap had it the hardest, as by now the hole was quite deep and a couple were floundering on their backs, desperately trying to right themselves.

‘They look so vulnerable,’ said Becky in an embarrassingly choked-up voice.

‘And they are, poor little sods. That’s why we run the Casino Nights when the turtles come up to lay their eggs and later, like now, when they hatch. Keeps people off the beach when they might otherwise want a romantic stroll under a full moon.'

'But none of your guests would want to harm them, would they?'

'Probably not. But it's this obsession with recording everything. It's as though nothing in this world counts for anything unless you can catch it digitally and post it on Facebook or YouTube or whatever.' He sighed then spoke more calmly. 'The flashes on their cameras can be fatal. The hatchlings get disorientated and head up the beach instead of towards the sea. If they haven't found the sea by dawn, then it's game over.'

'You could make it a special eco-thing. If people were told why they couldn't have flashes.'

'Other hotels do just that. They have special turtle nights. But I'm worried a couple of prats will take photos and then say innocently, "I didn't know that my flash went off automatically". I'd be so annoyed I'd probably deck them. So safer all round to dissuade people from coming onto the beach.'

Becky remembered Francesca's father complaining turtle was no longer on the menu. 'I can't bear to think of anyone eating them,' she said.

'Don't worry,' said Matthew cheerfully. 'Their flesh is quite toxic to humans, particularly that of the hawksbills. People can die.'

'Oh good,' said Becky, adding quickly, 'I mean if that puts people off eating them.'

She could tell Matthew was smirking. There was just one little turtle left, which had been flailing around on its back for a couple of minutes.

'I can't bear it,' she said.

'Go on, then.'

Becky reached forward to scoop it out of the hole and onto the beach, gently righting it at the same time. The turtle flopped where she'd laid it, exhausted.

Becky got up, scooped it up again in her cupped hands and set it down a few yards nearer the sea. This seemed to galvanise the turtle into action – it started its ungainly paddling over the sand to join its sea-bound siblings, some of whom had already reached the water.

Matthew joined her and they watched its slow journey down.

Becky felt a ridiculous sense of triumph. 'You know that feels like one of the most useful things I've ever done. Isn't that stupid?'

'Not stupid at all,' said Matthew. 'Especially from the turtle's point of view. Maybe that'll be the lucky one that will still be alive twenty-five years from now.'

'Wow.'

He was standing very close to her now. 'I knew you'd like Casino Nights.'

'I love Casino Nights.' She smiled at him. 'I'm only sorry it's taken me this long to know what they're about.'

'That's my fault. Sorry.'

They kept watching until Becky's turtle splashed into the water. Matthew gave a quiet cheer.

'God, I'm feeling quite emotional,' said Becky. 'Thank you for showing me that. This is one of the best nights I've ever had.'

'It's not over yet. Unless you want it to be?'

Was that a romantic proposal or a straightforward question? All Becky knew was she didn't want the evening to be over. She had never felt so alive in herself, so in tune with another person. Impulsively, she gave him a hug, wondering if he would return it politely then lead her back to the hotel, to the lights, to people, to a restaurant, to a world less alive. He hugged her back and when her hands slid from his shoulders he did not let go. Instead, he kissed her and she kissed him back like they had on the veranda a couple of nights ago. As his tongue explored her mouth Becky realised he was fighting an internal battle to control himself and take things slowly. They both paused for breath and he searched her face in the moonlight, as if unsure this was what she wanted, then picked her up and gently laid her on the sand.

He lay down beside her. 'I'm sorry,' said Matthew. 'I don't think I'm going to be able to stop. You'll have to scream "no" and throw sand in my eyes.'

Before she came to Barbados Becky might have done just that. Feeling Matthew's eyes on her she scooped up a handful of sand, held it as though weighing it and then opened her fingers, letting the sand grains drift away. Immediately he was unbuttoning her shirt, her trousers and tugging all her clothes off. She felt warm sea air gently exploring her nakedness as she watched him pull his own shirt off. Then he was leaning over her, kissing her again and she heard the metallic clink of his belt buckle being released.

Chapter Twenty-three

The house was hushed on Tuesday morning with an air of anxious expectancy. Even Clara was up much earlier than usual and unusually sombre. Today was the day they'd find out about the bid.

Becky found Matthew on the veranda and noted that he had donned a shirt for the special occasion, though evidently he still didn't think long trousers were warranted. When he saw her he got up and gave her a hug, only breaking off when Alex's car drove into the yard.

'Today he can manage to be on time,' muttered Matthew. He sat down and patted the cane chair next to him. 'Do you want to join us? Then the three of us can sit here in tense silence waiting for my lawyer to ring.'

'An irresistible offer,' laughed Becky. 'But I am going to resist it all the same. Sorry, but I must get to the computer – my rebels are calling me.'

'This rebel's calling you.'

She laughed at Matthew's rueful smile. 'You'll have Alex for company.'

She smiled at Alex as he came up the stairs, noting that he looked very strained and she didn't think it was due to a hangover. Maybe he had problems at home.

Becky went to the morning room and fired up the laptop. She'd decided to try and approach the Redleg story from a different angle by finding out what happened to those transportees who made it home. She had read somewhere that the merchants in England had complained that the loss of skilled labour had wrecked the weaving industry: they wanted the rebels brought back. Which was perfectly possible three years after the Battle of Sedgemoor as James II had been hounded off the throne and, within months, the rebels had been pardoned.

All she needed to do was to find testimonies from men who had been sent to Barbados but come back to England. They were bound to have given information on their lives as Redlegs and might even mention fellow rebels such as Randerwick or Pitcher.

But Becky found out something peculiar about Barbados. Although many of those exiled to islands such as Jamaica were freed and offered transport back to England, the plantation owners of Barbados seemed to have a special influence that allowed them to ignore the edict and hang on to their indentured labourers. Of the English, Scottish and Irish Redlegs in Barbados, it seemed none of them ever made it back to their homelands.

'You OK?'

Becky looked up to see Maureen staring at her quizzically. Only now did she smell the wood polish and realise that the table (apart from the patch occupied by her laptop) was shining; she hadn't even noticed Maureen come in.

'Yes, I'm fine, thanks. Miles away.'

She moved the laptop to one side so Maureen could finish polishing the table.

The phone rang and Becky and Maureen exchanged looks as they heard Matthew run in from the veranda to pick it up. Becky went into the hall to find Clara and Cook already standing there, waiting to hear the outcome. She noticed with slight surprise that Alex had stayed out on the veranda.

Matthew listened to the caller, poker-faced.

'Thanks for telling me,' he said and put down the phone. He turned round and looked surprised to find a female audience.

'The Carringtons got it.'

Everyone groaned. Clara put her hands to her face.

'How much did they bid?' Alex appeared in the doorway.

'I don't know. Let's hope it was five times what I was bidding.' Matthew smiled. 'Right. Come on everyone. That's it. It's over. We move on.'

Although he was smiling Becky knew how disappointed he must be; she had seen how much emotion as well as time and money he'd invested in the project. He really had thought the land was already his.

He noticed her looking at him. 'Really,' he murmured. 'It's fine.' He grinned. 'Of course I might need cheering up later.'

Becky blushed, which made him grin even more.

Alex seemed more affected by the news than Matthew. He looked ashen-faced. 'I'd better get back to the hotel,' he said.

'No, have the day off,' said Matthew. 'I'll ring Clarence; he can hold the fort for a day. Both of us deserve a break.'

Alex nodded.

By eleven o'clock, a strange party-like atmosphere had descended. Matthew had inveigled Alex into helping carry the cane furniture from the veranda to the garden, (so he could 'sit in the sunshine with my toes in the grass') and they'd enjoyed a tower of Cook's pancakes – her panacea for all troubles. Now Matthew had gone indoors and Clara and Becky were watching Alex clear a space on the table. Matthew reappeared and plonked down a jug of rum punch; it rattled with ice.

'Oh, Matthew. I'm not sure I should,' said Clara.

'Nor should I,' he grinned and poured four glasses. 'But I'm going to get hopelessly drunk and write off the rest of today. After all, "tomorrow is another day".'

Becky frowned. 'I would never have expected you to quote from *Gone with the Wind.* But I can't remember if Rhett Butler or Scarlett O'Hara said that.'

'It was Scarlett O'Hara,' said Matthew. 'She has all these voices swirling around her head. "The red earth of Tara." "Why land's the only thing that matters".'

Alex gave a bitter chuckle. 'I think she got to keep the land, didn't she?'

'I'll think of some way to get him back,' said Matthew, more grimly.

'Ah,' said Becky. 'You're not talking about Rhett Butler now.'

Matthew raised his glass. 'No. But it was a fair fight and they won. Here's to the Carringtons. Just a small sip, everyone.'

They drank tentatively. Becky couldn't remember having ever tasted alcohol this early in the day. She looked over to Alex, who didn't appear to have any qualms about drinking this early. Maybe this was hair of the dog for him.

Matthew raised his glass again. 'And now you're allowed a larger gulp. For here's to, "tomorrow is another day".'

'Tomorrow is another day,' they chorused more happily.

A car Becky recognised pulled in and came to an abrupt stop. Zena's mother got out and unbuckled Zena from her child seat. Her movements were hurried, slightly panicked.

'I'm sorry,' she said, rushing over, so that Zena – tethered by her hand – had to toddle along at a fair rate. 'My childminder's just been taken ill. I've got to leave Zena with her grandmother.'

'I'll take her,' said Becky, holding out her arms, which Zena ran into with a happy 'Weeeeeeee' cry.

'Thanks,' said Zena's mother gratefully. She ran back to her car and drove off. Zena sat on Becky's lap looking around at the less familiar adults at the table.

‘Aren’t you gorgeous?’ said Clara with a mixture of delight and unmistakeable longing. Becky wondered if Matthew was aware of his mother’s quiet grief at the absence of grandchildren. Zena, recognising another source of adult admiration, wriggled from Becky’s lap to Clara’s and started exploring Clara’s small bouquets of earrings.

‘You don’t have pierced ears, do you, Clara?’ said Becky, wincing at Zena’s rather urgent tugs.

‘No, fortunately.’ Clara anxiously checked the jewellery was still clasped to her ears. It was – but only because Zena had turned her attention to a half-eaten pancake on Clara’s plate and decided that her mouth was the best destination for it.

‘You didn’t want that did you, Mother?’ said Matthew, clearly amused.

‘No, I think that pancake went to a good home.’ Clara found a tissue and rubbed Zena’s hands and face clean of butter and maple syrup – another process the little girl seemed to find interesting.

When Clara had finished, Zena looked at the men at the table and wriggled down from Clara’s lap to investigate Matthew and Alex. She chose Matthew, who hurriedly pushed his glass of rum punch out of her reach.

‘You wouldn’t choose Alex who at least has some experience of children,’ he sighed, leaning over to study the little girl then pulling a fierce expression that sent her scuttling towards Becky. But curiosity got the better of her. She ran back to Matthew, reaching out to run her hand up his cheek and feel the rough texture of his hair then pulling back – her squeals a mixture of fear and delight – when he repeated his gargoyle-look.

They all laughed and Zena looked questioningly at them while happily grabbing handfuls of Matthew’s plaid shirt and examining the pattern. Then her attention was caught by a roofless jeep pulling up confidently onto the gravel. Matthew just managed to grab her before she leapt into the yard to welcome the arrival of this wonderful beast.

'It's Francesca,' said Clara, surprised. She asked Matthew something in French and he simply replied, 'non'.

Francesca got out and beamed. 'What a fabulous idea! Brunch on the lawn.'

In a cheerful rum punch glow the adults all called out 'hi' or 'hello' and Zena waved manically. Francesca stared at her, confused, then looked at Matthew.

'Pull up a pew,' he said cheerfully. 'We're toasting the Carringtons' good fortune.'

Francesca smiled in a puzzled way. She doesn't remember about the bid, thought Becky, or maybe Matthew had never bothered to tell her. Alex gallantly went up to the veranda and fetched another cane chair for Francesca but she automatically moved into his vacated chair (next to Matthew).

'Come and sit with me, Alex,' said Becky, trying to suppress a giggle. He gave her a rueful grin and put the chair next to her.

'I apologise for gatecrashing,' said Francesca, with a tinkly laugh. 'I'm afraid I just had to get away. My parents are over for a few more days and driving me quite mad. My father is convinced Barbados has gone to the dogs since they emigrated but then he thinks anywhere outside Philadelphia is a third-world country.' She gave another tinkly laugh.

Zena stared up at her in fascination. 'Hee-huh-huh-huhh.'

'What did you say, Zena?' said Matthew.

'Hee-huh-huh-huhh.'

Matthew looked quizzical. Clara and Alex both bowed their heads and Becky too was struggling not to laugh. It was so obvious Zena was trying to emulate Francesca's tinkly laugh. On her third attempt Francesca scowled at her and Zena looked anxiously at Matthew. He pulled her on to his lap from where she evidently felt brave enough to stare at the strange tinkly woman.

'She has quite an intense gaze,' said Francesca. 'Is that normal?'

'She must think you're interesting,' said Matthew, diplomatically, and he tried to distract Zena by walking his fingers up her tummy. The child's unrestrained laughter was infectious. Becky was surprised at how easy he was with the toddler, considering he had neither nieces nor nephews. By contrast Francesca looked like she wished Zena would go to some specially designated Child Space, far away.

'Granny,' said Zena, firmly, paddling furiously in Matthew's arms.

'Ah,' said Matthew. 'You're bored with me already.' He set her down and she made her way across the yard and up the veranda steps, hugging each stone spindle on the way and using it to pull herself up the next step.

'I wouldn't take it too personally,' said Becky. 'Zena really means, "Granny's often in the kitchen where there's lots of nice things to eat".'

Zena made it on to the veranda and went inside.

'Whatever childminders get paid it's not enough,' said Matthew. 'I'm exhausted.'

'Poor Matthew,' said Francesca. 'I have to say I can't really imagine you with children of your own.'

'Rubbish. He'd be very good with them,' said Clara.

'I'd better just check Zena's found Cook OK,' said Becky, getting up and going indoors.

There was no sign of Zena in the hall. Hopefully she'd gone straight through to the kitchen. But when Becky looked in there, Cook was sitting down looking at a newspaper spread out over the table.

'Has Zena not made it in here?'

'Zena, no, she's not due –'

'Your daughter-in-law dropped her off. The childminder's ill.'

Cook pushed herself to her feet. Becky did not wait for her but ran out to continue searching. Zena wasn't in the small bathroom next door, nor was she in the morning room or the dining room. Surely she could not have made it up the stairs?

'Maureen,' Becky called up to the landing. There was no answer. Maybe Maureen was right at the back of the house.

Becky heard Cook utter a cry from the lounge and ran in to see Zena rolling on the floor, her eyes wide, acutely distressed. Cook had her fists clenched to her breast wailing in horror. Becky knelt beside Zena and tried to make sense of her discomfort: there was no obvious blood, she didn't appear to be choking on anything and she was clearly breathing, albeit rapidly. Just as Matthew and the others ran in she spotted a can of furniture polish under a chair.

'I think we need an ambulance,' she said. 'Zena must have sprayed polish into her mouth.' Matthew headed for the phone in the hall while Alex, Francesca and Clara crowded in.

'Make her sick,' said Francesca.

'No,' said Becky, closing her eyes. She knew this, she was sure. She'd done a piece – one of several page fillers in the *Essex Gleaner* that masqueraded as first aid articles. For poison you should never make the victim sick but when to give nothing and when to give –

'Milk,' said Becky. 'I'll get some milk.' She ran to the kitchen. Matthew was still talking urgently on the phone.

Becky took a glass of milk back to the living room and propped Zena up while Francesca poured little sips into her mouth. Much of the milk streamed over Zena's face but Becky and Francesca managed to get her to swallow some.

Matthew came back in. 'It's going to take too long,' he said. 'There's no ambulance north of St Thomas.'

'Take the car,' said Clara, who was standing with her arm around Cook.

'I wouldn't trust myself. I've drunk too much. Alex?'

Alex was standing quietly in the background. He shook his head.

'I'll drive,' said Francesca. 'I think she's had as much milk as she can handle.'

She put down the glass and headed out to her car. Matthew picked up Zena and followed. 'Come on, Cook,' he said urgently. 'She'll want you.' Cook was clasping Clara's hand so Clara went too: with Francesca, Matthew and Zena in the front, Clara and Cook in the back, the jeep screamed away.

Alex and Becky looked at each other, emotionally drained.

'The milk must have been a good idea,' said Alex, soothingly. 'I thought she seemed in less pain after she had some.'

'I hope so.'

'What happened?' said a bemused Maureen, coming in to find out what the commotion was about.

'We don't know,' said Becky. 'We think Zena somehow swallowed some furniture polish.'

'Zena?'

'Her mother had to drop her off early.' Worried Maureen might blame herself, she added: 'the trouble is we weren't prepared for her. At least they're getting her straight to hospital.'

Maureen closed her eyes and looked pained. 'The hospital is all the way in Bridgetown. It will take them an hour.'

'Damn,' said Becky. 'I should have suggested the clinic.'

Maureen shook her head. 'If it was an emergency they would have sent her to the hospital anyway.'

Unable to settle at the computer again, Becky went out to the garden to bring in the rum punch. What a strange morning: from deflation about the failed bid to a sort of euphoric acceptance and then panic.

She turned to go back in and saw Pitcher standing in the yard looking up at the house and carrying that infernal piece of paper.

'Hello Pitcher,' she said wearily, traipsing past him up the steps, jug and glasses in hand.

'I have to go to the clinic.'

'Not today. Your appointment can't be today.'

He unfolded the paper and held it out. 'Look.' His finger was confidently (though randomly) jabbing the printed name of the clinic. 'That says, "Tuesday".'

Becky snatched the paper from him. Sure enough, he had an appointment today. There was no time given – perhaps the nurse realised that a fixed appointment would be pushing it – but to be fair Pitcher was getting the days spot on.

Becky sighed and went in to break the news to Maureen then found Alex in the office and told him they had to take Pitcher to the clinic and would be back as soon as possible. He nodded miserably.

Pitcher sat in the back of Maureen's car looking out at the passing fields. It was impossible to tell whether he picked up on the tense atmosphere: Maureen driving, stony-faced, Becky silent. Becky tried to feel more sympathetic towards him: it was hardly his fault he had an appointment on the same day as Zena had had to be rushed to hospital. She noticed that he had once more made an effort in the sartorial department in that he was wearing shoes and a clean shirt with all its buttons – or, more accurately, with an assortment of buttons filling the requisite number of buttonholes. At least Alex was still back at the house if there were any phone calls about Zena.

Maureen looked at her. 'Is this the last check-up?'

Becky unfolded the paper again and read it. 'Yes, it's the last time he sees the nurse. He's going to be gutted.' She looked at the handwritten note again. All she had taken in when she read it earlier was that the appointment was today. Only now did she spot the nurse's surname: *Mr Pitcher to see Nurse S. Thomson for final check-up*. Maybe that's what the receptionist had meant originally when she had heard Becky's surname and commented 'another Thomson'.

Becky tried to remember what the nurse's first name was – something beginning with 'S' of course. No doubt Pitcher knew it but he looked so serene it seemed a shame to disturb him. Becky searched her mind. The nurse had worn a name badge and she remembered noticing the name looked Indian. Sairah. It was Sairah. Sairah Thomson.

Becky shut her eyes and sighed inwardly: how could she have been so stupid?

They were soon at the clinic and Maureen dropped them off and went to find a parking space. As soon as he was out of the car, Pitcher was hurrying ahead like a dog straining at the leash.

'Hang on, Pitcher,' Becky called. He reluctantly slowed his pace. 'What's the name of your nurse?'

A shy beam lit up his face. 'Sarah.'

'Sarah what?'

'Sarah –' He looked confused. 'Thomas?'

Close enough.

'And what does she say to you?'

Pitcher gave a sheepish smile. 'Mustn't drink so much rum; women don't like men who carry on.'

'You said she was in that other place. Where is that other place?'

Pitcher beamed and pointed to the clinic. 'Right here.'

Becky nodded and picked up her pace to the main entrance.

'She want nothing from the Will, she get nothing from the Will.'

God knows what that was about. Maybe with his strong Bajan accent he was saying 'well' as in water rather than anything to do with a legal will. Maybe it was some Trinidadian nursery rhyme that the nurse had muttered to distract him from his painful treatment; Sairah Thomson could have realised Pitcher was a sponge – soaking up words and rhythms to the exclusion of other sensations.

'OK, Pitcher. Let's go in.'

But he was on a roll. 'Leave them stitches well alone if you want strong skin and bones.'

'Yeah, yeah. Come on.' Becky led him into the clinic.

The receptionist recognised them and directed them straight to the chairs, where Pitcher continued to mutter to himself. Becky tried to block him out and figure out what she felt. Disappointment definitely. Of course she had never really believed Pitcher was a spiritualist conduit to a woman who had been dead for over three hundred years but she had to admit she had loved the mystery of Sarah Thomas while it had lasted. Or maybe it had been a tinge of madness.

She should be satisfied that a silly little puzzle had been resolved. What else were you meant to do with mysteries but solve them? At the very least she should be laughing at herself for her gullible reaction to the collection of factors which had conjured up the ghost of Sarah Thomas in her mind. And yet she felt quite a sense of loss.

'I came on a boat, and I was all alone, then I met a man and we mek a home. Then the man died, and I'm back alone,' Pitcher told the floor.

A sad rhyme from Trinidad, possibly. Or a literal description of how the nurse had travelled from Trinidad to Barbados, maybe to take up this nursing post. Becky shut her eyes and tried to work out if Matthew and the others would have reached the hospital yet. No, they were probably still on the road. Not even a full hour had passed since Francesca's car had torn away from Copper Mill. She had to admit Francesca was the ideal driver for a mercy dash; she wouldn't let minor obstacles like speed restrictions or unhurried pedestrians slow her down.

'What does this Becky want from me? Why is she looking for me?' said Pitcher.

Becky's eyes snapped open. She'd forgotten Pitcher saying that. How could that be linked to the Trinidadian nurse? She looked at Pitcher's appointment note again as if it might hold a clue and realised she'd seen that backward-sloping handwriting somewhere else.

The door to the treatment room opened and the Indian nurse came out and called for Pitcher, who was out of his chair almost before she'd finished speaking. Becky rose too and saw the nurse semi-retreat into her room, poised to shut the door the minute Pitcher entered, but halfway there he developed a left limping gait, which he then corrected to a right-legged limp. Becky caught him up at the doorway.

'You don't have to come in, Miss Thomson,' said the nurse.

Becky put her hand on the door to keep it open. 'I'm afraid I do, *Mrs* Thomson.' The nurse reluctantly stepped aside to let them both in then shut the door behind them.

'Or can I call you Sarah?' said Becky, 'Is that how you pronounce it?'

Sairah nodded. 'Most people pronounce it that way. I don't mind.'

Pitcher looked dismayed to see Becky in the room too but was too placid to make a fuss. He sat down and put his right leg forward. Sairah bent over and began undoing his bandage. Becky sat on the chair in the corner.

'Does your mother know?' Sairah muttered.

'I don't know to be honest. I think she must have suspected but she never mentioned you. She didn't even mention my father much.'

'I meant about getting married to Philip. She knew about me.' Sairah unfurled the bandage and automatically started re-rolling it neatly round her fingers. 'You didn't know?'

'No, I didn't even realise they'd got divorced.' Sairah gave her a frightened glance and the penny dropped. 'Ah, I see. They hadn't.'

'There was no time. My family had got to hear of Philip. They were sending one of my brothers over to Barbados to make sure we were –' She searched for the right word, 'correct. We had to marry very quickly. I thought that's why you were looking for me.'

'I wasn't. I saw your card on his grave just a few days ago but I decided not to try and trace you. Before that I had no idea you existed, let alone were married to Dad.'

Sairah looked at her, obviously surprised. 'You really didn't know?' She looked down at the rolled-up bandage in her hand and said softly, 'We'd been married for just a year when he died. He talked a lot about you and Joe. I thought maybe you had found out and were looking for me.'

'Not at all. I really was just looking after Pitcher.'

'Will you tell them? About Philip's other wife?'

Who did Sairah mean by them? The authorities in Barbados? 'No. And even if I did I don't think you'd be in trouble. You could have married him in good faith, after all. But I won't tell anyone.'

Pitcher tapped his right leg impatiently to get Sairah's attention. 'You don't need another bandage, Mr Pitcher. Look how well it's healing.'

Pitcher looked mildly anguished. 'OK. A plaster. I'll get you a plaster.' Sairah went through a selection of plasters then rejected them all for a theatrically large piece of gauze, which she taped to his leg.

'How is Joe?' she asked.

Becky sighed. 'He's sort of OK. I don't think I realised how much he missed our father. I'll take him back photos of the grave. Maybe that will help.'

'I have something for him.' Sairah pulled a plastic bag from beneath her desk and handed it to Becky.

The bag contained a boxed car. Becky took it out and held it in both hands to study it. The name of the model on the box (a Holden LH Torana) meant nothing to her but it was a cheerful green and looked old rather than new, which rather added to its attraction. 'He used to bring back dinky cars for Joe but this is huge.'

'He said the colour was called "Barbados Green" – that's why he got it for your brother. I've kept it since … I've had it for twelve years. I couldn't throw it away.'

'It's great that you kept it all this time,' said Becky.

'I brought it here in case you came back.' Sairah dropped her head and corrected herself, 'in case we ever talked.'

'Thank you.'

'It was for his next trip home. I suppose Joe would have liked cars then.'

'He still likes them. He'll probably be as happy with this now, as when he was eight.'

Sairah looked at her. 'I'm sorry there's nothing for you. Philip was looking for the perfect present. He just couldn't find it. He did keep looking.'

'No worries. Joe's present is enough.'

Becky turned to Pitcher, who looked like he still wanted more treatment, and laughed. 'Come on. This excellent nurse has fixed your leg.'

Pitcher remained seated defiantly. 'When is the next time?'

'Sorry Pitcher,' said Becky. 'There is no next time.'

He got up and limped noticeably towards the door.

Becky and Sairah swapped amused but sympathetic glances.

'That man is not getting enough attention,' warned Sairah.

'I know,' said Becky, sadly.

She wanted to say a proper goodbye to the woman her father had loved but couldn't decide what was appropriate. Finally she stuck out a hand to shake. Sairah took it and pulled Becky in for a hug.

Chapter Twenty-four

'Still no news about Zena,' said Alex coming to meet them as soon as Maureen and Becky got back to the house. Pitcher wandered off limping worse than he had when he was first injured.

Maureen, Alex and Becky looked at one another. Matthew and the others must have reached the hospital by now. Maureen went into the kitchen, presumably to prepare something for them to eat when they got back and Alex headed for the office though Becky could not see how he was able to work. She sat at the table in the morning room and fired up the laptop but found it impossible to concentrate. She couldn't even think what to put in an email to Joe. She could hardly say she had important news about their father to share with him on her return: not when she wouldn't be back for almost another month.

One more month. She couldn't imagine not being here at Copper Mill. She couldn't imagine not seeing Matthew every day. Had he given any thought to their lives after she went back to England? Did he remember that she was due to leave in just four weeks?

Becky pushed these thoughts aside and remembered Zena. Hopefully she would be receiving treatment by now. But why no news? All Becky was aware of was the passing of time. The clocks in the house that she had barely registered before seemed to tick like synchronised bombs. She kept going into the hall and staring at the phone yet she jumped when it rang. It was Matthew.

'Becky? I just thought I'd let you know what's happening. Zena's being seen by a doctor now so we haven't heard yet. But she did get distracted in the car. Once she saw a few things on the way that grabbed her attention she certainly seemed less upset. I think she's going to be OK.'

'Thank God,' said Becky.

'Early days yet,' said Matthew, quickly. 'I'll phone as soon as I know anything definite. I'm going to take a wander now to see if I can find some coffee for us all.'

'OK, thanks for letting me know. I'll tell Maureen and Alex.'

She hung up and discovered Alex and Maureen were both standing behind her in the hall. They must have heard the phone ring too.

'Matthew thinks Zena's going to be OK. The doctor's with her now.'

Alex smiled and returned to the office. Maureen still looked concerned. She must be feeling responsible. Becky decided it would be a good idea to make a drink for all of them as well.

She was on her way back to the morning room with a mug of tea when the phone rang again. Had the doctor finished examining Zena already? It was Matthew on the other end but his voice was very different, very harsh.

'I've just bumped into that complete waste of space, Richard Carrington.'

'Richard?' Becky knew he was still at the hospital but that did not explain Matthew's angry tone. 'Yes, his brother said he'd be could be discharged today.'

'Do you know how much they bid for the land?'

'No idea, Matthew. How would I know?'

'Two point three million *and fifty* dollars.'

Becky was not sure what she was meant to make of that. She said nothing.

‘Why did you tell him?’ Matthew said, ‘did he get you drunk? Did he trick you? Why in God’s name did you tell him?’

Realisation slowly dawned. The Carringtons’ bid was only fifty dollars more than Matthew’s own. ‘I didn’t tell him. Why on earth would I?’

‘I’ve no idea. You tell me.’

‘I’m telling you I didn’t pass any information to Richard.’

‘You saw the amount I was going to bid. I know you did.’ Matthew sounded really angry now and the tenor of his voice reminded her of the man who had humiliated her at the Monmouth UK. She felt sick.

‘Yes, I saw it on the computer, but –’

‘You know how much that land meant to me.’

‘But I didn’t tell him.’

‘How else could he have known?’

Becky was already sure she knew who the culprit was and could imagine how he had been tricked into disclosing Matthew’s bid. But the truth wasn’t important: the point was that Matthew had immediately assumed she was to blame. She’d believed she’d seen a different side to him here in Barbados but clearly he was as unpleasant as she had first thought. ‘If that’s what you want to think then that’s up to you,’ she said. ‘At least tell me if there’s any news on Zena.’

‘She’ll be fine,’ he snapped. ‘They say Francesca’s trick with the milk made the difference.’

Before Becky could decide whether to correct him or not she heard a click: Matthew had hung up on her.

Becky returned to the morning room feeling furious but also deeply betrayed. So much for the man who was prepared to forgo profits to save endangered turtles. Had that all been an act to get her to sleep with him? And she had fallen for it. There was no way she could spend another minute in his presence. She felt badly about letting down Clara but she was going to have to invent some reason to go home.

Mechanically Becky sat down in front of the laptop and searched for flights from Bridgetown to the UK. There were two flights that evening to Heathrow; the latest left at 11 p.m. Was that soon enough to be gone before Matthew came back? The idea of seeing him – even at a distance – filled her with anxious dread.

But first she had to come up with a plausible excuse. Whatever it was it would have to be a lie, unless Matthew had shared his apparent discovery that she had revealed the bid to Richard Carrington in which case Clara herself might think it best that Becky leave Barbados early too.

As she started going through the booking process to find out if there were any seats, she heard the gruff engine of a jeep pulling into the yard. They couldn't have returned already. Becky checked the time on the laptop and was astonished to see she had been on the computer for more than half an hour. She went to the window and looked out, feeling a huge relief when she saw it was only Clara and Francesca.

A few minutes later they came in, Clara looking drained. 'Zena is going to be absolutely OK,' she said. 'Cook is staying with her and then her daughter-in-law will bring her back here tonight or tomorrow.'

'I think Matthew took it the worst of all of us,' said Francesca. 'Even when we knew Zena was fine he seemed to be …' She frowned. 'He seemed very upset.'

'He's staying at the hospital?' said Becky, hopefully.

'No, he wants to spend the night at the hotel,' said Clara. 'I don't know why.'

'Anyway,' said Francesca. 'I'll be off now.'

'Thanks Francesca,' said Clara. 'That was some very good driving.'

Francesca nodded her acknowledgement and walked out. They could hear her heels tapping across the hall.

'No need to look so upset, Becky,' said Clara. 'Zena's going to be fi –'

'I had a phone call when you were at the hospital. My mother's very ill; I have to go back to the UK. Today if possible.'

'Oh no,' said Clara. 'What dreadful news.'

The sound of heels on the wooden floor got louder again and Francesca reappeared in the doorway of the morning room. 'Did I hear right? That's dreadful, Becky.'

'I'm so sorry,' said Clara. 'But can it wait until tomorrow? Alex could sort out a ticket and Matthew could give you a lift to the airport.'

'There are still free seats on a flight tonight. I just need to book a ticket and get to the airport.'

'But who – actually, I suppose I could take you,' said Clara doubtfully.

'I'll take Becky,' said Francesca. 'It's the least I could do.'

Clara looked worried. 'Oh, Francesca, that's very good of you but you've been up and down the island already today.'

'It's no problem.'

'Thanks Francesca,' said Becky. 'Clara, I'm going to try and book the ticket on my credit card, but to be honest, I'm not sure what my limit is.'

'You will not. I wouldn't dream of it. You tell me when a credit card is needed and I'll sort it out.'

Becky refreshed the screen and was relieved to see that there were still seats available on the eleven o'clock flight. The screen that came up was asking for credit card details.

'So, I type it here, do I?' Clara gave the screen a rather worried look. 'It's quite safe is it? I mean it won't steal my card number.'

'It will be fine,' said Francesca. 'It's completely safe.'

Clara sat down and filled in the payment details. Becky pressed 'Confirm'.

'Done.'

'Really?' said Clara. 'Just like that? You've booked a ticket.' She peered at the confirmation screen. Becky was writing down the reference number.

'But I'm afraid I've got to get back for my parents so we'll need to leave pretty much now-ish,' said Francesca.

'I'll pack,' said Becky. 'I'll be as quick as I can.'

She ran upstairs and pulled her suitcase from under the bed, opening drawers and cupboards and stuffing the contents in. She left the black Léger dress in the wardrobe. She would have loved to take it and its empowering properties with her but just couldn't visualise a scenario in England where she would wear it. Anyway Matthew had clearly meant it to be a business prop, not a personal gift.

She decided to take the box with Joe's car in her rucksack.

Maureen appeared in her bedroom doorway. 'You're going?'

'My mother's ill.'

'When are you coming back?'

The question almost floored Becky. She didn't intend to come back. 'I'm not sure. I'll see how it goes.' They hugged and Maureen left quietly.

Becky made sure her passport and money were in her rucksack, closed her suitcase and hauled it downstairs.

Francesca was drinking a glass of water in the hall. 'Wow, I made that just ten minutes,' she said with a note of admiration. 'And you've got your passport?'

Becky nodded.

Clara looked as though she could cry. 'I'm just sorry that Matthew isn't here to say goodbye.'

'Please say goodbye to him from me,' said Becky. 'And say goodbye to Cook and Alex too. I won't disturb him now.'

Clara gave her a big hug. 'I will see you soon, Becky, I'm sure. You've got to come straight back. As soon as your mother's better.'

Francesca started twirling her keys around. 'You need to check in a good couple of hours before the flight and it could take us two hours with the traffic –'

'I'm ready.'

Becky lugged her suitcase down the veranda stairs, hoisted it into the back of Francesca's jeep and got in. Francesca drove them off without any ceremony. Becky hadn't wanted to look back but changed her mind; her quarrel was not with poor Clara. The older lady was standing at the bottom of the veranda steps, waving.

They were soon on the now-familiar main road to Bridgetown. Becky knew Francesca's assistance was not entirely altruistic; in fact it was downright self-serving. Even so she was grateful for Francesca's deviousness. Apart from getting her away from Matthew so promptly it also meant Becky was under no obligation to talk to the driver – and the driver certainly didn't want to talk to her.

So that was it – after two months of her planned three-month stay she was going home to England. She would think about how to explain her early return to her mother and Joe on the plane. For now she wanted to remember as much of Barbados as she could.

The fields blurred by as Francesca's car chewed up the road in front and spat it out behind. Snapshots of the last few weeks streamed through Becky's mind: gardening with Clara; little Zena playing with a Christmas worm; researching the Redlegs; finding out about Matthew's ancestors; the dreadful night of the attack on Richard; daily life at Copper Mill; finding out about her father's other woman.

And finding his grave. Becky groaned. She needed the photographs from Matthew's phone to show Joe. That meant she would have to contact him. She never wanted to speak to Matthew again but given Clara's technophobia she'd almost certainly have to. Would he be difficult or would she get a glimpse of the other Matthew: the one who had comforted her in Southbury Cemetery and shared the turtle run with her?

Amazing to think their time on the beach was only last night. It seemed like a lifetime ago when they were two different people. Becky set her jaw, determined not to cry. In the scale of things a broken romance was hardly a big deal: baby turtles had to face the gauntlet of predators on their hike to the sea and her father's 'wife' was clearly still alone.

And of course she was doing something the Monmouth rebels sent to Barbados could only dream of: she was going back to England.

Almost before she realised it they were at the airport.

'Shall I come in and make sure you're OK?' asked Francesca, revving the engine slightly.

'No need.' Becky got out and hefted her suitcase from the back. 'Thanks very much, Francesca.'

She headed for the terminal building without a backward glance.

Chapter Twenty-five

Naturally, Becky's mother and Joe were curious as to why she'd come home early but she was initially saved from having to give a full explanation because they were both out at work when she arrived back in Brentwood. Feeling incredibly tired after travelling for ten hours, she took her case and rucksack upstairs, lay down and fell into a deep sleep. She was woken by the sound of the phone ringing and staggered groggily downstairs to answer it.

It was Clara wanting to know that Becky had landed safely. Her voice full of concern Clara asked after Becky's mother. Becky said she was doing a bit better, relieved her mother was not at home for it would have been somewhat difficult to talk about her imaginary illness with her in the background, calling 'Who's that?'

"We all miss you," Clara said, wishing the whole family well and hanging up.

All except Matthew, no doubt, thought Becky. She definitely could not face speaking to him and had thought of a way around it on the journey home. She rang Alex's mobile, explaining she needed some photos off Matthew's phone and giving Alex her email ID.

'Do you want Matthew's phone number?' asked Alex, confused.

'Already got it, thanks,' Becky said.

Still sounding confused, Alex said he'd organise it and within the hour Becky received the photographs in the graveyard sent from Alex's email ID.

At that moment she heard her mother coming through the front door. Joe was not far behind. They sat in the front room with a cup of tea and Becky tried to answer their questions about her unexpected return truthfully, while deliberately giving them both the wrong impression. She told them Clara's pleurisy had meant little progress had been made with the book. She told them she had worked in the garden instead. She told Joe she had taken photos of their father's grave, which she'd show him later and, when their mother was in the kitchen cooking dinner, she brought out the model car. Joe was beyond delighted – he was ecstatic.

Of course he wanted to know how Becky had come by this present so she told him about their Dad's 'other partner' but decided not to mention the bigamous marriage. Joe took the news of their father's relationship more easily than Becky had originally.

To his insistent questions as to what Matthew was like she just said that he worked very hard. But her answers didn't really explain why – with her three-month term not up and no book written – she was back. Her mother said she thought Becky had been sacked because she wasn't up to the work, while Joe asked (more accurately) if there had been 'man trouble'. Becky didn't deny or confirm either of these suspicions but suspected both her mother and her brother thought their own assumptions were correct.

After dinner she went through the photos from Southbury Cemetery with Joe on the computer. Even their mother wandered in to look at a couple of the pictures of the gravestone, though without comment.

For the next few nights Becky dreamt of walking down the mahogany-lined lane towards the Darnley house but woke up before she could turn into the yard. It was a few seconds before she remembered she was back in England, in her old home, in her old bed. Sometimes she felt like a creature undergoing some sort of reverse metamorphosis, like a butterfly being squeezed into a confined chrysalis with only life as a caterpillar to look forward to. At other times she felt like a fraudulent imitation of herself, an insubstantial being who had strained conversations with her mother and Joe while her real self was sitting on a veranda, thousands of miles away.

After Copper Mill, Becky found their house and estate stifling. She took to having long, solitary walks in Brentwood's vast Weald and tried to figure out what she could do next. She had to find a way of shedding her recent past and starting anew. No more Matthew, no more Monmouth rebels. It was time to let go.

Towards the end of her first week back Matthew telephoned. He had barely said a word before Becky cut him short: 'there's nothing I want to say to you'.

She put down the phone with firm resolution and then spent the rest of the day wondering what he would have said if she'd let him. She had a pretty good idea: he probably knew by now it hadn't been her who had told the Carringtons what he was bidding and he would have apologised for leaping to conclusions and assuming she was the weak link. But whatever he'd have said it wouldn't have been enough: the hurt ran like a fault line through her whole being.

She tried to adapt to her old Essex life and studied the magazine racks in the newsagents to bring herself up to date on which publications were still in circulation. She wrote off to three editors. She held out little hope of success but at least one of them had accepted two of her articles in the past, which she'd offered for no payment when she was trying to build up a CV.

Despite her resolution not to think about the Redleg project Becky frequently compromised herself. She was like a gambling addict going back for one last fix – chasing the 'big winner' – each time telling herself it would be the last time but then urging herself to try once more to find a link she'd missed previously. She studied the online version of the book she had originally looked at in the

Somerset Heritage Centre; there was nothing she had overlooked in the details of the Monmouth rebels transported, other than that Randolph Randerwick was described as a 'plow man'. Becky hadn't missed any references to Sarah Thomas – she simply wasn't listed.

Next she searched for references to Sarah Thomas generally, wading through the many Facebook hits that came up for a multitude of contemporary women with the same name. But of Sarah Thomas in the seventeenth century there was nothing.

It wasn't until she decided to look for the complete list of owners of Copper Mill, starting, she anticipated, with William Darnley, that her addiction was finally cured. She remembered that the house had been called 'Copper Hall' rather than 'Copper Mill' in the past so scoured online book archives for plantation houses in Barbados with the name 'Copper'.

She soon found what she wasn't looking for.

The current Darnley residence – Copper Mill in the parish of St Lucy – hadn't been built until 1820. How could that be when William Darnley had taken on his indentured workers in January 1686? Unless he had lived in a completely different house. With a sinking feeling she googled Copper Hall and found a reference in an old book on Barbados buildings. Not only was Copper Hall a completely separate building, it had been built in St Philip – way down south. The plantation had been sold off for development in the early twentieth century and Copper Hall – by then a ruin – had been demolished to make way for a hotel complex.

The realisation shook her in more ways than one. It wasn't just that it exposed her lack of attention to detail in assuming there had been a single plantation house involved. She realised now how gripped she'd been with the fantasy of continuity: the idea of Pitchers working on the same land for three hundred years and the notion

Matthew had bought the same plantation house his ancestors could only dream of entering. Worse she had presented this fantasy to Clara and Matthew as history and they had accepted it.

But worst of all was the realisation that while she had been trying to solve this historical mystery she had felt alive in a way she had never felt before. Professionalism had gone out of the window while she built a fantasy world around Copper Mill, seeing only the facts that would support such a fantasy while ignoring the evidence that would have contradicted it.

It was in this mood of heightened sensation – in this fantasy – that she had got together with Matthew and it had seemed amazing. Now, when she looked back, she realised she couldn't trust her judgement on a single experience she'd had in Barbados: none of it had been real. Well, maybe meeting Sairah Thomson but if there wasn't the physical evidence of Joe's model green car even that would have seemed more like a dream.

She was feeling at rock bottom when Matthew rang again. 'This time please don't hang up on me.'

'Like you hung up on me from the hospital?'

A sigh came down the phone. 'I'm sorry. I could not have got it more wrong. Tell me how your mother is.'

Becky decided that her mother couldn't stay ill forever. 'She's much better.'

'Does she still need you to be there?'

Becky wondered if Matthew could hear the clattering in the kitchen which signified that her mother – having eschewed offers of assistance – was cooking a meal with a martyr's zeal.

'Probably not.'

'So when do you think you'll be able to come back here?

'I'm not coming back, Matthew.'

‘You’re not?’ He sounded surprised. ‘What am I going to tell my mother? What about her book?’

‘There isn’t going to be a book. There isn’t enough material.’ Especially in light of what she’d just discovered. ‘There’s nothing for me in Barbados.’

‘That’s not true,’ Matthew said. ‘I will do whatever it takes to get you back here. First-class flight and if you don’t think the book will work – I don’t know – you could run eco-tours round the island, anything you want.’

Becky had to smile at the idea of her running eco-tours. ‘Thanks. I can tell you’re serious and that does sound good.’

‘But?’

‘But it wouldn’t work. I had a great time but I realise now I was living a bit of a fantasy. I don’t think much of it was real.’

‘Not real?’

‘I can’t really explain but let’s leave it there. Thanks for trying. But really, it’s my problem, not yours.’

She put the phone down.

Chapter Twenty-six

Becky had been back for over a month. It was unusually cold for early October and if people had hoped for an Indian Summer it hadn't left the shores of India. Becky had had no more than a polite acknowledgement from one editor that they would 'keep her on their books but had no suitable position for her at the moment'; the others hadn't even bothered replying.

With time on her hands Becky decided to repaint the front room. Her mother had bemoaned the faded colour for many years – not in the hope of Becky or Joe doing anything about it – just because she seemed to think moaning was a valid exercise in itself. At the local DIY outlet Becky selected the colour that appeared to match what her mother had frequently described as her first choice and lugged two huge cans back in a biting wind. She really must learn to drive before she frittered away the money in her account.

Today was as good a day as any to start painting. Her mother was at her part-time job at the pharmacy and Joe was at the garage. She only had to go round one more corner to reach home but she had to set down the paint cans for a moment to give her arms a rest. As she picked the cans up again and rounded the corner, she noticed a car outside the house – nothing posh. It looked like a standard saloon with the logo of a car rental company on the rear screen. Drawing nearer she thought the profile of the man sitting in the driver's seat looked familiar. He looked up and got out hurriedly.

'Becky!'

‘Alex? What are you doing here?’

‘I was sent over to the UK with a list of messages to do.’ He grinned. ‘Oh, they look heavy. Do you want a hand with them?’

Becky nodded and they took a paint can each and went into the house.

‘Is your mother here?’ asked Alex in a hushed tone as they put the cans down in the hall.

‘No, she’s actually much better. She’s been able to go back to work.’

‘That’s good.’

‘So Matthew still has you flying over to the UK?’

Alex looked at her and made a glum face. ‘Never mind. One of my chores – though one of the nicer ones, I must add – is to reunite you with the things you left behind.’

‘Did I?’ Becky had subsequently realised she had forgotten her toothbrush but thought she had managed to grab everything else.

‘There were a couple of items,’ said Alex, vaguely. ‘And there were a few things Clara or Matthew meant to give you as presents, which obviously they couldn’t, um, under the circumstances.’

‘That’s sweet of them but not at all necessary. Are they in the car?’

‘No, they’re in the Magsab house. They were shipped over with some other stuff and I haven’t had a chance to sort it all out yet.’

‘What on earth is the Magsab house?’

‘It’s about, I don’t know, thirty miles from here.’ He frowned. ‘I think Matthew said you’d been there. It’s got a lake, if that helps?’

‘Oh yes. I only know it as Noak Hall.’

‘Magsab is our name for it. I’ll explain on the way.’

‘On the way?’

'If it's not too inconvenient it would be easier to take you there now, pick up what you want and then I'll give you a lift back here.'

'Are you sure? I don't want to put you out.'

Alex grimaced. 'I would like to get something right for a change. And besides I need the chance to make you a proper apology.'

She looked at him. He had his perpetual appearance of sleep deficit but he looked much better than when she had last seen him; his eyes and skin had lost their previous pink blotchiness. 'No need to apologise. I guessed what happened.'

'Right, I see. Even so, I'd like to fill you in on all the details as we drive,' said Alex, taking a step towards the front door. 'Matthew knows he owes you a major apology too. Now where is it?' He patted down his pockets before retrieving an envelope from his coat and handing it to Becky.

Becky opened it and read the note inside.

Dear Becky,

I'm going to leave it to Alex to explain the background to my very unfair accusation that you'd helped the Carringtons with the bid. The irony is they are now in a panic about cashflow and have already approached me to see if I'm interested so all's well that ends well.

I wish you would reconsider coming back to Barbados. You are being missed very much by everyone and I hate the fact we didn't say a proper goodbye. I'll try and remedy that when I'm next in the UK and will ring to see if you are free for a meal.

Very best wishes,

Matthew

P.S. Alex will reunite you with the items you left behind and will also pass on some presents my mother and I want you to have.

P.P.S. If you don't accept the presents, I will fire Alex. So no pressure.

Becky laughed. 'Still got his sense of humour, then.'

'It's not been obvious these past few weeks,' said Alex.

'OK,' she said. 'Let's get this over and done with.'

He breathed a sigh of relief and Becky realised he'd doubted whether she'd go with him. She picked up her rucksack, locked the front door and they went out to the car.

'I apologise now if I crunch the gears,' Alex said, letting her in. 'This isn't the normal model I rent.'

It was typical of him to put himself down; once they set off he drove quite competently. Anyway it was nice to see Alex again even if it was funny hearing a Bajan accent in Essex. She realised how much she'd missed the sing-song lilt. And despite wanting this 'over and done with' she also wanted to know how everyone was at Copper Mill.

'How's Zena?'

'Absolutely fine except she keeps asking where Becky is. We don't think she had more than a spray of that furniture stuff. It was just the initial burning in her mouth that made her so upset.' Alex glanced at her. 'I put Matthew right about the milk business. Francesca was acting like God's gift to first aid. I'm afraid it got on my nerves.'

'I'm sure she loves children,' said Becky, sweetly.

'Mmm,' said Alex. 'I'm sure she would love Matthew to think she loves children. But then if she thought Matthew was interested in, I don't know, bee-keeping she'd appear with a beehive on her head.'

Becky laughed.

'I also put him right about the party. You remember – the birthday party was Francesca's idea until she realised that Matthew was shattered and not enjoying it at all. Then suddenly it became your idea. Apparently she only went along with it because she felt sorry you hadn't had a chance to meet anyone in Barbados.'

'How sweet of her.'

Becky looked out of the window. In just fifteen minutes the urban sprawl of her dormitory town had petered out into Essex fields – like a lumpy patchwork quilt dotted with the odd farmhouse. The golden wheat fields that had been evident when she left England for Barbados had been replaced by acres of ploughed brown earth. It was only a gentle ache but she missed the little Barbados roads winding through verdant meadows.

'I don't think Matthew was ever fooled by Francesca,' said Alex. 'Not since he was a teenager, anyway. But I'm afraid he was fooled by Richard Carrington.'

'How do you mean?'

'You know it was my fault? About the bid?'

'Yes,' said Becky.

'I didn't tell deliberately of course. Derek Carrington was very devious. It was the end of an extremely trying day – a few problems with some difficult guests. Derek was complimentary about the food and insisted we have a drink in the bar later. We had quite a few drinks in fact. He said they'd already put in their bid and named a price ridiculously low. It became a game testing my reactions as he mentioned different bid prices. I don't know exactly what happened to be honest but I know that at some point I as good as came out with the actual figure.'

'Why did Matthew just assume it was me? Apart from his inability to trust anyone he didn't go to school with, obviously.'

'After what happened with Chris he's had to relax that rule. Anyhow Richard knew which buttons to press. From what Matthew told me, when they were waiting at the hospital for news on Zena, he bumped into Richard and congratulated him on the Carringtons' successful bid. Then Richard said he had had inside help and Matthew should be careful about the people he shared information with. All true of course but there was something in Richard's manner; he managed to make it sound like pillow talk.'

'What?' cried Becky.

Alex looked at her shyly. 'Apparently he implied you two got it on before his friendly visitors arrived.'

'I knew he was a spoilt brat but I didn't realise he was dishonest.'

'You have no idea of the rivalry between the two of them – I suppose between Matthew and all the Carrington brothers, though it seems most personal with Richard. He's very jealous of Matthew because he knows he would be useless without his family fortune or his older brothers whereas Matthew …' Alex didn't finish the sentence.

'Are you still overworked?' asked Becky. 'I mean that was the real problem, wasn't it? You always looked so tired.'

Alex looked at her. 'And I was silly about the alcohol. I was drinking just to try and get to sleep at night. It wasn't great. Especially for my wife.'

'So have things got better?' asked Becky.

'Definitely. I already had an assistant manager, a man called Clarence, who is more than capable but rather under-used. Matthew has finally accepted that I can't be the manager and his right-hand man; it was like having two jobs sometimes. So Clarence gets promoted and I can concentrate on being Robin to Matthew's Batman.'

Becky laughed. 'And how's Clara?'

Alex sighed. 'She really is missing you. You know I probably shouldn't say it, but …' His voice drifted away.

They had left the A12 and were winding along the B-roads.

'You've got to say it now,' said Becky.

'I'm sure she was very sincere about writing a book but I can't help wondering if it was actually you she wanted.'

'Me?'

'She's really fond of you. I think she genuinely believed that the history of the Redlegs should be told but I also suspect she had a bit of a fantasy that you and Matthew would get together.'

'I wouldn't have guessed that.' Though now Becky thought about Clara's reluctance to focus on the book it would make sense.

'Francesca turned up every day after you left, even when Matthew wasn't there. I think she was hoping to get in with Clara. Anyway she made the mistake of criticising you and according to Maureen Clara got quite indignant. Apparently she told Francesca: "Becky's the only daughter-in-law I would welcome." Francesca didn't take that so well.'

'And – if you don't mind me asking – you explained about the bid to Matthew?'

'Of course. It was uncomfortable, shall we say. But he didn't shout; didn't even get angry. He just looked, I don't know, beaten.'

Becky felt a pang of sympathy for Matthew. She couldn't imagine him looking beaten. Exasperated, tired, even haggard, yes – but never beaten. But she did remember his irritation when he thought people weren't acting efficiently.

'So he really wasn't angry with you?'

'No. He was just very, very angry with himself.'

'Why? Because he'd accused me?'

'Definitely that but something more as well. He didn't put it into so many words but I think what staggered him was realising he still had a bit of a hang-up about his start in life. Even though he's more competent than all the Carringtons put together. It can gnaw away at you, you know?'

They turned into the long tree-lined drive she had travelled down with a taxi driver in what felt like a previous lifetime. She saw the lake with its shining face lying in a sward of immaculate lawn dotted with clipped shrubs that looked like stalled Daleks.

'Go on then. Why do you and Matthew call Noak Hall the Magsab house?'

Alex grinned and turned the wheel to bring the car into the parking area at the side of the house. 'It stands for Meet and Greet, Schmooze and Booze. Sometimes it's better to entertain clients here than in the hotel.'

Becky sighed. Matthew had hinted at this in Barbados. 'So Matthew's lovely house is purely for business?'

Alex looked at her, surprised. 'It's not his house as such. He does have a stake in it but it's basically owned by a syndicate of companies. Matthew leases it back when it's needed. Other companies do the same. It's in use most of the time. A wonderful woman called Mrs Collie somehow manages to run it all.'

Her socialist taxi driver would have approved and so did Becky but she still felt a twinge of disappointment. Another fantasy balloon popped.

They got out of the car and walked round to the front of Noak Hall, both pausing to admire the stately solidity of the building. As if on cue smoke started drifting out from the chimneys.

'Alex, is it booked at the moment?'

'Yes, but it's fine. I've cleared it with Mrs Collie. It's booked for something later but we're not going to be long.'

They walked up the steps and across the courtyard to the ornate front door, which must have been unlocked as Becky noticed Alex just turned the handle to open it.

She followed him into the grand hall, obsessively wiping her shoes on the mat, and stared up at the high ceiling. She also peeked in the enormous living room where a log fire crackled discreetly in a walk-in fireplace.

'It all looks very inviting,' she said.

'Have a quick look at the dining room,' said Alex. 'Then we must go upstairs.'

He pointed out the doorway of another room and Becky stuck her head in. Ornate wallpaper stared down at a huge table covered with the whitest linen cloth on which silver cutlery gleamed. Clearly important guests were expected. Sumptuous smells wafted through from the kitchen. Becky could visualise Mrs Collie hurrying around getting everything ready.

'We'd better crack on,' said Alex. 'This way.'

Becky hurried up the carpeted stairs after him. She really did not want to bump into Mrs Collie and have to explain what she was doing at Noak Hall again.

From the landing she followed Alex into an impressively long corridor. 'Your things are in here,' he murmured, pushing open the first door on the right. Becky walked through and almost gasped. The bedroom – if you could give the huge room such a mundane name – had a king-sized bed covered with an abstract-patterned quilt in charcoal grey and burgundy. Rather incongruously her bathroom bag and her book about the Monmouth Rebels lay in the middle of it. Surely Matthew hadn't paid to ship them across the Atlantic? But as she got nearer the bed she could see beyond the bag and the book was the beautiful black bandage gown, in a cellophane wrapper, and next to it several more in the same style, except these were in new wrapping. The thin-strapped black bra had winged its way across the sea as well, which rather embarrassed her; had Matthew personally packed it? Next to it was a beautiful small velvet box.

'Matthew insisted you take the black dress. It's been dry-cleaned and is all yours, ready to wear.'

'OK,' said Becky, a little wearily. Was it all right to take a dress she would probably never wear again?

'But what are these?' She looked at the other gowns: there were a couple in burgundy, a couple in midnight blue.

'Matthew was absolutely insistent. He said you looked so good in the black dress it was only right that you should choose another colour as well. But apparently you'd cut the label out so he didn't know your size.'

That was true – she had been worried about the label showing so had cut it out before wearing the dress at Matthew's party.

'There are two sizes of each. Can you choose one that fits?'

Becky looked quickly at the labels. The measurements weren't recognisable UK sizes.

'Alex, it's a lovely idea but I'll have to leave these. I can't remember what size the black dress was and I can't tell from looking at the labels.'

Alex looked at his watch. 'I think you have time to try on a couple. I need to make some phone calls anyway. And whatever's in the little box is a present for you.'

He shut the door behind him, leaving Becky little choice but to gingerly remove one of the new dresses from its wrapper. The first midnight blue one she tried on was too loose but the second fitted perfectly. The black shoes were sitting next to the bed, having also made the journey across the Atlantic. She put them on, remembering how confident she had felt in this outfit and wanting to savour the moment.

She sat down on the bed to open the little velvet box. Inside was a necklace – a simple chain with a little silver turtle pendant. Becky could have cried. Underneath the necklace was a tiny piece of paper. She unfolded it and read in Matthew's handwriting: *It was real to me.*

Now she did cry. She couldn't even begin to separate the strands of her grief: loss of Matthew, loss of her father and loss of something else, something even more amorphous; maybe it was the loss of a version of herself who had felt alive, albeit just for a few weeks.

It was quite a while before she stopped crying. She put on the necklace and checked herself in the mirror. Unsurprisingly she looked like a young woman in a gorgeous dress and necklace who had been crying her eyes out. Becky went into the en-suite bathroom and washed her face then checked her reflection again: a little more normal.

Maybe one day she would have a reason – be it professional or social – to look like she looked now.

Or maybe the silver turtle would be forever marooned in the metaphorical sand of a drawer and the black and blue dresses would hang in her cupboard for years, dreaming of a night out that never came.

Ridiculous. She would tell Alex she couldn't accept Matthew's kind offer of the dresses and necklace. Becky put her hands up to unclasp the chain then heard a gentle knocking on the door, followed by a more insistent one. She opened it to see Alex with his customary worry lines etched on his face.

'Sorry to rush you.' He did a double take. 'You look, um, wow. But we're cutting it very fine now. Mrs Collie has just reminded me that one of the other companies has got a lunch scheduled. She's expecting guests – well, now.'

'Have I got time to change back into my things?'

'Sorry. Not really.'

Becky stuffed her discarded jeans, hoodie and trainers into her rucksack and Alex grabbed the black dress. The bathroom bag and book would have to be left to surprise the next guest who was lucky enough to stay in that room. She followed Alex down the stairs, moving slower in her party shoes. As soon as she joined him at the front door he opened it. The sun, previously whitely veiled, was now smothered in black cloud and it had started to rain.

Alex looked at Becky in her bandage dress. 'God, you'll freeze. Look, just get to the portico and stay there.

I'll bring the car round.' He gave Becky the black dress to carry and ran ahead.

Becky headed for the shelter of the portico as quickly as she could and arrived just as Alex brought the car as close to the bottom step as possible. He ran up, grabbed the dress from Becky and put it on the back seat, then opened the passenger door to let her in: the midnight blue Léger was not a dress to be washed in the rain. He slammed her door shut, got in the driver's seat and looked at his watch.

'We should be fine. I think we have a few minutes before the next lot arrive.'

He accelerated up the drive. Becky shivered – the dress was not designed for the British autumn – but she was more concerned about what she would tell her mother who would be home from work by now and ready to drop dishes at the sight of her daughter dolled-up like a socialite.

They had almost reached the road when Alex stopped abruptly and patted the pockets of his jacket. 'Idiot. I put my phone down somewhere. Maybe it was in the washroom. I daren't leave it. Sorry.'

He did a three-point turn and drove back down the drive at breakneck speed, screeching to a halt right in front of the portico. He leapt out and ran up the steps.

Becky could hear her own phone vibrating. She extracted it from her rucksack and was surprised to see it was Joe.

She pressed receive call. 'Becky, where are you?'

'Um. Just picking up some clothes. Why?'

'Mum rang me here – at the garage. She says someone has dumped a load of paint cans in the house and you've disappeared.'

Becky almost laughed. 'I brought home a total of two pots of paint to do the front room and I'm now with a friend.'

'Not exactly a crisis then? I've asked her not to ring work unless it's an emergency. And I told her firmly just now I am not my sister's keeper.'

They swapped exasperated goodbyes and Becky ended the call. If nothing else the Barbados trip had firmly cemented her relationship with her brother. It wasn't just about getting closure on their father. Joe had strayed way out of his comfort zone, getting involved in research to try and help her or simply keeping up her spirits by spinning his ridiculous tale about how Thomas Gehalgod had survived.

She couldn't help smiling at the thought of him pompously misquoting the Bible to their mother: 'I am not my sister's keeper.'

Something about the phrase sounded familiar. Becky thought back to the graveyard in Westonzoyland when she and Joe were crouching over Thomas Gehalgod's grave. They had assumed the epitaph on the headstone read 'My father was my keeper'. What if it said 'My *ſiſ*ter was my keeper' using the old-fashioned *ſ* for s?

There was still no sign of Alex. Nor of cars appearing down the drive. Becky closed her eyes. Why would Thomas Gehalgod have paid tribute to a sister?

The answer came like a thunderbolt. Maybe the captain of the *Betty* had pretended Thomas Gehalgod had died at sea rather than admit the officials had made a fairly fundamental mistake. No wonder she couldn't find any reference to Sarah Thomas boarding the ship. Thomas Gehalgod hadn't been thrown overboard; in fact he had never boarded the *Betty*. And Sarah Thomas, as such, had not existed before she set foot on Barbados. As Joe had told her: *The gaols had been chaotic ... the authorities barely knew who was who.*

At what point had Sarah Gehalgod swapped places with her brother? In jail? Or had she put on his clothes before the militia came looking for him? Had she realised the sacrifice she was making – that she would never come back home? At some point during this drama – it could even have been on the ship – Randolph Randerwick had made her acquaintance and helped her change into Sarah Thomas. Becky found herself hoping that their relationship had been solid and real and fulfilling.

She opened her eyes. She had told Clara that given time, she would trace Matthew's ancestors in England, and she had. Of course, she couldn't be sure she was right. Who could glean the truth after so much time had passed? All she could say with certainty was that whatever had really happened three hundred and thirty years ago had been more remarkable and emotional than anyone now could imagine.

She wished she could share her discovery with someone. There was Joe, of course, but she had a longing to talk to someone else. She fantasised about turning her head and seeing Matthew Darnley running down the steps towards her. He would be dressed to kill and carrying an umbrella to hold over her. Mrs Collie's sumptuous lunch would not be for corporate guests but a private banquet for her and Matthew and the whole debacle would have been a carefully planned ruse to bring her to Noak Hall, dress her up to the nines and create a perfect setting. The fire would have been lit in the huge hearth to throw out a smoky welcome through the chimneys – just for her. Alex's phone would have been safe in his pocket all along and Matthew would have flown over days ago to warn Mrs Collie that the 'waif and stray' would be visiting once more, this time as a guest, and he would conceal himself in the grand house until it was time to reveal his presence.

Becky sighed. It had been a nice fantasy.

She turned her head towards the house wondering what was keeping Alex. There was Matthew Darnley, dressed as if on Her Majesty's Secret Service, coming swiftly down the steps, unfurling an umbrella as he ran towards her.

THE END

For more information about **Marie Evelyn**

and other **Accent Press** titles

please visit

www.accentpress.co.uk

20601817R00225

Printed in Great Britain
by Amazon